Is this me?

Is this me?

Book one of the Being Me series

by Tricia Copeland

True Bird Publishing LLC

Is this Me?

Book one of the *Being Me* series
by Tricia Copeland

ISBN-13: 978-0692440056
ISBN-10: 0692440054

License Notes:

This book is a work of fiction. Names, characters, places, and incidents either are products of the author's imagination or are used fictitiously.

Edited by Tia Silverthorne Bach
Proofread by Mollie Turbeville
Interior Formatting by Jo Michaels
all of Indie Books Gone Wild

Cover by Daryl A. McCool of d.a.m. Cool Graphics
Published by True Bird Publishing LLC, Superior, CO

acknowledgements

At the start of this journey I would never have imagined just how many people would inspire me.

Many thanks are owed to my husband and kids for giving me the time to pursue writing.

To my editor and friend Tia Silverthorne Bach, there aren't words to capture how thankful I am for your friendship and expertise.

Thank you to my cover designer, Daryl McCool who contributed with enthusiasm to my vision.

To Jo Michaels, my formatter, thank you for pulling my vision together. Thank you to Mollie Turbeville for proofreading services.

To my beta readers Sara, Danielle, Kelly, Frances, and Cheryl thank you for your insights and support.

To my family and many friends who cheered me on, thank you.

For my daughter.

Never be afraid to be yourself.

Chapter 1

Waking to the sounds of pots clanging and the smell of bacon wafting up from downstairs, I scanned my now bare walls. Pancake breakfasts marked all our family's major events, and tomorrow I would wake up in a dorm room. I listened to the noise of my parents' laughter and morning news program coming from the kitchen. Although excited about being on my own, I knew I would miss my family. Fortunately my chosen college, Northwestern University, was only a two and a half-hour drive from my hometown of Champaign.

Out of the corner of my eye I caught the blur of Marissa launching herself onto my bed. I wasn't fast enough, and she landed spread eagle on top of me. "Get up." I pushed with every ounce of my strength to dislodge her. With her four inch and twenty pound advantage, she didn't budge.

"I can't believe I was up before you." She smacked me on the leg and pushed herself up.

"I was getting up."

"No, you were processing." She used air quotes when she said processing. With just eleven months between us, I vacillated between loving and loathing my younger sister. "Just like you do about everything. I hope they teach spontaneity at college, or better yet, being social."

Getting up, I pulled a sweatshirt over my head. "I'm social."

"If you use yearbook, debate team, or Spanish club as examples again..." She grabbed a brush off my dresser and raked it through her hair. I opened my mouth to speak, but she cut in.

"Everyone's face is buried in their screens at yearbook, all you talk about is how to argue for debate team, and all you do is talk in a language most people don't understand in Spanish club."

"Half the world speaks Spanish."

"No, half the world speaks Chinese." She put the brush down. "But I shouldn't say anything, that's probably next on your list."

"Girls, breakfast," Mom called.

Marissa wrapped her arms around me, nearly cutting off my oxygen, as we made our way down the stairs. "I'm going to miss you so much." She was such a teenager, razzing me one second and bemoaning my loss the next. "I wish you would wait a year. Mom and Dad are going to drive me nuts."

One more day of going to the same coffee shop and I was going to go bonkers. "No way."

"Who's going to help me with the cheerleader drama?"

"You can text or call."

"Like four times a day? I guess it's not like you'll be doing anything." She shoved me down the last few stairs. "Just don't end up a loner loser, okay. That would be pitiful."

"Your sister will not be a loner loser." Mom pulled me into a hug.

Marissa grabbed the coffee pot. "I can't believe I got up this early to help her move all her crap to school." She didn't like being up early any more than I did. Dad had agreed to let her miss a day of school to see me off, so she probably figured it was worth it.

"How's the country?" I asked Dad, ducking away from his huge hand descending on my head. I'd washed my hair last night and blow-dried it meticulously, there was no way I was letting him ruin it.

"We'll find out in a couple of months." Politics were as much a tradition in our family as the pancakes and Northwestern. "How's my newest Wildcat?"

"Good, but I'm thinking you helped with my scholarship because you wanted an excuse to go to the football games and hang out with your alumni brothers for four more years."

Dad lifted his hands, palms forward. "I was right about Tia loving it. I know where my daughters will be happy." Tia, my older sister, graduated from Northwestern two years ago. She'd married Ed, also a Northwestern alum, in June.

"And safely protected by the brothers." Marissa pointed at Dad. "You know that strategy could backfire." She hit me on the butt. "A lot of those frat guys are hot, she could fall for one of them."

Dad patted my shoulder and pointed at her. "Not this one. Plus, I've got Mark to keep an eye on her."

Marissa sat down in front of her plate of pancakes. "Yeah, but Lila is there. I think they cancel each other out."

Mark grew up across the street from me and Lila was my best friend. She was already at Northwestern having started summer quarter. Her dad had major guilt about not being with her mom anymore, and she'd begged him to let her go early to be with her boyfriend, Ross. A year ahead of us, Ross and Mark were now brothers at my dad's old fraternity

Hand to her hip, Mom raised an eyebrow at Dad and crossed the room with a plate of eggs. "Of course no Avery girl could possibly be caught under the spell of a Northwestern brother, scandalously running off to marry him before finishing school."

Dad, two years ahead of Mom, asked her to marry him when he graduated. She left Northwestern to finish her nursing degree near Dad's flight school. They were married two years later, just before he left on his first tour.

Dad cleared his throat loudly. "Things were different then."

"Tia met Ed her freshman year too." Marissa stuffed a fork full of pancakes in her mouth.

I rolled my eyes, like I had any interest in frat guys. I was not going to Northwestern to find a boyfriend! All I cared about was their international studies and language programs. Ever since I'd taken my first Spanish course in sixth grade, I'd been hooked. Thinking the CIA or military was a perfect career path for me, Dad insisted I minor in a science or engineering field. I accepted his requirement without much questioning, thinking it was a solid backup plan.

"Are we eating pancakes, or what? At least I'll only have two females in the house to gang up on me now!" Dad cut in.

After our celebratory breakfast, I dressed quickly and reviewed my list. My boxes were packed and ready to load into our sport utility vehicle. All that was left to go in the last bag were toiletries and my computer.

Mom came into my room and surveyed my boxes. "Ready, sweetie?"

"Think so."

She hugged me. "Oh, baby girl."

I pulled away. "Mom, I'm not the baby. You still have Marissa."

"She's too stubborn."

"We'll talk every day, and you'll be up for all the home games." I wasn't sure how I felt about Dad getting season tickets. Part of me was glad I'd see my parents frequently, but part of me wanted more space.

Mom smiled. "I'm happy you'll be so close."

"Okay, let's move out." Dad clapped his hands, pacing the hall. "Is Marissa ready?"

I put my ear to the bathroom door. "I hear the hair dryer."

"What does that mean? We have a schedule to keep." He was in officer mode.

"Twenty minutes, Marissa-time, sir." I stifled a giggle and resisted the urge to salute.

"How is it that I ended up with three girls?" He repeated his usual ranting.

Mom rubbed his shoulder. "It's okay, Charlie, we'll make it in time."

Dad shook his head and grabbed a box. "Yeah, yeah. The check-in appointment isn't until one."

As I was loading my last bag into our sport utility vehicle, I got a text from Lila: R U ON THE WAY?

SOON, I texted back.

CALL WHEN U GET HERE.

K.

Lila and I had decided not to room together, but I was glad we were in the same dorm. Although friends for years, we both knew it'd never work for us to be roommates. She'd been with Ross for two years, and they were nearly inseparable. I liked him, but I didn't want him in my room all the time or a roommate who was never around.

Finally on our way, my parents used the drive time to review all the dos and don'ts of being on my own. There must've been a hundred items, including don't do drugs, don't drink alcohol, no piercings or tattoos, never take an open drink, don't walk alone at night, pay attention to your surroundings, always have an exit route, and don't talk to strangers. The last one seemed like a vestige from childhood. Wouldn't everyone be a stranger?

"And don't have fun, whatever you do," Marissa added, cutting off their endless list.

As we neared Chicago, the farmland gave way to factories, row homes, and skyscrapers. In Evanston, home to the Northwestern campus, we left the strip malls and chain stores of suburban sprawl behind. Narrow streets were lined with trees and brick homes. Coming from a small town in the middle of Illinois, I probably overly romanticized life near a big city, but I was drawn to the constant activity.

We found my dorm easily, and I sent a text to Lila to let her know we'd arrived.

In my room, 215, come up, she texted back.

I checked in at the front desk, and we got everything up to my room in one trip thanks to the help of three muscular volunteers. Dad went down to move the car while we found Lila's room.

The door was open, and I crossed the room to hug her. Looking around, I was stunned at her progress. "Wow, you're quick." With a check-in time just an hour ahead of me, the loft for her bed was already together, and her dad was packing tools in a bag. The bed was made, and her mom was hanging curtains.

"Helps when you've done it before and,"—she scanned the room and leaned into me—"have an army determined to one up each other."

"What about your roommate?"

"She comes in this afternoon." She held up both hands in front of my face, crossing her fingers

Lila's roommate over the summer had been a struggling sophomore who slept most of the day and was up most of the night. It was so miserable Lila had basically lived at the frat house with Ross.

Because of her experience, I contacted my roommate, Elise, as soon as we were matched up. She was a senior, drum major in the marching band, and belonged to a sorority. In my book, all this equaled someone who was responsible and mature. Dad was happy she owned a microwave and fridge. She'd even volunteered to bring a television and stereo system.

Feeling the need to take advantage of my helpers, we left Lila and her two sets of parents and returned to my room to unpack. When we walked in, Dad was in the middle of a full blown rage against the loft pieces.

Perhaps cued in to our presence by the noise, a girl poked her head in through the bathroom doorway. "Hi, I'm Kate. I'm next door. I guess we share a bathroom." She bounded into the room offering her hand, her jet black hair bouncing on her head.

"Did you switch rooms?" I'd been given our suitemates names', Kyung and Emily, so I was confused.

Her nose wrinkled and she rolled her eyes. "My real name is Kyung, but I go by Kate."

I introduced my family, and we went over to meet hers. Her warm smile and enthusiasm seemed genuine, and I liked her right away. Dad got some pointers on putting the loft together, and we left her to finish unpacking.

Amazingly, within three hours we had my room fairly organized. We chose a restaurant close to campus for dinner before they headed home. Back at my dorm, we exchanged goodbyes in the parking lot. Mom was teary-eyed, and I promised to call before I went to sleep. Walking back to my room, I maneuvered around the droves of students, feeling both excited and apprehensive.

Assessing the last two boxes, I chose to unpack my books and movie collection. Halfway through, my phone buzzed in my back pocket. It was a mass text from our resident assistant reminding us of the mandatory dorm meeting starting in ten minutes. I finished off the box and found my brush and mirror.

At exactly seven, Kate knocked on the door. "You want to walk down to orientation together?"

I slid on my boots, and we joined the progression down to the basement. I wasn't sure which I dreaded more about the next few days, the orientation sessions or the social mixers.

Seemingly unfazed by the masses of people, Kate introduced herself to everyone we came across. We found Lila, and as I expected, she hated being there as much as I did. Hands on hips, she looked around. "This is stupid. I can't believe I have to be here. I went through this last quarter. I'm not going to throw myself out a window."

Excited about a party at the fraternity house, she was ready to ditch this meetup at the earliest opportunity. She knew the drill. We just had to stay for the presentation, sign the attendance sheet, and then we were clear. I was more than happy with being included in that plan. With the crowd of people, I was becoming more claustrophobic by the second and hoped the house party would be a smaller gathering.

We invited Kate to join us, but she declined. Signing the roster after the presentation, Lila and I headed for the elevator. She danced around me as we rode up to my room. "I'm so excited you're finally here, we are going to have so much fun! I can't wait to see all the clothes Marissa bought you. We'll find something awesome for you to wear."

"I need to change?" I looked at my outfit as we got off the elevator. I'd just changed before dinner, and I thought I'd done a pretty good job.

"Tomorrow they have to clean for the alumni barbecue, so this will be one of the biggest parties of the year. All the brothers and potentials will be there."

I had no clue what potentials were, and my hope for an intimate hang out with Mark, Lila, and Ross vanished like a puff of smoke.

In my room, Lila browsed through my closet. Finding something awesome to wear really meant she would choose what she wanted me to wear. This was a long tradition in our friendship, and I didn't fight it. She always looked great, although sometimes a little risqué for my tastes. I'd learned how to make her happy without sacrificing my standards. Picking an outfit from the many choices Marissa had added would just give me a headache anyway.

Lila held up a pair of jeans and a skirt. I pointed to the jeans and she frowned. She was constantly trying to get me to wear more skirts. Pants helped my legs look longer. Only reaching five-two, looking taller always equaled better in my book. In the end, Lila threw a dark pair of skinny jeans, a spaghetti-strapped blue top, and strappy wedge sandals at me as she walked out the door. I dressed and touched up my makeup and hair. She returned not minutes later, in a short dress and wedges. Looking in the mirror, she added darker liner and shadow to my eyes.

Taking the elevator down to the lobby, she opened an app on her phone. "You have to get on this. It's the best way to get a ride."

After sitting in the car half the day, walking was more appealing to me. In my heels I'd probably only make it two blocks, so I followed her lead. "Are you sure about this? Is it safe?"

"Sure, I've been doing it forever."

"You never did it in Champaign."

She rolled her eyes. "Okay, well since I came here. We're not going to end up in a dumpster. Well I'm not, you're the one with bad luck." She handed me her phone with the company's safety information.

"If we're going by the superstition that bad luck comes in threes, I'm done."

"You're counting Law?"

"Course." These days I was counting every incident I could to believe I was finished with my run of bad luck. I scrolled through the safety information and realized it was totally legit. I passed her phone back to her.

"See, your dad's got you paranoid."

"Isn't it expensive?"

"How much do you make tutoring? Twenty-five an hour, right? This is five bucks and the bus will take an hour on the weekend."

A car pulled up, and she opened the door and waved me in. The driver routed through the deserted main campus. The streets and lawns grew more crowded as we neared the Greek houses.

I fidgeted with my necklace, and Lila batted my hand from my neck. "You met a good number of the guys this summer. You remember Bill, right?"

"Sure." I reminded myself that one reason for coming to school here was to meet new people.

Lila paid the driver, and we took a narrow path that ran along the side of the building to the back of the house. Mark and Ross were playing volleyball in the sandpit, and we greeted them with a wave. Mark was a great player and loved the game. He'd tried, mostly in vain, to improve my skills over the summer.

As we sat on the grass to watch the match, a yellow lab lumbered over to me and rubbed against my legs. I patted her head and she curled up at my feet. If Kate counted, I'd made my second new friend.

The guys made the game look easy, expending little effort in lofting the ball back and forth over the net. I recognized Bill from this summer. Two exceptionally tall guys on his team stood out, and I could've watched them play all night.

Defeated by Bill's team, Mark and Ross sauntered over to where we were sitting. Mark collapsed on top of my outstretched legs, displacing the dog who circled behind me.

"Eww, sweaty boy!" I tried to push him off, but it was like pushing against a brick wall. I gave up. "Decent game, you only lost by three." He rolled off, standing to replace his shirt.

Bill and the taller guys from the other team approached us, retrieving their shirts from the lawn. Mark motioned them towards me. "Hey, you guys should meet Amanda."

I stood quickly, fighting the urge to brush away any grass that might be clinging to my pants.

"Hi, I'm Bill. We met this summer."

"Right, good game." I shook his outstretched hand.

"Thanks." He motioned towards the house. "Sorry, I need some water."

"This is Doug, our president," Mark continued.

Still shirtless, Doug held out his hand towards me. Purposely making eye contact, I slid my hand into his.

"Avery, right, your dad's an alum."

With olive skin and dark wavy hair, my Bubbe would've said he was Greek. But she had a thing for Greeks. He sported a perfect five o'clock shadow, and his deep blue eyes were focused on me. I forced myself to concentrate.

"Right." I nodded not knowing what else to say. My face felt like it was engulfed in flames. Seriously, couldn't Mark have waited to introduce us until after they had their shirts on?

"And this is Zack," Mark pointed tc the super tall blond beside Doug. "He's our VP."

Having to look nearly straight up to make eye contact, I shook his hand as well. He must've been at least six foot four. Where did these guys come from? They looked like they stepped out of a magazine.

"You stink, and I already took a shower." Lila squealed, bringing me out of my trance. Ross grabbed her and slung her over his shoulder, carrying her across the lawn and towards the house.

Mark tapped me on the shoulder. "Hey, I need a shower, too. I'll be back in a few minutes. Do you want to hang out here?"

He's abandoning me? In front of two good-looking, shirtless strangers? "Sure," I heard myself say.

Thankfully, he stood there a minute longer. "I'll grab a round of drinks." He darted away.

"Nice spike there at the end," I commented to Zack.

"Thanks. I see you have a shadow." He bent down and patted the dog still glued to my leg.

Excusing themselves to replace their shirts, Doug and Zack once again towered over me. Even in my wedges, the top of my head barely reached the middle of Zack's chest.

Zack spoke before the silence became obvious. "So, Amanda Avery of the famed Avery sisters?"

"In the flesh." I waved my hands past my legs, not quite sure where he was going with the conversation. Obviously they knew their alums.

Doug continued in an Elizabethan tone. "The beauty of the Avery girls has inspired many brothers to greatness."

"I'm just glad no one remembers when I flashed everyone on the front lawn when I was three."

"Your reputation is still intact." Doug winked at me with his blue eyes.

Mark approached with three plastic cups filled with amber liquid. I wondered if this counted as taking an open drink from someone. At the very least, it went against the no alcohol rule. Not even six hours in, and I was already contemplating being an illegal drinker. Maybe I needed that orientation more than I thought.

Even though I didn't like beer and had never drunk a whole glass, I wasn't going to stand there and do nothing. The sip I took tasted bitter, and I hoped my face didn't betray my attempt at a relaxed facade.

"Not that great, is it?" Doug asked.

"It's relatively cold."

Zack held up his cup. "Cheers to that." Doug and I did the same, and we clunked the cups together. "If I may, my lady, I'm not sure you're going to maintain your virtue drinking that."

Doug punched Zack. "Dude."

I winked at Zack. "Maybe you should stick with flattery and leave Shakespeare to Doug. You have to stay in your niche."

I was surprised how comfortable I felt with them. Their knack for humor immediately put me at ease, despite their magazine model aura. "So do you guys do this routine on a regular basis?"

Zack held his cup out. "This is a one-time only special showing. If we hope to win the heart of an Avery girl, we have to be creative."

"And there are only two of us left to be wooed."

"We would be nothing without your inspiration." Doug bowed towards me, one hand over his heart.

Zack and I both faked a cough.

Doug grabbed a Frisbee from the lawn. "Frisbee?"

The lab followed me as I slid my wedges off and propped the beer between them. Doug and Zack were better coordinated, playing with their cups in one hand. Mark returned and joined us, and we tossed the Frisbee around a few more minutes before Doug and Zack excused themselves for showers.

As they left, Lila and Ross approached. Lila made sure to untuck my hair from behind my ear. "Why do you do that when you get nervous?"

I fluffed my hair out and stuffed my free hand in my pocket with my phone. "Better?"

"Much." She kissed me on the cheek.

We hung out, talking and milling through the crowd. I was introduced to almost every brother and potential there. A potential, I learned, was a potential pledge, usually an entering freshman with an alumni connection. Feeling guilty about ditching the dorm social, I was glad I was at least meeting some freshmen.

After drinking half the beer, being social was easier, and I enjoyed the evening despite myself. Later, Mark started another volleyball game. Looking around, I noticed Lila had disappeared. Thirsty and tired, I went inside to find her.

Not seeing her downstairs, I made my way up to the common area in the middle of the second floor. She was nowhere to be seen, so I leaned against the sofa to text her. I could hear my parents' voices in my head: Freshman lesson number one, always have a trustworthy buddy. Either they had missed one, or I had stopped listening. Then again, their rule about no drinking parties would have covered this situation.

"Nice phone. Looking for Mark? I think I saw him playing volleyball." Doug stopped in front of me.

"Oh, thanks." I turned to him, tucking my hair behind my ear. "I was looking for Lila. We were supposed to get a ride back together."

I made sure to distance myself from Mark. As if it would've mattered to Doug. *Seriously, what am I thinking? Like the president of the fraternity is interested in me?* A gorgeous senior like him probably had an equally beautiful girlfriend. The alcohol was clouding my thought process.

He leaned on the back of the couch beside me. "So you're not into drunk volleyball?"

"Well, volleyball in general, but definitely not drunk volleyball."

He pointed to the mostly full cup I was holding. "Do you need something else to drink?"

I'd carried around the second beer Mark had brought me most of the night. "Water would be great."

"I have some in my room. I'll take that for you." He held out his hand.

Taking my cup, he darted into the kitchen area and returned a few seconds later.

"Since your drink was warm, I'm guessing you're not much of a beer drinker."

"It's the same one I've been holding all night."

"Good strategy. So, you're more of a..." He motioned for me to continue.

"...wine drinker. Yes, sadly, I'm an eighteen-year-old wine snob."

He laughed, but his expression appeared wary. "This way." He motioned down the hall.

I followed him until he stopped in front of a door at the end of the hall, unlocking it. He held the door open, and I stepped inside. It occurred to me this had been another item on the don't-do list: letting a stranger come between me and an exit. But was he really a stranger? I wasn't sure.

It was a typical fraternity room, or at least like Mark and Ross's, except there were huge posters covering one wall from above the desk to the ceiling. As I looked more closely, I realized they weren't just scenic images. Instead, each included one or more people who set the tone. On the left was a picture of what I guessed was the Amazon. A man paddled a boat away from the camera. Although the colors were vibrant and bright, the photo had a serene feel to it. Beside it was a picture of the Eiffel Tower. A couple, centered in the foreground, walked towards the structure holding hands. Although there were many others in the picture, the way the couple was centered made it seem intimate.

"These are amazing. Did you take them?"

He handed me a bottle of water. "You knew they weren't stock?"

I looked at him, and his blue eyes seemed to be boring into me. "Well, the tone of each makes them seem personal." I looked back at the scenes. "You've been to really cool places."

"No one has noticed that before. Are you into photography?"

"Sort of, although my shots are nothing like this."

A photo on his desk caught my eye. "Is this your family?" I pointed to the print. Five nearly identical looking men stood in front of the Great Wall of China.

"Yeah, my brothers and my dad. We were there this summer. It was incredible."

I continued to study the photos. "You really have a gift for this."

"I guess. It's just something I do. Have you traveled much?"

"Nowhere this exotic, just Mexico and Europe a couple of times. My dad gets special deals as a pilot. What city is this?" I pointed to the picture on the far right.

"Tokyo. It's my favorite city."

I turned back to face him. "I'd love to see more of your shots." As soon as the words escaped my mouth, I wanted to take them back.

He turned and grabbed his computer from his desk. He held the laptop out and motioned towards the futon. "Here, I'll show you the ones from my trip this summer."

"I don't want to impose if you need to get back to the party."

He waved a hand in the air. "We're good."

He held the computer on his knees and narrated. As he talked, he grew more animated, pulling up maps of where he'd been.

I was totally engrossed and jumped when there was a knock on his door. Zack appeared in the doorway. "Should've known I'd find you here."

I stood quickly. "He was showing me his photos. They are amazing!"

He ambled towards us. "Yeah, yeah, Doug and his amazing adventures. Always a babe magnet."

Doug stood and set his computer on the desk. "Are you crashing here?"

Zack motioned to where I'd been sitting. "That's my bed." He lumbered towards me, and I had to dart away to avoid his descent onto the futon. He sprawled out, his feet hanging over the end.

"Okay, well, that's that, I guess." Doug opened the door. We stepped out into the hall, and he shut the door behind us.

I slipped my phone out of my pocket and checked the time. It was after one-thirty. "Wow, I didn't realize it was so late."

"Do you want me to help you find Lila or Mark?"

"Umm?" I looked around, disoriented for a moment. We made our way down the hall to the common area.

"I can drive you back to your room."

"Oh, wow, I don't want to put you out. I can get a car." I started a text to Lila and Mark.

Just then, Mark sauntered into the room. "There you are, Manda." His words were slurred. He wasn't going to be any help.

"Have you seen Lila?"

"They turned in a while back." He collapsed on the couch.

"Maybe you should too."

"Sounds like a plan." He stood and loped down the hall.

I picked up my phone, finding the app for the car service. "I'll get a car." I hoped I sounded more confident than I felt.

Doug looked at his watch, "Right about now, everyone wants a car. You're going to wait half an hour and pay double. I can drive or walk you, it's not a problem."

I finally accepted his offer, and we walked down to the parking lot. The lot was completely full. "I was afraid of this. Unfortunately, Zack's is blocked in too. I can walk you."

"I'll call a cab." I looked at my phone again.

"I don't mind walking with you." He placed his hands on my shoulders and turned me back towards the house. His hands were warm, and I shivered at his touch.

We walked on the path around the house to the street in front. Quiet and lit by the soft glow of street lights, the campus felt peaceful. Tall trees lined the streets, and a few changing leaves glowed orange and yellow.

"Thanks for showing me your pictures, they're amazing."

"Thanks."

Tired, I couldn't think of anything else to talk about. Fortunately Doug spoke.

"So you and Mark aren't together?"

"No, just friends. We've known each other since we were little."

"That's pretty rare."

"I guess. His family lives across from mine. He's more like a brother."

"That's cool. And you grew up with Lila and Ross?"

"Just Lila. Ross is an add-on."

Within fifteen minutes, we were at my building. "Thanks so much for walking me back," I told him as we approached the door. Turning to face him, I shuffled my feet and looked at the ground.

"No problem." He waited for me to unlock the door to my building. "Goodnight," he said, holding the door open for me.

"Goodnight." I waved slightly and ducked inside, fighting the urge to turn and watch him walk away.

Changing into my pajamas, I crept into the bathroom, using the light from my room to see. Having washed my face, brushed my hair and teeth, I climbed up into my loft to sleep. I checked my messages on my phone, realizing I'd neglected to text Mom. I'd never hear the end of it if I left a message after two though. All my muscles ached but my mind was abuzz. Even if I had broken a few rules, it had been a good first day. Listening to music, Doug's images, smooth voice, and chiseled chin danced through my mind until I floated off.

Chapter 2

My alarm jolted me out of sleep and upright. Startled by my unfamiliar surroundings, I fought a moment of panic. Gasping for breath, I exhaled and sank back into my pillow. I looked at my phone. Seven was way too early. Still, even with barely five hours of sleep, I didn't regret a single second of last night.

Getting my bearings, I checked for messages. As expected there were a string of texts from my parents and Marissa. I barely had time to shower, dress, and get to the student union by eight so I started a pot of coffee. Thankfully I'd had the foresight to bring a coffee maker, or I'd be a zombie. I got off a text to Marissa, Mom, and Dad while I waited for it to brew.

In the bathroom, a chime from my phone indicated a new text message. I picked up my phone seeing it was from Lila.

Morning, u up?

Just.

Mark said you were with Doug.

He walked me home after you bailed.

Ooh la la. She ignored my dis.

He was just being nice. Knowing she would analyze every second of my time with him, I chose not to elaborate about the evening. It wouldn't do to have her think I was crushing on someone after the first night here. Are you at the dorm? Want to walk together?

I'll meet you there. She must've still been at the fraternity house.

Sipping my coffee, I knocked on Kate's door to make sure it was okay to shower. Kate was already dressed and busy organizing her things. We made plans to walk to orientation together.

As we made our way to the building, we were in agreement about the cruelty of the early start time. In my rush, I hadn't thought to grab anything to eat and hoped they had food. We parted inside the student union, each making our way to our appointed sessions. The day was just as mind-numbing as I thought it'd be, but at least we got lunch and a chance to stretch our legs on the campus tour.

We were released at four, and I met up with Lila to walk back to our dorm. "You look like hell."

"Thanks to you." I shoved her off the path, chastising her for being MIA the night before.

"So, Doug Taylor?" Fortunately, her query was interrupted by a chime from her phone. Reading the screen, she grabbed my arm. "Everyone's going into the city for dinner. You have to come."

"Everyone?" The question came out before I could stop it. Seeing Doug again was definitely something I wanted.

"Yes, even Doug." She bumped her hip into mine, smiling.

"As if?" I rolled my eyes. There was no way he was available, especially to me.

"Yeah, he's totally hot, but he's a senior and can have anyone he wants."

In the dorm elevator, Mom called. Lila got off on her floor holding up six fingers. I shot her a thumb's up. Making my way to my room, I apologized to Mom for not calling the previous night. She was happy that I was meeting people and let me off the hook. When I got to my room, a girl was unpacking boxes with who I assumed were her parents. I put Mom on hold and introduced myself.

Excusing myself to finish the call, I recounted my evening to Mom. Of course, I left out drinking a beer, being abandoned by my best friend, and hanging out with a hot senior till after two.

As I reentered our room, Elise jumped over to me right away. We stood eye to eye, a rarity in my world. Her dark hair was smoothed back into a bun decorated with ribbons of our school colors. If she'd been wearing makeup and anything other than a band T-shirt and khakis, I would've sworn she was a cheerleader.

After introducing her parents, she started detailing her dorm organization protocol and decorating ideas. It was hard to keep up, as she barely paused to breathe. Her excitement felt authentic, and I liked her right away.

Thankfully, after an hour of unpacking, her parents decided they needed dinner. I declined the invitation to join them, figuring I had just enough time for a power nap. Setting my alarm, I lay down on my futon and was asleep within minutes.

Knocking sounds woke me before my alarm. Lila stood at the door holding her makeup bag. Yawning and stretching, I excused myself to shower. By the time I finished, her makeup and hair were done and she had picked out my outfit, a flowery, light, V-neck sleeveless shirt, a pair of black fitted pants, and strappy pumps.

After she did my eyes, she wound a few strands of my hair around a curling iron. "Maybe you should leave more of your natural curl in." She stood back from me, spraying my hair with her favorite hold product. Even with my low style aptitude, I could see how the flowery, ruffled tank worked with the curls.

I felt bad about leaving Elise on her first night and wrote a quick note to her on the white board she'd put up. Lila and I made our way downstairs through what seemed like an endless sea of kids and boxes. Waiting on the walk for the guys, Lila straightened my blouse and untucked my hair from behind my ears. I ducked away from her, trying to remember if she'd always been this picky.

It wasn't long before a silver sport utility vehicle pulled up with Zack in the driver's seat. Mark jumped out of the back seat to let us in.

"Did you recover from last night?" Zack asked, looking into the rearview mirror at me.

"Barely, we had to be at orientation at eight. How bout you?"

"Brutal." He shook his head. "Yeah, I was good. Rowing at eight cures all hangovers."

"You guys were up at eight?"

Zack shook his head. "We were on the water by eight."

I made a mental note to apologize to Doug. I hadn't realized he had to be up so early.

It was a twenty-minute drive into the city, but finding a parking place took a while. As we walked from the parking lot, I caught up with Doug.

"I'm sorry about last night. I wouldn't have kept you so late if I'd known you had rowing so early."

"No problem, I would've been up anyway."

The restaurant was nestled in between other shops, now closed for the evening. It was crowded, and we waited at the bar for a table. I was chatting with Mark when small shot glasses with a dark liquid inside were handed out. I hadn't even been carded. Drinking at a fraternity house was one thing but in public was a completely different story. Chicago was nothing like Champaign, where they carded everyone.

I looked around nervously, trying to decide whether to drink it.

"Don't worry." Doug's smooth voice spoke into my ear. The warm air sent chills down my spine, and I had to square my jaw not to shiver. "I know the owner."

Even though I was nearly frozen, I managed a smile. "Thanks." I swirled the glass, studying the dark liquid.

Zack lifted his glass to toast. "To brotherhood." Everyone's, including Lila's, drink went up in response. I studied the empty glasses. Lila had never been a drinker in high school, but maybe being here all summer had changed that. Mark, seated to my right, shook his glass at me. Doug bumped my elbow, and held his glass, still full, up to me. His blue eyes were seemingly fixed on mine.

"What are you guys waiting for?" Zack called from down the bar.

Doug lifted his glass and winked in my direction. I hoisted my glass, threw my head back, and let the searing liquid slide down my throat. Sweet and bitter, it warmed a path down my chest.

Zack hit the bar with his hand. "Now that there aren't any more virgins, the fun can begin."

Eyes fixed on the glass, I set it on the bar. I took slow breaths, trying to abate the heat rising towards my cheeks. Distracted by my conversation with Doug, it didn't seem long before we were shown to our table. I took a seat near the open windows ending up between Mark and Doug. When the waiter approached, he spoke in what I assumed was Japanese. Doug joked with him as if they were old friends, mixing English and Japanese. Not even lifting a menu, he ordered for the table.

They got another round of shots, and I fully intended to let mine sit. Mark shook his empty glass at me. "What are you waiting for, Amanda?" *So much for my dad's theory that Mark would be a good influence.* I didn't consider myself someone who was swayed by peer pressure, and wondered whether they cared if I drank it or not. Still, I was uncomfortable, and the drink would cure that. What the heck, I thought and downed it in one swift motion.

"So you speak Japanese?" I asked Doug, setting the glass slowly on the table, trying to cover my shakiness.

"Just enough to order food and be social." He motioned to the two waiters who placed several dishes on the table. "I'm focusing on Chinese right now. I'll take Japanese winter and spring."

Zack pointed at Doug. "He's sort of a language genius."

Mark elbowed me, nearly knocking me from my seat and into Doug. "Maybe we found someone who knows more languages than you."

Ross pointed between Doug and me. "That's right."

Zack held a bite of foods towards me. "What you got, Amanda?"

Doug looked at me. Normally I would've preferred to disappear rather than admit I was eighteen and knew four languages, but the two shots were definitely working in my favor. I glanced at him first and then around the rest of the table. "Spanish, French, Italian, and German…"

"Impressive." Zack put a fist up in front of me, and I knocked my hand against his. "I think you guys are tied, especially since I'm not sure Spanish counts for Doug. He's like half Puerto Rican."

"Like half Puerto Rican?" Doug hit Zack on the head. "Watch it." His tone bordered on being playful, but his face showed no signs of humor. I guessed he was indeed half Puerto Rican, which made sense with his coloring. Puerto Rican, not Greek, I told Bubbe in my head.

Curious, I turned to Doug. "So spill. What are yours?" I had to remind myself this was not high school and intellect had value.

"Yo habla Español," he rolled his eyes as if that were obvious, and then he continued in French. "French, Italian, you heard my Japanese, and I'll finish Chinese II this quarter. I actually don't get many opportunities to speak in French, so this is good practice for me."

I continued to speak with him in French. "Impressive. I hear Asian languages are tricky to learn."

"More so to read or write. Growing up in a bilingual home definitely was an advantage. I hope to work in Asia after I graduate."

"So you really liked China and Japan?"

"Especially China, my internship in Hong Kong was a great experience."

"From what I've heard, doing business there is challenging."

"You really have to be sharp. Are you taking any language classes this quarter?"

"Only the intro to international studies course. They wouldn't let me sign up for more, something about core classes." I rolled my eyes, surprised I was feeling so confident. Either the shots or speaking in French served to ease my anxiety.

"How do you practice?"

"I tutor, but I'm not sure how I'm going to keep that up."

"We have a Latino graduate club, and I think there's some sort of tutoring group. What age do you work with?"

"All ages, even preschoolers."

"Really, preschoolers?"

"They're so fun. It's my favorite age to teach. Some of the older kids aren't motivated, but the younger kids don't even know they're learning. To them, it's just fun."

Zack interrupted our conversation. "Umm, guys with the weird language, food's here."

Doug ignored him and continued in French. "Those stupid Americans."

I laughed and winked at him. "They don't know any better." Was I flirting?

Zach stood up. "Okay, enough of the brainy stuff. Doug, switch with me."

Doug got up, and they switched seats. "You're just jealous. I told you to learn a language. It's a chick magnet." Doug winked at me as he sat.

"But with all my other attributes, it would give me an unfair advantage." Zack pushed up his sleeve and flexed his biceps.

I reached out, felt the muscle, and fanned myself.

Zack laughed. "See, they'd melt like butter." He leaned into me. "So you look pretty fit. Are you into sports?"

"I play tennis and ran cross country. Mark coached me in volleyball all summer, but I'm not that good."

"You should play co-rec volleyball with us. It'll be epic!"

"Wow, epic?" I wasn't sure if he was joking.

"Well, maybe not epic, but you should play."

"Maybe. So what about you? You're on the rowing team, I know nothing about rowing." I hoped to keep the conversation going since I'd talked to Doug the whole night. Although I definitely was, I didn't want everyone to think I was interested him.

Zack's major was a sports medicine. I had no idea what sports medicine was, and one simple question sent him into an in-depth explanation of the field. When he asked about my class schedule Mark jumped into the conversation.

He did his best spin on some foreign language. "She has the primo schedulo due to el scholarshipo."

My face suddenly flushed, and I rolled my eyes at him and pinched his cheek. "You should stick to English, sweetie."

"You're on scholarship?" Doug asked.

"She's such a princess she doesn't have a single class before ten," Mark answered for me.

Thanks to Mark, my face was now a fire ball. I began plotting his demise.

"Sweet, so you can work out with us!" Zack said.

I wasn't sure if it was a real offer or if he was just being nice. Who wouldn't want to work out with them? Of course that could lead to becoming just one of the guys, and that was not what I wanted. "I'm not sure I can keep up with you."

"I'll get you on a circuit, and you'll be buff in no time." Zack lifted my arm and felt for muscle. "You should start by upping your protein." He slid the sushi plate towards me.

The food was amazing and hanging out with them was really fun. When we drove back to campus, Zack dropped Lila, Ross, and Mark off at the house. Doug and Bill were staying at Zack's due to their early morning on the lake. Pulling up in front of my dorm, Doug jumped out and opened my door before I could reach for the handle. "I'll walk you to the door."

"Don't worry, it's not far." The front door of my dorm was maybe fifty feet and the sidewalk was well lit.

"Don't fight it," Zack said. "He's the last Southern gentleman alive."

"My mom is very traditional, and my dad grew up in Virginia." Doug placed his hand on my lower back as we turned towards the dorm.

His hand radiated heat, and instinct taking over, I slid closer to him. It would have been so easy to lean into him and rest my head on his chest. I caught myself before I reacted to that thought. My lack of sleep and two shots were catching up with me, but it was more than that. Two days and already I was captivated by him. I was in big trouble.

"So, will you be at the house tomorrow after the game?" he asked when we were almost to the door.

Was he interested in seeing me, or was he just making small talk? Not wanting to seem like a stalker, I gave a long-winded answer about my family being up for the game and the alumni event at the house. Feeling a little ridiculous, and realizing he already knew my dad was an alum, I unlocked the door quickly and thanked him for walking me to the building.

With the excuse of waving to Zack and Bill, I watched Doug walk to the car. He was hands down the most amazing guy I'd ever met. Leaning against the wall in the elevator, I could still feel the warm imprint from his hand on my back. I walked down the hall to my room in a haze, thinking I loved this college. Exhausted and still slightly buzzed, it didn't matter that the room still felt foreign, and I fell into a deep sleep quickly.

Every year since I could remember, my family had attended the alumni barbecue at Dad's fraternity. He still kept in touch with many of his brothers, and this event was their annual ritual. Walking from my dorm, I found their tailgating spot easily. Tia and Ed were parked in the spot beside my parents, and it felt like a huge family reunion. After reintroductions to all the friends, Marissa and I opted to sit with Mark, Lila, and Ross at the game. Dad insisted we go to the barbecue together, so we met them outside the stadium afterwards. We walked the short distance to the fraternity house. On the front lawn, Doug, Zack, and Bill intercepted us.

With a quick smile and nod in my direction, Doug greeted Dad. "Mr. Avery, Doug Taylor. Good to see you again."

Marissa nudged me, cocking her head towards the guys in front of us. We'd sat with Mark, Lila, and Ross at the game, and I hadn't had a chance to fill my sister in on my first few days. She had no clue that I'd spent two nights in a row with them.

Dad shook Doug's hand. "Doug, good to see you again. Please call me Charlie. I believe we met last year when you were president-elect."

"Yes sir, that's right. But I don't think I had the privilege of meeting your whole family?"

"Maybe not. Do you remember my wife, Claire?"

"Yes. Mrs. Avery, nice to see you again." Doug shook her hand.

"And these are two of my daughters." Dad introduced Marissa first.

Doug shook her hand and turned to me. "Amanda, I'm glad you came." He smiled at me.

"You've met?" Dad inquired.

"Mark introduced us," I answered.

Doug smiled at me before turning back to Dad. "So your Northwestern tradition continues. Your older daughter graduated a couple of years ago, correct?" Trying not to read too much into his facial expressions, I concentrated on the conversation.

"Yes, and she also married an alum earlier this summer."

Just then I felt something cold and wet against my calf and jumped. Blondie, the house lab, had found me again. I rubbed her ears and received a lick in the face as thanks.

Bill leaned down and grabbed her collar, pulling her away from me. "Sorry, she's supposed to stay in the house. She must've gotten out."

Standing up, I heard Dad continuing his conversation with Doug. "So, I believe you and Amanda have a few things in common. You're an international studies and business major if I remember correctly?"

Before the conversation could go any further, I was captured from behind in a bear hug. Mark picked me up by my middle and spun me around. Luckily, he was considerate of the fact I was wearing a sundress and didn't throw me over his shoulder like usual. At least I was saved from Dad's academic major conversation.

Marissa rolled her eyes. "Drink much? We just left you like thirty minutes ago."

As Mark put me down, Doug introduced Zack, who winked at me. "We won't judge you by association with Mark."

I smoothed my skirt and looked up at him. "Thank you!"

"And this is Bill McKenzie, the new president-elect." Doug introduced Bill as he rejoined our group.

Dad gripped Mark's shoulder. "I hope our Champaign boys have been pulling their weight."

"Of course, Mark and Ross are great for the Chapter. Mark is even heading up the intramural teams this year."

"Good to hear."

"I was hoping to add some co-rec teams this year with Lila and Amanda on board," Mark told him.

"What sports are up for the fall?" Dad asked.

"Flag football and volleyball."

"Those might be a little risky for Manda. Do you remember the volleyball incident last year at school?"

Did he have to bring that up?

"We'll make sure Amanda is taken care of, sir," Doug said.

I looked at him and our eyes met briefly. Then he turned to look squarely at my father. Doug was pledging to take care of me? I wasn't a child that needed to be looked after.

Dad motioned towards Doug. "Are you gentlemen athletes?"

"We're on the rowing team."

"Beautiful sport. It looks almost as peaceful as flying. Well, it was nice meeting you gentlemen." Dad shook Bill and Zack's hands. He turned to Doug and did the same. "Great to see you again Mr. Taylor."

"Always a pleasure, and don't worry about Amanda, she'll be safe here." This was beyond embarrassing. I felt like a school girl.

"Thank you." Dad turned, wrapping his arm around Mom and walking towards the Chapter house.

I was reeling. Doug's pledge—was that what it was?—struck me as odd. Some guy I'd just met two days ago was promising to take care of me, make sure I was safe? I tried to write it off as some type of brotherhood thing. I hoped I didn't come across as frail and fragile. Dad had made sure we could protect ourselves. Although I was small, I could hold my own.

Lagging behind our parents, Marissa linked her arm through mine and leaned into me, faking a whisper. "I'd let those three keep me safe anytime. I might even have to fake something if I were you, Manda."

I elbowed her in the ribs, but I couldn't help but laugh.

My parents went off in search of their friends while Marissa and I found Mark, Ross, and Lila. There were a lot more brothers in attendance today, and Mark took it upon himself to introduce us to all those I hadn't met. Two hours later, with cheeks sore from smiling, I was more than happy to have a break when Dad texted me to meet them at the front door.

As we were leaving the house, Dad made an effort to find Doug and say goodbye. "Mr. Taylor, the house looks great. You have done a lot of good work."

"Thank you, sir. Are you heading home tonight?"

"Yes, we have a bit of a drive."

"Well, I hope to see you again soon. Be sure to come by the house if you're in town."

"We'll be up for all the home games. Thanks again for everything." They shook hands.

As we started to walk away, Doug reached out and tapped my shoulder. His touch sent tingles down my spine, and my contradictory feelings for him frustrated me.

"Most of the brothers will be hanging out later if you want to stop by."

"Okay, thanks," I managed. We made our way to the car and back to my room, where I introduced them to Elise. Mom and Marissa were impressed with how we'd organized and transformed the room with matching curtains and pillows. Dad was anxious to get home, and I was ready for them to be gone. I'd had enough of his fatherly oversight.

As I waved goodbye to them out front, I got a text from Lila. BBQ over. band starting. Are u coming?

Yes! Be there in half hour! I wrote back. I needed an outlet for my anxiety and dancing would be perfect. Plus, I wanted to see Doug and figure out what this whole pledge thing was about.

Tonight I didn't need fashion advice. I knew I wanted to look sexy. I found a tight pair of blue pants, cream lacy tank, and the best push-up bra in my closet. Touching up my makeup, I added bright lavender liner and dark mascara to my eyes. I curled the ends of my hair and slid on some bangles and a long necklace.

As I was pulling on my high heeled sandals, Elise looked up from her show. "Where are you going?"

"Fraternity party. You can come if you want." I stood and smoothed down my pants, feeling like I was bailing on her again.

"No, I'm beat, and those parties really aren't my thing."

"I'll be quiet when I come in." I stuffed my phone, ID, and key into my back pockets, pushing my questions about what she was thinking to the back of my mind. I had enough spinning around in there already.

I'd reserved a pick up from the car service, proud that I was breaking out of my comfort zone. At the house I found Lila first, needing to get out everything going through my brain.

Unfortunately, she didn't have any better explanation than I did for my Dad's or Doug's comments.

"I need a drink," I told her as we reached Mark's and Ross' room.

"Finally!" She slid her arm around my waist. "Realizing the benefits of alcohol are we?"

"She wants booze," Lila said to them inside. "The good stuff."

Mark retrieved a bottle of vodka from his bottom drawer, and Lila mixed it with a Diet Coke for me.

Mark let me finish half of it before asking any questions. "So what's your deal?"

"Did you hear my dad?"

He started laughing, and I punched him on the shoulder. He stood, starting to act out the scene for Ross and Lila.

I didn't let him get the whole way through before I pulled Lila up by the arm and dragged her out the door. Drinks in hand, we slid through the crowd making our way downstairs and to the dance floor. Near the stage we found an empty pocket and danced the whole set.

Hot and close to breaking out in full sweats, we headed in the direction of the back door. As I neared the exit, I noticed Doug standing against the wall, arms folded over his chest, looking directly towards me. Thinking there must be some hot girl behind me, I turned around. Seeing none, I returned to my former course only to slam right into his chest.

Feeling his rippled muscles below his shirt, I was temporarily distracted. "Sorry." I recovered, stepping back and to his right. He moved in the same direction, blocking me. Hands on my hips, I looked up at him.

"I'm hot." I fanned myself. "I was getting some air." Those drinks had done exactly what I wanted and lowered my inhibitions. This thought was a little distressing, but I ignored it.

He held up a bottle of water.

"Oooh, thanks." I said, almost forgetting that I meant to interrogate him. I moved to slide around him again, but he hooked me around the waist with his arm. I was trapped, and he was touching me again. "I was going outside with Lila." I pointed in the direction she'd gone.

"You want to go with Lila?" he asked, pointing her out to me. She was already wrapped around Ross. Darn that girl. "You should stay inside. It's much safer."

He was so close I could feel the heat radiating from his body, but I stood as tall as I could. "Does this have to do with that freaky pledge you made to my dad?"

He laughed. How dare he laugh? This was serious. He turned me around, facing me towards the back door. A campus police car was turning around in the lot. Staying inside made sense now. He spun me back around. "Your dad was worried about his daughter being away from home for the first time, and I eased his mind."

When he explained it like that, it sounded like he was just being nice. I decided to forgive him. He ushered me towards the window, and I sat down on the sill next to him. As I sipped the water, he peppered me with questions about my schedule, my classes, and major and minor. Like before, I was mesmerized by his aura and thought nothing of answering each one with total honesty. Eventually he ran out of topics, and I was able to learn more about his travels and family. His dad took him and his three brothers on exotic vacations each year. I could've listened to him for hours.

Finishing the water in my bottle, I looked around and realized the band was gone along with most of the people. Bill materialized in front of us. I wanted to stand, but my body felt like it was defying movement.

"I'm surprised you're still down here. I thought I was the only rower up so late. Just wanted you to know the house is all locked up, and I'm turning in. Can I get a ride to the boathouse in the morning?"

"Sounds good," Doug said. "See you at 7:30?"

"See you then," Bill said. "Night, Amanda."

"Goodnight," I replied.

Looking at my phone, I was shocked to see it was after one. "I kept you up too late again."

"No worries, I would've been up anyway. I'll drive you home." He held his hand out, and I took it. Leading me upstairs to his room, he retrieved his keys and Blondie. We walked down to the lot and found his car. I was surprised to see Doug drove a Honda, especially after being in Zack's forty-thousand-dollar sport utility vehicle and seeing the lot littered with expensive sedans.

The cool air had sobered me up, and as I opened the door, I hesitated, remembering my recent incident with Law. I shook my head trying to ward away the memory.

"You okay?" he asked from the other side.

He's president of the fraternity, and he told your dad he'd take care of you, I reminded myself. Still, suddenly I froze. "Sure, just a minute." I stepped back and pulled out my phone.

DOUG GIVING ME A RIDE BACK TO MY DORM, I texted Marissa.

I stepped back to the car and opened the door. He got in his side, and Blondie jumped in behind him taking my seat. "Hey, that's not for you," Doug said, pushing her into the back seat.

We rode the short distance in silence with Blondie's head between us. I had to crane my neck around her to see him. "You can just drop me at the curb."

"My grandmother would roll over in her grave if I did that."

He parked directly in front of the door, turned the car off, and got out. Before he reached my door, I had propped it open and thrown one foot out. He shook his finger at me and laughed. "I'll let this one slide."

Like the night before, he waited for me to unlock the door and held it open.

"So tomorrow's the last day freshmen are allowed inside the houses, and I suspect Lila will be taking advantage. We have tons of stuff going on if you want to come by."

When I turned around to answer him, I was surprised he was only a foot from me. "Ooh." I ducked back.

He laughed, letting the door close. "Wow, my charm must have taken a night off. I don't think I've ever had someone jump away from me so quickly."

"I didn't realize you were right there." I felt silly, but I wasn't sure what else to say.

Just inside, I watched him walk to his car. Blondie had jumped into the front seat, and he rubbed her head before driving off. Taking the stairs two at a time, I tried to shake the nervous energy I felt from being close to him and the way my hand felt wrapped in his. I did a quick reality check. I'd been introduced to at least a hundred guys, and I liked the first one I met? He was a senior, president of the fraternity, the hottest brother, and a guy who just happened to speak four languages. Of course I was into him, who wouldn't be? I was seriously delusional if I even entertained the thought of him being interested in me. He probably had a super-hot girlfriend who had yet to return from summer break.

Falling for him was not a good idea, as there were three possible outcomes to this story. First, my initial attraction to him would fade and we'd end up friends (that was unlikely and seriously a downer). Second, he'd fall madly in love with me and we'd live happily ever after (in what universe would that happen?). Or third, the most likely scenario, I'd fall hard for him (not that I hadn't already), but he wouldn't be into me and I'd be left crushed. They were called crushes for a reason. No matter how many years of drama and debate clubs were in my past, I wasn't good enough to pull off seeing him on a regular basis if he blew me off.

Turning my key quietly in the door, I saw it was dark inside. Snoring sounds came from Elise's top bunk, and I was glad to be a heavy sleeper. I washed my face and crawled into bed, still berating myself for thinking about Doug's huge callused hands and hard chest. A ding from my phone saved me from my mental spiral.

It was a text from Marissa. DOUG, NICE! ANYTHING I SHOULD KNOW?

WE HUNG OUT.

THAT MAKES 3 NITES IN A ROW!

If I got into it with her now I'd never get to sleep. NEED ZZZs. TALK 2MORROW.

Chapter 3

On Sunday morning, I talked Elise into running with me. I could tell I was starting to get edgy from so much socializing, and running was always therapeutic for me. I knew I shouldn't do a long run alone, and I doubted Lila would be up for it.

It was a gorgeous sunny day, warm with a light breeze. It would be windier by the lake, but it would feel good when we got there. Elise had a slower pace, but I was content to match hers. I had a loop mapped out, taking us by the fraternity house in each direction. It was juvenile, but I wanted a chance to see him.

"So I'm guessing you've met tons of hot guys hanging out at that frat house. Anyone caught your fancy yet?"

Her choice of words was hilarious. Caught my fancy? Who talked like that? It sounded like something Bubbe would say.

"I've only been here like three days." I evaded her question. Doug was way out of my league and what did I really know about him, anyway?

Elise broke my mental anguish. "So, no boys?"

I got the sense she didn't believe me. "No," I lied.

"Girls?"

"No, I like guys," I corrected.

"Had to ask."

For the next mile or so, she told me about her dating dilemmas and how she'd had a series of semi-steady dating runs, but all had fizzled. Eventually she grew too tired to talk and run, so I was rewarded with the silence I was craving. My breathing evened out and my thoughts stopped racing.

By the time we passed the two-thirds mark, I could tell Elise was really pushing herself. I felt bad and offered to stop and walk, but she was determined to run the whole way. Just as we passed the house for the second time, a silver sports utility vehicle crossed over and parked on the curb in front of us.

"I thought that was you, Manda." Zack jumped out of his car, using my nickname.

Bill climbed out of the back, and Doug came around from the other side. Dressed in workout clothes, they must have just come from rowing.

Elise and I slowed, and she doubled over, holding her side. I didn't think she would object to stopping for a bit.

"How far are you guys running?" Zack asked.

"I was trying to kill my roommate to get the room to myself, so I took her on a loop around campus. This is Elise." I motioned to her. She righted herself, smiled, and waved, sweat pouring down her face. "Are you okay?" I asked when I noticed she was as red as a beet.

"Yeah, never better," she said, trying to control her breathing. She offered her hand to Zack. "Hi, I'm the roommate who will die of a heart attack very soon." I was relieved her personality was kicking in. At least that meant she wasn't really in distress.

"Good thing we were here, then. I'm Zack."

I introduced Doug and Bill, and Elise managed to smile and stay upright.

"Would you guys like to come in and get something to drink?" Doug asked. "I have Gatorade and water in my fridge."

Elise looked at her watch. "I've got to get back."

Before we turned to go, Zack spoke up. "We're grilling this afternoon. You coming?"

"There will be a lot of people around. Elise you're welcome to come too." Doug added grabbing his bag form the car.

Elise interjected before I could answer. "Thanks for the invite. Sorry, Amanda, I need to get back."

"Okay," I said to her. "I'll see you guys later," I said, turning back to Zack and Doug. I was still undecided if the invite was about me specifically or having girls at the house to mingle with the potentials. Mark had mentioned that idea the previous night, and I'd been turning it over in my head. But there was no fighting the blaring truth that I wanted to see Doug again.

Making our way back to the dorm, Elise collapsed on the floor of our room.

"I'm guessing you're never going to run with me again."

"If we see hot guys like that, I'll run with you anytime."

"I can't guarantee the scenery."

"You know who you're hanging out with, right?" She didn't let me answer before continuing, "Although I'm not really into the scene, for those who are, Doug and Zack are like the most eligible guys on campus. Well, Zack I guess. Doug has been with Zoey for like two years."

I bit my lip. The proverbial shoe had dropped. "Zoey?"

"You haven't met Zoey."

"I haven't even heard of her."

With one hand on her hip and the other waving through the air, she took a huge breath. "Let me get this straight. You've been hanging out with these guys for three days and there's been no Zoey, no mention of Zoey, no Zoey anything?" Out of nowhere she had a Southern twang, must have been her South Carolina background coming out.

Still stunned, I shook my head. My mind was reeling, of course Doug had a girlfriend. Elise whipped her yearbook out from under a stack of books. She turned through the pages. "Okay, so this is the lowdown as I know it. Zack is a player, so don't even think about him. Actually, don't even look at him, although I know it's hard. Doug hasn't been available for two years. If he's on the market, oh my goodness, you don't even want to be in on that."

I wished this conversation would end, or actually had never happened. More than that, I wanted not to care. "I've just been hanging out with my friends."

"Good, because Zack will spit you out like hour-old gum, and Doug is..." she started but paused for a moment. "There aren't words for that boy."

I had lots of words for that boy. My phone buzzed, and I picked it up when I saw it was Lila. After Elise's revelations, I just wanted to hide under a rock. I mentally berated myself for ever considering Doug might be flirting with me. When I told Lila I was thinking of going to the dorm cookout, she badgered me to come to the house until I caved. By the time I finished my shower, she was already looking through my closet.

"Any epiphany?" I began to towel dry my hair. Whether or not Doug was taken, I wanted to look good.

"What if you wear shorts with heels? That's totally in."

"No, jeans," I said. I hated that my skin was so white. There would be no way I could pull off nonchalant, and I was determined to, if I wasn't comfortable in my clothes.

We chatted about roommates while I did my hair and makeup, and then we walked over to the house. The back lawn was crowded with people but we found Mark and Ross playing volleyball opposite Doug and Zack. I pulled my shades down wishing to be invisible. We sat down on the grass near the sandpit. I wished I could relax and not think about the fact I'd been hanging out with a guy who might already have a girlfriend.

Doug and Zack won, but it was close. Ross and Mark waved to us, but showed no sign of moving off the court. Volleyball was their passion, and they could play for hours. The game ended but Mark didn't leave the court. "Who's playing next?" he yelled from across the pit. "Hey, Manda, Lila, come play."

Zack and Doug made their way over. "Is that guy obsessed or what?" Zack asked.

"More like addicted," Lila said.

"Hey, glad you came, Manda," Zack sat down next to me. "I thought I might have to come drag you out of your dorm."

He'd adopted my nickname already, and it took me a second to acclimate. Nobody except Marissa, Mark, Lila, and Ross called me that. I recovered, pointing to Lila. "Your little cohort over here got to me first."

"You're asking Amanda to play volleyball?" Ross asked, plopping down beside Lila.

Mark ran over and started pulling me to my feet. "Sure, she played with me all summer."

"How'd you get her to play volleyball after the chin incident, much less the prom fiasco?"

I didn't like where this was going. I scanned the faces and all of them were trained on me.

"My girl is tough," Mark retorted.

Lifting my glasses, I looked over at Ross. "I'll play. Lila, come play." I made my way into the sand pit, hoping they'd follow me. In bad luck incident one, I'd slit my chin playing volleyball. Incident two included my now ex-boyfriend, Carter, making out with half the girls' volleyball team a week before prom. These were not facts I wanted advertised.

"I thought you hated volleyball." Ross snickered.

Zack jogged into the pit. "This sounds interesting, I'm playing with Amanda. Doug?"

Everyone was standing now, and Lila pushed Ross towards the pit. "That's enough," I heard her say to him quietly.

Mark and Ross rounded up a couple more guys to make the teams. Our team huddled and when we broke, Zack took a spot beside me. "So what does volleyball have to do with a chin and prom?"

Deciding it was better to just come clean, I quickly told my stories. Repeating them out loud helped me feel in control again. Besides the incident with Law, these were the most embarrassing things Ross knew about me.

Zack held a fist up to me. "Athletic injuries are cool, makes you look committed. So are we going to annihilate them or what?"

I tapped my fist on his. "Sounds like a plan."

"Take it easy on her," Mark yelled from the other side of the net. "We want her to play co-rec."

"Fat chance!" Ross said, laughing again.

Doesn't he ever take a break? I was up first to serve. It was the one skill I was consistent at. Although I'd had bruises on my arm for weeks, I could heave the ball over the net with some accuracy.

My first serve landed where I wanted, right in the middle of the court. Despite my annoyance with Ross, I started to relax. Zack and Doug weren't nearly as intense as Mark, and the team fell into an easy rhythm. Because no one on our side cared whether we won or lost, Mark and Ross got their victory.

"Nice serve," Ross commented to me as we walked out of the pit.

"Thanks. Oh, and thanks for that walk down memory lane." I elbowed him in the ribs.

"That's what I'm here for."

Mark came over and put an arm around me. "Hey, I thought that was my job."

After a few more playful jabs, everyone broke to mingle. Retrieving my shoes, I was startled by a hand on my back.

"Did you eat yet?" Doug pointed towards the food. "I'd stay away from the hot dogs, but the burgers are pretty good."

His touch stunned me, and all I could muster was a quick agreement.

He kept his hand on my back, walked with me towards the grill, and then offered to brave the crowd to get me a burger. Why was he being so nice? It was useless to speculate, so I stood by and let him take the lead. When he got to the condiments area, he was holding them up to figure out which ones I wanted. A comical dance ensued, and I was laughing hysterically by the time he got back with our plates of food.

Zack came over to us, scarfing down his own burger. "So, do they do that all the time?"

"If you're asking if my friends love to humiliate me in front of strangers. Yes."

Doug left without saying anything, and I was mad at how much it bothered me.

"We're strangers? I'm offended." Zack pretended to be hurt. "But, seriously, you take it well. I remember Mark scrambling for a tux last spring. He took you to prom, right? But you guys aren't together?"

"No, just friends." I caught sight of Doug walking towards us, two water bottles in hand.

Zack looked away and then back to me. "I thought you guys might be a thing."

Doug returned with the water, and put a hand on Zack's shoulder. "We need to be social."

The next hours flew by as I hung out with the potentials and brothers. Remembering names, faces, and relevant facts from earlier encounters, I was surprised to realize I was enjoying myself. It was after six when Lila found me talking with some potentials. As soon as I excused myself, she dragged me up the stairs by the arm.

I pulled my arm from her grip. "What's going on?"

Walking backwards down the hall in front of me, she tugged at my hand. "I'm not sure where everyone is going, but there is going to be a huge party." I rolled my eyes wondering if, in Lila's mind, there was any other kind.

As we approached the common area Zack announced they were heading to his place. Mark tapped me from behind. "You in?"

Zack's apartment was off campus where they could drink more freely. I remembered the other night, and I didn't want to be stuck getting back alone, or worse as a designated driver. "I'm going to pass."

Zack was beside me in a second, grabbing my hand and spinning me under his arm. "Come on, we've been here all weekend. Come hang out with us."

"It sounds like fun, but do you mind dropping me at my dorm on your way?"

"I think you're making a big mistake, but yes I will."

I looked down the hall towards Doug's room. Noticing it was open, I walked to it and poked my head inside. He sat at his desk in front of his laptop, so I knocked lightly.

He spun around in his chair. "Oh, hi, I was just sending off some emails."

"I was just leaving. Zack said he'd drop me off at my dorm."

"Is everyone going to Zack's?"

"Yeah, but I'm bailing."

"Hold on a minute, okay?" He punched a few more keys on his computer, and then turned back to me. "I'm on house duty. Do you want to hang out here? I went through some more of my photos if you want to see them."

Bill appeared behind me. "Sorry Amanda, I need to talk to Doug for a sec."

"No problem." I made my way back to the common area. Not seeing Lila, I went to Ross's room, and thankfully, she was alone. I bit my lip and tried to decide if I was actually going to ask her. She'd been at the house all summer, so she was sure to know if there was a girlfriend. Don't be a wuss, I told myself, but something inside me told me to hold my tongue. Being exposed was not in my nature.

I retrieved my bag and followed her to the common room. Still unsure of my decision, I hung back.

As people started filing out, Zack nodded to me. "Amanda, you ready?"

Doug crossed over to me. "Did you want to hang out here?"

Mark, Lila, and Ross all turned to look at me, Lila with eyes as wide as saucers.

"Yeah, sure." I tried to sound nonchalant.

"Cool."

"Kay." Zack shrugged and followed the others out.

Mark and Ross headed down the hall with no reaction. Before she was out of sight, Lila turned and shot me a thumb's up. There would definitely be an inquisition tomorrow.

Doug and I went back to his room. Blondie was standing just outside the closed door. "I guess she might need a walk. I'm hungry too. You mind walking to get some food?"

"No, that sounds nice." Movement was good for anxiety after all.

We walked across campus with Doug reviewing points of interest. He must've realized I'd know where everything major was, because we passed through sections I'd never seen before. He was easy to talk to and our conversation flowed easily. By the time we got to the restaurant, I knew all about his family and the trips he'd taken. He got dinner at a sandwich shop, and by the time we got back to the house, it was after nine.

In his room, I sat down on the floor beside Blondie while he went to fill her water bowl.

When he returned, he laughed at me. "What are you doing, you don't have to sit on the floor."

I slipped my shoes off and moved to the futon.

He picked up one of my shoes as he sat down beside me. "I made you walk an hour in these. I feel horrible. Why didn't you say anything?"

"I walk in them all the time."

"Really?" He picked turned the shoe over. "You're probably ruining your feet."

I shrugged, and there was a short bit of silence before he spoke again, "So, why didn't you want go to the party at Zack's?"

Realizing I'd acted more conservatively than the previous night, I tried to recoup. "We have orientation tomorrow, and I didn't want to end up with no one to get a ride back with."

"For being eighteen and having newly acquired freedom, that's pretty mature."

I wasn't sure if his comment was meant as a compliment or if he was making fun of me. "My Bubbe always said I'm an old soul." Wow, that had just left my mouth without my permission. How much of a geek was I?

"Your Bubbe?"

"Sorry, my grandmother; she was Jewish." Wow, that was more info than I planned on sharing too. I released my hair from the ponytail I'd been wearing, shaking it out. "You worked on some of your pictures?"

He reached over to his desk, retrieved his laptop, and sat back down beside me. I moved closer, and Blondie got up and stuck her nose in my lap. I patted the cushion, and she plopped down next to me.

Doug put the computer on his lap and stretched his arm out behind me. "I do have one more question for you, if you don't mind? What was the volleyball thing Ross was talking about?"

I winced. If I never had to tell those stories again, it'd be too soon. Given my dad's need to pass on his paranoia, if that's what it was, about me getting hurt, I decided to avoid talking about my injury. I recited the part about my boyfriend and the girls' volleyball team.

"How long were you dating?"

"Four months." I pushed a stray strand of hair behind my ear and looked down.

"I'm sorry, too personal?"

"No, he was a jerk."

"What was the chin thing?"

Ugh, I thought he'd drop it! "I dove for the ball in gym class. The floor won. It wasn't pretty."

"Broken bones?"

I lifted my chin to show him the scar. "Just a cracked chin."

"I'm guessing that's what your dad was referring to with his comment yesterday?"

"Wait, that's three questions." I wanted the spotlight off me, especially since we were cataloging my most embarrassing moments. "But, yes." Ready to move on, I took the computer off his lap and set it on mine.

He reached over and started opening files, showing me more photos of the Amazon trip he and his brothers had taken. Even though he claimed it was a new camera and it was his first stab at photography, the images were brilliant. We looked through over two hundred photos, with me snuggled between him and Blondie. Eventually she woke, and started nudging me. Doug looked at his watch.

"Wow, it's after eleven. I'll drive you back, since I already walked you around campus in your heels."

"That'd be great." I stood and stretched.

Blondie rode with us in his car again, and they both walked me to my door.

I unlocked the door to the building. "Thanks for showing me your pictures."

"I'm surprised you didn't fall asleep." He held the door, leaning towards me.

"Course not, they're brilliant." What I meant was that he was brilliant.

"Okay, now I know you're toast. You should get a good night's sleep." He laughed and waved as the door shut.

Elise was combing her hair when I came in. "I'm surprised you're still up."

"I just got back from our sorority meeting. It took forever," she complained, climbing into bed. "How about you?"

"Just hanging out."

"I don't blame you. The views at that house are amazing!"

The views were amazing. However, if you were just looking at the view, you wouldn't see the whole picture. Maybe this was only my interpretation, or maybe I was delusional, but Doug seemed to be a different person with me.

Chapter 4

I slept in till eight the next morning, and it felt like heaven. Due to my scholarship status, I wasn't scheduled for an orientation event until after lunch. When I grabbed my phone to check for messages, there were several texts from Mom, Marissa, and of course Lila, who wanted every detail from last night.

Getting a cup of coffee, I called Mom first. Deciding to go to the campus athletic center for a run, I was responding to the texts when I was snatched up and swung over a huge shoulder.

I saw Doug and realized Zack had me. "She's a bird, she's a plane, she's Amanda Avery, Super Mini-Girl." He spun me until I was dizzy.

I tried to focus on a static object, and Doug stood with his arms crossed over his chest right in my line of view. "I would put her down. She looks green."

"I just had Cheerios," I threatened.

"Super Mini-Girl with the weak stomach being put down gently now." Zack backed away.

I lowered my head between my knees. "Super Mini-Girl?" I asked, taking slow breaths.

"It fits, don't you think?"

"Was that premeditated, or did it just pop into your head?"

"Just popped in there." He held his hand out to me and pulled me up when I took it. "You should've come last night. It didn't get too out of control. What'd you guys do?"

"I showed her some of the images I worked on," Doug told him as he held the door open.

"Wow, great hookup moves there, big guy." Zack punched Doug.

This was the third comment Zack had made about Doug's hookup moves. Surely Zack wouldn't have made that comment if there was a girlfriend. Elise had said Zack was a player. I wondered if Doug had been before Zoey and if he would be again?

Inside, Zack stopped and turned to me. "So what's your thing? Have you been here yet?"

"Just on the tour. I was planning to run on a treadmill."

"We can start there. Okay with you, Doug?" Zack started towards the stairs and we followed. "How many miles are you planning on running?"

"Six," I told him unzipping my jacket.

"Hard core runner, eh? Not bad. You should do weights with us after." He pinched my small biceps between his fingers.

"Maybe." We stretched before we climbed onto the treadmills, Doug on one side of me and Zack on the other.

Zack did most of the talking as we ran, and they slowed and stopped after three miles. Zack gave me directions to the weight room as they toweled off.

I completed my run and found Doug and Zack on the rowing machines.

"That was fast, Mini-Girl," Zack commented as I came over to them. He hopped off his machine.

"Here, try."

"I think I'm good for today."

"Come on, it's good for you. I should know." He tapped his temple.

Thinking I was in store for a good dose of humiliation, I climbed onto the machine and waited while he adjusted the seat and switched the tension to the lowest setting. Even then, I could barely move the handles. By the time I got them all the way down, we were laughing so hard I could barely breathe.

"Okay, well that's my embarrassment for the day." I jumped out of the seat.

"It's your first day. I'll make you a training plan."

"What's she training for?" Doug asked.

"She's rowing."

"That's a good one."

"No, look at her." Zack put a hand on each of my shoulders and spun me towards Doug. "She's tiny. She'd make a perfect coxswain. If she got in shape, she could sub."

I put my hands up and took a step back. "I'm going before I get hooked into any more sports."

"So what are you guys doing tonight?" Doug asked. "No freshmen inside the house, remember?"

My stomach did a flip and I tried to sound nonchalant. "Yeah, I know. Lila is super bummed. We have this orientation mixer. I'm not sure what we're doing after that." He hadn't exactly asked me to hang out, so I left my answer open and vague.

"We can always hang out at my place again," Zack said, popping Doug with the towel.

Excited to have an option for the evening that included Doug, I phoned Lila on my walk back to my dorm. There was no getting around recounting my evening and workout.

"Wow, you are like hot guy central these days."

"The brothers are all really nice." I tried to be non-specific.

"I told you."

After returning to my room, I showered and hung out with Elise until it was time for more orientation torture. The sessions ran till five, when we had an hour break before the dinner and mixer. Lila and I walked down to the buffet dinner together. "This orientation and the no frat house rule are seriously depressing," she said, surveying the spread. Freshmen weren't allowed inside fraternity houses for the first two weeks of the quarter. Today was day one, and she was already imploding. It was going to be a long two weeks.

"If they're feeding us every two hours, how are we supposed to avoid the freshman fifteen? It's not a myth, either. I gained like five pounds over the summer." I studied her carefully, realizing she did look a little heavier. It was a new issue for us. We'd never had to worry about our weight in high school. Between her cheerleading, tennis, and my cross country, we got plenty of exercise.

Lila decided she needed a shopping trip to lift her spirits. Skipping the meal, we socialized for a half hour, signed the roster, and used the driving service to find a ride.

Finally alone, she started in with her interrogation. "Okay, so you can't tell me there isn't something between you and Doug. What happened last night? Any physical contact I should know about?"

I tried changing the subject. "We just hung out. Really, it's nothing."

"That was some major flirting at the barbecue. And that man is crazy hot!" She went into a five-minute dissertation on how he was the most perfect man on Earth. These were not things I needed to have cataloged for me.

We pulled into a shopping center, and she instructed the driver to stop in front of one of the clothing stores.

I held the store door open for her. "So you've been here all summer, what do you think of him?"

"Doug?" Assuming correctly, she smiled at me. "We never really hung out with him. He's only been back at the house for a few weeks. He's usually quiet, unless he and Zack get going."

We went through one store and moved to another. She was determined to find the perfect clothes for the fraternity party the next night. Lila had me try on several outfits, but they all looked too fancy for a lawn party. We finally settled on a pair of dressy jeans and a blue print silk top for me and a pair of black pants and green top with spaghetti straps for her. We were at the register when she got a call from Ross.

"They're at Zack's, and it sounds like they're already drinking. It might be a pretty wild night. I'm assuming you want to go to see what Mr. Taylor is up to."

"Do you think I'm way out of my league?"

"Definitely, but one can dream. I haven't seen him with anyone since he's been back. You guys have a lot in common and obviously some chemistry. I'm not surprised you like him. He's totally your type."

I wasn't sure if that was a bad or good thing. Since my disastrous relationships with Carter and more recently Law, I had no confidence in my choice of guys. To be fair, both of them had pursued me. Carter was cute, but I never felt really strongly about him, which made it easier when things went bad. Law was just psycho.

Going out with Law had been a huge mistake. I met him at the gym where Mark worked. I told him I didn't want anything serious, and on our second date, he drove way out of town and parked in a field. He was majorly pissed when I told him I didn't want to have sex. He wouldn't drive me home, and I ended up threatening to call 911. He left me alone in the middle of the field, and I had to call Mark to pick me up.

"Stop biting your lip. You do that way too much." Lila's voice tore me from my thoughts.

We paid for our purchases, and she detailed the rest of the week's events as we waited for a car to drive us to Zack's. His apartment was more crowded than I would have preferred, especially since I didn't recognize most of the people. Zack gave me a tour and introduced me to everyone. I was more disappointed than I wanted to be that Doug didn't seem to be there. Trying to kill time, I went to the restroom to check my makeup. As I made my way back to the main room, someone called out my name.

I stuck my head in the room to see who it was. Doug stood there, shirtless. "Sorry." I quickly covered my eyes.

He laughed. "I stopped you, remember."

"Right." I lifted my hands off my eyes. It was hard not to appreciate his perfectly defined abs, and trim waist. He turned away to put on his shirt. Three Chinese symbols were tattooed on his lower back.

"How was the rest of your day?" He faced me again and my face felt flush.

"Fine," I shrugged. "Nothing exciting, I got my PO Box."

He motioned to the door, and I backed out of the room, into the hall. As we moved through the crowd, he put his hands on my back to guide me to our friends who were congregated on the deck.

Lila scooted over beside me. "They're already drunk."

"I'm just starting my second, baby." Ross grabbed her around the waist and pulled her to him.

She put both hands on his chest and pushed back. "Wow, this is going to be a doozy. I may go to a movie with Amanda and leave you guys to your drinking."

"You gotta stay. Someone get this girl a beer," he yelled at no one in particular.

Mark jumped up. "We can't lose the women folk."

He grabbed cups and started filling them, handing one to Lila. Despite the threat of leaving, she took a long sip. Mark held a cup up to me, but I waved it off.

Doug slid closer to me, leaning down to speak into my ear. "Do you want to get out of here and get something to eat?"

Had he just asked me out? It sounded like it. "Sure." Whether it was a date or not, getting away from drunk Ross and Mark seemed like an excellent idea.

Doug cocked his head in the direction of the exit, and I held up a finger to indicate I needed a minute. I whispered to Lila that I was going.

She hugged me, whispering in my ear. "Have fun, even too much if you want."

"We're out of here guys." Doug put his hands on my shoulders. Suddenly I felt like there was a spotlight aimed at my head.

"Where are you guys going?" Zack asked.

"To get something to eat," Doug said.

Zack held up his phone. "We're ordering pizza."

"I haven't been out of the house since Thursday, and I've had all the pizza I can handle. I want something good."

Zack shrugged. "Okay, more pizza and beer for us."

"Bye," Lila called in a sing-song voice.

"Be good," Ross pointed a finger at me.

Doug took my hand and led me through the packed living room. Not only was I ecstatic he'd sort of asked me out, but I was beyond glad I didn't have to hang out in this crowd tonight. Halfway to the door, I heard Mark's voice over the music. "Hey, where'd Manda go?"

I looked back and saw Ross pointing towards me as he yelled, "You turned around and your woman is gone."

Mark was already making his way towards us. Face burning, I motioned for Doug to go ahead.

"So, Doug? I'm not sure—" Mark started as he wrapped his arm around my shoulder.

I pried his arm off. "It's just dinner. Have fun drinking with your friends."

Ross materialized behind Mark. "She'll be back."

"Soon?" he asked.

I looked to Ross. "You guys are cutting him off, right?"

"Yeah, no more beer for this guy, and we'll get some food into him."

I mouthed a thank you to Ross, and found Doug waiting at the door. Outside, we made our way across the parking lot to his car. I turned my phone over and over in my hand. I couldn't decide what was making me more nervous, Mark's state or Doug. I looked back to the apartment, second guessing myself, wishing Mark hadn't made a scene.

Doug had asked me out, right? Had he wanted me to come with him or just someone who wasn't drunk? Was he just being nice? Was this about his pledge to my father? And where the heck was my self-confidence? Seriously, I was smart and cute. After seeing Zoey's picture in the yearbook, I downgraded my looks to a seven on a ten-point scale. I figured I lost a point for being short, one for not being perfectly curvy, and a third for having small breasts.

I looked up, refocusing on Doug. Nearing the car, he took a couple of long strides ahead of me, and opened the passenger's door. "You're quiet. Are you worried about Mark?"

"It makes me nervous to see him like that."

As he closed my door, he reassured me they'd take care of Mark. Getting into his side and starting the car, he suggested a Chinese place in the city. On the drive, we chatted about courses. Soon, I recognized the area. We were close to where we had sushi the other night. After parking, we walked the couple of blocks to the restaurant.

On the way, he pointed out a tall building several blocks ahead of us. "That's where my mom lives. I grew up there." We were just north of downtown, and the building was at least twenty stories high. I couldn't even imagine how much his condo might cost.

Finding the restaurant, he opened the door for me. At the hostess stand, a small Chinese woman, just about my height, dropped all her menus and crossed the space to greet us.

"Mr. Doug…" She wrapped her arms around him, patting him on the back. "Your mom says you go to China, how you like?"

He spoke to her in what I assumed was Mandarin. She smiled widely, nodding to him and replying in the same language. Then, she turned to me. "You bring friend." She beamed, looking between us.

Doug stepped beside me. "This is Mrs. Chen. Her family owns the restaurant. This is Amanda."

"Nice to meet you." I bowed slightly to her.

She bowed to me and led us to a small booth beside the front windows.

"I bring you drinks." She hurried off.

"You okay with a drink?" he whispered to me. "To be polite?"

I nodded. She came back with two glasses and a bottle of wine and spoke with Doug again. After a few exchanges I couldn't understand, she smiled and wrapped an arm around my shoulder.

"Beautiful hair." She rubbed her hand down the length of my hair.

Normally I would have recoiled from someone touching my hair, but she radiated warmth, and obviously adored Doug. One arm still around me, she used the other hand to make a circular motion around my face, speaking to Doug in Chinese.

"She wants to know where you get your coloring," he translated.

My cheeks warmed, and I hoped I wasn't blushing yet. "My father is German and my mother is Norwegian." I'd always felt my fair skin, dark hair, and hazel eyes, made for an odd combination. Unlike my blond-headed, blue-eyed sisters, I exhibited features from both my eastern and northern European grandmothers. To help me blend in family photos, Mom often suggested highlights for my hair and clothing to bring out the blue in my eyes.

Mrs. Chen nodded and said something else to Doug. To my surprise, he blushed and lowered his head. "She thinks we'd have beautiful children."

Now, my face definitely felt hot. I took a sip of the wine to regain my composure. She left our table laughing.

He tasted his wine and set his glass down. "What do you think?"

It took me a second to figure out he was asking about the wine. "It's good."

Mrs. Chen came back with soup and asked him a few questions I couldn't understand.

He turned to me. "What do you like?"

"I'm not picky."

"She usually brings me whatever is best that day. Does that work?"

"Of course," I nodded. The soup was amazing, so I wasn't too worried. Plus, I was starving.

He spoke to her again, and she retreated from our table.

"Just to warn you, she'll bring lots of food."

"She does realize I'm little, right?"

"In China that wouldn't necessarily predict how much you could eat."

"Right now I feel like I could eat a horse."

He laughed. "I wouldn't say that too loud." He winked, and I pretended to be shocked.

At regular intervals, Mrs. Chen brought more food. I'd never tried some of the dishes, and it was fun to be able to sample different things. The conversation flowed easily and after the second glass of wine I got up the courage to ask about his tattoo.

I leaned towards him. "Can I ask a personal question?"

He raised an eyebrow. "What type of personal question?"

"I was just wondering about your tattoo."

He explained he'd gotten the tattoo, with Chinese symbols, representing body, mind and soul, just two weeks before. "Does this mean I get to ask questions, too?"

"What do you want to know?"

He studied me for a few seconds. "What are the three things that you enjoy most?"

"Besides my family and friends?" He nodded. "I think you already know them. Languages, travel, and running."

"Really running?" He looked at me like I was crazy.

"It's therapeutic," I defended. "How about you?"

"Languages, travel, and rowing."

"See you have rowing, and I have running. So, on that topic, would it be possible for me to go rowing sometime?" Since the first day we'd met and he'd described the sport, I'd wanted to ask.

He studied me again. "Are you a good swimmer?"

"Yes."

"Well, the boats are owned by the team, and officially you should have a swim test and sign a waiver, but I could arrange it."

"Cool, thanks." I smiled at him.

Mrs. Chen came to the table. "You like?"

Looking down at our spread, I realized we'd, well mostly Doug, had eaten almost all the food. "Yes, very much," I told her.

"Good, I'll be back with fortunes."

I looked to Doug who was shaking his head. "What?"

"She picks the fortune she wants you to have."

She came back to our table with the cookies, handed one to each of us, and left chuckling.

"How much do you want to bet we have the same one?"

I started to open mine. "I'm not betting."

Reaching for my cookie, he lowered his voice. "You don't want to do that."

I held it up in front of him. "Tattoo parlor needles, no problem, but beware the fortune cookie. Really? You first."

He looked around the room, popped the cookie in half, and pulled out the small paper. Looking at it, he glanced up at me and back to the paper. "Your heart will soon find a home," he read.

Okay, so maybe he was right, these weren't your typical fortunes. It was a little heavy for a first date, if that's what this was.

My cheeks felt hot as I lifted my fortune to read it out loud. "Your soul mate is near."

He cleared his throat. "See, I told you they were rigged. I think she likes you."

As if on cue, Mrs. Chen appeared. "You like fortune?"

We both nodded, and she asked him a few more questions in Chinese. After a few phrases back and forth, she threw her hands up and walked away.

My eyes followed her retreating form. She was still shaking her head, and I looked back to Doug.

"She tends to have strong opinions about certain issues." He wiped his brow, emptied the last of the bottle of wine into his glass, and downed it. "You ready to get out of here?"

I nodded and followed him outside into the crisp air. "Do you mind walking for a bit?" Before I could answer, he stopped and looked down. "Wait, what shoes are you wearing?"

"Flats." I wiggled a foot to emphasize my point.

"Great, want to see the skyline from my building?"

"Course," I said, matching his swift pace. In a few blocks, we reached the entrance to the high rise. Doug took out a key, but a doorman jogged up to the door, opening it for us.

He greeted Doug and crossed towards the elevators. "Your floor, Mr. Taylor?"

"No, the roof please, Phil."

He turned a key to unlock the elevator and stepped in, using another key to allow us access to the roof. At the top he wished us a goodnight.

We stepped out of the elevator room, and the view took my breath away. I ran to the east edge, amazed at how the city's light bounced off the lake.

He joined me, keeping his distance. "I can't believe you grew up here. This view is amazing. If I lived here, I would never leave this roof."

"It is spectacular, but the wind can be annoying after a while."

Walking to the west side, the view didn't disappoint. Doug followed behind me, hands stuffed in his pockets, and I had to force myself to look back towards the sky. If you'd asked me to describe a perfect date, this would be it. As he reached the edge, I studied him. His hands were now clenched around the railing. I wondered if he was afraid of heights. "I guess it would be cold in the winter."

A gust of wind blew my hair into my face. He ran a finger across my cheek and tucking my hair behind my ear. "See, windy." When he touched my face, I froze. It'd been a sweet gesture, but his tone was tense. "We should go." He turned away from me.

My buzz still in full effect, I skipped back to the car to keep up with him, asking about every building we passed. On the drive back to campus, I fiddled with the radio and chatted about sports. "You are really animated when you're buzzed," he told me as we pulled into my dorm's parking lot.

I hopped out of the car before he could walk around to open it, but unlike the previous night, he didn't seem to notice. "Thank you, that was really fun," I told him as we walked to the door.

His smile seemed forced, and I raked my hair over my left shoulder, wondering why he'd become so distant. At dinner, we'd been sharing dishes, even passing bites across the table to each other. "So, I'll see you around."

He held the door for me. Okay, so this was definitely not the end to this night I'd hoped for. "Sure."

I turned and walked inside, purposely not looking back.

It was nearly midnight, but Elise was sitting on the futon listening to music when I entered the room.

"What happened to your hair?"

"I don't know." Puzzled, I hopped into the bathroom to look in the mirror. My cheek still tingled along the line where his finger had traced. I was definitely buzzing. Focusing on my image, I realized my hair was a tangled mess. No wonder he'd disappeared so fast.

"It was windy in the city," I told her.

She rolled her eyes. "Sure, the wind." Shaking her head, she walked over and grabbed a strand of my hair. "Never mind. Hmm, I never realized you had so much curl in your hair. No wonder you spend half an hour blowing it out."

"Not everyone can have beautiful, smooth hair like you."

"It's all about the product, baby." She ran her hands down her straight, shiny hair.

I grabbed my comb, toothbrush, and toothpaste and headed back to the bathroom. It took ten minutes to get the tangles out of my hair, but it gave me time to think. Not having orientation until nine, I set my alarm for seven, thinking of getting a run in before another long day of torture. With only one more day before classes started, I was excited about diving into my coursework. As someone who liked routine, I felt I'd be more comfortable once I got into the groove of my schedule.

"You're not a morning person, are you?" Elise asked the next morning after my third nod and second yeah in reply to her chatter about campus life. She turned down my invitation to run, and I went to the gym, ignoring my phone altogether. I wasn't ready to talk to anyone about last night.

During the run, I picked through the night in my mind, racking my brain trying to decipher what had derailed the evening, but it didn't come to me. Unfortunately, I'd forgotten to hydrate, and my body wasn't particularly happy about the six miles, but I pushed myself. I took a quick shower afterwards, so I'd have the required half hour to blow dry my hair. Lila had stressed how important the lawn party was tonight, and I wanted it to look perfect.

The last day of orientation wasn't as bad as it could have been, as I was in a couple of sessions with Lila and Kate. Kate, Elise, and I made dinner in the evening, but as the sky darkened, I grew more apprehensive about seeing Doug. Thinking that I was content with a night in my dorm room, I decided to see a movie with Kate. Ignoring texts from Lila, we'd just started the film when my phone rang.

I didn't recognize the number, but I answered anyway. A somewhat familiar male voice spoke. "Where are you?"

"Who is this?"

"Who is this? Super Mini-Girl, it's me, Zack. Who else? Lila gave me your number, and told me to tell you to get your butt over here." Telling him I was watching a movie had no effect. "If you're not here by nine, I'm coming to get you."

Figuring he would make good on his threat, I relented.

"Who was that?" Elise asked when I finished the call.

"Zack."

"From the fraternity? Is there something going on between you guys?"

"No, he just offered me a ride."

"Uh, huh. I told you about him, remember?" She pointed a finger and looked bug-eyed at me.

"I know. It's not like that."

I invited Kate to come with me, but she declined, reminding me we still had a half day of orientation the following morning. I dressed quickly and touched up my makeup, adding my favorite brown wedge heels to the outfit Lila and I had picked out.

"Wow, nice outfit," Elise complimented pulling on her own sweater. "Here." She handed me a coffee tumbler filled with some liquid.

"What's this?" I asked, taking a sniff.

"My own private concoction. You are way too uptight, I haven't seen you smile all day. I hope this isn't a pattern, but..." She pointed at the drink. "That will help."

I took a sip and the fruity but potent drink warmed my throat. "What are you drinking for?"

She rolled her eyes. "Smoozing."

As Elise and I were both headed to the same side of campus, we shared a car.

"Have fun," she shouted as I jumped out at the fraternity house. "But not with Zack." She got in just as I closed the door. Although he wasn't bad looking, and seemed nice enough, he wasn't who I was stressing about.

I could hear the music from the street, and I took the brick path to the back of the house. Bill stood beside a table, serving as the greeter. "Finally," he said to me. "You better find Zack before he calls 911."

Looking for tall people had its advantages, and I quickly spotted Zack and Doug standing beside a table near the band. They were studying some kind of list. As I approached, I tapped Doug on the shoulder. He turned and smiled at me, none of the previous night's tension in his face.

"You're here!" Zack scooped me up and spun me around. He took my drink when he set me down. "What have you got here?"

"Elise made it for me."

He took a sip. "Hmm, girlie."

I guessed we were at the sharing drink stage of our relationship now. I reached for my cup. "I am a girl."

"We've got something other than beer when you need a refill."

"Thanks," I replied, not meaning to take him up on it. I could already feel the effects of this one.

Doug offered to store my bag in his room, and then they pointed me in Lila's direction. I sipped my drink as I made my way through the crowd to find my friends. It seemed to be a never-ending labyrinth as I couldn't see beyond the person in front of me.

Lila found me first and pulled me to the edge of the crowd. She motioned to the outfit. "Love it. Zack's been going nuts. What's up with that?" She linked her arm through mine and led me further away from the band. "So, last night? Spill."

"It was fun." I shrugged.

"And?"

"That's it." I tried not to me her gaze.

"Really? I totally thought he was into you."

"I think he was just being nice."

"Are you completely bummed?" She leaned down to look directly in my eyes.

I'd never done it before, but I looked into her eyes and lied. "No, he was being nice, and it was fun so..." I shrugged, letting the words hang in the air.

She stared into my eyes for a half-minute longer. "Well, okay then, finish your drink and let's dance." She bounced in front of me. I downed the rest in one gulp, took her hand, and followed her to the stage. Packed in at the front of the crowd, we danced the whole first set. As the last song finished and the crowd thinned, something cold was pressed onto my back. I ducked away, spinning around to find the culprit. Grinning from ear to ear, Doug held a water bottle up in front of my face. Twisting the top off, he handed it to me.

Every bit of me melted. Taking the bottle, I stood on my toes, leaning into him. He leaned down so that I could whisper in his ear. "That was cruel."

"You looked hot." He twisted my hair up and held it off my neck.

Okay, there was no mistaking it. This was flirting. "Thanks," was all I could manage. If I'd been thinking faster, which I obviously wasn't after Elise's drink, I'd have come back with something sexier. As it was, I had nothing.

Having finished their shifts at the greeter table, Doug, Zack, Bill, Mark, and Ross joined our dance party. As time passed, there were fewer of us dancing. The song changed into a ballad, and I looked for Lila, but she seemed to have disappeared. As I stood searching the crowd, a huge pair of hands locked onto my hips.

"May I have this dance?" Doug asked. He didn't wait for my reply, guiding me to the center of the dancing crowd. I'd taken formal ballroom dancing, and his form and lead were excellent. Our steps flowed seamlessly into each other. "You're a good dancer."

I vowed to never complain about the many hours in dance lessons again. He dipped me when the song ended, and we made our way to the edge of the crowd. Nervous, I scanned the crowd for my friends.

Doug must've noticed my confusion. "Most of the brothers went inside, but I'm not sure where your crew went. Do you want to go find them?"

I shrugged. I didn't want to find them, because I wanted to dance with him. Still, I refused to be obvious or desperate. The band had started another ballad. Without hesitating, Doug swirled me back towards the stage. "So, you've had lessons, I'm assuming?"

"One long year of Fred Astaire."

He pulled back from me, holding up two fingers.

"Two years?"

He nodded and pulled me back to him. Everything about him became intoxicating: his smell, his warm arms around my back, the smooth skin on the back of his neck.

He switched to the tango when the song changed. I was definitely falling for him, which couldn't be good. When the music ended, he squeezed my hand and spun me away from him. I leaned back into him, and he rested his hands on my hips. I would've been content to stay like that all night.

The band, finishing with their concert, thanked the crowd. Doug stepped away from me. I turned around and he stretched, straightening his back and lifting his chin, surveying the crowd. "I should get your bag." He was instantly more formal. He motioned me toward the back entrance to the house. "Do you need another water?"

"I'm fine." Like the previous night, his demeanor had done a one-eighty. What was the problem? Couldn't he figure out if he liked me?

"I'll be right back."

I leaned up against the wall, not knowing what to do with myself. Blondie bounded up to me, wagging her tail ecstatically.

Grateful for the distraction, I bent down to pet her. I was just about to text Lila when he returned.

Doug handed me a water bottle and my bag. "Wait here. I have to pay the band, and then I'll walk you home."

His tone was abrupt, and I didn't want to impose on him. "I can get a ride."

"No, I'll walk you. Wait here." With that, he was gone.

I sat down on the wall surrounding the patio. Blondie rested her head beside me.

I texted Lila. DOUG IS WALKING ME BACK. I wasn't sure where she was, but she texted back immediately.

EVERYTHING OK?

COURSE. I texted back a quick reply to ease her mind.

"It's good to be a dog, eh?" I said to Blondie, rubbing her head.

Exhausted and bothered by throbbing feet, I took my shoes off and stretched out my legs. After a few minutes, I got up to look around. The wind had picked up and it started to sprinkle. I ducked under the eaves for shelter. Thankfully, Doug materialized within a minute.

"She likes you." He reached across to rub her head, before looking to the sky. "Do you need a jacket? We should be able to get someone's car out of here."

"No, I'm fine." We sprinted out to the edge of the lot. His car was blocked, but Zack's was clear at the back of the lot. We dashed to it, in the now heavy downpour.

"You can just stop in front. I can run in." I told Doug as we neared my building.

"No, I'll walk you up."

He seemed set on some unsaid plan. In my mind nothing good could come of a situation where one minute you were dancing semi-intimately and the next you were being escorted to your front door. Chivalry could be taken too far. I crossed my arms over my chest.

Unlike previous nights, he followed me inside the building. In the lobby, he started to speak, but a large group passed us and he hesitated.

"Do you want to come up? Elise is at her sorority party." I looked at my watch, praying she was still out.

"Okay."

We walked into the elevator, and I hit the button for my floor. The silence was driving me nuts. "That was a great band tonight." I said as we got off the elevator.

"Yeah, we used them last year."

"Entrée vous." I unlocked the door to my room, ushering him in.

"Wow, you guys really gave this place a makeover."

"Elise has this down. After four years in the dorm, she's sort of a professional."

"I would say," he replied, looking around. "So you're voting Republican?" He motioned to my signed poster of the party nominee.

"Not such a popular view around here." I pointed towards the bathroom door. "I'm getting a towel for my hair."

"Sure, go ahead."

I hurried to the bathroom and brushed my teeth. I splashed some cool water on my face and dried it with a fresh towel, glad I hadn't worn much makeup. I dried my hair with the towel as I walked back into the room. He was standing in the same position I left him in, but now was only in his white undershirt. This boy was pure torture.

"My shirt was wet." He picked it up from the chair and replaced it. "You have a lot of movies."

I sat on my futon, deciding to be direct. "My mom is sort of a movie buff. Do you want to sit?"

He complied, and I crossed one leg under the other and turned to him.

"How do girls do that?" he asked.

"Zack doesn't have you guys doing yoga stretches?"

He shook his head. *Well that didn't cut the tension at all.* Where was Blondie when you needed her?

"The past week was pretty intense," he started.

"I guess." I wasn't sure where he was heading.

"Well, I just wanted to be sure we were clear." He waited for me to respond. I didn't.

"We hung out like every night," he started again.

Where is this going? "I guess." Again there was silence. I decided to not be a coward. "And?" I looked him straight in the eyes this time.

He sighed and raked his hand through his hair, obviously frustrated. If he was trying to break up with me before we even started dating, I wasn't giving in. If he thought I'd step in and save him the awkwardness, he was mistaken. I'd done that with Benjamin, my first boyfriend, and regretted it.

"I don't have much time with classes and the fraternity. I just didn't want you to think..."

Think what? That we had some sort of thing? That he liked me? "Of course." I shrugged and stood, smoothing my jeans. There was nothing else to say.

He shook his head and stood. "Of course..." It was half statement, half question. "Okay, then, I guess I'll go." He motioned towards the door.

I wasn't sure what he expected me to say. How many different ways did we need to clarify the situation? I didn't particularly like where this went, but it wasn't my call.

For an awkward moment, he stood there. Then, I remembered I had to walk him down. The no unescorted males rule was mandatory. This night couldn't end fast enough. I moved forward too quickly, and I bumped into him. He caught me before I fell backwards.

"Sorry." My pulse raced at his touch, and I had to catch my breath. I recovered, and he let go. We tock the elevator down. I really had no idea what to say to him. "See you around" seemed wrong since he'd just told me he didn't have time to see me.

"Goodbye," I said when we got to the exit. He stuck his hands in his pockets and dashed out into the pouring rain towards the parking lot.

Angry, I got ready for bed. Was I mad at him or myself? Picking his shirt up, I flung it on the futon. I was too exhausted to process the evening. It just didn't make sense. We seemed to have connected on so many levels.

He'd said something about the week being intense. I thought about it as I lay in bed staring at the rectangles above my head. I was getting oriented to my new life. But he was just trying to get through an intense week of potential recruiting and alumni catering. We met in a contrived environment, and the relationship that I'd formed with him in my mind wasn't real. He was just being nice. How could I be so stupid? He probably thought I was some kind of crazy stalker. At least I hadn't initiated any of the contact.

Chapter 5

Avoiding a guy was not how I wanted to start my first quarter at college. But it seemed like the only solution, as there was no way I would risk looking like a stalker. Attending Mass followed by a run seemed like a solid plan and centering start to my day. I went to Mass every weekend at home and hadn't been since I'd moved. Seeing as I had hours to fill with non-fraternity activities, it would be a good routine to start. Having no idea what Doug's rowing schedule was, I prayed today was an on-the-river rather than a gym day.

Although the rain had stopped, it was still cloudy and humid enough to make doing my hair pointless. I confirmed the schedule and location for the Sheil Catholic Center on my phone, and threw on some running clothes and a jacket. Jogging to the chapel, I slipped into the back pew as the priest made his way to the altar.

Impressed with the number of students present, I scanned the room. My gaze stopped when I recognized Doug seated in the first row on the other side. *So much for my centering start.* Dodging him was going to be difficult. If I'd really thought about it, I would have realized he was probably Catholic. What were the chances that he would choose today to come to Mass?

After the homily, as we got up to receive communion, I snuck out the back. I didn't even make it out of the lobby before I heard my name. Taking a deep breath, I turned around to face him. "Doug, hi, I was just going to squeeze in a run." I wasn't sure what else to say. It wasn't a good excuse for skipping Holy Communion, but it was the only one I had on the fly.

"Yeah, I try to get this in before crew." I wondered if this was every day or just today. He opened the door for me. "You should go to the gym. It's pretty quiet this early with no classes."

Does he have to act like he cares? "That was my plan."

"Good, well, I've got to get going. See you around."

No, you don't have time to see me, remember? I ranted in my head as I jogged to the gym. My run was good, although it didn't take my mind off the current dilemma. There really was no point in analyzing the events of the past week, since the outcome would still be the same. All I had to do was act as if it never happened.

In my room, I got off the required texts to Mom and Dad, then showered and washed my hair. Lila bailed, but Kate and I walked to the dorm social event together. The weather cleared up, and it turned out to be a pretty fun afternoon. I even played a game of volleyball with some people Kate knew.

As we walked back upstairs afterwards, I couldn't ignore Lila's stream of texts demanding details about last night any longer.

Apologizing to Kate, I sent Lila a text message. ON MY WAY BACK UP TO MY ROOM WITH KATE.

With impeccable timing, she met us at my door. As we walked inside, Elise spun in her chair to face us, raising Doug's shirt above her head. "Whose is this?"

I walked toward her, reaching out for it. "A friend's. It was raining, and he must have left it."

Lila grabbed it from me. "That's Doug's shirt from last night, he was in your room and you didn't tell me?"

Dang, did I have a good reason for him being here other than ditching me? "For a minute, his shirt was wet so—"

"When were you going to tell me this?" She shook the shirt at me.

"Nothing happened."

"She doesn't say much, does she?" Elise spun back to face her computer.

"Never has," Lila tossed the shirt to me. "So, nothing else?" She put a hand on each of my shoulders and stared into my eyes.

"Like I said, his shirt was wet from the rain. I got him a towel. He must've forgotten it." It wasn't a complete lie, just an omission of facts.

"No dramatic hook up? You like him. Maybe you should've made a move. He must be interested at least a little."

Thank you, Lila, I thought. This was not information I wanted Kate, and especially Elise, to have.

Fortunately, I was fast on my feet. "Throw myself at Doug Taylor? And be like every other girl?" It was true. I'd watched him at the parties, every girl he talked to at least touched him. Many of them draped themselves all over him.

"Okay, so maybe I see your point." Lila plopped down on my futon. "You are so boring." She got back up. "I need a nap," she announced and left for her room.

Needing some quiet distraction, I read a chapter in my intro to international studies book and reviewed the first lesson for calculus. Afterwards, Elise and I made dinner, and she left for her sorority meeting. All the Greek organizations had their chapter meetings on Wednesday nights, so Lila joined Kate and me for a movie in my room.

Mark called after their meeting. It was good to hear his voice, since I hadn't really connected with him since I'd gotten here. He invited himself over to see my room, and when he and Ross arrived, Lila and I went down to meet them. Mark greeted me with a big hug. "How are you girl?"

"Good," I lied. What was I supposed to say? Disappointed? Depressed?

Ross started in right away. "Hey, Marko, maybe she's not your girl anymore." He hit Mark on the shoulder and winked at me.

Mark batted my arm back and forth in the elevator. "So, you and Doug?"

Mark's involvement was the last thing I needed. "No, we were just hanging out."

"Yeah, every night. Then, dinner and dancing," Ross put in.

He was annoying me. When did he get so nosy? "He was just being nice."

"Last time I checked, Doug doesn't have time to be nice," Ross said, getting off the elevator. Okay, that stung.

"So, are you guys like seeing each other?" Mark asked as we walked down the hall.

I made sure to keep my voice even. "No, like I said, he was being nice." I shrugged for extra effect and put my key in the lock.

Entering my room, I retrieved a bag of chips to distract them from the current topic. I learned a long time ago this always worked with guys.

"I totally thought you'd be into him. He definitely seems your type, but what do I know?" Ross said, stuffing a handful of chips in his mouth.

The other topic of the evening was the co-rec teams, which Lila and I were supposed to sign up for. They invited Kate, too, but she was already committed to the dorm teams.

The guys had early classes and didn't stay long. Not wanting Elise to overhear my conversation, I went down to the lobby to recount my Doug story to Marissa. At least I had her to vent to.

I awoke just before seven the next morning fully committed to my avoidance strategy. Skipping breakfast, I blasted off a short email to Tia, who I'd ignored for the past week, and called Mom on my way to the gym. Usually I was pretty forthcoming with them, but crushing on a totally unattainable guy wasn't something I wanted to admit.

Is this me?

I was just over four miles into my run when I felt a tap on my shoulder. I squeezed my eyes shut and prayed for the miracle that it was anyone but Doug. When I turned my head, I saw Zack beside my treadmill, gym bag in hand. Doug and Bill stood behind him. My avoidance score bounced to zero out of two.

I removed my earphones and slowed my pace. "Hi, guys."

"You're here early. Were you trying to get out of doing machines with us?" Zack asked.

"You caught me. No rowing this morning?" I asked, hoping to get some idea what the schedule was.

"Classes mess everything up. Mind if we run with you?"

His vague answer did nothing to help with my planning. "Course not." I lied, thinking I'd rather be sticking needles in my eyeballs.

Zack took the treadmill next to me, and Doug and Bill took machines on the other side of him. Thankfully, Doug was the farthest from me. I resumed my normal eight-minute mile pace, and they followed suit. When we were done, Zack was ready to strike.

"Just do three machines with us. We have an odd number."

Like I could spot? Before I could answer, he took my arm and led me with them. I'd always wanted to do more weight training, and here was a free personal trainer thrown in my lap. Besides, Zack was fun to be around. What girl would pass up working out with three hot guys? Still, I was convinced I was a masochist.

We started with the leg press. There were three machines, so I climbed on one while Doug and Bill took the other two. Zack set the tension on what he deemed to be low and told me to watch Doug for positioning and form. I'd been trying really hard not to look at or think about him, and now I was supposed to study his form? Couldn't a girl catch a break? I forced myself to concentrate and tried to push the weights. Nothing happened.

"Okay, guess we'll cut this weight in half then," Zack said.

"How much is he doing?" I pointed to Doug.

"Don't worry about him." Zack adjusted the weight. "Concentrate on you." When he had it set, he told me to try again. This time it was easier, so I did three reps.

Several machines and many instructions later, I was still watching Doug's form. Doug caught on and started making fun of Zack, pointing to his muscles and pretending to swoon, sending me into fits of giggles.

"Hey, hey, pay attention." He clapped his hands, demanding attention.

I looked to Doug, and he immediately put on a serious face, making me laugh harder. "He's making faces," I tattled.

"I'm going to separate you two." Zack pointed between us.

Please, I thought. "I'll be good. I promise." I traced a cross on my chest, continuing the charade.

"Okay, ready?" I raised the weight. It was a little heavy, but I could lift it. After ten reps, he lowered the weight and I did two more sets. Then we moved to an arm machine. After almost an hour, my muscles were screaming at me. I picked my bag up, packing in my towel.

"Come on, finish with us, you can just spot." Zack pulled my arm as before.

"This is fun, and a good workout, but I need to go." I pulled on my jacket.

"So are we good for Mondays, Wednesdays, and Fridays?"

I looked to Doug, but he looked away, starting a conversation with Bill. "I don't want to mess you guys up."

"You won't, right guys?" He motioned for their attention and they shrugged. He feigned a whisper, "It'll motivate them."

Despite that it was in complete opposition to my avoidance strategy, I agreed. Jogging back to my room, I tried not to think about how I'd just put myself in close proximity to Doug for at least three hours a week. In my room, I showered quickly, washing my hair and blowing it out smooth.

I walked to the main campus, and found my calculus class easily, thanks to careful studying of the map before I left. I recognized several faces, although no names surfaced in my memory. An hour and a half was a long time to look at math, and only having grabbed a latte, I felt shaky by the end. Fortunately, I had a half-hour break to grab a bagel before my next class.

In English, a girl I recognized from calculus sat down next to me. Her name was Vivian, and she began telling me about herself. From a suburb west of Chicago, she lived at home, commuting to school every day. Enjoying the distraction, I let her chat. Within the five minutes we had before class, I knew how many siblings she had, how old they were, and what her parents did for a living. She was a bit intense, though nice enough, and we traded numbers.

After English I had my international studies class. The lecture was interesting and the professor seemed approachable, so I introduced myself after class. I hoped to initiate a connection to the language program and felt successful after he talked to me for fifteen minutes. He even gave me some places to advertise my tutoring services. I was late meeting Mark for racquetball but glad I'd taken the time engage the professor. Due to my weight-lifting session, my legs and arms felt like they were seizing by the end of our game, and Mark beat me easily.

As he was walking me back to my room, he asked about me joining the co-rec intramural teams again. I agreed to play flag football but was hesitant about volleyball.

"Come on, you're decently good and I need girls. Besides, Doug and Zack are playing and no one else will have to do much." Would every activity in my life involve Doug? Mark's voice brought me out of my worry. "So, you're in right?"

For some reason, I always had a hard time saying no to him, so I agreed to play on both teams. I reminded him I couldn't come inside the frat house to fill out the paperwork and got out of a walk to the house with him. I loved that rule!

"Tomorrow, lunch." He made me promise. "On another sports-related topic, I heard you're working out with Zack, Doug, and Bill?"

"Yeah, Zack roped me in."

He stopped walking and turned to face me. "Can I ask you something?" His voice sounded an octave lower, and his tone seemed more serious. "So you thought Doug was nice, and that's all?"

Mark and I had always been honest with each other, but I didn't want him to know the details of this particular relationship. With them being brothers at the same house, it was too complicated. I chose my words carefully. "I'm not pursuing him." I rolled my eyes for effect.

"Good. You should steer clear of Zack, too." He resumed walking.

"Because?" I stretched the word out like I knew nothing.

He grabbed my arm, spinning me around to look at him. "Zack is a player, Amanda. He's not your type."

Pulling my arm back, I held my hands up in surrender. "Okay, got it."

I showered and ran some product through my hair, thankful I hadn't worked up too much of a sweat playing racquetball. Elise came in, and with too much already in my head, I wasn't in the mood for her exuberant personality. The first day of classes, with three syllabi outlining work for the whole quarter, was a little overwhelming. Adding the Doug issue to that put me over the top. I needed some space. After getting a quick rundown of her day, I packed up my books and walked to the library.

Thirty minutes into my study session, a huge hand plopped down on top of my book. When I looked up, I saw Zack with Doug and Bill a few feet behind him.

"What are you doing here?" Zack asked.

"What people do in a library?" I pointed to my book. "Studying."

He looked around. "You're like the only person here!"

I rolled my eyes. "You're here." *Score one for me.* "If you must know, I'm avoiding my overly perky roommate."

"Trouble in paradise already?"

"No, she's just chatty, and I'm overwhelmed by these test schedules."

Bill hit Zack on the arm. "Hey, we gotta get to it."

Zack turned to Bill. "Yeah, just a sec." Then he turned back to me. "See you tomorrow at eight sharp, right Manda?"

"We worked out today?"

Backing away, he pointed at me. "Monday, Wednesday, and Friday. We'll just do a light run tomorrow, no weights."

After two hours of reading, I took the bus back to my dorm. Walking into the building just before ten, my phone indicated I had a text from Lila. EVERYONE GOING OUT, SHOULD WE PICK YOU UP?

JUST TURNING IN, I sent back.

I'LL LET THIS ONE SLIDE BUT BTW, THURS IS THE NIGHT TO GO OUT, she replied.

They certainly went out a lot. No wonder she'd gained weight, she drank a lot.

It was finally Friday, and I was ready for the weekend. I talked to Mom, ate a bowl of cereal, did some biology reading, and got to the gym just before eight. I warmed up and started running, but kept a watch out for them.

"You're here!" Zack knocked on my treadmill.

Stopping my machine, I took off my earphones. "Sure, I said I'd be."

"The only other place I saw you was the library. You not into going out with us anymore?"

"I had stuff to do."

"Right." He shook his head.

Even though I was dying to check Doug's reaction, I kept my eyes fixed on Zack. Since the avoidance strategy had failed completely, pretending Doug didn't exist was my back-up. Our half-hour run passed easily, and I left them to their rowing machines. I showered quickly and still had time to review a chemistry chapter and skim through the first chapter of biology again.

Realizing we had the same Chemistry lecture, Kate and I walked to the building together. In the lecture hall, she introduced me to a couple of people, including Jeremy, who sat with us. It turned out we were all in same chemistry lab and he was in biology with me too.

After class, I met Mark at a sandwich cart to fill out the co-rec forms. He handed me the paperwork, and I filled it in using Elise as an emergency contact. Reading through the information, I came upon the location for the volleyball games. "The games are in a gym?"

"Where'd you think they'd be?"

"I was hoping for sand so I don't end up on a stretcher."

He put his arm around my shoulders. "I told you. You just have to stand there and look pretty."

After lunch I had biology. Thanks to the time spent reading ahead, I wasn't completely lost. Since Jeremy's dorm was adjacent to mine, we walked together. In my room, I changed quickly, calling Marissa as I made my way to the house for football practice. Contrary to my attitude when my family left Saturday, I was happy they were coming up for the game the next day. I made plans to stay with them at the hotel to catch up with Marissa, glad to have an excuse to opt out of hanging out at the fraternity house.

Approaching the back lawn of the house, I saw no signs of Doug. No one, except Mark, was too serious about practicing on a Friday afternoon. We warmed up and went through some simple plays. Mark handed out a playbook and the rules sheet. As Lila and I were the only girls, we'd have to play full games. Thinking I could have taken a PE course if I wanted to spend this much time on football, I reminded myself that it was a social activity that didn't include Doug.

As practice ended, so did my Doug-free afternoon. As we broke huddle, he walked out of the house carrying a cooler full of Gatorade and water bottles. I was glad I'd thought to bring water, so I could avoid proximity to him. As we rested on the lawn, he came over and sat beside me. Couldn't he tell I was avoiding him? Wasn't that what he wanted?

He leaned in close to me. "Didn't your dad have concerns about you playing co-rec?"

"It's flag football." I stood with the intention of walking away, but I didn't have the guts to actually do it.

He stood too, bending over to speak in my ear. Dang he smelled good. "On a turf field."

I shrugged. "Details."

"Okay." He shook his head and walked away.

Mark saved me by asking me to catch some balls with him. We threw for a while, and everyone started making plans for the night. I faked having a dinner with Elise and Kate to avoid a night that possibly included Doug.

The game Saturday started at eleven and my parents, along with Tia and Ed, were in their tailgating spot by nine. Having had such a heavy workout schedule, I did an easy three miles on the treadmill at the gym and got in some studying before meeting up with them. Marissa and I met Mark, Lila, and Ross outside the stadium to sit with the fraternity for the game.

Doug sat several rows away, and I berated myself for looking for him. As per Dad, the barbecue at the house afterwards wasn't optional, but the crowd made it easy to steer clear of Doug. I saw Dad talking to him and wished I had a bug planted to overhear the conversation.

That evening, the whole family met up at my parent's hotel room. I felt more balanced after seeing them and filling them in on my classes and the people I'd met. Things at school were going well. I realized I'd let this hiccup with Doug overshadow everything. Not all of the students I met belonged to the fraternity. Some of those, like Kate and Elise, were becoming friends. I'd posted a tutoring ad and gotten a call already.

On Sunday morning I felt rested and refreshed. After brunch with my family, I spent the afternoon cleaning, doing laundry, and studying. Lying in bed that night, I felt more centered than I had two days ago. I missed Doug, an idea that sounded crazy after only knowing him for five days. The anxiety around seeing him was slowly subsiding though, and no one save Marissa had any idea I'd been jilted, thank God!

Chapter 6

On Monday, Elise noticed I was perkier. "Hey, you're talking to me. I like it," she told me, gathering her things for her eight o'clock class. Not having exercised Sunday, I had plenty of energy for my workout. Seeing Doug, I wanted to talk to him and find out how his Mandarin and other classes were. Instead, I kept my distance and ignored his existence. Thankfully, Zack was always a good distraction.

After my quick shower, Kate and I walked to class together. I met Mark after the lecture, as he wanted to go to student organization day booths with me. I could see him bouncing on his toes as I walked towards him. He hugged me quickly and started in right away. "You should check out a Spanish or French club, maybe even the College Republicans."

Along the way, Mark greeted a few friends and introduced me. I found the NU Heights booth first. They tutored local elementary and middle-level students, and the members seemed really nice.

Two tables down was the Graduate Latino Club's booth. Two dark-skinned girls sat chatting in Spanish to each other.

"Hi, can I get some information about your group?" I started. Eyes scanning me, one of them plopped a clipboard in front of me. With only thirty seconds to decide whether to speak in English or Spanish, perhaps I'd chosen wrong. I wrote my name and email down, and they handed me a flyer without uttering a word.

"Thanks," I said to them, still not getting a reaction.

Too shocked to move, Mark put an arm around me and guided me away. "Wow, they were nice. I think you better start with the tutoring group."

We walked down the sidewalk to a few more booths. I was about to ask Mark if he was ready for lunch when he grabbed my arm. "Hey, there's Doug at the College Republicans' table. Come on. This is definitely for you."

Wonderful! Had Doug said he was Republican? I needed another activity with Doug like I needed another cracked chin.

"I have a volunteer for you guys." Mark pointed to me as we reached the table.

Doug turned to us. "Are you up for helping these guys out?" He motioned towards the students standing behind the table.

I noncommittally looked over the info and put my email down. Doug excused himself and walked away. I was glad I had Mark as a distraction from feeling totally disappointed. Was I really expecting Doug to change his mind?

Mark's politically incorrect commentary on each of the organizations entertained me as we surveyed the rest of the booths. In the end, I had just enough time to grab a sandwich from a cart before my next lecture.

Lila and I walked back to the dorm to change for volleyball practice after our lab. We hadn't had much time together since our shopping trip, so it gave us a chance to catch up. There was still a week left before freshmen were allowed back inside the Greek houses, and it was driving her nuts. I, however, was thinking I didn't ever care to step foot back in that house.

Walking across the crowded gym that evening, I could see Doug already warming up with Mark. Suddenly nervous, I looped my finger around my ponytail.

Lila grabbed my hand. "Relax, you're not going to bust anything. Your Dad needs to take a chill pill." Glad she attributed my anxiety to the sport, I focused on being calm.

As with football, we were the only girls there. Mark hadn't been completely honest about the participation required by us, and I was a little peeved. It seemed there had to be two girls on the court at all times, and one of us had to touch the ball each play.

The pressure was on, and I reviewed all Mark's coaching tips in my head as we warmed up. At one point, I was playing back with Doug directly in front of me. A high ball came down just in front of me, and I jumped for it. As soon as I did, I realized that Doug had stepped back to get it too. Fortunately, he saw me, and looped his arm around me as we collided, catching me before I fell.

Mark went ballistic. "See, that's how you're going to get hurt. These guys are bigger than you. Give them this much room," he yelled, spreading his arms out wide and spinning around in a circle.

Stunned at crashing into Doug and nearly falling, I'd grabbed his arms as they'd encircled me and we stood frozen while Mark finished his tirade. When I realized I was still gripping Doug's arms, I let go. He didn't.

"Let them get the ball, for God's sake." Mark threw his hands up and stomped off.

"You okay?" Doug looked down at me.

Inches from his chest, I managed a weak nod. He released me, and I backed away. I glanced around, realizing we had an audience.

Having circled back, Mark took my arm and repeated Doug's question.

"Yes, I'm good." I pulled my arm from his grip. "Sorry, my bad." I looked to Doug and then back to Mark.

"Okay, water break and then back in five," Mark called to everyone.

Lila came straight over to me. "Oh my God, are you okay? Mark lost it out there."

I was angry, but I wanted the whole incident over. "He was just worried about me."

Our practice continued without any more drama, and I felt confident again by the end. Doug didn't say another word to me and walked out alone as soon as practice was over.

Tired, sore, and still a little frazzled, I took a long hot shower when I got back to my room. Drying off, I noticed Doug's shirt still draped over the back of the futon. As I tossed it in my laundry bin, Elise spoke up.

"You know you're not fooling me with this whole nothing-happened-with-Doug nonsense." She stood, putting her hands on her hips.

There was no need to come clean about Doug now. It was over. "I forgot to wash it yesterday."

"You can't just wash it. They dry clean their shirts so they look perfect. Light starch."

"Really?"

"My friend Josh cleans at least five shirts a week. Plus, I think I got hair product on it."

Now I had to get it cleaned? What a pain! Fortunately, Elise and I picked up salads and I dropped the shirt at the cleaner's beside the grocery store that night.

Our first co-rec football game was on Tuesday night. Thinking of the previous day's incident, my stomach tightened as Lila and I walked onto the field. I could see the brothers standing in a loose group talking. Two heads, belonging to Zack and Doug, towered above the rest. I didn't expect Doug to be there, and his presence made me even more anxious. My cognitive processes seemed hijacked in his presence.

"You ready for this?" Lila asked.

"Bring on the humiliation."

"It'll be fun. Just pretend we're playing in the field back home."

This thought calmed me, and I reminded myself that football practice had gone well.

Zack noticed us first. "SMG!"

I guess we were back to the Super Mini-Girl moniker. Doug looked up and I fought the urge to look away.

We warmed up and then huddled for a strategy conference before the game started. As we broke from the circle, Doug squeezed my arm and pulled me aside. "Remember, you don't have to do this. We can get someone's girlfriend out here." He motioned toward the group gathered on the sidelines.

How dare he pull this big brother thing on me? "Play? Of course I'm playing. There are only two girls registered on the team."

He motioned towards the other team. "These guys are big."

Hadn't we been over this before? Before I could make a dramatic exit, a ball hit me on the head. I turned around to see Ross laughing.

"You're an idiot." I yelled at him.

"You playing or flirting?"

Now I was mad. "Playing." I threw the ball at him as hard as I could.

We won the coin toss, and Mark chose to receive the ball. Doug watched from the sidelines. At least I was on the field and not standing there trying to ignore him. Often Lila and I lined up against the girls from the other team. We didn't do much but were able to grab a couple of flags. Each team scored in the first half, keeping the game close.

As the night grew cooler and dew started to form on the turf, I could feel my shoes sliding. I didn't own cleats and was assured, by Mark, it wouldn't be a big deal. Still, I wished I had something on besides my running shoes. As the amount of dew on the field increased, I was slipping more and more. The chance of me pulling a Charlie Brown and ending up flat on my back seemed pretty high.

In the second half, Mark decided to mix it up, incorporating Lila and me into plays the other team might not expect. I caught a couple of short passes, and Lila made a few short runs. We were third and nine when Mark called a play for me to cut across the field and catch the ball. When the ball was snapped, I concentrated on running the pattern and then turned around to watch for his throw. It was a little high, so I took a few running steps backwards. I caught the ball and put all my effort into turning in the direction of the goal. A player came in from my right, and I jumped to the left to avoid him. As my left foot hit the ground, I slid. There was nothing I could do to stop the momentum I had built up. With the ball tucked in my left arm, my knees hit first, followed by my elbow. Pain seared through my arm, and I ended up falling face down with my chin scraping the ground.

After the initial shock, I flipped over fast, not thinking of my wounds as much as my pride. I stood up, but my head was spinning. Leaning over, I closed my eyes and resting my hands on my thighs to reset my balance.

Mark was the first one by my side. "Are you okay?"

"Sure, just a few scrapes," I replied, grimacing.

Looking around, everyone seemed to be moving towards me with caution. Each of their expressions was a little off. Out of the corner of my eye, I saw Doug running onto the field.

"Let's get you to the sideline," Mark suggested, putting an arm around my shoulder.

I was confused. Sure, I had scraped knees and elbows, but it didn't seem like they warranted this much concern. "I just need to walk it off." I said as we reached the sideline.

"Maybe you should sit down." Mark motioned toward the grass.

Everyone crowded around me. "I'm good. It's just a scraped knee."

Lila looked me up and down. "It looks pretty bad."

I finally looked at my knees and blood was pouring out of huge gaping holes just under my kneecaps. I turned my arms over and saw that my elbows were also covered in blood. Feeling sick, my ears began to ring and everything turned dark.

I heard voices. I wanted to answer, but the hum in my ears consumed me.

"I think she's coming to. Did she hit her head?" I heard a deep voice question.

"I was watching her; she didn't hit her head." I knew that voice, I would recognize it anywhere. That was Doug.

"She usually faints at the sight of blood," Lila said.

"That's right. Remember that time in cooking class, and the one at the blood drive." Of course Ross would bring that up.

"Are you guys sure?" Doug asked.

"She's been out a full minute, we may need to call 911," said the unfamiliar deep voice.

I forced my eyes open and saw a referee, Doug, Lila, Ross, Mark, Zack, and Bill leaning over me.

"Amanda?" Doug asked, waving his hand in front of my face to make sure I was focused on him. "Can you sit up?"

I tried, but nothing was happening fast.

"Put your head between your knees," instructed the referee.

I tried to take deep breaths. The air felt cool against my skin and I shivered. "I'll be okay. Just give me a minute," I managed. "Go play." I motioned them away.

It seemed like my words had some effect since several shadows retreated from my view. But, Mark, the referee, Doug, Lila, and Ross still hovered.

"Amanda?" Lila started, taking my hand. "They think you should go to the medical center."

I looked at the bandages on my knees and elbows. "Do I need stitches?"

"Probably, but you should go to the hospital, not the campus med center," the ref said.

"Really?" I stood, trying to look better than I felt. I just wanted to be out of the spotlight.

Doug scooped me up before I knew what was happening. "Lila, come with us," he instructed. Carrying me across the field, he lifted me into the back seat of Zack's SUV. Lila climbed in the other side. She tried to help me with my seat belt.

"I got it," I said, embarrassed and annoyed.

"Here, drink this," Lila insisted, handing me a Gatorade as Doug started the car.

Now I was lucid enough to feel the burning on my knees and elbows and see the blood-soaked bandages. I scanned the car for anything to keep my mind off my wounds. I was seated behind the driver's seat, and I looked into the rearview mirror and realized I could focus on Doug's face. Moving through traffic, he kept a watch on his mirrors and caught my stare. He lifted an eyebrow and shook his head. "Is this what your dad was worried about?"

"Maybe." I rolled my eyes and looked away, fighting back tears.

Lila waved her hand in the air as if this was no big deal. "Well, you're not getting out of this. If I have to play, you have to play. You'll be fine." It was exactly what I needed to hear.

My phone rang way too early.

Memories of the previous night came flooding back as I reached for it. Doug had driven me to the Northwestern University Hospital emergency room where I'd gotten seven stitches in each knee. They'd determined I'd probably fainted due to a dip in blood pressure, a reaction to the trauma.

At one point, Zack, Bill, Doug, Lila, Ross, and Mark were squished in between the dividers that formed my room. Lila, Mark, and Doug stayed with me until after eleven. I couldn't figure out why Doug was there. He spent three hours pacing, hovering, and critiquing. It was equally endearing and unnerving.

My phone screen showed Zack was calling, and I picked it up.

"I guess you're not working out with us. We did win the game, by the way. We need to get you some cleats." In that moment, I realized how much I liked Zack. He was upbeat and easygoing.

"I'm playing again?" I asked in disbelief.

"Of course, you're our ringer. We're getting cleats tonight. Besides, you'll need them for soccer in the spring."

"Soccer? Did you hit your head last night?" The guy was absolutely crazy. Maybe I didn't like him that much.

"Ha! No. But Mark says we need you on the team."

"Fine, what time?" I relented. There was no getting out of cleat shopping.

"How bout after your lab. You're out at like five, right?"

I was impressed he remembered my schedule, and we planned to meet at the house.

Since I was up, I called Mom. She answered on the first ring. I considered not telling her about the ER incident, but I realized there would be too many paper trails. It wasn't like me to keep things from her, but I didn't want my parents worrying.

After reassuring her for the hundredth time that I could get to class, I headed to the kitchen. I was starving and couldn't remember the last time I'd eaten. Needing something easy on my stomach, I toasted a bagel and smeared some butter on it. I'd just settled back in my room with my plate and my orange juice when I heard a knock on the door.

"Entrée," I called.

Lila let herself in. "Hi. You look better."

"Thanks, and I'll feel even better once I eat this and get a shower. And thank you for waiting with me at the ER last night. I'm sorry I passed out like that."

"Are you kidding, even Zack was freaked out by the blood, and he's pretty much the toughest guy I know."

"He called this morning."

She seemed surprised. "Wow, really?"

"You gave him my number, remember? We're going cleat shopping."

"You're going to keep playing?"

"I'll look even wimpier if I quit, right? It was kind of fun up until I got hurt."

"It was. Did Doug call?"

"Should he have? He doesn't have my number."

"He asked for it, so I gave it to him." This was getting to be a habit of hers.

"Oh," was all I managed. I finished the last bite of bagel, thinking I would've been better off not knowing that last piece of information. Now I was really depressed.

Making my way to the house after lab that afternoon, I found Zack out front waiting. He drove us to a sporting goods store not far from campus.

"Okay, you'll need soccer socks. What size?" he asked, looking down at my feet as we entered the store.

"I can't just wear these like I do for running?" I lifted my foot to show him my socks.

"No, you need these." He picked a pair off a rack as we reached the shoe department. "They'll probably come over your knees, but that's a good thing." He nudged me. "Now, cleats." He led me to the women's athletic shoe aisle.

As we were going over the choices, a sales guy appeared. Unfortunately there was limited selection for women's size six cleats so we moved to the children's department.

Wonderful, now I would be wearing girl's cleats! Zack picked up a black pair of cleats with pink stripes. "What do you think?"

"Really, pink stripes?"

"Do you have something against pink?"

"I haven't worn pink since the fourth grade."

"They're cute, don't you think?" He held them up for me.

"I'm not really aiming for cute."

"Just try them on." He handed me a box of size sixes.

The sales guy brought out several more styles in my size from the back, and I tried on all of them. Much to my dismay, the pink striped ones actually felt the best.

Zack wanted to browse so I followed him around the store as he surveyed all the equipment for every activity from inline skating to camping. We tried on skates, looked at skis, sat in kayaks, lay inside tents, and tried out every type of ball. He was fun to hang out with, and a welcome break from my serious life.

We spent over an hour in the store, and I was amazed we got out of there without a whole stack of things I, according to him, needed.

"Hey, I'm starving," he said as we got into the car. "Want to grab something to eat?"

"Sure," I said, realizing I hadn't eaten since breakfast.

He pulled into a gourmet burger place, and I ordered a grilled chicken salad while he got some sort of huge hamburger. "So, you not into burgers and fries?" he asked as we sat down.

"Not really." I crinkled my nose. "I don't really like fried food."

"What? Not even French fries? Everyone loves fries. And these are amazing."

With an oil and herb coating, they looked really greasy. "Yeah, I don't know, I just never liked them," I confessed, ducking my head.

"What?" He was nearly yelling now.

I looked around to see if anyone was staring and put a finger to my lips. "I'll eat one if you drop it."

"Done." He picked up one of his biggest fries, dipped it in some mayonnaise sauce, and passed it to me.

Figuring now was not a good time to mention I hated sauces, I took a bite, and he grabbed the rest back, popping it in his mouth.

"What was that about? I can't tell if I like it from one bite."

"I wasn't going to waste it if you didn't like it. But truly the best thing you've ever eaten, right?"

I shook my head at him and went back to eating my salad. Zack was late for the house meeting and I hung out with Lila till it was over. Afterwards, the guys trickled out to the back patio.

Mark greeted us first. "What took you guys so long?"

I hugged him, returning to my seat on the wall. "Miss me?"

"Did you guys know Mini-Girl here doesn't eat fried food?" Zack asked.

"She's just weird." Ross said.

"I got her to eat a fry!" Zack bragged.

That was it. It was just the thing to get Ross going.

"She ate a fry, no way!" he exclaimed, putting up his hand for a high five. "That's nearly like getting her to sleep with you."

How did we get from food to sex? Truly guys only thought about two things.

As they continued with the razzing, Doug got up and left. I figured now was my chance to thank him for the ride to the hospital and apologize for getting blood on his T-shirt, so I followed.

He was nearly to the door when I caught up. "Doug?"

He turned around. "How are you?"

"Fine. A little sore, but good. I wanted to thank you for last night."

"No problem. You thanked me last night. So you have cleats and you're sticking with the football?"

"Yes."

"What does your dad think? You did tell him, right?"

"He was on a flight. I told my mom."

A brother approached us with a question for Doug, saving me from further interrogation. Couldn't he just let it go?

I rejoined our circle, sitting next to Zack. "Are you well-versed on my food preferences now?"

"Who knew you didn't like fried foods? What a rookie mistake!" He rolled his eyes. "At least we're past that awkward first sex stage, though." He winked at me.

I hadn't seen a sex comment coming, and my face instantly felt like it was on fire.

"Aw, there's the Manda we know and love. I thought you'd grown immune. Should I drive you home?"

"You should," Doug said, sounding annoyed. What was his problem? He was probably anxious to be rid of me.

Zack dropped Lila and me off. Sitting down in my room, I realized how exhausted I was. Elise wanted a full account of my injury, and I let Lila take the lead. Halfway through, Kate joined us. Lila finished by telling them about Zack and the cleat expedition. She took my pink pixie cleats, as she called them, out of the bag and held them up.

"Aren't they so cute?" Lila barely took a breath before switching topics. "So what happened with Doug just now?"

"I thanked him." I left out that he'd asked about Dad. She didn't need to be included in his paranoia or whatever it was.

"And?"

"That's it."

"You're so boring." She turned to Elise. "You have a boring roommate."

After getting the dorm gossip from Elise, Lila and Kate retired to their rooms. As soon as they were out the door, Elise wanted to talk about Zack.

After the third time I swore on my Bubbe's grave that he was just a friend, Elise believed me. I washed up, changed into my pajamas, and took my English book up to my bunk. I must have fallen asleep somewhere in the first chapter, and when I woke the next morning, it was after seven.

"Morning," Elise said as I climbed down. "You slept for ten hours. I was starting to get worried."

I grabbed a bowl of cereal and sat down with her. When she left for class, I answered an email from Dad, sent one to Marissa and Tia, and then called Mom. With three classes in a row, my day passed quickly. In the evening, I got in an hour of studying before walking to the gym for the volleyball game. I could see the team already on the court warming up. Doug stood on the sidelines with Mark.

Mark walked over and gave me a fist bump. "Hey, you're late. I was worried."

Then, Doug came over. "She shouldn't be playing with those knees." So he wasn't even speaking directly to me now?

"We don't have any more girls. She's tough." Mark turned his attention to me. "Just don't bend your legs too much."

"Yeah, I'm good." I waved him off.

Mark walked away.

"You are so stubborn," Doug said.

"What?" I couldn't believe my ears. "Why do you say that?"

"Because you don't listen. You can barely bend your knees."

"I just took an Advil. It'll kick in." What I wanted to say was, "Why can't you just leave me alone, I can take care of myself."

"I saw you earlier at the library. You looked like you were in pain then, too."

"And you didn't even stop to say hi?" I swung my hair around my shoulder on that side. It was a train of thought comment. I regretted it instantly, but it derailed him for a minute.

"I was running late to class."

Frustration and anger took over. I glared at him. "Stubbornness can also be perceived as perseverance or dedication."

I wasn't mad about him calling me stubborn. I was mad at myself for hoping he'd change his mind about having time for me. After all, he'd stayed the entire three hours at the emergency room. What was that about? I was glad I had his stubborn comment as an excuse to vent my frustration.

"Dedication is an admirable quality, but you're just being stupid about this."

Stupid! Did he just call me stupid? I folded my arms over my chest, completely done talking to him.

Walking over to his bag, he returned with bottles of water and orange juice. "At least drink one of these."

I'd been so consumed by our drama I didn't see Zack approach. "Mark said I should break up your little lover's quarrel and tell you to get your butts on the court."

Doug turned and jogged to the court, leaving me holding the two bottles.

"Wow," Zack said. "I thought Mark was just kidding. You're really mad, aren't you? Glad I'm not Doug."

Stunned, I took a few sips of the water and walked onto the court. I had to serve first, and I tried not to be nervous. Mark tended to take sports way too seriously, and I didn't want to let him down. Thankfully, my first serve was good and we played well, winning the game.

Afterwards, I let Lila convince me to come out with everyone, so we ran back to our room, showered, and changed. I needed to blow off steam after my week anyway, and I hoped this event would not include Doug.

Not an hour later, Zack picked us up in his SUV that was already packed with Doug, Ross, and two other team members. Thinking I should shoot myself and get it over with, I squeezed in the back row with Mark.

At the pub, Doug sat beside me. Really? Couldn't he just disappear along with his shirt? I leaned as far away from him as I could.

"Nice game." He said to me.

I looked at him for a good half-minute. "Thank you."

"How are your knees?"

"They're fine."

"Good."

This was driving me crazy. I couldn't stand chitchatting with him. "I'm not really that accident prone. I just got hurt that one other time," I said, feeling the need to defend my reputation.

"What about cooking class and the blood drive Ross mentioned Tuesday?"

"That's different. I fainted." I crossed my arms over my chest. "I don't know why my dad's worried about me. He's never been like this before."

He leaned forward. "As I said, his daughter is away from home for the first time."

Since we were having a semi-normal conversation, I figured it was safe to bring up the shirt. "I have your shirt. I got it cleaned."

"Oh, thanks." he rubbed his hands along his thighs, repositioning himself in his chair.

"Will you be at the house tomorrow afternoon? If so, I'll bring it by then." I wasn't sure how I would get it there undetected. Maybe I would hire a courier to deliver it. Ha! I was going mad!

He nodded. "Yep, should be."

The waitress came and we got pulled into other conversations. He didn't speak to me the rest of the night. Although I should've been relieved, I was just disappointed.

The next morning I folded the shirt as neatly as possible and put it in my backpack, planning to deliver it after classes. As Lila and I walked out of the chemistry building, she jumped in front of me. "I knew you were lying about Doug."

"What?" Where had that come from?

"Don't look, but he's standing right there."

I was surprised to see him but recovered quickly. "And you weren't obvious at all." I rolled my eyes at her. "I have his shirt, remember?" I walked over to him, unpacking it from my bag.

"Thanks," he said as I handed it to him.

"Sure." I nodded. "See you around." I turned around and walked back to Lila, who stood with her mouth agape.

"Dang, that was cold."

"It's a shirt." I shrugged. "Hey what are you doing this weekend?" I asked quickly, trying to divert her attention. Starting tomorrow, freshmen were allowed back in the Greek houses, so she was thrilled.

I attended the first Latino club mixer that night. It didn't go any better than the booth encounter had, with only one guy talking to me the entire time. I was pretty sure he was hitting on me, so I really didn't count that. At least the NU Heights information meeting had gone well. Two and half-weeks post Doug and life wasn't half bad.

Chapter 7

Lila and I were one minute late to the gym for our volleyball game the next Thursday and Mark barked at us. The other team was supposed to be good, and even in warm up he was in crunch time coaching mode. Since the other team had tall players, Mark had both Zack and Doug in rotation the whole game. He placed me between them, and although we had gained another girl, he kept me in for both matches.

We won the first match by two, but the other team won the second. As we huddled, Doug handed me a bottle of water. It didn't escape me that he'd noticed I'd chosen that over the orange juice the previous week. But I pushed that thought out of my mind.

Starting the match, the other team hit the ball high from the front row. I moved forward and jumped up to place it to Zack, who popped it over the net. They returned it, hitting it long again. I jumped for it, and Doug must have done the same. We slammed into each other mid-air. His momentum and size were overpowering, and I was knocked to the floor. Instinctively, I reached out to break my fall. As the ball of my hand hit, a sharp pain shot up through my wrist to my elbow. My shoulder and head hit, leaving me temporarily frozen. Reacting to the shooting pain, I rolled onto my back, clutching my arm to my chest. The pain consumed me and I curled into a ball, trying to make it stop. My heart pounded inside my skull.

"Don't move," Doug said.

I couldn't focus. The pain in my head and arm weren't subsiding, and I wasn't sure I could comply. I wanted to uncurl and find a way to make the pain stop, but no part of my body moved. Zack popped into my view. He lay beside me on the floor about a foot from my face.

He repeated Doug's words. "Don't move."

Because no muscle in my body seemed to be responding, I complied.

"Look at me," Zack insisted.

I noticed Doug move away and my eyes followed him.

"No, look at me," Zack said again. I closed my eyes. "Look at me," he repeated.

The lights and noise were suddenly too much. I felt a humming in my ears and the brightness grayed.

I heard Lila next. "Manda, listen, you have to focus." I forced my eyes open. Lila's face was next to Zack's. "Sweetie, you're okay, you just hit your head."

In the background, I somehow picked out Doug's voice from all the rest. "Don't tell her we're calling 911."

Zack and Lila's faces were still only a foot from mine.

"I can hear Doug," I tried to say, but I couldn't tell if they heard.

It was as if I could only focus on one sense at a time. The shooting pains in my arm, and wrist took first stage again.

"No!" Lila's piercing voice brought me back.

Her expression mirrored my pain. I was struck with fear and gasped for breath. My eyes must have shown my panic.

Zack put his hand on mine. "Amanda, you're going to be okay."

My body was overwhelmed with sensations. My head was throbbing, and it felt like my ears were filling with fluid. Stabbing pains shot down my arm, and a low hum vibrated through my head.

Doug's face appeared next to Zack's, relaxing me. "Damn." I heard him say.

Blackness took over.

"Beep. Beep. Beep."

The sounds echoed through my head, and I opened my eyes to a room, dark, save a green glow. I felt something in my nose, and moved my hand to take it out.

A hand held my arm in place. "Easy, you need that." Doug.

Turning my head towards him, the pull of a bandage taped on my neck caused me to stop. Lifting my arm to inspect the dressing, his hand stopped my movement again. Annoyed, I balled my fist and pulled my arm quickly away from his grip. Two IV lines were taped to my arm. Okay, so keeping that arm still made sense now. But the sound of the beeps felt like a sledge hammer hitting my brain. I tried to lift my left arm and found it casted from my thumb to above my elbow. I leaned back and closed my eyes trying to process.

His hand touched my arm again. "What do you need?"

I didn't open my eyes for fear I would cry. "The beeping hurts my head."

"You can hear, that's a good sign." I opened my eyes and turned to look at him. His words sounded like an attempt at humor, but his face showed none. He held up the control for my bed, pushing the button to call the nurse.

"I can see." I looked towards my feet, wiggling my toes. "I can move everything."

My attempt to lighten the mood didn't bring a smile to his face. He rested his forehead on the bed beside my arm. "You're okay." I wasn't sure if the words were meant for me or for him. The exhaustion, evident in his bloodshot eyes and slumped shoulders, suggested how serious my condition might have been.

I couldn't think about that right now. Blinking back tears, I asked about Lila and Mark.

"They left a couple of hours ago to get some sleep. Your dad and Marissa, too. Your mom just left to get coffee. Do you want me to call her?"

I wanted to get my bearings. "No. What time is it?"

"Nearly eight in the morning."

"Friday?"

"Yes."

As he answered a man in scrubs came in. "I'm Ryan. I've been taking care of you. Do you mind if I turn on the lights for a minute?" He turned them on, and light flooded the room. "Wow, Dr. Carpenter wasn't lying. You have the brightest blue and green eyes I've ever seen."

I looked to Doug, who rolled his eyes. Ryan pushed a button on the monitor above my head, and the beeping noise finally stopped. He checked all the monitors and left saying he would let the doctor know I was awake.

Once he was gone, I turned back to Doug. "Did you get any sleep?"

Ignoring my question, he detailed the night's events. The EMTs had taken only five minutes to get to me, and Mark rode in the ambulance. They did a CT scan, and detected a hemorrhage in my brain, and had to operate immediately.

Panicking, I moved my hand to my head, feeling for my hair.

"Your hair is fine." He lifted a strand of my hair for me to see and then took my hand. I let him hold it. "The incision in your neck is where they relieved the pressure. They operated on your arm in the same surgery. They had to put in several pins and two plates."

I lifted my left arm, turning my cast over, just noticing the bandages sticking out from the edges.

"After your surgeries, we expected you to wake up, but you didn't."

The anguish in his eyes was too intense for me to acknowledge, and I wiggled my hand until he let go. "I shouldn't have gone for that ball. Mark must be livid."

He shook his head and half-laughed. "Yeah, there was some pacing." He patted my arm, leaving his hand there.

I rested my head on the pillow. Unlike the previous ER visit, he was comforting. I knew Mom would be a bundle of nerves, and Dad would question every detail. I let my mind drift. So here I was not three weeks into my freshman year, and I'd already had two hospital visits. Even for me, this was a record. I exhaled slowly, wanting nothing more than to curl up and sleep. If only my head would stop throbbing.

"Does your head hurt?"

Before I could respond, Ryan came in along with a female in a white coat.

"Hi, I'm Dr. Bridgestock. I've been taking care of you. I'm glad to see you're awake. Ryan said you woke up about twenty minutes ago." I nodded. "Is your head hurting?"

She asked about my pain and went through a series of questions aimed at assessing my long- and short-term memory, or so I guessed. She reviewed the list of tests scheduled for the day. If everything looked good, I would be released that evening.

"Do you have any questions?"

"I don't think so." I looked to Doug for confirmation. In my half-comatose state, I couldn't be sure I'd think of everything I might need to ask. Doug shook his head.

"Okay, then I'll see you after your scan." She left and Ryan followed, saying he would be back with the pain medication.

Doug took a seat beside me again, and I closed my eyes to try and ease the pain. I heard movement, and I opened my eyes. Ryan had come in with a syringe.

He hadn't lied. The medicine relieved the throbbing within minutes. With my headache gone, other issues began to seep into my thoughts. What about the classes I was missing? I had tests in almost every subject next week, and I couldn't afford to lose my scholarship. As I voiced my concerns, Doug held up my computer, assuring me all my professors and even the dean had been emailed.

"Thank you. So, what time is it now?" The time thing was bothering me. Some moments seemed to pass too fast and others too slow.

"Eight twenty."

In that moment, I realized I loved him. I shouldn't and wished it wasn't true, but it was. "Will you say goodbye before you leave?"

I barely registered Mom kissing my forehead just before drifting off to sleep. The day was long and tiring, and my body craved sleep. Mom, Dad, Marissa, Lila, and Mark were in and out. As I expected, Mom wrung her hands and Dad paced the tiny room.

Mark and Lila weren't much better. She cried and he scolded me, but I could tell his heart wasn't in it. He harped on my two supposed infractions. First, going for the ball when I shouldn't have, and second, hiding my alleged relationship with Doug.

"The guy has been here all night, holding your hand. Explain that."

I couldn't, as I had no idea why he was there either.

Is this me?

They released me just after nine that evening with a long list of instructions and medications. I had to be watched twenty-four-seven for two days, but I didn't care. All I wanted was to be somewhere in a normal bed, with no lights, sounds, nurses, or doctors.

I barely remembered riding to the hotel or crawling into bed. I wasn't comfortable with my huge cast and the pain in my head never left, but at least it was dark and quiet. Several times during the night, someone woke me. Eventually the pain in my head overtook my need for sleep, and I opened my eyes to a day almost half over.

Marissa helped me get a bath and wash and towel dry my hair. The hotel had a nice big tub, and it felt good to be clean and have normal clothes on. Mark, Lila, and Ross stayed most of the afternoon from what I could tell. Zack and Bill came by and brought me a Northwestern hoodie as a gift from the fraternity, but Doug never showed. I convinced myself he was a ghost or an angel, and I'd just dreamed he was sitting beside my bed the previous morning.

After my next dose of medicine, I drifted off and had no clue what time of day it was when I woke to Marissa shaking me. "Doug will be here in fifteen minutes."

His name was like a shot of adrenaline, and I pushed myself to a sitting position. Once the spinning slowed to a tolerable level, I inched to the bathroom to freshen up.

As soon as they were gone, he looked at me. "You're annoyed."

"I don't like having to be taken care of. I'm hungry, and my head hurts."

"Good thing I brought pizza. You're cranky when you're hungry."

"Aren't you?"

"Good point."

The pizza was reasonably hot, and we ate it straight out of the box. Although I had only had a bagel all day, I barely ate one piece before I felt full.

"So, how was your day?"

Was he serious? I wanted to think about anything but me. I'd been semi-conscious or sleeping for most of it, and the rest was depressing at best. "Weird, I'm not used to being an invalid. My family is hovering. No one is acting normal, except Marissa."

"You gave everyone quite a scare."

"I feel horrible. Mark wouldn't stop apologizing. Ross only criticized me to stop Mark from apologizing."

"You should've been at Zack's apartment last night. It was like a morgue."

"And now I feel so much better," I told him, rolling my eyes. "What about you? You're acting normal."

"I'm good at detachment." He almost smiled.

"What? So you're just acting normal for my sake?"

"It helps you, right?"

Why was he here? Didn't he know I was falling more in love with him? It was so much easier to ignore my feelings when he was mean.

"Okay then. What do you want to do? Watch TV? A movie?"

I shook my head. The noise and light would kill my head. I pointed to his backpack. "What did you bring?"

He reached for his bag and opened it, pulling out his computer and some books.

"What's in the Chinese literature book? Is it all in Chinese?"

"Yes. It loses a lot in translation, but they're interesting stories."

"Will you read me some of them?"

"In Chinese or English?"

"English, please. Read one you haven't read yet, so at least you can get something out of it."

As he began, I rested my head on the arm of the couch and put my legs up on the table. I wasn't sure how many stories he read when he stopped. I opened my eyes.

"You're squinting. Is your head hurting badly?"

"Yes, but finish."

"It's after ten. You can take your pain meds now."

After the medicine took effect, he showed me pictures of his trip to France. The next thing I knew I woke to the sound of my family's voices. My back rested on the side of the couch and my legs were draped over his. Doug put his finger to his lips. Noticing I was awake, he lifted my legs off his lap and stood. My face felt hot, and I was sure it looked flushed.

I remembered him leaving but not moving from the couch. When I woke I was in the bed. Lying there, I tried to identify the voices in the other room. I picked out Mom, Dad, Marissa, Tia, Ed, and Doug. How late had I slept? I looked at the clock. It was nearly eleven. I'd slept twelve hours, so why didn't I feel better? Reminding myself the doctor said it could take weeks for the headaches to subside, I pushed myself up.

Fighting nausea from my spinning head, I went to the bathroom and gently brushed through my hair. I gave up on getting it in a ponytail and brushed my teeth.

Mom jumped up and hurried over to me as soon as I opened the door. Glancing around the room, I saw Doug seated on the couch. He was too much to process. I greeted everyone and moved towards the suite's kitchen. Mom hovered not inches from me and Tia, Ed, and Doug followed.

I picked up a bagel and knife, but Mom took them from me. I opened the cabinet for a glass, and she left the bagel and reached over me to get it. Leaving her to tend to those, I retrieved the medicine bottle from the table. She was right behind me, slipping it from my hand and laying the dose in front of me. Giving up, I sat down at the table across from Ed.

"So, hey there, Crash," he started, motioning to me.

"Really? Crash?" I rolled my eyes at him. At least he was acting normal.

"So how do you know each other?" He pointed between Doug and me. Hadn't someone prepped him? Mom sat the cut bagel and the glass of water in front of me. Tia pointed a finger at Ed and raked it across her throat. How did I answer that question? I had no clue who he was. I looked at Doug, meeting his gaze for a second. He looked to Ed about to speak.

Dad jumped in, patting Doug on the back. My eyes were trained on him, and his face tightened at Dad's touch. "Doug stayed with Amanda the whole time and made sure we knew her status." The word detachment echoed through my thoughts. "He's the president of the fraternity, the Greek Council, and student body." Dad removed his hand and sat beside Doug, who looked down at the table. "He's an international business major like Manda, even knows four languages." Did Dad have to love him, too? It was all too much.

"Mark rode with me in the ambulance," I blurted out without thinking.

"I'm the one that crashed into her on the volleyball court," Doug added.

"Sweet, good job, Crash ." Ed faked a punch to my good shoulder, chuckling. Tia dragged him into the next room.

After a few bites of the bagel and taking my meds, we went down to the hotel restaurant for brunch. It was nice to be out of the room, although sunglasses were a must. I hoped it looked like I was hung over. But with the cast on my arm and bruising on my face and neck, I doubted I could pull that off.

Mom insisted on getting me a plate from the buffet. "We have our room until four. Before we take you home, we'll drop by your dorm room and pick up whatever you need," she said as she placed the plate of food in front of me.

It took me by surprise. I hadn't thought past today. Was she suggesting I leave school? I couldn't. I wouldn't. I would go nuts. My mind raced. If they were set on this course, it would be difficult to convince them to let me stay. What if the school wouldn't allow a medical leave? What if I lost my scholarship? I'd made good money tutoring, but it would only last me a year tops. My parents were still paying for Tia's wedding. With Bubbe's illness, she'd needed a lot of medical care. It ate through her money as well as a good portion of my parents' retirement funds. Dad had already sold his plane and doubled his flights to make up for it.

"I don't need to go home."

She took my fork and knife and started cutting my waffle. "Of course you do, sweetie. It's not a problem. I can take some time off and be with you. You need to heal. You just had surgery two days ago." Mom wasn't going to go down easy.

I tried to keep my voice even and sound factual rather than hysterical. "I already feel better, and the meds are working." It wasn't a total lie. "The doctor only said I needed to be watched for two days, and today is the second day."

Dad chimed in. "I think your mother's right. You need someone to be with you, and you won't have that here."

At least I knew how to argue with my father. I'd rarely had to do it myself, but I'd learned from Marissa and her many disputes with him. The key was to have facts. Emotional pleas, or whining, lost every time.

"Elise is almost always in the room, I'm friends with our suitemate, Kate, and Lila is right down the hall. Between the three of them, I can have someone close by at any time." My parents looked at each other and then back to me, so I kept going. "Between Elise, Kate, Lila, Mark, and Ross, we could put together a schedule so no one person would be over-burdened."

I hadn't included Doug on purpose. He'd already gone over and above, and I couldn't have him sacrificing any more time, especially with our undefined relationship. He tapped my leg under the table. I looked at him but couldn't get a reading on whose side he was on.

"I'm a graduating senior sir, so my test schedule is somewhat more relaxed. I can help make sure Amanda is okay."

Dad looked between me and Mom, his gaze finally settling on me. "Well, it seems that you have answered all of our concerns. I guess you are staying, for now."

Mom jumped in. "Charlie, are you seriously letting her stay? She needs to recover."

"She's got it covered." He told her.

Mom rubbed my back. "I hope you're right." She looked away wiping her eyes.

I squeezed her hand. "I'll be fine Mom."

They dropped me off at my dorm just after four. I'd convinced Elise to keep her camping plans, so she wouldn't be in till late. Not sure how much motion or chatter I could handle, I was glad to have time before she got back.

Doug took charge immediately, surveying our food stores and starting a grocery list. Even with my dizziness, curiosity sent me to check the contents of the fridge. Only a nearly empty jug of milk and some condiments were left. Our plastic milk crate pantry shelves held only stale bread, half a box of pasta, and an empty box of cereal. I shook the coffee jar.

Doug pointed a finger at me. "No caffeine, doctor's orders. Sit down. You're white as a sheet."

"I'm always white." I told him but obeyed. With every bit of my body aching, I just wanted to sleep forever. He sat next to me, typing a list into his phone. Finding my wallet in my bag, I was surprised to see a stack of twenties. My parents must've fortified my funds.

I handed him some money. He popped it in his wallet and sat back, turning his phone in his hands. I pulled my knees up to my chest thinking that he may be just as bad as my mom. He handed me a blanket, and I folded it next to me. "Are you going?"

"Waiting on Lila."

"Oh." Was all I could think to say. I guessed he wasn't leaving me alone, but I didn't have the energy to fight it. Leaning my head back I closed my eyes. I'd learned it helped the headache and dizziness to keep them closed. Soon I heard a knock, and he got up to get it.

Lila crossed over to me right away, wrapping her arms around me. "Hey, you look so much better." I shuddered at the thought of what I looked like yesterday.

Doug left, and Lila helped me take my medicine as Doug had instructed and get a shower. We found some plastic grocery bags, and secured two around my cast to keep it dry. She put my hair up so it wouldn't get too wet. The warm water felt good, but my head was throbbing within minutes. A rush of queasiness hit me hard, forcing me to sit on the edge of the tub. A bath might've been a good idea, I thought.

Thankful to at least be able to soap and rinse, I sat on the side of the tub and shaved. With a little awkward maneuvering, I was able to get on the tank and yoga pants Lila had left on the counter. Looking in the mirror, I realized I'd need something to hide all the bruising on my neck, back, and arm. Thankfully, Lila had a cowl neck sweater waiting for me when I came out of the bathroom as Mark had materialized.

I was glad he came, but I was already struggling to pretend to be okay for Lila. Hopefully the meds she gave me would kick in soon.

"Look at you!" He wrapped his arms around me, giving me a gentle hug once Lila had helped me into the sweater. "You look so much better. I tried to call all day, but you weren't answering your phone."

Sitting, I found my phone in my bag. There were three missed calls from Mark and two from Zack, along with a string of texts from both of them.

"Sorry," I told him, sending a text to Zack.

"No worries. I was just checking in. So what's up? You settling back in?"

"I guess. Doug is grocery shopping." I wasn't even sure why I said it.

"Doug?" Mark looked at me then Lila with raised eyebrows. Lila shrugged and motioned towards me.

"I don't know." I played with the fringe on the pillow my arm rested on. "He told my dad he had a light schedule. I think it's the only reason Dad let me stay." I prayed Mark would take some pity and avoid giving me any grief. I had no explanation for Doug's behavior other than guilt.

"Right, okay, we'll just play along with your whole you-don't-have-a-relationship game." He rolled his eyes.

I didn't have energy to figure out if he thought I was lying to him. Timed perfectly, there was a knock on the door. Doug was back with the groceries.

"You showered?" he asked as soon as he looked at me.

I felt my hair, realizing it was in ringlets from the humidity of the shower. I was surprised at the sound of concern in his voice, which of course was warranted after my near fainting spell in the bathroom. "Lila was here. I was fine."

"As long as someone is close. Did you take your medicine?"

I nodded and Lila concurred. Mark took the groceries and put them away, and Lila saved the plastic bags for my next shower.

Doug went to work right away putting together a salad for our dinner. My stomach still fest queasy from the shower and possibly the meds. Their movements seemed to make it worse, and I closed my eyes and rested my head on the back of the futon.

Within a few minutes, the medicine kicked in. When I opened my eyes, Doug sat down beside me and handed me a bowl of salad. Across the room, Lila and Mark were eerily quiet as we ate.

"Amazing what a little medication can do, isn't' it?" I tried to ease their anxiety.

"We'll have to see if you can take your meds closer together." Doug said, making a note of it on his phone.

After our salads, we went over my schedule to figure out how I would make it through my three tests. Between Mark, Lila, and Doug, it seemed I had my own tutor team.

There was a knock on the door, and Kate popped her head in. "Wow, I'm so glad you're okay." She crossed the room and hugged me.

Thankfully, she and Jeremy had already organized chemistry and biology study sessions. Now I just had to figure out how to concentrate with my head pounding and the room spinning.

Kate, Lila, and Mark excused themselves to get some studying done.

"I forgot what it was like the first two years," Doug commented after they left. "I can't believe you guys have this many tests in one week."

I felt bad about how much of his time I was taking up. "You don't have to stay."

He wouldn't leave, and I decided I could at least pretend to look at a book. I chose math first, wishing I could somehow have a data upload. My definition of feeling well had drastically changed in the past three days. I tried to focus but lasted barely fifteen minutes before I needed to close my eyes and take a break.

The next thing I remembered was Doug moving my legs from atop his lap.

"What time is it?"

"Almost ten."

I'd been out for over an hour? How had that happened? "I'm sorry, you don't have to stay. Elise will be back soon, and Kate is next door."

"You already told me I didn't have to stay, but I don't mind."

I was in too much pain and too tired to kick him out. Fortunately, it was time for my next medication dose. I'd testing just taking Advil earlier in the day and realized the codeine was the only thing that reduced the pain to a tolerable level. Within twenty minutes, I was functional again and pulled out my computer to work on my English paper. I had to adjust the brightness, but at least I could get something accomplished.

"What're you doing?" Doug craned his neck to see my screen.

The effect of the codeine was wonderful, leaving me feeling weightless. I pushed his face away. "It's my English paper, but it's not finished."

Mom called to check in for the second time, and I filled her in on my past three hours. Marissa got on the phone for a minute and had to mention how hot Doug was, like I didn't know.

"Music?" Doug asked when I hung up.

"What do you have?"

Doug scooted closer to me, scrolling through the list on his phone. "Green Day, The Fray, One Republic, Cold Play, Imagine Dragons. What are you in the mood for?"

His tastes were similar to mine, and I left the choice up to him. He retrieved a speaker from his bag and set it on my desk. He paced around the room. "So what's a language major doing taking so many science classes anyway?"

"Chemistry is a good background for CIA agents." Had I just told him that?

"CIA?"

"I know, odd." I stretched out so I was lying flat on the futon. "My dad's really into civil service. He says I'm the only levelheaded one of his girls."

"Levelheaded?" He leaned against my desk.

"Yeah, anyway, I'm thinking this injury is the perfect experience for being a CIA agent." It was an odd feeling to hear yourself say things and wonder why you said them.

"What doesn't kill you makes you stronger?"

"Something like that."

"You don't have a masculine cell in your body."

"Really?" I sat up. "I'm not nearly as girly as Lila or Marissa."

"What about your hair? It's always perfect!"

"I do love my hair." I raked my hand down the length of it. Thankfully, Lila had run some product through it to stop the frizz.

"Do you really want to think about a career as an agent?"

"Sure, why not? I mean, it's another option besides translating or diplomacy protocol."

He sat down beside me. "What about teaching? I mean, do you hear yourself when you talk about tutoring? Your face lights up. It's obvious you love it."

I stretched, considering his assessment. I'd always thought of tutoring as a means to an end. Although I loved working with kids, I'd never considered it a career path.

"I mean, you're going to take two years of chemistry, biology, five levels of calculus, and physics. Do you really like science and math that much?"

"I do well in them."

"I didn't say you didn't. It's just an interesting choice." He handed me a pillow. "So, I'm going to change the subject and ask you about the English paper you didn't want to tell me about."

I started to tell him and stopped mid-sentence. "So what is this medication anyway, some kind of truth serum?"

"Don't you always tell the truth?"

"Yes, but I don't go around telling people I'm levelheaded and want to be a CIA agent."

He laughed. It was nice to hear him laugh and see him smile. "And that you love your hair. So, about that English paper, I'm supposed to be helping you with it, so spill."

"Promise not to laugh?" I grabbed my computer and inched closer to him. "It's pretty girly."

Studying his face, I realized I felt different around him than anyone else I'd ever liked. Pain meds or no, I was comfortable with him and willing to put myself out there. In an odd twist, I was willing to be unguarded with the guy who was unattainable. Perfect.

With the computer on my lap and sitting so close to him, I got warm. I started to pull off my sweater.

"I'll help you with that." He pulled it from around my hair.

When I was free of it, I noticed a weird expression on his face. "What's wrong?"

He pointed towards my shoulder. "Those bruises must hurt a lot."

"Not right now." I got up and found a cardigan to slip on. Wanting to talk about anything else, I diverted back to my paper. "Do you want to hear about my paper or not?"

He wiped his brow, but nodded. I tried to be engaging, folding my legs yoga style as I sat. "We're reading Shakespeare, and I was wondering if romances need a second love interest, a rival, to be interesting."

"I guess you could argue most do, but you'd have to find one that didn't as well." At least he acted interested. "Quite an endeavor for your first college paper, don't you think?"

"I guess." A long yawn interrupted my thought process.

"Sleepy?" he asked.

"I want to wait up for Elise." The truth was I didn't want to miss any time with him.

"Good luck with that. Here, let me read your paper while we wait."

I handed him my laptop and settled back against the pillows. The next thing I remembered was him lifting my legs off his lap and onto the futon.

"I'm going," he whispered in my ear. "Elise is here. I'll see you tomorrow."

The only thing missing was a kiss.

Chapter 8

I awoke, reprimanding myself for that last thought.

"Hey there." His voice startled me.

"Where's Elise?"

"She went to class. You're stuck with me again."

The shades and curtains were drawn, keeping it dark in the room. "What time is it? How long have you been here?"

"Almost ten, I've been here since seven-thirty."

"You missed your workout?"

"It's okay."

"Isn't Kate here?"

"Yeah, but I know your meds so..."

All I wanted was for him to lie beside me and sleep for another twelve hours. Shaking off the thought, I sat up. One movement at a time, I swung my legs over the side of the futon and stood. I went to the bathroom, and leaning against the counter, splashed cold water on my face and brushed my teeth. I would have to deal with my spiraled hair later. Right now I had to get something to make my head stop pounding.

I returned to the futon, hoping that sitting would ward off the dizziness that was escalating. Doug set a bagel beside me and offered a glass of orange juice. After I took the cup, he passed over the next dose of pills. I ate a couple bites of the bagel with them and got up to figure out what I could wear to class. Looking down at my yoga pants, I decided they would suffice. I pulled on my sweater and started putting things in my backpack.

"You're getting ready for class? Do you feel up to it?"

"Yes," I lied. There was no way I was losing my scholarship.

"There is an issue." This stopped me short.

He pulled up an email from the dean notifying me I'd been put on medical leave. I realized I'd never asked him how Doug got into my email, but I didn't have the energy to care. I had to be cleared by a University medical center doctor before returning to classes or taking any tests.

"Well, it's not like they are going to bar me from going to lecture, right?"

"Probably not, but you're definitely going to have to get this sorted out before your test tomorrow."

That sounded logical to me. Once the throbbing in my head dulled, I ate the rest of the bagel. I went back into the bathroom to brush my teeth again. Putting some lotion on my face, I ran some product through my hair to keep the frizz at bay. Realizing I'd never get a tie in it to make a ponytail, I slid the elastic on my wrist for Lila to deal with.

Back in my room, I slipped on my high top sneakers.

"Wow."

"What?"

"Just impressed with your efficiency."

I wasn't sure if he was making fun of me. Taking my packed bag from him, I surveyed the contents. He'd packed my electronic tablet, a pad of paper, phone, sunglasses, and an apple. I grabbed my math book off my desk and slid the glasses on my face. Locking my room door, we headed downstairs.

I was nervous about taking the shuttle, since I'd only taken it once before and had no clue of the route or schedule. Even though Doug was with me this morning, I'd have to figure out how to get back to my dorm. I was relieved when he explained there was only one loop.

On the ride, Doug sent me the details for the medical center visit that he scheduled for the next day. I thanked him, realizing I'd completely forgot about it already. We got off the bus at the main campus, and Doug handed me my backpack. Just then, Lila came running up.

She hugged me gently. "Doug texted me you were coming. Are you sure you're okay?"

I looked at Doug. He waved a hand at me. "Bye."

I watched as he walked away.

"I swear Amanda that man is pure torture. How can you stand it?" So it wasn't only me. "Wish I had him for a personal assistant, or really any personal assistant."

In the lecture hall, I focused on one stair at a time, making my way down to where Kate had saved us seats. After a minute or two my dizziness mostly abated. I hoped the professor wouldn't be offended by my shades, as they were a must with the lecture hall lights. They were a two for one in that they also hid most of the bruising on my cheekbone. I couldn't really follow the lecture, but I forced myself to take notes. Hopefully I'd be able to make sense of them later.

After chemistry I would've loved nothing more than to sit with Lila in the warm sun. But even with my sunglasses, I barely made it ten minutes. I excused myself to find a darker spot in the library. I set my timer to make myself study calculus for fifteen minutes. By the end, I was only staring at the numbers on the page and wondered if I was doing more harm than good.

After my biology lecture, Professor Nolan approached me as I was putting my notepad away. He pulled me aside and asked about my medical clearance. Embarrassed to be caught breaking the rules, I decided on straight up honesty. Fortunately, he understood my desire to be in class, especially when I told him I had a medical appointment the next morning. Still, he reiterated the need for the clearance to take the test.

Lila helped me through our chemistry lab assignment, as I'd apparently passed my activity limit for the day. I sat on the stool, gripping the countertop in an attempt to control my dizziness, afraid I'd hurl on the lab bench. Sitting at the bus stop in the cool air afterwards helped. Lila sat with me but kept checking her phone.

"Are you missing something?" I asked. I was so in a fog I could barely remember what day it was much less what she or I would usually be doing.

"Flag football practice, but it's not a big deal." She waved her hand in the air.

"You should go. All I have to do is get off the bus and ride the elevator to my room."

She hesitated, but not for long. "Are you sure? I'll come by tonight."

I nodded. After a quick hug, she ran off.

Waiting for the bus, it occurred to me that maybe I was due for a dose of meds. I'd taken them when I woke up six hours ago. Was I supposed to take it at six- or eight-hour intervals? I couldn't remember. On the bus, the motion made me queasy. I closed my eyes and rested my head on the seat cushion, trying to concentrate on not puking. After what felt like an eternity, a guy tapped me on the shoulder.

"Hey, Amanda, I think this is your stop." He walked me into my building and made sure I got on the elevator.

Walking to my room, I realized I didn't even get his name and wondered if he knew me from classes or the fraternity.

Inside, I shed my backpack and shoes and laid down on the futon, my head pounding. The next thing I knew there was a buzzing sound coming from the floor. I woke enough to realize it was my phone, and sat up and retrieved it from my backpack.

"Amanda?" I heard a male voice say my name.

"Yes?"

"Where are you? Are you okay? I've been calling for ten minutes." I finally recognized Doug's voice and the intensity of it. "It's nearly six. How is your head? You can take your meds now."

"In my dorm. I'm fine," I managed, lying back down as a wave of nausea hit.

"Eat something before you take it. I'll be there in half an hour."

Sitting up and getting my bearings, I realized I barely remembered getting to my room. Who was that guy on the bus, and how did he know my name? I reached for the pill bottle from my desk and tried the cap. I held it with my right hand and tried to turn the cap with my left, but with only two fingers I couldn't get a grip. I switched and tried to hold the bottle with my left hand, but that didn't work either.

Head throbbing and stomach churning, I knocked on Kate's door. There was no answer. I went to find the resident advisor. She wasn't there either. Not wanting to ask a total stranger to help me open a prescription bottle, I gave up and went back to my room. Frustrated, I paced the room looking for a solution. Did this have to be this hard?

On the verge of tears, I needed a distraction. I was not going to cry. Instead, I scanned Elise's pictures on her tack board. Inadvertently, I tapped the mousepad on her computer. There, at the top of the school newspaper's website, taking up nearly the whole screen, was a photo of paramedics lifting a stretcher off the gym floor. The caption read: Freshman Critically Injured in Co-rec Game. You couldn't see my face, just my long dark hair, my left arm splinted on my chest, my horribly white legs, and my right hand hanging limp over the edge of the stretcher. I sat down in her chair, straining to read the words with my blurred vision. "Amanda Avery, a freshman international studies major," the article started. I didn't need to read more. Taking deep breaths, I focused on not crying.

There was a knock on the door, and Doug poked his head in, rushing towards me when he saw me sitting at Elise's desk.

"What's wrong?" He knelt down beside me.

It was too much. Funny how you can hold it together until someone asks you if you're okay. I'd always been that way. It annoyed me to no end. I took some deep breaths, raked my hand through my hair, and held the pill bottle up.

"Childproof cap."

"What? Why didn't you call?"

"I tried to find someone to help me open it." Tears were threatening to pour.

He opened the cap and handed me two pills. I took them with a swig of water from the bottle he handed me.

"We'll take these to the medical center tomorrow and get the bottles switched. Did you get anything to eat?"

"No." I tapped on Elise's mousepad and motioned towards the screen. "Is this how a random guy on the bus knew me?"

"Maybe, but not everyone reads that."

Was he kidding? I had started getting the emailed links the day I was accepted.

I stood up, pushing past him. "Did you see Lila? Is she still coming? What about Mark?" I wiped my cheek where a tear had escaped.

He looked at me, his eyes round as saucers. All I wanted was someone who could give me a big hug and tell me everything was going to be okay.

"She said she'd be here after she got dinner. Not sure about Mark. I'll get you something to eat. You'll feel better soon." He was in action mode, and I retreated to my futon. Why was I feeling this vulnerable, this helpless, this out of control? This was not me. I got up and paced the room to keep the tears at bay. My head was killing me but I convinced myself that it was better than a full-out cry in front of Doug.

When he came back with dinner, I ate while surveying Elise's books, movies, and pictures to distract myself. He'd topped the bagels a mile high, so I could barely finish one half. My phone rang, and I noticed it was Mom calling. Even though I was feeling a little steadier after the food, I was nowhere near ready to talk to her without waterworks. Turning the phone so Doug could see, I shook my head. He rolled his eyes and answered the phone.

"Hello, Mrs. Avery." There was a break. "Yes, this is Doug."

He went on for a few more minutes, explaining how I was in the shower and was doing well. Then, he continued to tell her about the medical clearance and the caps on the medicine bottles. Finally, he said, "I'll make sure she calls you tonight before she goes to sleep."

As soon as he hung up, he handed me the phone back. "What was that about?"

I didn't look at him. "I can't talk to her right now."

"Can I ask why?"

"No."

My feelings were all over the place. Most of all, I was angry. Why did this have to happen to me? Afraid I'd cry from pure frustration, I was desperate for a distracting conversation. I said the first thing that popped into my head and instantly regretted it.

"Are we friends now?"

He didn't say anything for what seemed like forever. Then, he said, "No."

I took a minute to think things through. He was helping rehabilitate me from a critical injury, but we weren't even friends? Could he be more confusing?

He held up a finger. Instead of jumping in, which was my usual reaction, I waited.

"It seems, you have issues telling your friends when you need help, so—"

"But—" Before I could finish, he held his finger up for me to wait again.

"I'm not being your friend."

I sat back on the futon pulling my knees to my chest. "Fine," I told him, feeling frustrated and defeated.

"Fine? Let's see. You couldn't get your medicine bottle open, you didn't call anyone to help, and you haven't eaten since breakfast. What am I forgetting?" He raised his eyebrows.

I looked up at the ceiling. Now I was really close to tears and drained of all energy. I considered what he said. As much as it pained me to admit it, he might be right. Still, I had the same word for him. "Fine."

"Wow, I thought this was going to be a fight."

"Do I look like I have enough energy to fight with you?"

"No, but for once, I wish you did." Looking at him and seeing he was serious, I couldn't help but smile and realize again that I loved him. "That's what I like to see. So what would you be doing tonight if you weren't stuck here?"

"This might actually be better than what I'd be doing."

"How is that possible?"

"Right about now," I lifted my phone to check the time before continuing. "I would be enduring my second Latino club meeting." I explained my whole Latino club experience and my good-old-college-try approach to it.

"I can't believe they wouldn't talk to you?"

"Look at me." I held my arm up to his. "See how white I am? Plus, look at my light eyes. It makes me look like a wanna-be. No one spoke to me at the intro mixer, except some guy named José."

"And you think the Latino club members don't talk to you because you don't look Latino or Hispanic?"

"Definitely," I said.

He didn't respond for a minute. "How about, when you feel better, I go with you?"

I'd go anywhere with him. But I'd keep that thought to myself. "Really?"

"Sure, no problem. So, why were you so anxious to make sure Lila was coming?"

Not willing to answer his question, I gave him my best confused stare.

"Just wondering." Instead of pushing for an answer, he moved on. "Ready to call your mom?"

It was the last thing I wanted to do at the moment, but I knew she was worried. I summarized my day for her, leaving out the zoning out on the bus and cap incidents. While I talked, Doug rubbed my back. As a result, I only caught half of what she said. His hand on my back felt equally like Heaven and Hell. Heaven because he was touching me, and Hell because I knew I was only falling harder for him. Detachment, I reminded myself. As I was reassuring her for the tenth time that all was good, I heard a knock on the door.

I looked up to see Lila. "Hey Mom, Lila's here. I have to go. I love you, and I'll call you tomorrow."

She sat down beside me, giving me a big hug. "How's your mom?"

"Worried and neurotic."

"Of course she is. She's your mom. Turn around, and let me brush your hair."

Doug got up to sit at my desk. Lila found my brush and began pulling it through my hair. She'd told Mark I was too tired for a visit, which I was grateful for. Recapping football practice, she complained about Ross giving her a full body hug, leaving her sweaty from head to toe. I enjoyed listening to her talk, grateful for the distraction.

Partially dozing until I was able to take the codeine, I barely remembered Elise coming in and Lila and Doug leaving.

"Amanda?" Elise's voice played through my mind, and I felt tapping on my arm. "You have to get up. Doug won't go to rowing until you do."

Registering Doug's name, I opened my eyes. Elise waved my phone in front of my face. I took it and squeaked out a hello.

"Hey, sleeping beauty, you awake?" Doug asked.

"Yeah, I'm awake." I pushed myself up.

"Okay, I'll see you at the medical center later."

"Got it." I heard commotion in the background.

"Is that Mini-Girl?" Zack's voice came through. "Let me talk to her."

Doug must have handed Zack the phone, because his voice came through the line. "Mini-Girl?"

"Yes?" I answered.

"Hey, nice morning voice, sounds very sexy."

"What? Give me the phone." It was Doug's voice. He must've won the phone battle, because he came back on the line. "See you at eleven-thirty."

I put down the phone and thanked Elise for waking me.

"You got that boy wrapped round your finger, girl." She started stuffing items in her backpack. Quite, the opposite, I thought. "You remember the rules, right?" she asked pulling on her shoes.

"Rules? I have rules?"

"Yes, you don't remember this? Well there's really only one."

I was not allowed be alone at any time. This morning, Mark was coming to help me study and escort me to class. After my morning calculus class, I had my appointment at the medical center. Then, after my English and international studies classes, I was supposed to go back to the house and hang out with Mark.

"Okay, no unsupervised time. Got it."

"Kate is in the other room till Mark gets here. Doug thinks you were in pretty bad shape yesterday."

"It was just the meds bottle."

"I don't make the rules," she told me walking out the door.

Perhaps I should have been concerned about not being able to recollect the conversation from the previous night. But, I now lived in a world dominated by pain management, and as long as I could sleep and get to my classes, I was content.

Mark came in during my obligatory call to Mom. I had breakfast with a side of pain killers, and got in a good half hour of studying before class. Calculus was uneventful, except for Vivian, who doted on me like a nervous grandmother. She followed me halfway to the medical center before noticing she was heading the wrong way for her next class.

Entering the medical center, I found Doug standing right inside the door. He crossed the room to me.

"Good morning, you look better than last night." He took my backpack. He looked at it and looked at me. "Does this hurt your shoulder?"

I shrugged. "Hi, thanks, a little, I guess." The backpack on my shoulder was the least of my pains. I made my way to the registration desk and checked in.

"Are you nervous?" Doug asked when I came back over to him.

"Why?"

"You're biting your lip."

"I don't like doctors."

"Good thing I'm here then." He handed me a sports magazine.

Within a few minutes, a young male dressed in a white coat called my name. I followed him back to a room where he pulled up my file on his tablet. He took my vitals and conducted a neurological exam. Next, he reviewed the list of post-concussion care instructions. He asked questions about my roommate, friends, and how classes were going. Finally, he determined I could be medically cleared. I was required to schedule a session with a counselor and a follow up with him, but I accepted those conditions relieved that I could take my tests.

He walked me back to the lobby and to the registration desk. As I was scheduling the appointments, Doug approached with my medicine bottles. Ugh! I'd already forgotten those. The doctor led us into a supply room and switched my bottles to some with pop top lids. "Anything else?"

"No, I think that's it." Wishing Doug weren't there to witness me scheduling the counseling appointment, I was grateful to have someone as a backup.

"Good. I'll see you next week, Ms. Avery."

Doug and I made our way through the lobby. "So?" He moved his thumb up and down.

"You didn't think he would clear me?"

"No, I . . . I don't know what is normal."

"I can walk in a straight line and put my finger to my nose."

"Only when you're on the meds. So you passed?"

"Yes, except I have to see the counselor about posttraumatic stress. I don't think he thinks I have friends."

"Well, Lila and Mark, right?"

"And Elise, Kate, and Zack." It was mean, but I put Zack in there on purpose. Now that I had a little energy, I felt hurt by his unwillingness to be my friend.

He stopped mid-stride, putting his hand out in front of me. "Amanda, Zack's not—"

I didn't let him finish. I wasn't going to listen to him tell me Zack wasn't a good guy. "Zack and I work out together. We're friends, end of story." Not sure I could fake not being warned about Zack, I knew Doug would probably guess I knew about Zoey.

It was cloudy out and Doug sat with me in the courtyard while I ate my lunch. With little appetite, I got through half my sandwich and then handed him the rest. I probably wouldn't have bothered at all if he hadn't been there.

With my medical clearance, I had no problem taking my calculus test. Knowing I had limited concentration time, I skimmed through and did the problems I knew first. There were three out of the twenty I had to go back to. I only finished one of those, but nothing could be done about it.

Mark met me outside the building afterwards. "I didn't realize I had an escort this afternoon," I said, realizing that it was possible someone had thrown that information at me this morning.

"Doug's rules, remember? I told you this morning?" He rolled his eyes. "He called me at lunch to make sure I was meeting you. I wish you would come clean about him."

My energy level tanking fast, I diverted. "Can I go back to my room now?"

Lila and Ross were expecting us at the house, but he agreed to come back to my room with me. All I wanted to do was sleep. In my room, I slid off my shoes, shed my backpack, and slunk onto my futon, happy to not be vertical anymore.

Mark reminded me I had to eat something and take my meds. Not wanting to make him my slave, I pushed myself up with my good arm and retrieved half of a pita. He handed me the pills after I had eaten a bit, and I lay back on the cushion.

"You can go. I know you want to warm up before the football game."

"This really sucks for you. You're missing all the fun. Are you sure?"

"Look at me, I'm totally good. I'm just going to take a nap."

"Doug said he'd be by after class. Do you want us to stop by after the game? Zack asked if he could come by, too." Mark shot me one question after another.

"You should go." I pushed him off the futon with my feet. "Tell everyone to come by later."

The repeated hammer strikes on the anvil grew in intensity, and the last blow forced me awake. The smell of chicken hit my senses next and I sat up. Doug sat on the floor in front of me, two Styrofoam bowls beside him.

"You got me chicken soup?"

"So this you wake up for? I've been here for two hours."

"Thanks for getting dinner." I looked around, trying to get my bearings, and noticed it was already dark out. Picking up my phone, I saw it was after eight. I had three missed calls from Doug and two from Mom. I'd been asleep for five hours.

"I talked to your mom for you."

"Thanks." I told him, thinking he'd probably hate me for the rest of his life.

After the soup and another round of medicine, I felt better and was able to study for an hour before my head started throbbing again. This was going to be a long week.

✗ ✗ ✗

Wednesday morning I missed Doug's first attempts to wake me via phone, but Kate finally was able to rouse me so I didn't miss the chemistry test. I used the same strategy I had for the Calculus test, again finishing about eighty-percent of it. I just hoped I got most of what I finished correct. Feeling as if I was getting more confused as the week went along, I wondered if I was trying to cram too much into my brain. I wasn't used to using short term memory for test taking. With a biology test and English paper to get through, I worried about my grades.

Thankfully we didn't have to dissect anything in bio lab. The embalming fluid would've put me over the edge. Taking the shuttle back to my room, Doug was knocking on my door before I could even unpack my bag.

"Did I know you were going to be here?" I asked ushering him in.

"Nope." He was smiling for a change. Could this man be any more irresistible?

"Where's Lila?" I asked, thinking we were supposed to have our regular Wednesday girl's night in.

"We tried Lila and Mark. It seems you have issues with your friends."

"And those are?"

"You always talk them into leaving you alone."

I walked away from him, grabbing a bottle of water and my medication bottle. There was no use arguing with him. I liked being with him anyway. We ordered takeout, and I studied until my head felt like it would explode. I leaned back on my pillows, watching Doug read his Chinese literature. When he looked up, he caught me staring. I hoped he assumed I was staring into space.

"Chemistry got the best of you?" He reached out and rubbed my leg.

Although I could've watched Doug all night, I was worried about monopolizing his time. I wondered when Elise would be back. With all her band and sorority activities, she'd been out a lot this week. "What are you missing tonight?"

"Wednesday house meeting."

Wednesday, right, I knew that. "You should go, Kate is probably next door."

He assured me Zack could handle it.

"Wasn't Zack supposed to come over last night?"

"Yep, you fell asleep. Actually, he should be over after the meeting. Want me to read to you until he gets here?"

I nodded. He smiled and opened his book. I closed my eyes and listened to the story.

Zack's voice woke me. "Wow, you guys are having a hot night hitting the books." He snatched Doug's book. "Chinese literature? Of course you'd fall asleep to this. You guys are the biggest geeks at this school."

Doug tried to come to our defense. "Lights and noise make her head worse, so—"

Zack didn't let him finish. "I can't believe you're my best friend. And you, Mini-Girl, I would've expected more."

Normally I would have come back with something smart, but I really had nothing tonight.

Doug stood up. "So what should we have been doing? Making out?"

Looking between us, Zack slid a hand through his hair. "No, I guess not."

"Is everyone else coming?" Changing the subject, I got up, and started cleaning up.

Lila, Mark, Ross, and Bill showed up a few minutes later, and my room was packed. With the noise and commotion, my head was spinning and pounding within half an hour. Thankfully, Lila walked them down after just an hour's visit.

I wasn't sure if he ever left or not, but he was the first thing I saw the next morning when I woke. He sat on the floor, leaning his back on my futon, not a foot from my head. I reached out to touch his shoulder and he jumped.

"Sorry." I sat up, hoping my hair wasn't completely a mess. A wonderful smell, one I couldn't quite place, assaulted my nose. "What did you bring?"

He lifted a cardboard drink carrier and brown bag. "Decaf mocha and egg and ham croissants."

"You're an angel," I told him, excusing myself to freshen up.

Following breakfast and all my meds, I finished my English paper and had Doug review it. I emailed it to the professor with ten minutes to spare. We rode the shuttle to the main campus, and Doug walked me to my class. Handing me my backpack, he reviewed the schedule he'd entered into my phone. It felt like a long six hours, but just as planned, Zack was waiting for me after class that afternoon.

He took my hand immediately, pulling me to him and wrapping an arm around my shoulder. I was already on overload from the day, and I stiffened. My Tuesday and Thursday classes were grueling. Other students started to realize I was "the girl" from the gym accident. Without Lila, Kate, or Jeremy as buffer, I had to talk to more people than I wanted to. It was shocking what classmates would say to me, with "Wow, you're lucky you're not dead," being the most popular. Who says that to someone?

He released me. "You are way too tense. Close your eyes." He turned me around and proceeded to rub my shoulders. The warmth from his hands felt amazing, and I had to remind myself that we were standing in the middle of the main square.

He motioned me to the closest bench. "Ready for Zack-sitting?"

"Do you have to call it that?"

"Mandatory stuff out of the way first. Have you taken your meds?"

I sighed and pulled my pill case out of my backpack along with a bottle of water and an apple. We sat as I ate the apple. "So, what are we doing today?" I knew the routine, but after fielding so many questions in my classes, I didn't think I could go back and stare at my four walls. Maybe I was actually starting to feel better.

"I have a surprise. Do you feel like walking?"

"How far?"

"Couple of blocks."

He picked up my backpack and slung it over his shoulder. "So, I have one thing to say concerning last night."

"That is?" I asked, standing and following him.

He took my hand. "I'm much better at making out than Doug."

Oh my goodness, he hadn't just said that. I burst out laughing. "I'll have to keep that in mind." Zack might be a player, but he sure knew how to lighten a mood.

We rounded a corner, and I realized we were at the stadium.

"Would you like to watch the guys practice? I have connections."

Seeing the stadium and team scrimmaging from the field was beyond amazing. I took some pictures for Dad, and afterwards, the players autographed a football jersey, football, and posed for photos with me. It was super cool to meet the players and the perfect mood lifter. They were all so nice, telling me how glad they were that I was okay, and offering tips on concussion management and elbow and wrist rehabilitation. It was so fun, and I was so excited, I couldn't help texting Marissa and Dad as we walked out of the stadium.

Zack reeled me in, taking my phone from me. "Please don't text and walk." He guided me towards the shuttle stop.

I thanked him profusely while we waited. On the bus, Zack's phone buzzed and he took it from his pocket. He looked at it, and held it up in front of me. There were six missed calls from Doug. "We're busted."

Taking out my phone, I realized he'd been trying to reach me too. I sent him a text so he wouldn't worry. AT THE STADIUM WITH ZACK. HEADING TO THE HOUSE NOW.

When we got there, Lila, Mark, Bill, Doug and the rest of the co-rec volleyball team were congregated upstairs. As I showed off my jersey and football, they surprised me with a gift. The team had gotten me a zip-up hooded sweatshirt, embroidered with the frat's letters. I put it on, my face blazing from the attention. An extra-small, it fit perfectly. I thanked each one of them as they filed out for dinner.

Doug cornered Zack and me, concerned about the appropriateness of our outing. I reassured him I felt okay. It wasn't the total truth. My head never really stopped hurting and the bus ride had made me nauseous, but these sensations were becoming background noise. At least they weren't debilitating today, and it was a much-needed break from my dorm room.

Zack ordered dinner, and we ate up in the common area as the brothers ate downstairs. "I could get used to this. I got gourmet while they got cafeteria. I'll have to invalid-sit more."

I hit him on the arm. "I'm not an invalid."

Zack was driving everyone to the volleyball game and dropped me at my dorm on the way. Having confirmed that Elise was in our room, Doug went with them to the gym. Unpacking, I showed off the jersey and football as well as the hoodie from the house. Looking at my pictures with the team, she was speechless for the first time since I met her.

It didn't take her long to recover. "So, Mr. Walters is stepping up his game?"

I put my phone down. "No game. We're friends."

"Mr. Taylor seems less intense today," she continued as I took out my books.

"Yeah, I'm feeling better, so I think he's relaxing. I'm sorry it's been so crazy around here."

"Hey, I'll take broken arms with a side of hunk any day. Not that you're not cute and everything, but the views from over here have never been better."

I laughed, but she got me thinking. Once I was back to normal, I wouldn't need Doug. He said he wasn't my friend. Would he just disappear again?

"You like him, don't you?" she asked, bringing me out of my thoughts.

"Doug?"

She nodded.

There was no use denying it. "Yeah."

"You're in so much trouble."

"Can we not talk about it?"

"No problem." She sat down in front of her computer.

I seemed to have turned a corner as I was able to read for two hours with only a five minute break. My phone buzzed and the display indicated a call from Doug. I answered on the second ring. "How'd it go?"

"It was fine." He sounded out of breath. "I'm showering and heading over along with the rest of the crew. Is that okay?"

Checking with Elise, I confirmed the plan with him. I freshened up, glad that my head wasn't imploding from staring at my biology text. Lila made it by first, followed by Ross, Mark, Zack, Bill, and Doug. Kate heard the commotion and came over. It was great to actually feel good enough to enjoy hanging out. With pub choice discussion ensuing, it almost felt like a normal Thursday night.

With a destination settled upon, everyone save Doug trickled out.

"I can stay, if you'd like. I brought my books. My guess is you're crashing pretty soon anyway."

"You should go out, do something fun."

"I need to study, so I'm not going out. I might as well do it here."

I craved being with him, but my worry about whether he would vanish surfaced again. More time with him would only make that feel worse. I couldn't read anymore, but I got out my notes and pretended. After sneaking glances at him several times, I noticed he kept rubbing his right arm.

"Did you hurt your arm?"

"It's sore from the game. It'll be okay tomorrow."

"I'll rub it for you. Sit down here." I pointed to the floor in front of me. He gave me an odd stare but obeyed. I scooted over so I was behind him. "Take off your shirt."

He complied, and I propped a pillow behind his back. I started rubbing his neck, unsure of how effective the massage would be with only one hand. "You don't have to do that." He pulled my hand away.

"No, it's fine." I traced down his neck to his back, back and forth over his shoulder blades. I reached his biceps, and my fingers barely stretched halfway around his arm. When my hand tired, I handed him his shirt.

"So how do you pack so much muscle into these tiny fingers?" He took my hand and held it up. "Do you do finger flexes or something?" His hand felt good encircling mine, and I tried to force the thought from my brain.

He let go and stood, and I moved back to my corner of the futon. He put his shirt back on and checked his watch. "You should probably take your meds if you want to wake up at a decent hour tomorrow."

"I might try to sleep without the codeine tonight."

He was shaking his head before I was halfway through my sentence.

"You need rest. You'll wake up in the middle of the night and be in pain and won't be able to get out of it." He reached across me, popped open the medicine bottle, and handed me a pill.

As the meds kicked in, it was all I could do not to touch him again. Reviewing my schedule for the next day, he reminded me about my counseling appointment.

Thinking I'd rather get stitches out a million times than sit in a counselor's office, I excused myself to the bathroom. As I brushed my teeth, Elise texted she would be out late. The meds weren't inducing the same sleepy state they usually did, and it made me anxious.

For the first time, I wished he'd go and leave me alone. He also seemed fidgety as he kept opening and closing his book.

"What would you be doing if you were at the house?" I asked.

"Watching TV, probably." He flipped the pages of his book.

We'd never watched anything together, so it hadn't occurred to me he watched TV like a normal person.

"What do you watch?"

"Whatever. Usually it's some reality thing everyone's into."

He closed his book. "What do you like?"

"I'm more of a movie person." I stood and motioned to the movie collection on the shelf above my desk. How stupid was I? He'd stood right here three weeks ago staring at this shelf. I couldn't figure out anything fun to talk about. "You should go. I'll be fine."

He grabbed my good hand and pulled me down to a sitting position.

"I'm not leaving."

I sighed. "Really, you should go meet up with everyone."

"They're drunk by now."

"Elise has some wine." I got up to find it.

He pulled me back. "I'm not drinking and neither are you." He fluffed the pillow and ordered me to lay back on it. He settled in beside me. I wondered why he was doing this. Then it hit me. Tonight marked one week since my accident. This was the first time they'd been on the court since my accident. Lila hadn't said anything about the volleyball game. What had he said about the game? It was fine, was he remembering last week?

His eyes were closed, so I propped myself up on my good arm and whispered to him. "How was volleyball?"

He didn't open his eyes. "I told you it was fine. We won."

"No, I mean, how are you?"

He opened his eyes but he still didn't look at me. "I'm as good as you are."

Unsure of how to interpret his words, tears started to form in my eyes. I blinked to keep from crying. How was I? I was better, I reassured myself. Even if better only meant I'd moved from zombie-state 10 to 8, I was better. He didn't say anything else so I let it go.

He was as good as I was. My mind circled back to my earlier thought, and I prayed he wouldn't leave me again. How selfish was I asking God for a guy, especially this guy?

Chapter 9

I woke to the smell of coffee and eggs. Doug was lying beside me as he had been the night before. It threw me for a minute. Surely he hadn't been there all night. Focusing more, I noticed he was wearing a different shirt.

Doug lifted his cup of coffee as if to toast. "Morning."

"Please tell me I can have some of that."

"Half and half." He handed me a cup. The warm liquid tasted like heaven. I pulled my phone out to see if I'd missed any messages and noticed the time. It was almost ten.

"Oh, God!" I sat up quickly, nearly spilling the coffee. "Chemistry."

"Taken care of. You're cutting chemistry today."

Breathing a sigh of relief, I closed my eyes and tried to calm my racing heart. "I like the way you're thinking today." I took another sip of coffee. "Amazing the things you miss when you don't have them."

"What else do you miss?"

"Don't laugh, but Diet Coke. I'm sort of addicted."

"Wow, you do live on the edge, don't you?"

"Do I smell eggs, too?"

"Lila mentioned you like eggs. Is it Diet Coke or diet soda in general? And how do you like your eggs?"

"Why the sudden interest in my food and drink preferences?"

"Just gathering a list of all things Amanda." He was in a good mood, and it made me happy. We ate our sandwiches and drank our coffee in silence.

"Thank you." I said once we were done with breakfast. I wanted to say more but anything else seemed superfluous. "If I could just get over the dizziness and headaches, I'd be good as new."

He looked offended. "You didn't tell me you got dizzy. You need to stop and rest when you get a headache, remember."

"Only when I stand up." That probably didn't help. I did remember the headache rule. Not willing to put my life on hold indeterminately, I'd ignored it.

He shook his head at me. "Zack will be here in ten minutes if you want to do something to your hair."

"Is it a mess? Why didn't you tell me?" I hoisted myself up and checked the mirror. My hair looked like a bird's nest.

"You must have slept badly. Are you tired?"

"No, I feel good. Why is Zack coming?" I asked as I ran some product through my hair.

"You missed your study session while you were at the stadium. He's helping you study bio."

"Won't he miss class?"

"He doesn't mind. If you haven't noticed, you have Zack wrapped around your little finger."

Pulling some clothes from my closet, I ignored his assessment.

Zack helped me study, and then we all rode the bus with Kate to biology. I was surprised to see Zack again after my test. "You're off to the medical center to see the shrink, right?" He greeted me, taking my bag from me.

"Two-thirty, I have a couple of minutes." He walked with me towards the medical center. "You don't need to come in with me," I said just before we reached the entrance.

"I don't mind. I can wait for you."

"I'll be fine, and I can take the shuttle to the house after." I hoped he would take the hint. I really didn't want an audience for this.

"I should be helping to clean for tomorrow, but Doug will cut me some slack if I'm with you."

I fake punched him on the arm. "That's pretty lame. Go work."

Waving goodbye, I walked into the lobby and checked in. Within minutes, a young brunette woman came into the lobby and called my name. Settling in her office, she introduced herself and asked me general questions about my family, friends, and school activities. I repeated the information I'd given the doctor earlier in the week.

"Dr. Rumack noted you had a friend with you when you came in for your medical clearance appointment." Her voice rose a little as if she was asking a question.

"Yes, that was Doug."

"Did he come with you today?"

"No."

"Is he your closest friend at school?"

"One of them." We weren't officially friends, but it was the best definition I had. Our relationship classification only made sense to Doug.

She asked if I was dating and a few more questions about my family, roommate, and how my courses were going. She wrapped up, reviewing information about posttraumatic stress disorder and saying she thought I was doing well. I hoped she wouldn't feel the need for me to see her again, but she asked that I schedule three more sessions.

After scheduling the appointments, I took the shuttle over to the house. Some of the freshmen were out front raking, and inside, others were mopping floors. I found Mark, Ross, Lila, Zack, and Bill sitting in the common area drinking beer. Mark and Bill made room for me between them on the sofa, giving me a hard time about seeing the shrink. As other brothers joined our group, the conversation turned to next week's Homecoming schedule.

Events started Monday, with competitions every day, leading up to the parade and game on Saturday. The fraternity would have a breakfast that morning before the game, and a barbecue and band party afterwards.

Doug wandered in taking a seat across from me.

"So, you're coming, right?" Zack asked hitting me on the leg.

"I guess, my family will be in." I hadn't thought about tomorrow much less a week from tomorrow.

"You have to come with us," Zack said. "It won't be the same without you." Then his expression changed completely. He turned to Doug. "Hey Doug, you don't have a date, right? You can take Amanda."

Doug looked at me. "That would work."

"It's settled. You're coming with us." Zack pointed at me as he crossed to the refrigerator and grabbed a beer.

Wait, what just happened, I wondered. I was Doug's date for Homecoming?

Doug and Zack excused themselves to take care of some fraternity business and Mark, Lila, Ross, and I made our way back to Mark and Ross's room.

Mark closed the door behind us. "Do you guys sit around and plan how to stage these things? Is Zack in on it too?"

"What are you talking about?"

Lila rolled her eyes. "He still doesn't believe you and Doug aren't together."

I shook my head. "Do you think I'm lying?"

"Yes and no. Even though you're like glued at the hip these days, you aren't really Doug's type. You know, tall, built, savvy, sophisticated." He sat down taking a long sip of his beer. I shot him my best mean look, but he continued anyway. "I hate to say this Manda, but you'd come up about a six on Doug's girl-o-meter."

I was beyond offended. I was hurt and angry. Mark's tone was totally harmless, but his words stung. We'd always bantered. Still,

I felt like I'd been kicked in the stomach. On the heels of my counseling appointment, my psyche wasn't in the best place. It didn't feel good to think I was a six, much less hear Doug may be that shallow. Wouldn't my ability to speak five languages count for anything?

I needed to go somewhere and clear my head. "I'm supposed to meet Elise for takeout soon." I stood up.

Lila came over. "Do you want me to ride the shuttle back with you?"

"No, that's stupid. I'll catch you later or tomorrow."

I was glad to find that the shuttle was empty, as was my room. By the time Elise got in, I'd taken a long hot shower, washed my hair, talked to Marissa and Mom, turned off my phone, and was nearly back to a normal psychiatric state. The evening with Elise was just what I needed, simple and quiet. It turned out she was the perfect person to complain to about boys. Although I tried to tell her it wasn't a real date, she was ecstatic about my plans with Doug. That night, as I settled under my blanket, pain medication in full effect, I found I didn't even care about Mark's comment anymore.

Sleeping in until nine, I felt rested when I woke. My phone showed several missed calls and texts from the previous night, along with a call from Doug this morning. I replied to all via text and turned my phone off again. Nothing was going to derail my perfect day of sleeping on my futon. After my week, it was exactly what my body and psyche needed.

The day was punctuated by my family's visit before the game. When they left I got in another nap after an hour of studying. They returned after the game and we went out to dinner in Evanston. Dad had invited Doug, and he met us at the restaurant. With a full day of rest and solitude, I felt the best I had since the accident. My rocky week had left me wondering if I'd made the right choice about staying at school. It was good to be able to look my parents in the eyes and feel like I'd made the right decision for myself.

Elise had a small dinner party Sunday night, and I was surprised Doug seemed excited to come. After dinner with my family the night before, I thought for sure he'd bow out. Unfortunately, he and Zack had to leave pretty early, and I was left to face a slew of questions from Lila and Mark.

"So, are you finally coming clean or what?" Mark asked, finishing his last sip of wine.

"Remember, I'm only a six on the Doug-scale." I couldn't help but throw his comments back at him.

"Yeah, sorry about that one," Mark said. "But seriously, you aren't together?"

"No, for goodness sake, I'm practically an invalid." When against a wall, go to humor.

"Good point," Ross said, laughing.

Fortunately, Elise and Lila started cleaning up, and the conversation died. But after Mark, Lila, and Ross left, Elise was ready to pounce. "He better come to his senses soon, or I'm going to have some words with him. Isn't he going with you to that Latino club tomorrow night?"

I cut her off by distracting her with questions about her own social life. Doug had set boundaries around our relationship before, and I didn't want to allow myself to hope those walls were down.

For the first time since my accident, I fell asleep without codeine, and the next morning I felt more like me. I wasn't drugged up floating me, just headachy dizzy me.

Doug's presence helped with the Latino crowd that night. Everyone spoke to me in Spanish, except Maria, who promptly engineered him into a corner and held him captive most of the evening.

"I guess you were right about not looking Latino enough for them," he said as we walked back to his car after the meeting.

"Thanks for coming with me. I hope you weren't completely miserable."

"Why, because we pretty much needed a crowbar to pry Maria off me?"

"She seemed focused."

"Well, we'll definitely have them talking for a while."

"What do you mean?" I was waiting for the other shoe to drop, and tonight seemed like a pretty probable time. I figured it was best just to get it over with.

He leaned in close as he opened the car door. "Maria spent half the time telling me why she was the one for me, and the other half giving me examples of why you weren't."

His face was only inches from mine, and my pulse raced in reaction to the intensity of his words. I had to really think to come up with a reasonable reply. "Sounds painful." I liked our new level of friendship, and I didn't want it to end. "You don't have to come with me again."

He stepped back. "It wasn't that bad, besides, if my Spanish gets rusty, I won't hear the end of it from my mom."

I got in the car, and he walked around to his side. We drove in silence for a minute. "So, the stitches come out tomorrow right?" he asked.

A shiver ran down my spine. "Ugh, don't remind me. I feel faint just thinking about it."

"Don't worry, I can be there. Zack and I will be working out beforehand, so he may tag along."

With the vision of Zack and Doug escorting me to my appointment with Dr. Rumack, a laugh erupted before I could stop it. They'd probably look like the Italian Mafia, flanking the Mafia princess. Maybe I'd wear black with heels tomorrow. "That should only add an extra week to my counseling at most."

"Dr. Rumack did seem to think we had some twisted thing going."

"The counselor mentioned something too." I was impressed we'd moved our relationship to this level of honesty and grateful he seemed comfortable with it. Questions flooded my brain. Were we friends? Was there a chance this could lead to something more? Should I even ask? He spoke before I could decide.

"So, I was thinking as Maria was rambling on, we could probably be friends now if you agreed to behave."

I clenched my hands into fists. "Behave?"

"Yes."

"Sure, why not?" The words came out more sarcastically than I'd intended. What else was I supposed to say? No?

He shook his head. "No reason, obviously."

What was he thinking? Did he really just want to be my friend? Why was this so hard? Maybe I should just kiss him. Then at least this would be done for good, and the torture would be over one way or the other. But that wasn't really what I wanted. I needed him in my life, even as a friend, because the absence of him would be unbearable.

So caught up in my thoughts, I didn't realize we were already at my dorm. He parked and flew around the car before I could get the door open. I waited and let him open the door for me.

"See, behaving." I pointed at the door.

He cleared his throat. "Funny."

He walked with me to the front door. In the movie in my mind, he took my hand, pulled me to him, and kissed me. Then, reality hit, and I realized he was waiting for me to get my key. Instantly, my face felt hot. "Thank you again for coming with me, and thanks for offering to come to my doctor's appointment."

"No problem." He placed his hands in his pockets and turned and walked away.

In the elevator, I tried to figure out how things could've gone differently. It was no use, as I would probably give myself more of a headache. Elise was out studying, so I was able to do some reading without answering one hundred and one questions about my evening. The adrenaline from my night perhaps helped me have more stamina, because I was able to read for two hours straight. I even had energy left over to send emails to Mom, Marissa, and Tia.

Is this me?

The sun was pouring in my window when my alarm went off at eight thirty the next morning. Elise must have opened the shades and curtains. Details of the day ahead trickled into my thoughts. I decided to focus on English and not think about my appointment. My headache and dizziness were routine, and I ignored them, taking the prescribed maximum dose of Motrin with my breakfast. Thankfully, my head was barely aching by the time I walked down to the shuttle stop.

In class, the professor returned our English papers, and I was thrilled to see a glowing A minus at the top of mine. Vivian walked part of the way to the medical center with me again. I was thankful for her company, and her chatter kept me from being too anxious. As I approached the building, I saw Doug and Zack standing out front laughing.

Zack was two steps in front of Doug as they walked towards me. "There you are. Wow, this guy's as nervous as a rooster in a hen house." Zack took me in his arms.

I hugged him back with my one good arm. He kept it around my shoulder as I stepped back to greet Doug.

"Hey, I'm not the one who was going into withdrawals so badly he was willing to spend an hour at the medical center." Doug motioned towards me. "You good?"

"I'll be better when this is over." We walked into the medical center, and I checked in at the nurse's station. Finding seats, I asked them about their morning workout.

Zack jumped in first. "Lover boy here told me about having to pry Maria off him. You should watch your back. She's been after Doug since freshman year." I looked at Doug, and he rolled his eyes. "Did you guys ever hook up?" Zack continued.

Doug shook his head. "Are you crazy?"

A nurse called my name, ending my brief snippet into Doug's life. Doug picked up my backpack, and they followed me towards the door she held open.

"We only need Ms. Avery," the nurse said.

I froze for a minute. There was no way I was doing this by myself. I straightened my back and raised my chin. "I would like them with me." I kept my eyes fixed on hers. Without saying a word, she turned and opened the door leading to the exam rooms.

She stopped in front of a scale, placing one hand on a generous hip. "We need your weight and height."

I stepped on the scale without hesitation. If she was trying to intimidate me by having my weight broadcasted in front of two handsome guys, she had the wrong broad.

"Ninety-one," she said and then tapped the information into a tablet.

My lack of appetite was taking more of a toll than I thought, as I was four pounds down from August. Still, I felt like I looked good now that my bruises were healing, my color was returning, and I wasn't so dehydrated from the meds. If my weight was going to change, down was the only acceptable direction anyway. She asked me my height and motioned us down the hall.

With the three of us plus the nurse, the exam room felt tight. I leaned against the exam table and she whipped out a blood pressure cuff. After several attempts to use the adult cuff, when I clearly needed a smaller one, she gave up. She took my pulse and my temperature and typed the numbers into the tablet.

"The doctor will be in soon," she announced before leaving.

"What was all of that about the blood pressure cuff?" Zack put his fingers around my bicep. "You are pretty small, I guess. You'll have to start working out with us again when you're up to it."

As soon as there was silence, I started pacing. It made me light headed, but it took my mind off what was about to happen.

Zack's hand caught my shoulder. "Okay, you're making me dizzy."

I leaned back against the exam table again. There was no way I was going to sit on it with my legs dangling like a small child, not with Zack and Doug in the room.

Zack came over and hoisted me onto the table. "I just realized you probably couldn't jump up there with one arm."

I slid back so my knees were comfortably at the corner of the bench. It wasn't two seconds before I felt the need to swing my feet back and forth.

"Ms. Avery?" Dr. Rumack peeked in the door. "I heard male voices, so I wasn't sure," he said, entering the room. "Mr. Taylor, right?" He stepped forward to shake Doug's hand. "And you are?"

"This is Zack. He's my comic relief."

Dr. Rumack seemed confused for a second, but he quickly recovered. "Everyone needs some of that, I guess."

"I tend to be a fainter, so I figured distraction would be a good thing."

"Okay, then, let's take a look at those stitches." After a neurological exam he examined the stitches on my knees and neck quickly and turned to retrieve his instruments from the cabinets.

Looking around the room, I tried not to focus on what was about to happen. Doug came over and leaned on the table beside me.

Zack rolled around on the exam stool. "How was English this morning?"

"Good, I got an A on my paper."

Dr. Rumack came over and started the procedure. He pulled the stitches from my knees first. With the lacerations healed and the stitches over two weeks old, I barely felt them come out. I pulled my hair to one side so he could access the site on my neck. As he started, I could feel the strings pulling through my skin and dug my fingernails into my palms, trying to create a distracting sensation. There was a slight tug and I flinched, pulling away from him.

Dr. Rumack put down the scissors and moved my hair to inspect the site. "Wow, this is impressive."

Suddenly I felt hot and cold at the same time, and leaned on my good arm. I closed my eyes, trying to take slow steady breaths.

Zack got up, crossing the room so he stood in front of me. "I know, have you ever seen so much hair on a person's head."

Doug tapped my hand. I looked at him and he smiled.

Dr. Rumack sighed. "I was commenting on the surgical site. The incision is much bigger than I would've thought. It's at least two inches long. They used a lot of tiny stiches though. The scar will barely be noticeable under your hair."

My face flushed and everything went black. When I opened my eyes, two dark figures were hovering over me. The light that outlined their forms blinded me, and I lifted my left arm to try make out their faces. The light went off and a hand lowered my arm away from my face.

"She's awake," Doug said. His voice was smooth and calm. I turned my head his way. "There you are." He smiled, squeezing my hand.

Zack piped in from the end of the exam table. "You weren't kidding about the fainting thing."

Dr. Rumack's voice was soothing and reassuring. "You've been unconscious. I need to ask you some questions. Okay?"

I nodded and patiently answered the questions he asked. Finally, he seemed convinced that I was indeed just a fainter.

"How long was I out?"

"Just over twenty minutes," Dr. Rumack said as he checked the monitor above my head.

I scanned the room, trying to get my bearings. A nurse was checking a drip bag hung above my head, and two uniformed men stood against the wall. I lifted my arm studying the IV taped to it.

Dr. Rumack put his hand on my arm. "We're consulting with Northwestern Hospital. Let me update your condition with them, and then we'll go from there."

Doug leaned in closer to me when Dr. Rumack stepped away, addressing the uniformed men.

"Who are they?" I asked.

"EMTs, they were ready to transport you to Northwestern."

I looked up at the light, suddenly overwhelmed with how serious they were taking this fainting spell. This would have been my third ER visit since I'd been at school. What did Doug and

Zack think of me? I had to stop my train of thought, or I was going to end up crying. Tears were already starting to form. I blinked my eyes and looked around for distraction.

Doug leaned in close. "This'll all be over soon. They just need to confirm this was nothing more than a fainting spell, and then you'll be out of here. Okay?"

"Please tell me the stitches are out." I couldn't handle anything else.

"They're out."

Zack rubbed my calves. "You know you're making me look bad here. I'm losing it if I can't hold an audience for more than two minutes."

Doug's phone rang. He squeezed my hand and then let go to retrieve the phone from his back pocket.

He looked at the screen. "It's your dad." Answering the call, he was silent a minute and then spoke into the phone, "She actually just woke up. Here, I'll let you talk to her." He handed me the phone.

I sighed and tried sounding cheery. "Hi, Dad."

"I'm glad you're okay. I haven't told your mom yet, so you'll have to tell her tonight."

I sighed. That would be a long phone call. "Thanks, Dad. Love you."

"Love you, too. Can I talk to Doug again?"

I handed the phone to Doug and he nodded as my dad spoke. "Yes sir, take care," he said before ending the call.

Out of the corner of my eye, I saw Dr. Rumack shake the EMTs hands. One of them nodded and walked towards me.

"Ms. Avery, looks like you're in the clear, so we're heading out. Try to stay vertical, okay?"

Dr. Rumack came over and explained he'd be releasing me after the IV fluid bag was finished. Then, he led us through the dos and don'ts of the next twenty-four hours. Once again, I wasn't to be left alone.

Zack deemed it safe to make an exit, but Lila and Mark showed up only minutes later. When would the humiliation end? I just wanted to disappear. I argued my way into going to class, much to Doug's dismay. After verifying that Mark would walk me to the classroom, Doug left for his own lecture.

This quarter had been nothing like I thought it would be. I dug my fingernails into my hand to keep from crying as Mark escorted me to my class. He met me afterwards too, and we took the shuttle to my dorm. Lila joined us not long after. I would've rather crawled onto my futon and been left alone for the remainder of the evening, but she convinced me to take a shower and wash my hair. The hot water felt good, and I stood under it until the skin on my fingers started to shrivel. Thinking I'd have liked to stay in that shower forever, I dressed in my favorite jeans, tank, and sweater. I brushed my teeth and towel-dried my hair. I took time to do Marissa's five-minute make-up routine figuring the better I looked the better I would feel. As it was, I looked like a total zombie. I continued to towel dry it as I walked into my room, stopping short at the sight of Doug.

Lila jumped up. "I'd dry your hair for you, but we have to get some dinner before our game." She was leaving me? She hugged me. "Sorry, but it's hard to find girls to play football."

"So, you're good?" Mark asked rocking on his heels.

"Course." I sat down on my futon. I really didn't care if he left. I was still annoyed that he thought I was lying about a relationship with Doug.

Feeling disappointed Lila was gone, I turned to Doug. "If you want to get some dinner, Kate's probably next door, so I'd be okay." I just wanted to be alone.

"What about your dinner?"

"I'm sure I have something in the fridge."

He opened the fridge. There was leftover spaghetti, which made my stomach turn, but I had no intention of eating anything anyway.

"Um, gross. Anyway, I was thinking sushi and a movie at my place. You need to get out of here."

It sounded like a normal person's evening. Too bad all I wanted to do was hide under my covers. "I just want to have some soup here. You should go get something good, though."

It felt like the words came out of someone else's mouth. He wanted me to do something fun with him, and I was begging him to leave. What was wrong with me? I wished I could ignore the feeling of wanting to be alone, but it was overwhelming. Was I depressed? Who wouldn't be in my situation?

He stood in front of me, hands on hips. "Do you remember what we talked about last night?"

Great, a memory test. I wasn't good with recalling things lately.

He sat down beside me. "You're supposed to be behaving yourself."

"I didn't realize behaving meant doing everything you said."

"Of course, what did you think it meant? Now, dry your hair. I'm hungry."

"Fine," I gave in. "But this could take a while."

As I was starting the process, Zack knocked on the door. How did these people get in my dorm? "Hey Mini-Girl." He gave me a hug. "What's up with the hair?" He twirled a piece around his finger.

"Jewish grandmother." I pointed to my head.

"Sweet." He took a seat beside Doug. "Continue," he said, pointing at the blow dryer."

I sighed, resigning myself to the fact that I was going to have an audience for this process. Why was he here? They talked while I dried. I hurried, stopping before it was completely done. The end result was a mostly dry, wavy look, but it would have to do. When I finished they stood up.

They both were staring at me. Doug spoke first. "You look different."

"Wavy hair?"

"Maybe that's it. Ready to go?"

All I needed was a jacket and shoes. Searching in my closet, I spotted my black Converse high top sneakers. They were perfect for my dark mood. The three of us went down in the elevator, and we dropped Zack off at the field. Thinking about my pink striped cleats, I realized I probably would miss the rest of the games.

Doug told me all about his afternoon as we drove to the restaurant. It was a rare glimpse into his life, and I soaked in every word. It was easy to see how much he loved his chosen major. Even I, who had little knowledge of economics or business, found his review of his class topics interesting.

As we got out of the car, Mom called. I followed Doug down the sidewalk and stood outside the sushi place talking to her while he got our order. Although Dad had told her about my fainting spell, she was determined to get a full account from me. She told me again how I should be home having her take care of me. I listened politely, although I was really just watching Doug inside talking to the staff, probably in Japanese.

"Mom, I'm actually at this sushi place with Doug," I said when she let me get a word in. Maybe because I was out doing something normal, she decided I was indeed okay. Only after I promised to call her first thing the next morning did she release me from the conversation.

When we got back to the house, it took a good twenty minutes to make it to his room. One brother after another stopped us to chat. Once we were in his room, Blondie in tow, Doug leaned against the closed door and exhaled.

He pointed to a cabinet behind me. "Wine."

I opened it, and handed him one of the bottles. He handed me two glasses and took the bottle, opening it. I'd never seen him so intense, but I did remember him saying he was starving. It must've been as trying a day for him as it had been for me.

"You didn't get lunch, did you?" I asked.

"No." Handing me the bottle, he stuffed a piece of sushi into his mouth. I poured the wine and handed him a glass. He chased his bite down with the entire glass.

"I'm sorry about today."

"It wasn't your fault. We told him you were a fainter." He passed me his glass, and I refilled it.

We sat on the futon and ate dinner, mostly in silence. Choosing a movie, Doug finally seemed to relax. I watched for a while, but the wine made me drowsy.

Zack's booming voice woke me. "Wow, sushi, wine, and a movie. You guys actually seem normal tonight."

As I came to, I realized my head was resting on Doug's shoulder. I was warm and comfortable nestled there between him and Blondie and didn't want to move.

"Oh, sorry," Zack said in a more hushed voice.

Reluctantly, I opened my eyes and pushed myself up on my good arm. Zack shooed Blondie away and sat in her place. "Must've been an amazing movie. You can always count on Doug for those."

Doug's hand reached behind me and hit Zack on the back of the head. I was still in too much of a fog to respond.

Doug tapped me on the leg. "Ready to go back to your room?"

"She looks like she'd rather just go back to sleep right here," Zack said.

Doug stood and extended his hand to help me up.

Zack stood too. "I'll take you home. My car's still warm, and I have heated seats."

"That'll work." Disappointed, I'd wasted an evening with Doug sleeping, I retrieved my bag from Doug's desk.

Doug pointed to the bag. "Your phone's in the front pocket. You have several texts."

Marissa had probably heard from Mom about my fainting incident and getting sushi with Doug. "Thanks for dinner and the movie."

"No problem." He stuffed his hands in his pockets.

If we were a couple, he would've pulled me in for a kiss. Again, the movie played in my head. Now I was depressed and neurotic. I shut my eyes to clear my thoughts.

Zack drove me home, recapping the game. They'd won, and he was sweet to add it wasn't the same without me. In my room, I forced myself to think of anything but today. Crying myself to sleep wouldn't solve anything. I sent a simple reply to the last of Marissa's five text messages: WILL CALL TOMORROW.

I twisted my codeine bottle around in my hand. Sinking into oblivion would be nice right about now. Deciding I would pay for it tomorrow, I turned on some music.

Chapter 10

Before I knew it I woke to the sound of my phone buzzing. I picked up my phone and looked at the information on the screen: five missed calls and one new text message. Leaning back against a pillow, I closed my eyes. My phone started buzzing again immediately. I picked it up. Doug.

"Hi."

"It's after ten," he said.

Realizing I was due in class in less than an hour, I threw my blanket off. "Wow, umm, thanks. See you later." I heard him laughing as I hung up the phone.

Riding the shuttle alone, I realized even with my little setback I was doing better. The headaches and dizziness weren't nearly as bad as they had been just a few days ago and my arm didn't hurt much at all anymore. Thanks to nearly ten hours of sleep, I made it through my classes and lab feeling I had energy to spare. Jeremy and I walked out of the lab building to find Zack waiting for me.

Jeremy pointed towards Zack. "Is that boyfriend number one or two?"

I couldn't tell if he was being funny, so I ignored his comment, thanked him for his patience with my slow brain, and said goodbye.

Zack approached, wrapping his arms around me. He pulled the sweatshirt the fraternity team had given me out of his pack.

"How'd you get that?"

"Elise let me in. Want to have some fun?"

"Definitely." I traded out my sweater for the hoodie. We ended up in a student parking lot along with probably half the student body. He took my hand and led me through the crowd until we found the brothers standing outside a roped-off area.

"Look over there." He pointed to the center of the lot. A number of guys sat on tricycles behind a painted line. It was the Homecoming tricycle race event, and Doug was front and center.

"You put the tallest guy on a tricycle."

"Hey, I'm taller. But it's his favorite event."

Doug looked happy, and I was glad to see him like this. With a gunshot, the race started. Going fast through the turns, many of the trikes fell over, spilling their drivers. Doug and his brothers were able to stay on, and Doug crossed the finish line in first place by half a tire.

After the awards ceremony, all the brothers walked back to the house together. Doug carried his tricycle, and Zack carried me on his back. A cookout replaced their normal Wednesday night house meeting, and I stayed until after ten, socializing with the brothers.

The next day marked two weeks since my accident, and I let Lila talk me into going to the volleyball game. If it'd been up to me, I would've never set foot in that gymnasium or seen a volleyball game ever again. Realizing that was a bit impractical, I put on a brave face.

We had dinner together, and she insisted I put on skinny corduroys and a waffle crew shirt. She cut the left arm off up to the elbow so I could wear it with my cast. When I grabbed my fraternity hoodie out of the drawer, she snatched it away, handing me a tan mid-drift jacket. It felt good to be in normal clothes, and I braved wearing some low-heeled boots. It was chilly, but we walked over to the sports center.

Entering the gym, the sounds of the balls bouncing off the floor resonated in my head. The boom of the balls and the glaring lights triggered the memory of me lying on the floor, frozen in pain. I rubbed my neck, fully expecting to see blood on my hand. Clutching my arm, I looked up at the ceiling to blink the memory away. Looking back down at the floor, I fully expected to see my half-crushed body writhing in pain. Self-preservation kicked in and I kept pace with Lila, thinking I'd be okay if I could just make it to the stands.

There were two short whistle tweets, and I was lost in that night again. Unlike today, there was a long shrill whistle and then all was silent. The balls stopped, and all I could hear was a low hum and my pounding heartbeat. Then images of faces, Doug, Zack, and Lila's, flashed through my brain. Their voices were whispers floating into my ears. Damn, I heard Doug say. I shivered and closed my eyes tight, trying to stop the flood of sensations.

Something gripped my arm. "Amanda." Lila shook me, bringing me back. Her hand was like a vice on my arm, and I pulled away.

The face in front of me was one that had just surfaced in my memory. "Amanda, hi I'm Stephen," he held out his hand, "you may not remember me but—"

I didn't let him finish. "No I remember. It's good to put a name with a face."

Lila's eyes, wide as saucers, relaxed, and she exhaled and smiled, squeezing my elbow. "We run into Stephen at the gym all the time."

Wondering if Lila was introducing us because she thought I might like him, I looked back to him. He was the ref who'd helped when I got hurt on the soccer field. It was his whistle that brought everything to a halt the night I'd crashed onto the floor.

He turned to Lila. "So, I'm on your game tonight."

I looked beyond Stephen and found Doug. All I wanted was to be wrapped in his warm arms.

"You're okay." His voice echoed in my head.

I forced myself to focus on Stephen and Lila. With this behavior, I was going to end up being the girl that got hurt and went crazy.

Lila smiled, looking between us. "Great, well I have to go warm up." She jogged towards their court.

If I knew Lila, he would be refereeing all their games from now on. Could she be any more obvious? I doubted she cared. We followed her over to our court. With dark skin, dark wavy hair, and an athletic build, he was fairly handsome. Not overly muscular, I would guess he was about six feet. Lila and I usually found the same types attractive. If I'd been looking for a guy, she'd chosen well.

Stephen lingered beside me. "So, how are you?"

"Good." I gave my standard answer reserved for strangers. It was uncomfortable for me to discuss my injury. More than that, I was sick of thinking about it at all. Fortunately, Zack and Doug saved me.

"Mini-Girl!" Zack captured me in a bear hug from behind.

Doug wrapped his arms around me next. He whispered to me, holding me against his warm chest. "You didn't tell me you were coming. Are you good with this?"

I looked up at him. "Mostly." At least I was now that I was encircled in his arms. He didn't loosen his grip, and I was content to stand there and be held.

Zack smacked Doug on the arm, and he released me. "Okay, lover boy, we're here to play."

Doug hit Zack on the shoulder, and they rejoined the team for warm ups. I noticed Kara, who I'd learned Zack was seeing, had joined the group. Unlike me, she was tall and formidable, the perfect volleyball type.

Once the team moved to the court, Stephen crossed back over to me. "So I think we have a common friend. My roommate is Jeremy."

"Wow, small world I guess." Fortunately, he was easy to talk with. He'd grown up in a small town in the central part of the state, about an hour from Champaign. A freshman too, he planned to major in mechanical engineering. Unfortunately, standing there with the balls flying around, I was getting dizzier by the minute.

I excused myself to sit down and watched them warm up. Growing overwhelmed by all the stimuli, I tried to focus on just one image, the door at the other side of the gym. Stephen blew his whistle to start the game and I jumped.

Doug sat down beside me. "You okay? You're as white as a ghost."

Fighting nausea and déjà vu, I waved him off. "I'll be fine."

He got up and grabbed a bottle of water from his bag. "At least drink this." I sipped the drink and it helped. My head pounded from the echoes of the balls hitting the floor, but I was determined to see this through.

Doug sat beside me when he rotated out. "The ref seems to be interested in you."

Really, he was going to talk to me about other guys? This would definitely put us in the friend zone, a place I didn't want to be. I rolled my eyes. "I think Lila had something to do with it."

"He's not bad. He was pretty with it when you got hurt."

I looked him straight in the eyes. "Are we really going to talk about this?"

He looked away and then back. "No."

Mark yelled over to us. "Are you two fighting again? Actually, it doesn't matter because you're in, Doug."

Mark sat beside me, but I was in too much turmoil to have a conversation with him. With my headache, and the issues with Doug, I was glad when the matches were over. Lila invited Stephen to go out with us. His refereeing gig wasn't up until ten, but she happily gave him her number to call when he got done. At least she hadn't given him mine.

As luck would have it, Stephen's games went fast and he showed up early. Squished between him and Doug at the table, I figured it served me right for wanting the unavailable guy rather than the free one. I talked to Stephen for a while and enjoyed the conversation. Still, the whole set up thing was just too much pressure. If I were smart, I would concentrate on my classes and forget the dating scene. My GPA needed some serious attention anyway.

Looking over to Zack, I noticed Kara didn't join us. Thinking I'd rather concentrate on someone else's love life, I asked him about it. He explained she felt we were too tight of a clique to break into. But she was still coming to the Homecoming game with him so that was something.

The conversation turned to the Homecoming game, and Stephen asked what everyone was doing.

"The fraternity has a block of seats," Mark answered.

Stephen turned to me. "What about you?"

"Yeah, I'm going with them." What an awkward situation. I didn't add that I had a date, or that said date was sitting on the other side of me. It seemed a bit cruel.

"Oh," he said, moving back in his chair. But, after a minute he engaged me again. "Hey, the dorm Halloween party next week sounds cool."

"Yeah, Kate was talking about that."

Mark grabbed a celery stick from the appetizer plate in front of me. "You have to have a date or special invite for the fraternity Halloween party, you know."

What was he doing? Trying to force me into the dorm party? If I'd had a stun gun right then I would have blasted him.

Bill, who had been silent as was his usual MO, spoke up. "I don't have a date for Halloween yet, you could come with me."

"Thanks Bill, I'd like that." I dipped a celery stick in the dip and took a bite, doing a mental victory jig. It was mean to say in front of Stephen, and I felt bad, but I wasn't going to be bullied into dating someone by Mark or Lila.

Standing, Zack gave me an exit. "You want a ride home, Mini-Girl?"

Doug who had been talking with another brother, stood too. "I'll drop her off." He didn't say anything until after we pulled out of the lot. "So, you look stressed."

Why did this boy care so much? I shook my heading, trying to forget the déjà vu neurotic flashback in the gym. "There was a lot of drama tonight, and it's not really my thing. Mark seemed miffed about something, Lila seemed weird, I haven't even met Kara, and then the thing with Stephen."

"It's always like this. You've just been too out of it to notice."

"Great, can I go back into my bubble now?"

"You don't need to worry about Kara. Zack's a big boy, and they've only been dating like two weeks. As far as Stephen, he seemed to throw in the towel. One vulture down."

Putting my hand to the dashboard, I turned to face him. "Vulture? And one? I don't see a line, but you aren't allowed to comment on them anyway." I crossed my arms over my chest and didn't look at him the rest of the drive. Whatever he thought about my outburst, he didn't voice it. Arriving at my dorm, he walked me to the entrance as usual. God this boy was unnerving, but at least he was consistent.

Lying on my futon after changing, I couldn't relax. Too many thoughts swirled through my head. Stephen probably wouldn't pursue me after tonight. Did I care? Not really. Was that wrong of me? Obviously Lila thought I should be dating. Should I be? Was I crazy? Yes I was. As if wanting Doug wasn't enough, the psychotic episode at the gym had me convinced. He was the person I wanted, but I had no clue if he was interested. I decided the only way to sleep was to read something totally distracting. Chemistry fit the bill, and I needed to catch up on it anyway.

My phone buzzed just after midnight. It was a text from Lila: YOU UP? CAN WE COME BY?

We? Great, that meant at least her and Mark, probably Ross too. I decided it was better to let them get out whatever it was, so I texted them to come over. The knock on my door was almost instantaneous.

Mark sat down next to me. "So we're doing an intervention." Obviously he'd had a few drinks and wasn't going to beat around the bush about anything. "We set up the perfect opportunity, and you messed it up."

"So I'm not supposed to get a say in whether I was interested in him or not?"

"He's really nice and was really into you. What more do you need?"

Tracing my finger around my phone screen, I took a moment to catch my breath. I knew Mark and Lila cared about me, even if they were trying too hard. "Guys, I appreciate the effort, and I'm sorry. Just so you know, though, I can handle things."

Lila sat down on the other side of me. "We were just trying to help you meet someone."

"I'm going to the Halloween party with Bill."

Mark threw up his hands and crossed the room. "Fine, whatever." As he opened the door to leave, Elise stood in the doorway, ready to insert her key in the lock.

Lila hugged me. "We just want you to be happy."

Elise slinked by them as they left, dumping her bag on her futon. "What was that about and since when are you up past midnight?"

"I had a weird night." I needed to talk to somebody, and it was too late to call Marissa. "Lila tried to set me up with this guy, and then Doug and I had an awkward conversation about it."

She sat down on her futon facing me. "I thought you and Doug didn't do that."

"He broke the rules."

"And now you're up studying way past your bedtime?"

"I probably would've been up anyway. Lots of stuff came up tonight, and I need to sort through it."

"It sounds like you're catching up from being out of commission for two weeks."

"That's what Doug said."

"Well, I think he's right. You should get some sleep."

She climbed up in her bunk. For once I was happy to be down in my futon. I could leave the light on without bothering her too much. After finishing my chemistry chapter, I decided to text Zack and Doug to make sure they wouldn't drag me out to go to the gym the next morning. It was the first day I was cleared for physical activity, but there was no way I was getting up at seven-thirty after being up until after one. I'd just turned on some music to clear my mind when Doug replied.

WHY R U STILL UP?

CAN'T SLEEP.

WHY?

THINKING.

NOT ABOUT THE VULTURES I HOPE, he texted.

I bit my lip. Did I continue this conversation? Texting felt safer than a face to face conversation. This way, I didn't have to look at him or hear his voice. VULTURES SELDOM ATTACK HEALTHY ANIMALS BUT MAY KILL THE WOUNDED OR SICK.

GET THAT FROM WIKIPEDIA? YOU DON'T REALIZE YOUR APPEAL. SORRY ABOUT THE VULTURE THING, BAD REFERENCE. IT JUST POPPED INTO MY HEAD. CALL ME.

My breath caught in my throat. ELISE TRYING 2 SLEEP, I wrote back.

We chatted via text about classes and music. I liked these easy conversations with him. Maybe I should just accept that friends were all we'd ever be.

Eventually I relaxed, said goodnight to Doug, and was able to sleep.

The next sound I heard was my phone buzzing.

The text was from Doug. ZACK AND I R ON THE WAY UP.

My clock read five after ten. Ugh! I barely had time to make it to class. Standing, there was a knock on the door. Doug and Zack stood in the doorway, and Doug pulled a coffee from behind his back.

"Thank you." I took the cup and ushered them in.

Zack leaned in for a hug, and I stepped back. "You woke me up." I motioned to the restroom and ducked in to brush my teeth.

"Rough night, kitten?" Doug asked when I returned.

I was a kitten now? "Why do you say that?"

"Well, your hair's a mess. Usually it's untouched when you're dead to the world."

Looking in the mirror, I saw my hair was a curly mess. "I had these horrible dreams about circling vultures."

"Kittens are easy prey."

I rolled my eyes. Zack came up behind me as I ran product through my hair. "Bed hair is sexy."

Finishing my hair, I found jeans and a sweater and was ready within minutes.

Deciding to walk to class, we took the elevator down. Outside Zack pulled me towards him. "Okay, I seriously need to know about kittens and vultures."

"Believe me, it's not that interesting."

"I'll get to the bottom of us." He looked to Doug, who shook his head.

Nearing the classroom building, Doug leaned in and whispered in my ear. "Told you you'd need an escort." He pointed up ahead to a waiting Jeremy.

"Nope, not a vulture."

"You sure?"

"Vulture's roommate."

We stopped a good ten feet from Jeremy. "Brutal."

"I know."

Zack cut in. "Okay you guys have to stop. Manda, I need your playlist. Give me your phone. Doug says you have good taste."

I made Zack promise to return it after class and then handed it to him.

"Wow, that's trust," Doug said, backing away. "See you this afternoon?"

"Sure." I didn't have a plan for this afternoon, but seeing him was always at the top of my list.

Zack met me right after class to return my phone. "So, interesting texting between you and lover boy."

I kept my face still and voice steady. "No."

"Damn, you didn't even flinch. You are stone cold."

I let go of the breath I'd been holding and hoped he didn't notice. That afternoon, I had my counseling session. I'd considered not revealing my psychotic episode but it had freaked me out and I didn't want to have another one. Fortunately, they were normal for someone "like me".

Mom, Dad, Marissa, Tia, and Ed were all dressed in their Northwestern best when they arrived at my dorm at nine the next morning. Marissa wanted to help me with my hair and makeup. As soon as we were in the elevator, she started opening garment bags filled with outfit choices. In my room, she spread out two bags of makeup and hair products on my futon. She was a pro, so it took her only half an hour to do my hair and makeup. We caught the shuttle outside my dorm so we only had to walk a block to the fraternity house. It was the first time since the accident I'd put on heels, and I wasn't taking any chances. It was a perfect fall day, and we walked arm in arm the last block to the house, crunching the leaves on the sidewalk like when we were kids.

Nearing the house, Marissa leaned over and whispered in my ear. "Oh my God, you are dating the most gorgeous guy."

I followed her gaze. Doug was standing on the sidewalk talking to what Tia would call a gaggle of girls. With khaki pants, a light purple shirt, and navy blazer, he looked like he just stepped out of a clothing ad. Looking in our direction, he smiled.

Feeling like Cinderella at the ball, I decided I was going to enjoy this day and worry about how much my psyche would suffer tomorrow. Doug started towards us. As he approached, he closed the distance with a few quick long steps, scooping me up and spinning me around. "You look awesome!"

I grabbed his bicep to try and stop his motion, and he quickly realized his mistake. "Sorry, I forgot, no spinning." He put me down gently, keeping his arms around my waist. I focused on the ground, waiting for the dizziness to pass. He bent down and studied my face. "Wow, you look really pale."

Marissa pointed a finger at him. "No twirling the merchandise. This took me a long time."

"My compliments to the artist!"

"An artist is only as good as the canvas." She replaced a strand of my hair that had fallen in my face.

We walked up to the house. The main hall was packed with people, and Marissa left in search of our parents. Doug slid his hand down my arm and took my hand. I was nervous about being his date, but his affection towards me seemed unforced and it put me at ease. I reminded myself that that's what people did on dates, they held hands, and his actions meant nothing more than being a good date.

Following him through the crowd, he stopped halfway across the room. "My mom ended up getting tickets for the game. She wants to meet you. Zack's been talking to her, so be prepared."

Doug pointed to the back room, and we made our way to his mom and stepdad. Tapping his mom on the shoulder, he introduced us before excusing himself to find my parents.

Paula gently hugged me. "It's so nice to meet you. I feel like I know you already. Doug told me all about your accident, and Zack has been going on and on about you. How long have you been at Northwestern?"

Zack was bragging? I focused on her question. "I'm a freshman, this is my first quarter." I'd barely gotten the words out when Doug returned with my parents. He squeezed in beside me and introduced them.

Paula put her hand on my arm. "Amanda, I assumed were older since Zack couldn't stop talking about your language skills."

Dad, always eager to brag about his girls, explained how I'd loved languages since I was young. Fortunately, he didn't get too far in his story before he was interrupted by the alarm on Doug's watch.

A grin spread across Doug's face and he squeezed my hand, letting go to silence the alarm. "It's time to head to the game. We should get you out of here. Mom, Mrs. Avery, do you want to wait with Amanda on the front lawn?"

I was at a loss for the need for me to be outside, but both women agreed. Doug took my hand and led us out the front door. I followed Mom and Paula to the sidewalk in front of the house. I leaned in and whispered to Mom, "What's going on?"

Before she could say anything, a loud roar erupted from the house. Images from my childhood flashed through my memory, as I recalled sitting on top of my dad's shoulders when the chant went up. Later, as teens, Marissa and I had stood outside rolling our eyes at the silly tradition. Now I wished I could be inside with Doug.

When the door opened, he was the first one out. He walked straight to me and took my hand. "I didn't think the noise would be a good thing for your head." He whispered in my ear. Zack, Bill, the other officers, and their dates caught up with us, and we led the fraternity towards the stadium.

Like Zack's date, Kara, the other dates were all tall and gorgeous. For a second, I felt out of place. But Doug squeezed my hand and smiled at me. "This is awesome." Feeling excited to have these traditions now be my experience, and to share them with him, I pushed that thought out of my head.

As we walked, the brothers overtook us and led the fraternity to the stadium. Inside, we made our way up to the assigned section. Just climbing the stairs left me feeling light headed, and I didn't dare look down at the field. I held a firm grip on Doug's hand and halfway up he turned around to me. "Lookin' a little pale there, you okay?" He slipped behind me, keeping a firm grip on my waist the rest of the way up.

As we found our seats, he smiled and whispered in my ear. "Don't look down."

"I won't."

His arm didn't move from around my waist save the two times he went to get drinks and once when I went to the restroom with Lila. Yes, today I was Cinderella, and tomorrow would be brutal.

Northwestern won the game, and we made our way back to the house, weaving through the happy crowd. The fraternity hosted a barbeque on the back lawn, and the adrenaline and caffeine from the soda Lila slipped me supplied enough energy to get me through the day.

Doug worked the crowd most of the afternoon but found me later. "Your parents are going to dinner, and they invited us. Should we join them?"

There was no way I was asking him. "If you want."

"Sitting down for a quiet meal would be nice."

I agreed, realizing the band party would run late and I'd only see them for brunch before they headed home tomorrow. Dinner with my family was fun, save Ed's ribbing about my fainting incident at the medical center. My parents dropped us off at the house just before nine, leaving time to get set up for the party.

Lila had me help her at the greeter table. "Okay, so you two looked really cozy."

My face instantly heated. Were we becoming a couple? He'd been really affectionate today, but I didn't want to assume. When the band started, I stayed as far away from it as possible without being anti-social. Lila was bummed I wasn't up for dancing with her, but empathized with my plight.

Doug and I danced a slow song, and we switched partners with Zack, Bill, Mark, and their dates for a few more songs. Afterwards, he kept an arm around my waist as we watched everyone dance. Leaning into him I yawned, and he wrapped the other arm around me. "It's after midnight, are you going to turn into a pumpkin?"

The band was loud and I stood on my toes and whispered into his ear. "That was the carriage. I turn into a vampire."

He moved his hands to my hips. "You do have the complexion for it."

I rested my hand on his chest. "I'm going to take that as a compliment."

He shook his head laughing. With me still on my toes, our faces were barely a foot apart. Our eyes met for a brief second.

He stiffened and looked over my head. "I have to stay here. I can get Zack or Bill to drive you home."

Inwardly, I screamed. I stepped back, and after a deep breath, looked up at him. "Today was good. I had fun." Lila's voice screamed at me, *just kiss the boy!*

"Me too." He put out his hand then dropped it to his side. "There's Bill." He pointed towards the door.

In the car, I thanked Bill for driving me home and offering to be my date for the Halloween party. At the dorm, a lot of students were still milling around in the common area. I put my head down and slinked to the elevator hoping I didn't see anyone I knew. The elevators were packed, so I took the stairs up. My head pounding, I regretted it after the first flight, but pushed on. Opening my door, I was glad to see Elise was still out. All I wanted was to be alone.

Wondering why I thought today may be different; I freed my hair from the pins. I slipped out of my clothes and into pajamas berating myself. With a washed face and brushed teeth, I pulled my favorite blanket around me. Scrolling through pictures from the day, I realized I couldn't keep hoping that Doug would decide he wanted me. I had to accept we may always be friends.

The next morning Lila, Mark, and Ross came to brunch with my family. Thankfully, after spending Homecoming day with us, Lila and Mark were convinced Doug and I weren't a couple. I hid my disappointment from them, glad they decided to stop bugging me. Conversation flowed to the Halloween party, and Marissa and Lila decided we needed to go costume shopping. Even though the guys protested, we walked around until we found a costume shop. Lila ended up with matching medieval queen and king costumes for her and Ross. Mark bought a Zorro costume, which was hilarious because he had zero Latino swagger. Much to Dad's distress, Marissa chose a sexy red devil costume. Torn between Cat Woman and Snow White, Dad bought me both just to get us out of the store.

Next to Homecoming, Halloween was the biggest social night of the year. With the events back to back, the whole two weeks felt wasted academically. I banished all hopes of a romantic relationship with Doug from of my mind. The party was about having fun with my friends. I was Bill's date after all. Doug hadn't so much as batted an eye at that fact.

Trying not to get behind, I studied until Elise and her friend came in. She was the most excited I had ever seen her, and as she didn't stop talking. Deciding that my I study session was over, I joined in their conversation. For costumes, she and her cheerleader friend switched roles. Her friend put on Elise's drum major uniform and Elise squeezed into a cheerleading skirt and top. Clipping a long ponytail hair piece over her own short ponytail, she tied purple and white ribbons in bows around the base. Then they both painted a wildcat on one side of their face and NU on the other.

Holding my costumes up in front of the mirror, I couldn't decide between Cat Woman and Snow White. My broken arm detracted from the Cat Woman look, but the long skirt of the Snow White costume was annoying. I put on one and then the other.

Having finished her outfit, Elise pointed a finger at me. "Decide already!"

I slumped down on my futon. Maybe I wasn't up for this. Everyone would be kissing someone except me.

"You need a drink." She took a cup and poured me a glass of the drink they'd made. She crossed the room, holding up the Snow White costume. "How much did this cost?"

"My dad paid for it."

"Do you care if I cut it?"

I shook my head, and she whipped out a big pair of scissors from her desk. Cutting in a large zig-zag pattern, she snipped off the bottom half of the skirt. I slid it on and it fell a couple of inches above my knees.

She grabbed the boots Marissa had bought for the Cat Woman costume. "Put these on." I slipped them on and looked in the mirror. It actually wasn't bad.

Elise handed me the cat ears. "See, a Snow White Princess Kitty. Perfect."

Looking in the mirror, I had to admit I was impressed. A fair, dark-haired princess with nine lives, or in my case seven, was the perfect costume for me. We shared a car and they dropped me off at the fraternity house along with a second one of her special drinks. "Full report tomorrow," Elise yelled out the window as I got out of the car. "I supply the booze, you talk."

"Got it." I shot her a thumb's up.

Bill was at the front door, and he greeted me with a hug. He stepped back and looked me up and down. "You look great, but who are you?"

I twirled around. "Snow White Princess Kitty."

He laughed. "Of course, how did I not get that? Does your date get the first dance?"

"Definitely." A group of people came in behind me, and he motioned over to where the band was setting up. "Zack and Doug are at the music table. They want you to help with the music."

I found the band table. Doug was dressed in blue scrubs, and he'd let his stubble grow out to a nine o'clock shadow. He looked sexy, really sexy. This was not going to help me rid my psyche of attraction to him.

Doug hugged me. "You look great."

Zack stepped back, looking me up and down. "I'm confused."

"Snow White Princess Kitty." I took a huge sip of Elise's drink concoction, and spun around. The first already in full effect, I was feeling pretty weightless.

Doug took my drink and smelled it. "You need to go easy on this." He set it across the table from me. I opened my mouth to tell him that it was a party but thought better of it. Behaving, right?

Zack pulled a long piece of white fabric out of his back pocket. "I made you something." He held it up. The letters SMG had been printed inside a diamond shape halfway down.

I traced my fingers down the length of the fabric. "Super Mini-Girl, sweet."

He held it up to my head, but I ducked away. Headbands were definitely out since my injury, so I held up my arm. He tied it around my bicep and wrapped his arm around my waist, having Doug take a picture.

"Do I get to wake the princess first?"

"Zack." Doug stepped toward us, his tone suddenly serious.

Before I could react, Zack's lips were on mine. The kiss was soft, warm, and insistent all at the same time. He released me, and our eyes met for a brief second. My cheeks flooded, and I tried to recover by reaching for my drink.

"Wow," was all I could manage after taking a sip.

"Great work, Zack, her color is gone." Doug put his hand around my waist. "I think you better let me take over."

Zack's phone buzzed. He picked it up with one hand and kept his other arm on me.

"Oh, Kara's here."

"Okay, didn't see that one coming." I turned to Doug.

"So, Snow White Princess Kitty?"

"Multiple personalities, I know. But it fits, right?"

"I'll give you that." He smiled a smile I'd been sure was only for me. Shaking his head, it was gone. I helped with the song list for the band, and he went over the party schedule. He had me down for judging the costume contest with him and Zack.

"I'm going to find Lila and Mark. Can I put my stuff in your room?" This was inevitable. There was no other place I could stash my stuff where I knew I'd be able to get it when I wanted it.

He handed me his keys. "You got a place to keep these and a phone in that get up?"

I stuck my leg out, flashing him the secret interior pocket in my boot.

He leaned into me. "I expect you to text me back."

So, he was planning on texting me? He wanted to keep up with me? Instead of one quick blow, like the first time, I guessed it'd be slow and painful this time.

I found Mark, Lila, and Ross upstairs. My phone buzzed not a second after I sat down with them.

Doug: Do U Copy?

Me: Yes.

Mark hit me on the leg. "Who's texting you?"

Kara and Zack came up behind me. "Twenty bucks says it's Doug."

My phone buzzed again. ZACK'S LATE FOR HIS DOOR POST. I read the message out loud.

Kara stayed behind to hang out with us, and everyone headed downstairs when the band started. When I parked myself along the wall, Bill hung back with me.

"You're not dancing?"

"Find me on a slow one."

Doug saw me standing alone and waved me over to his post at the door. There was a line now, and he motioned for me to take the other side. When the line dwindled, I moved back beside him.

"You're not dancing?"

"Not up for that yet."

"How's your head?"

"Not bad, considering." I pointed to the band and crowd.

Just then a group of four very tall and beautiful girls came in the door. Doug's demeanor instantly changed. He stood rigid beside me, his brow creased. Anyone else probably wouldn't have noticed, but I'd spent too much time studying his face not to. I recognized them as the same girls talking to him in front of the house Homecoming morning.

"Hailey, Anna, Sam, Lexi, it's nice to see you again," he greeted them.

The first girl in the line gave him a hug and quick peck on the cheek. "What's up with you? Homecoming is the only time we've seen you all quarter." She looked at me and then back to him.

The girl next to her motioned to me. "Isn't this your date from Homecoming?"

Doug turned to me. "Yes, Anna, this is Amanda."

I smiled and shook her hand.

She took a step back, studying me. "Amanda? Wait, is this the girl Zack is always going on about? You're the one who got hurt playing volleyball."

I jutted my chin out, looking her square in the eyes. "Right," was all that came out, though. Feeling lost, I cut my eyes to Doug, hoping for clarification.

"Anna lives in Zack's apartment complex."

Anna looked back to me. "Are you going to rush next quarter?"

Before I could respond, Zack came up with Kara. I was glad to be saved from the rush question. Although Tia had loved her sorority, I wasn't attracted to the whole idea.

Zack leaned in and hugged Anna. "You met Amanda."

She rolled her eyes. "I did, finally. You need to have another party so we can hang out."

He saluted. "Will do, chief."

Her friends started moving towards the dance floor. "Well, I'll catch you guys later. Nice to meet you, Amanda." She followed the other girls.

Just then an alarm went off on Doug's phone. "Wow, that was fast. My shift's over."

Zack went in search of Ross and came back with Ross, Lila, and Bill.

"Hey, listen, a slow one." Bill motioned for me to join him on the dance floor. "Mark says you're a good wingman," he commented as we danced.

Maybe I shouldn't have come to college with one of my best guy friends, because he gave away all my secrets. "I have been known to serve that purpose," I admitted.

As the song ended, Bill took my hand and led me over to a group of brothers. Over the course of the next hour, I played wingman for him and at least five other brothers. Finally, Zack came to my rescue, drink in hand. Thirsty from talking and smiling, I drank half of it in one sip. I looked up, and he was staring at me, dumbfounded.

Kara laughed. "Maybe you should've put a warning label on that drink."

I sniffed the drink and took another sip. "Rum and Coke?"

Kara leaned into me. "It's okay. I made him use diet soda, so it's low calorie. Not that you need to worry about calories. The wind could pick you up."

I looked back and forth between them and realized they looked different. Maybe it was the alcohol, or, maybe they'd had a quickie. I hoped for Doug's sake it wasn't on his futon. The band announced a break and the room quieted down. My phone and Zack's buzzed simultaneously.

Zack held his phone up to me. "Must be lover-boy." For a split second I wished I were super woman and could blast him with a laser.

Just then two large hands grabbed me around the waist. I jumped.

"We're up!" Doug said into my ear, and I melted from head to toe, dang blasted hormones.

Judging the costume contest was fun, and somehow Mark won. The band started back up and I reclaimed my wingman position at the bar. Nearing the end of the band's second set, I found myself leaning against the bar alone. Needing some water, I ducked behind the bar to find one.

Doug's voice came from behind me. "You're not playing bartender, are you?"

"Just looking for water."

"Want some of mine? I think we're out down here."

I took the bottle from him and finished half of it. None of the brothers had hit on me, even in my sexy getup. I wondered if everyone assumed Doug and I were together. On the one hand, it kept me from meeting guys I might like. However, it was also a bit of a safety net. College dating seemed much scarier than high school dating, and I definitely didn't want another experience like Law.

He took the bottle back and drank from it. The music switched to a slow tune and he slipped his arm around my waist. "Want to dance?"

We moved towards the dance floor. "So you didn't want to go to the dorm party with Stephen?" There was barely an inch of space between us, and Stephen was the furthest person from my mind.

"No, why?"

"I figured Lila and Mark were giving you a hard time, so you'd cave."

"I've had years of experience dealing with the two of them. I don't cave when it matters."

"Good to know."

We moved on and off of the dance floor, depending on the speed of the song. Even with the noise, we chatted. I lost track of how many songs we danced to, but I assumed it was close to midnight. The band started playing "Viva La Vida" by Coldplay, and Doug pushed me towards the dance floor.

"Come on, it'll be fun. Not too much spinning or dipping, I promise." He tilted my chin so I could see his face. No one, and certainly not me, could resist that look.

He placed one hand on my waist and another on my shoulder and started a waltz. I tried to stop smiling and make a serious face. It was impossible.

"What?"

"Isn't this spinning?"

"Well, it's not spinning in one place. Would you rather do a tango? It fits better anyway."

We switched styles, and he pulled me closer. At the end of the song he dipped me then pulled me back to standing. I was in heaven. Unfortunately, a fast-paced song followed and a massive amount of people flooded the dance floor.

He didn't let go of my hand. "Want to play some pool?"

I looked at him like he was crazy and pointed to my arm.

"We'll make it work." We made our way to the pool room. One game was near the end, and Doug called to play the winner. He took a stool and pulled me closer to him so we could hear each other. Being close to him was intoxicating, and I repeated my mantra in my head. He wasn't interested in me that way. I wasn't going to make a move one way or the other.

When it was our turn to play, he stood with his right arm wrapped around my waist and his left arm extended to help me hold the end of the stick.

As the other team took a turn, Zack and Kara came in the room and sat down. "So, you guys playing or what?"

"Yeah, look, Amanda here is winning the game for us."

Zack stood. "I have to see this."

We showed off our pool trick. Kara whispered something in Zack's ear. He rolled his eyes. "Okay, well, we're going to dance now, you guys have fun."

I turned back to Doug. "They look happy."

"They do."

I was enjoyed a nice buzz thanks to the several drinks I'd had. This left me with the courage to whisper what I'd been thinking earlier. "Changing your sheets would probably be a good idea."

"You're up," a guy from the other team called.

"A minute." Doug waved the guy off.

Doug sat me on the stool. I took another sip of my drink and he leaned into me. "Did you seriously just say what I think you did?"

"They were oozing hormones."

He smiled his best sexy smile and turned around to finish the game. From my perspective, it wasn't an I-think-you're-cute smile, it was an I-see-you smile. Having forgotten my mantra already, and happy with my play, I took another big swig of my drink.

Coming back, he took my cup. "Where'd you get this?" He took the last sip.

"Hey, I'm thirsty. What do you have?" I tried to grab his drink.

"Never mind this." He held it out of my reach.

I stood in front of him with my hand on my hip. Maybe it was because I looked so determined, but he lowered his cup. It looked like a club soda, and I took a decent-sized sip.

"Vodka and tonic?" I asked.

"You recognize vodka?"

I shrugged my shoulders. "I'm Russian remember."

"No, you're not."

I grabbed his hand. "Are we fighting? Come on, I hear slow songs again." The alcohol was definitely lowering my inhibitions.

Before we got to the dance floor, we ran into Anna.

"I thought you guys had already gone," he said.

"We were upstairs hanging out." She stepped forward and gave him a kiss on the cheek. "Thanks for another fun party." She turned to me. "Let me know if you want to talk about rush. Oh, and make these guys put together a party at Zack's."

She and the rest of her entourage each took turns hugging and kissing Doug and then stumbled away.

"Wow, drink much, do they?" he said as he pushed me into the dancing crowd. "You're not going to rush, are you?"

I shook my head no. As we danced and mingled, he became irresistibly charming. When the band came back and announced their last set, the dance floor became packed again. He led me back to the bar. "I need water. Want to come up?"

I nodded, and he led me upstairs to his room. He closed the door behind us, and the quiet was instant. He crossed the room to retrieve two water bottles from his fridge. I leaned against his counter, smoothing my skirt.

He stood in front of me and set the water bottles down, one on each side of me. "Tired, princess?"

I stretched. "Not really."

He moved a strand of hair that had fallen into my face and secured it behind my ear.

"Is my hair going everywhere?"

"It's curling quite a bit."

He leaned in so his legs touched mine, and I could feel his breath on my forehead. I dared not move. His fingers brushed over my scar and he wrapped his hand around the back of my neck. I hooked my fingers through his belt loops and he leaned in closer. I closed my eyes as his lips touched my forehead. I could feel his breath on my eyelids, my nose, and then my lips. I pulled him to me, tipping my chin up to kiss him, but he backed away. I opened my eyes and his face was still only inches from mine, his hand still laced around my neck. I didn't dare move.

"Sorry." He released me and stepped back.

It was the last thing I wanted to hear. I looked up to the ceiling to keep the tears from forming. What was I doing here? I really had fooled myself. Our friendship had come so naturally, but where was I now? Just the place Lila and Mark said I would be. Anger kicked in, and I barely squelched the scream building inside.

"Sorry! Sorry for what? Almost kissing me or not kissing me?" I pushed past him, retrieved my backpack, and moved towards the door.

He grabbed my arm. "What are you doing? We should talk."

I didn't want to talk to him. Things seemed pretty obvious. "I'm going."

He tried taking my backpack from me. "We should get some coffee."

"I don't want coffee." I pulled my pack back from him.

"You're upset. Let's talk. Come down with me for a minute. I'll get Bill or Zack to take care of the band."

Already to the door, he blocked my exit. As pissed as I was, there really wasn't any use resisting. It'd just make things worse. Even after everything, I didn't want to lose him as a friend.

Downstairs he went to pay the band, and I took my phone out and checked the time. One forty-three. I could see Zack dancing with Kara in the front of the room near the band. Bill, Ross, Lila, and Mark were on the dance floor, too, but I kept my distance. I tried not to think about Doug, but it was futile. I was a first-class idiot.

When I looked up again, Zack stood in front of me. "Hey, I haven't had a dance yet." He pulled me onto the dance floor.

"Where did Kara go?"

"Gone. It's over."

"What? But you guys…" I didn't finish; I didn't have the energy. "I'm sorry."

"It's okay. It wasn't working anyway. So, how's your night?"

"Fine."

He raised his eyebrows. "Fine?" He pulled me closer to him and spun me around the other way. I could see Doug talking to

Bill. Zack squeezed my arm, and I looked up at him. He tipped his head towards Doug. "He might surprise you, you know."

I tried to play dumb, but I couldn't get myself to look away from Doug.

"Hey, I didn't get a dance," Mark said from behind me.

Would my agony ever end? I thanked Zack, and Mark slipped in. All the while I kept Doug in my sights. When the song ended, I walked straight towards him.

Doug held my backpack up. "You ready?"

I took a deep breath and nodded. All my fight was gone and only sadness was left.

Chapter 11

We darted through the rain to his car. It wasn't far but my dress was almost soaked through, and I could already feel my hair forming ringlets.

He started the car, blasting the heat, and reached into the back seat, retrieving a towel. "Here, dry off."

"Where are we going?"

He dropped the towel in my lap. "There's a diner over by the hospital."

"I'm dressed as Snow White Princess Kitty. Can you just take me back to my room?"

"I'm hungry, and they have great pie. Besides, it's two on Halloween. Everyone will be in costume."

There was no way he was letting me out of this. I hated not having control.

It was only five minutes to the restaurant. We walked in, and I could see Doug was right. The crowd was quite diverse. A vampire waitress showed us to a booth in the back. I was glad to be tucked away. It felt safer somehow, less exposed.

"What do you want? Their apple pie is the best."

"Just decaf."

It was awkward. I tried not to meet his gaze. He had insisted on this, but he couldn't make me eat or listen. He ordered two decaffeinated coffees and two apple pies.

"I'll eat yours if you don't want it," he said after the waitress left. His hands resting on the table, he vacillated between looking at them and at me. It seemed like minutes before he spoke. "I'm sorry."

My anger reappeared and I wanted to scream. Did he bring me to a diner so I wouldn't? I was sick of him being sorry. I folded my arms across my chest.

He stared at the table. "That shouldn't have happened."

I waited because I realized I needed him to say it. No more ambiguity. Otherwise, in the morning, I would wake up wondering if I'd just imagined it or misunderstood. He didn't continue. "Which part?"

He looked at his hands again. "We shouldn't have gotten this close."

Leaning towards him, I gripped the edge of the table. "Why? Because I'm eighteen, because I'm a freshman, because you promised my dad you'd take care of me?" I threw up my hands. "What?"

I was startled by the waitress, who set the coffee and plates of pie in front of us. I slid back in my seat. Looking at the pie, my stomach turned, and I pushed my plate away. He took a bite of his and I waited for him to finish it. "So?"

His studied his fork, turning it over and over. "You're a freshman and I'm a senior. In seven months, I'll graduate and get a job, hopefully in Asia."

I folded my arms across my chest. "Two months ago, you told me you didn't have time." Clearly that'd been a lie. Who was I kidding? I was walking around in circles. I studied my mug. If I had to see him nearly every day, seven months sounded like an eternity of torture. But after he graduated I may never see him again. I wasn't sure which was worse. Suddenly, I felt hollow. Refusing to cry in front of him, I lifted my mug and took a sip of the coffee.

He pointed at my pie, and I pushed it towards him. Hesitating as he lifted his fork, he continued, "I shouldn't have gotten this close to you, and tonight shouldn't have happened. I was drinking, and you're a very hard person not to be around."

I wasn't letting this go. My age and his impending graduation weren't good enough reasons. "If I were older?"

"No, even if you were older, if I hadn't promised your dad I'd take care of you, and if you weren't best friends with one of my brothers."

Clearly he was attracted to me, he'd basically said as much, but it wasn't enough. I dug my nails into my fist to get out my next question. "So, where does that leave us?"

"As you pointed out, this is the second time we've been here."

Again, I conjured an image of having a laser beam, but I wasn't sure if I wanted to aim it at him or me. We sat there a minute in silence. I didn't dare exhale, knowing that only emptiness would fill the void. He was only half done with my piece of pie, but I didn't care. "Can we go?"

He stared at me for what was an awkwardly long time before nodding. I wondered what he saw. So many emotions were coming at me at once: anger, fear, desperation, loneliness. The mixture was akin to what I'd felt after I fainted at the medical center. I knew this would be worse, much worse, because there would be no Doug to catch me.

He paid at the register while I waited beside the door. With my cold dress clinging to my skin and the distance between us, the drive was torture. He slowed as we neared my building, stopping for pedestrians. "Can you just drop me off?"

When he stopped the car, I looked at him. It pained me to think I wouldn't see his face tomorrow. Blocking the thought from my mind, I grabbed my backpack, swung the door open, and closed it behind me. Reaching the building, I didn't look back.

I'd meant to dash to the elevator, but lobby was crowded, the dorm party still at full throttle.

"Amanda! Snow White!" I heard a male voice call.

I turned to find Jeremy and Stephen walking towards me. I forced a smile.

Stephen pointed towards me. "Great costume."

Jeremy reached out and grabbed some strands of my hair, examining it. "Wow, your hair is…"

"Curly, from the rain."

He put one hand on Stephen's shoulder and pointed at me with the other. "Did you know her hair curled in the rain? Did you know she's my lab partner?"

Stephen removed the hand from his shoulder. "Yes, you told me that." He turned back to me. "Are you just coming from the fraternity party?"

"Umm, yeah," I hedged. It wasn't a total lie. I did come from the party via the coffee shop.

Jeremy pointed at me. "Doug or Zack probably dropped you off. Whichever one, he's an idiot if he just dropped you off."

Jeremy was right. Doug was an idiot.

Stephen motioned towards the crowd. "Do you want to join us?"

"Thanks, but I'm pretty tired. I'll catch you later."

I rode up the elevator, squished in a crowd of drunken students. My hall was packed too, and I had to maneuver to get to my door. I slipped inside, unzipped my boots quietly, and placed them on the floor next to my closet. I listened for sound from Elise's bed. Hearing her snores, I leaned against the door, and slid down to the floor. Finally taking a deep breath, I folded my knees into my chest. My phone buzzed and I picked it up, seeing a text from Marissa. I turned off my phone and let it slide onto the floor. I exhaled, feeling the hollowness of my loss. Quietly I let the tears flow, gripping my chest to control sobs that begged for escape.

How long I sat there I couldn't be sure. Cold and exhaustion finally won over. Shivering, I stripped off my dress and found some pajamas. Systematically I forced myself to brush my teeth and wash my face. I pulled my hair back and burrowed under my blanket, dreading ever having to wake again.

Light from the window woke me. Please God let it be at least noon, I prayed. Thursday, ugh! I had class at ten, but at least it would be a distraction. Rolling over, I noticed Elise was already gone. I dared not turn on my phone. It was too early for that, if I ever turned it on again. Maybe I'd get a new number.

I looked at the clock on Elise's desk. Seven fifty-three. Really? Only seven fifty-three? Scanning my room, I realized I couldn't be alone here. What to do? Gym! I was cleared for physical activity, and Doug would be rowing. Trying to ignore the ache in my chest, I brushed my teeth and pulled on gym clothes. I took some Motrin and applied Marissa's anti-puffy stuff on my eyes. Boycotting my phone, I grabbed my old MP3 player and stuffed it in my gym bag.

Outside, the gray sky fit my mood. I pulled my hood on and tried to ignore the tightness in my chest. Maybe full on cardio wasn't the best idea, but I needed something. As I expected, the gym was deserted. I headed straight for the treadmills. Never mind that I hadn't run in three weeks, I was ready to go. I stretched and started the machine at a slow run pace. I put my earphones on, trying one song and then another but finally giving up on music altogether.

After a few minutes, a figure appeared beside me. Noticing it was Stephen, I stopped my machine. "How long have you been standing there?"

"Not long. You seemed pretty focused."

"Are you running?" I pointed to the treadmill beside me.

"I didn't want to disturb you."

"No, it's fine."

"You're not usually here on Thursday mornings."

"I just got cleared for exercise."

He set his speed to match my slow pace and we started running. Stephen's presence made me think of Doug and his vulture comments. Forcing myself to breath evenly, I realized I had to think tactically. First, Lila, Mark, Ross, Zack, or Bill couldn't know about last night and how upset I was. Wow, that list was long! I hated to lie to my friends, but there was no way I was letting my stupid crush go public. Second, I had to minimize seeing Doug. This meant staying away from the house, the gym on workout days, co-rec games, and possibly Thursday nights at the pub. My three tests and paper would be good alibis. But I'd have to see Doug on Monday morning when we volunteered to hand out the Republican Party pamphlets. That was going to be painful.

"Amanda?" Stephen's voice broke into my thoughts. "How far are you planning on running?"

I looked down at my readout and saw I'd run over five miles.

"Maybe you should take this exercise thing slow. You look a little pale."

Great, another caretaker! I had enough of those. I stopped the treadmill and got off, my chest heaving. I tried to change the subject. "You're up early for such a late night."

"I always work out four days a week." He handed me a Gatorade from his bag. "Will you please drink this?"

I took a couple of sips.

"It would make me feel better if you drank more of that."

I put the bottle down. "Do I look that bad?"

"Just pale."

"I'm always pale."

"I know, but now you look really pale. If you're heading back, we can walk together."

I drank more of the Gatorade and gathered my stuff.

He held the door for me. "So, are you coming to the gym tonight?"

I had my excuse ready. "No, I have to study."

"Well, if you want a break, I think we're going out again."

Usually, I was good at small talk, but not today. We finished the walk back to the dorm in silence. When we parted, I headed for the shower. It felt good to have the hot water beat down on me. Having braved turning my phone back on, it was ringing when I stepped back into my room.

Lila didn't even give me time to say hello. "Manda, for goodness sake, I've called like five times. What are you doing? Why didn't you answer? Where did you go last night? Did you and Doug hook up?"

"What? No, you know we're just friends. I just got back from the gym and was in the shower." I forced the words out quickly and smoothly, hoping they sounded light and breezy.

"Oh, I thought Mark said—I guess not. I guess you're still you. Well, are you coming to the v-ball game tonight? We're going out after."

"I have an insane amount of studying to do."

"Okay, well there will be lots of people missing you."

"Is she coming tonight?" I heard Mark say in the background. Lila must've told him I declined, because he immediately said, "Good, she won't distract Doug."

I wished for laser beam powers.

Lila was back. "Call me later."

Looking at my phone, I saw there were three text messages from Marissa. I'd have to wait until she got out of school to talk to her. At least I had one person I could talk to about the breakup.

I couldn't be in my room. Pulling my hair up, I wished I could do something different with it. Look different, be different, anyone but myself.

Zombie-like, I moved through my day. In class, I had to talk to Vivian and some football players who thought they knew me after the scrimmage. Between lectures, I hid in the library, praying I didn't see Doug.

Wishing I could retreat to my room, I met Mark for racquetball. Keeping up appearances was crucial to my charade. Back in my room, I showered quickly. All I wanted was to be under my blanket, alone with my misery. I pulled my covers over my head, and exhausted, fell asleep. I woke when Elise came in but lay there pretending to be asleep as she made dinner.

With a grumbling stomach, I finally had to get up. Elise greeted me but I pointed to the bathroom. Once there, I splashed cold water on my face and applied concealer around my eyes. Dawdling as long as I could, I finally had to emerge.

"Oh my goodness, how was last night? I didn't even hear you come in. You did sleep here, right? Are you totally hung over? Did you sleep all day?"

I avoided eye contact, passing her to get a bagel. "No! I had classes all day. I wasn't that late, just like two-thirty."

She grabbed my arm. "And..."

I wasn't going to be able to keep it from her, so I told her the ending. She made me go back and start from the beginning of the night. It hurt to relive it, and I was gripping my chest and fighting tears by the end. I had expected a huge reaction from her, but she sat calmly until I finished detailing my strategy for dealing with my friends.

"I am not happy with that boy, and, I'm not going to be able to hide that." She gathered her dishes and took them down the hall.

When she came back, I went downstairs and found a quiet corner to talk to Marissa. It was a good strategy, as being in a public place kept me from crying. I returned to my room, determined to rid thoughts of him from my brain. Deciding to study math first, I got in an hour of calculus and then one of biology before I was interrupted.

My phone rang, and the caller ID indicated it was Zack. I debated whether to answer it but figured if I didn't he'd probably come find me. "Why didn't you come to the game, and why aren't you coming out?"

"I didn't get much done with Homecoming and Halloween this week."

"I know. Intense, right? Okay, are you working out with us tomorrow? I heard you ran today with Stephen."

"I don't—"

"That doesn't get you out of our workouts. I'll pick you up if I have to. Got it, Mini-Girl?"

"Yes," I relented.

"Good." He hung up.

Trying to think of anything but tomorrow, I dove into my English paper, read for international studies, and reviewed the chemistry and biology chapters for the next day.

The next morning my alarm sounded at seven-thirty. Brushing my teeth and flinging on clothes as fast as possible, I tried not to think about what torture might lay ahead at the gym. I got the gym early and was two miles in when Zack and Bill showed up.

Zack hit me with his towel as I ran. "So where's Doug?"

I removed my headphones. "I don't know."

"You're not playing me, right?"

I looked between him and Bill. "Why would I know where Doug is?"

Zack leaned over my treadmill. "You guys left together Wednesday night."

I looked him straight in the eyes. "We got coffee, and then he dropped me off at my dorm."

"Seriously?" He studied me for what felt like a full minute, shrugged, and set his gym bag down. We ran another three miles. My muscles were begging to stop, but I pushed through. As we got off the treadmills, Doug came in. Looking at him would do me no good, and I forced myself to focus on my cool down.

Zack went over to talk to him, and I finished stretching with Bill. "Want to go do the machines?" I nodded, and we made our way to the weight room. After a few machines, Zack and Doug appeared. They started on the rowing machines at the other end, and I was able to slip out undetected.

Running back to my dorm, I barely had time for a shower before class. I stacked my day like that on purpose, leaving little time for socializing. Fortunately, Lila also had her own schedule to keep and hadn't noticed my avoidance tactics yet. Again, I hid in the library till my next class and zipped to the medical center afterwards. Waiting in the lobby with sick students was better than risking seeing anyone from the house.

The last place I wanted to be was in a room with someone focused on how I was feeling. I'd learned it was hard not to be completely transparent with the counselor. Inside her office, she gestured for me to sit down.

"Any more flashbacks? How were Homecoming and Halloween? Are you ready for your next round of tests?" She paused after each question and I gave short answers to each: no, okay, and I should be.

"Your recovery seems to be going well. Is there anything else you want to talk about?" This was the big question. I was drowning, but did I really need to tell her? Could I relate the story without crying? My hesitation had her looking at me with an odd expression. I had to say something soon, and I couldn't lie to her.

Relaying my predicament as succinctly as possible, I didn't even take a breath. I hoped getting it out fast meant it wouldn't hurt so much. But it did, and tears formed in my eyes before I could stop them. Concerned I hadn't shared my story with Lila or Mark, she encouraged me to do so. Ironically, she was able to help me in my endeavor to fill my time with non-fraternity activities. She had a friend who needed a sitter.

I left her office on edge, feeling raw and exposed. Another run was out of the question, so I walked the long way to get back to my dorm. As I climbed the stairs to my room, my phone buzzed.

Seeing that it was Lila, I answered the call. There were lots of voices in the background, and she shushed them. "Hey, where are you? Are you coming over to the house?"

Fortunately, I was ready with my excuse that Elise and I were hanging out. Lila complained she had no one to talk to but didn't launch a full out assault. Finishing our conversation with the promise that I'd call the next day, I sent my sitter resume off, updated my tutoring profile, did my laundry, and cleaned my room. Thankfully, Elise got there before I went into a compulsive organizing binge.

That night we had pizza and wine and watched Elise's self-proclaimed heartbreak recovery movie. I was in tears before half the movie was over. Never having been a crier, I hated being out of control of my feelings. Would this ever hurt less?

The next day Elise went hiking in Wisconsin with some friends. Relieved I had the day all to myself, I started coffee and tried to figure out how to keep busy. My sitting job wasn't until five. I couldn't go to Mass, but I could go to the gym. As I sipped my coffee, my phone rang. It was Mom, and I'd dodged her calls from yesterday, so I had to answer. I got up, brushed my teeth, washed my face, and put on my gym clothes while we talked. It was just the diversion I needed to get myself out the door. Still on the phone, I walked to the gym. I paced outside the building, trying to appease her need to have a full update of my life. Stephen approached, and I lifted a finger to signal I'd be done soon.

"Hey, Mom, I'm supposed to meet a friend at the gym, so I have to go now."

"Oh, anyone I know?"

"No, Mom, I'll talk to you later." I turned to Stephen. "Sorry, my mom freaks out if I don't talk to her every day and I missed yesterday."

He shook his head. "I'm not sure whether to feel used or flattered."

We walked into the gym and up to the treadmills. Stretching out, and beginning our runs, I tried listening to music. Every song just made me upset. Stopping the music, I went through my week mentally. I'd be in pretty good shape for my tests if I studied all afternoon. But I still had a whole Sunday in front of me. Then there was Monday morning and volunteering with Doug and the College Republicans. What would I do about that? I had to go so Doug didn't think I was devastated. I'd seen him yesterday without breaking down. I could make it an hour, right? Tuesday I'd be clear, and Wednesday was my regular date with Lila. We usually met at the house, but I could work around that. On Thursday, I'd skip the volleyball game. How had I gotten to the point where I was rearranging my schedule to avoid seeing a guy?

Suddenly a Gatorade bottle was thrust in my face. I hit the stop button and looked at the readout. Oh, I was a crazy person! I'd run almost six miles in only fifty minutes.

Stephen shook the bottle. "Are you trying to kill yourself?"

I took off my headphones. "Exercise is good for you, right? Endorphins, adrenaline, cardiovascular health."

"Do you ever hydrate, or eat?"

"This week is just bad, I have a lot of tests. I really need to do well to keep my scholarship." It was the truth, just not the whole truth.

I took the Gatorade, and we walked back to our building. "So, would you like to grab some breakfast?"

He wasn't bad company. Maybe it would be fun if I wasn't in the middle of this personal crisis. "Another time?"

"Okay, I'll see you around." He walked towards his side of the dorm.

After a shower, I spent the day on my futon studying. I only talked to Lila long enough to provide an excuse for the rest of the weekend. I was proud that I got up the nerve to take a car service to my sitting job. The family was nice, and the kids got to bed fairly early, giving me even more study time than I'd budgeted.

It was after midnight when I got back to the dorm, and Elise was already snoring. Glad I didn't have to face her, I quietly got ready for bed. If I'd let myself think about it I could have had a huge pity party over the state of my life. Focusing on strategies to avoid anything Doug related, I drifted off.

Slipping out before Elise woke up, I found Stephen was waiting in the dorm lobby.

He held out a bottle of Gatorade towards me. "I didn't have you number but figured I'd wait five minutes."

Sipping my coffee, I waved off the Gatorade. We chatted about our weekends on our walk. During the run, I made a mental note to be present. I tried to find tolerable music on my player but gave up after the fifth song. Figuring I must have looked like a nut case, I picked one fast-paced funk song and set it to loop.

After the second mile, I found my rhythm and relaxed. Stephen tapped my arm and asked me how far. I held up five fingers, and he nodded in agreement. My training had started out well but over eagerness had left me sore after the first few days. Setting a goal of a comfortable seven miles by Thanksgiving would put me in great shape for a 10K in Champaign over the holiday. It wouldn't be the half-marathon I'd hoped to do, but it was better than nothing.

We took our time stretching out and cooling down before we went out in the cold. Again, he invited me to brunch. Again I declined, citing needing a shower before my study groups as an excuse.

"You do eat, right?"

I faked a laugh. "Amazingly, I do. Maybe next week." I wasn't in any shape to be forming a new relationship, platonic or not. I took the elevator up and took a hot shower.

In the afternoon, Kate and I met up with Jeremy to go to the library. The study sessions were the perfect diversion as they included nothing that reminded me of Doug.

Being with Elise was harder, but I forced myself to go to the grocery store with her. She was chatty as usual and thankfully didn't mention Doug once. She did take notice when I picked up a six-pack of Gatorade.

"I've never seen you drink that stuff."

"I owe Stephen several." Feeling the need to explain, I continued, "I guess I look pale when I run."

"Stephen, the referee guy Lila tried to set you up with?"

I tried to minimize the connection. "Yeah, turns out he runs on the weekends."

"What's the plan for tonight? How are you going to get through two hours with your friends without telling them? And what's your excuse for hiding all weekend?"

I stopped short. "What?"

"You do remember we said last week that we'd do dinner again this week right?"

"No, I forgot. Maybe everyone forgot." I took out my phone that I'd failed to turn on after our study sessions. There were messages from Lila, Mark, and Zack, confirming dinner. There was no way I was getting out of this.

"Okay, so I've been studying my ass off. It's the truth."

She stopped and leaned toward me. "You know how I get. I'm really not happy with that boy, so it's going to be hard not to say anything."

"I know, I know. If you're tempted to say anything, you could just make an excuse and leave the room."

"You are going to owe me."

The task of cooking dinner distracted me from panicking about who would show up. As with any food event, my crew was right on time, minus Bill and Doug.

I refused to ask about Doug. "Where's Bill?"

"Studying," Mark said.

Lila cleared her throat. "Lots of studying going on this weekend."

They all looked between each other. "So, where's Doug?" Zack finally asked.

His question caught me off guard. The pressure on my lungs returned, and I pushed my nails into my palm to steel my expression. "I haven't talked to him."

Mark bent down so that we were eye level. "You sure?"

Everyone was looking at me. "What are you saying?"

"Well, you were both studying all weekend." Lila made quotes around the word studying. "You left together Wednesday night, and we haven't seen either of you since, so we figured—"

Mark threw up his hands. "You were together. It sure looked like it the other night."

I motioned towards Zack, trying to keep my voice steady in my panic. "I worked out with you guys on Friday. I haven't talked to Doug since the party."

"What's the Gatorade for?" Ross pulled the bottles from under my futon.

What was this boy, a blood hound? It was a well-known fact I loathed the stuff. I would've welcomed the subject change if it hadn't involved another guy and me nearly passing out on the treadmill.

"Stephen spotted me some, so I'm replacing it."

"So Stephen is a good choice." Lila hit Ross on the arm.

"We just ended up at the gym together. You know hardly anyone goes on the weekends."

"Yeah, only huge losers like you, obviously!" Mark said, chuckling and pushing me into Zack.

Lila locked her arm through mine. "So what'd you do the rest of the day. I called you to come to brunch but your phone was off."

Fortunately, Elise brought in the appetizers, saving me from further inquisition. My phone buzzed and Lila grabbed it, looking at the screen. "Oooh, speak of the devil." She tossed me the phone.

I looked at the screen. Doug's text read: R U IN FOR 2MORROW?

I didn't want to think about our volunteering gig. I'd have to watch as every girl on campus flirt with him. It would be hell, but I was going. I shot back a quick text to confirm.

Zack leaned into me. "He not coming?"

I shook my head, thinking it was embarrassing that Zack witnessed my inquisition. But I corrected myself, realizing he was part of it. The rest of the evening was smooth, but the earlier conversation had opened a gate and he was all I could think about. The others' validation of our connection was beneficial in confirming I hadn't created a relationship with Doug in my head. But he didn't like me enough to make it more. Further, he felt what we'd had wasn't worth the complications that plagued us. The depression lurking on the fringes of my psyche descended. Cleaning up kept me busy until it was late enough to justify bedtime. I slid into bed, and let the tears flow.

Chapter 12

I'd set my alarm for eight to have just enough to get ready. My eyes were puffy but I showered and put a cold compress on them. Determined to look amazing, I selected my fitted corduroys, turtleneck, leather jacket, and boots. Ignoring the tightness in my chest and cramping in my side, I did my hair and makeup meticulously.

Anxious, I walked to the student union. It felt good to stretch my legs, and the cool air and open space helped my breathing. Too preoccupied to interact with the other students, I waited outside the office door. I had no interest in discussing why our candidate was losing the election.

I got a text from Elise: BE STRONG.

When I looked up after responding, he was walking toward me. The sight of him caught me off guard, and my breath caught in my lungs. His empty gaze, the absence of the smile, the one just for me, ripped through my chest. I gripped my phone and remembered: be strong.

I forced a smile and greeting. He simply nodded, brushing past me to the door, and I followed him into the office. Finding our pamphlets, we made our way down to the main level of the student union. At first I couldn't focus, all I could think about was him. Could I have done something differently? Yes I could, I berated myself. I could have not danced with him, and not played pool when he asked. If I hadn't fallen in love with him, then we would still be friends.

Determined to look unfazed, I put on my best smile and focused on the task. I forced myself to interact and be upbeat and animated. If anything, I talked to more people than I ever had. When the crowd thinned, I looked around, not finding him. Feeling a tap on my shoulder, I turned to see he was right behind me.

"You looked like you were enjoying yourself."

I let his words hang in the air. What was I supposed to say? Since our time was nearly up and he was out of handouts, we walked up the two flights of stairs to the office. Ready to be away from him, I retrieved my bag and headed for the exit. My first choice would've been to go back to my room and hide under my blanket for a week, but I had chemistry with Lila.

He'd been trailing me, and just outside the door he mumbled something I couldn't understand. Angry that he dared to speak to me, I turned to clarify. Bumping into his chest, his hand gripped my arm, stopping my motion. His scent flooded my senses and my chest seized. I used all my willpower to step back from him.

He shoved his hands in his pockets. "How was your weekend?"

Was he kidding? I put my hand to my hip. "Why?"

"You didn't tell any of your friends."

Why did he care? Couldn't he tell I wanted nothing to do with him? "No."

"Why?"

Because you're a jerk, and I didn't think you'd want the world to know it. "Nothing happened, what was there to tell? You didn't tell Zack."

Before he could answer, a set of hands covered my eyes from behind. Only one person did that. Kate.

Turning around, I forced a smile. "How was your camping trip?"

She looked between us. "It was good. How was your weekend?"

"Fine," Doug and I said at the same time.

She started to back away. "Okay, well, I'll see you in class then."

My adrenaline still at full throttle, I spun back to him. "Just so you know, I did tell Elise."

"So, I should definitely look out for her. She's probably ready to kill me."

"Pretty much." I looked away. Was he trying to be funny? I couldn't do humor with him, because no part of this was amusing. What I really wanted was for him to tell me he'd made a mistake and changed his mind. "I have to go." I turned to leave.

"So, are you going to the Latino club meeting tonight?"

Why was he still attempting small talk? I didn't want to go, but I needed to keep up my Spanish. It was a just over a month until Christmas break, and I needed to be sharp for my tutoring gig.

Exasperated I turned back to him. "Probably."

"Everyone will be talking politics."

"No, then." I would have said thank you but I had no gratitude for the boy right now. Not giving him any more opportunity for conversation, I walked away. Nearly late for class, I considered bailing. Scholarship, I repeated in my head, sliding into the seat Kate saved for me.

As soon as we were out of the lecture hall, Lila cornered me. "Kate says you were fighting with Doug."

I tried not to look directly at her. "Why is this news?"

"Spill," she ordered.

I used my best breezy voice. "You know how Doug and I are. He's always finding something to give me grief about."

"No, Mark gives you grief. Doug? I don't know what Doug does to you or why you stick around for it."

"So, you don't like Doug?" Not that it really mattered, but it was an interesting development.

"No, I like Doug fine. I'm just wondering if you're still torturing yourself by being friends with him. Maybe you should just force him to be in or out."

"Doug and I are clear on that."

"Clear? As in you're clear he's not going to be your boyfriend, and you're moving on? Or, clear as in he's not going to be your boyfriend, but you're still hanging out with him?"

I couldn't look away from her, and I tried to take slow breaths so tears didn't form. "He's been a good friend."

"Yes, I get that. You've always had guy friends. I don't want to see you hurt."

I didn't want to full out lie to her. "I know, can I go eat now?"

"You're not going to fight me on this?"

"No, and I'm starving."

"Did you skip breakfast again?"

Why did everyone care whether I had breakfast? It made me never want to eat again. "Yes," I admitted. "Can I go now?"

"Okay, I'll see you in lab."

I grabbed a sandwich and joined Kate and Jeremy at their table.

"I hope Lila told you what a big mistake you're making with that Doug guy." Jeremy started.

I couldn't believe he'd said that. Was he trying to be funny? I tried to breathe. It wasn't Jeremy, I was mad at myself. I knew it would end that way. I had chosen to maintain a relationship I knew would harm me. "We're not—"

Kate jumped in. "Maybe you talk about something that is your business."

Jeremy shrugged. "Just sayin'."

Thankfully, she switched topics detailing her weekend camping trip.

⁂

Having to interact and be normal with people in class was torture. But filling my days with tutoring, workouts, and studying, provided excuses for other social events. It was a pretty sad existence, but I saw no other way through it. The absence of him was like a vortex. My only goal was to not get sucked in.

Tuesday was Election Day, yet another reason to want to stay under my covers. Unfortunately, I had to go to classes and meet Mark for our now regular racquetball games. That night, Elise and I watched the election results come in. She took pity on me and offered a glass of wine. I didn't care that much that my candidate lost, but the election reminded me of Doug. Everything did. Trying to sleep, I listened to the celebration outside my dorm, tears streaming down my face.

I awoke Wednesday morning with more issues than the election results. It was workout day, again. Zack had texted the night before to gloat about the election and make sure I would be at the gym the next morning. Doug would be there, but I liked my workouts with Zack. I wasn't going to let avoiding Doug rule my entire life.

I got there early as usual so I could run a few miles before the guys showed up.

Zack started in with the ribbing right away. "Working off a little steam from last night's election results?" He and Bill took the treadmills flanking me.

"Something like that."

We focused on our runs, and Doug still hadn't shown by the time we finished.

"Doug must be crying in his latte," Zack said as we headed towards the weight room.

He steered me to the arm machine. With one hand on my hip, I waved my cast in the air. "How am I supposed to do this?"

"One-armed." He demonstrated for me. "Then we'll work your back and legs."

It was fun working out with the two of them. Zack always brought up obscure topics, and Bill talked more than he ever had. The conversation was light, effortless, and exactly what I needed. Just as we started the third machine, I saw Doug come through the door carrying a cup of coffee. He stopped, scanning the room. I should have looked away, but I couldn't. The short stubble on his cheeks and the curls in his hair I loved were gone. I exhaled and looked away, trying to take slow even breaths.

"You made it," Zack feigned a punch to his shoulder as he approached. "We thought you were probably crying in your latte about last night, and I see we were right."

Doug glanced in my direction. "I don't drink lattes." He turned around, removing his shirt, and sat down on the rowing machine beside me.

What was I doing here? I was certifiably insane agreeing to workout with Zack. Elise would probably have me committed on the spot. Zack and Doug went back and forth with stabs at each other while I kept plugging away on my back machine.

"So, um, maybe you need to pay a little more attention to your trainee over there. Her color looks a little off," Doug said, pointing at me.

Why did he care if my color was off? We weren't friends. We weren't anything to each other.

"Nah, she's looked like that all morning."

Bill came over and stood in front of me. "So how are you these days?"

It never failed. I'd be fine until someone asked. A lump caught in my throat, and my eyes started to water. I bit my tongue and blinked a couple of times. When I was fairly sure the tears weren't going to spill, I looked back at him.

"Fine, yeah good."

"Okay, then." He shook his head and led me to another machine. After that last set, we got water and Zack and Bill started towards Doug.

"I'm going." I pointed towards the exit not breaking my stride.

"Wait," Zack said. "We're just saying goodbye to Doug."

"I need a shower."

"Okay, well, you'll be at the house tonight, right?"

I hadn't thought that far ahead. Lila and I usually did our girls' night on Wednesday. "Not sure, I have a math test, so..."

Zack stopped me. "You're coming to the game tomorrow and out after, right? And working out with us on Friday?"

I shook my head. "I have two tests on Friday."

Zack put his hand to his chest. "Aww, you're killing me. How can I be your trainer if you aren't working out?"

"Next week." I waved as I jogged away, relieved to be away from Doug. Grabbing a quick shower, I made it into my saved seat just before the professor started his lecture. I resumed my normal hide-in-the-library strategy between classes and my afternoon sped by.

In the evening, I studied in my room, putting off calling Lila for as long as I could. She called me precisely at six-thirty. "Where have you been? I've been waiting an hour."

"I was wondering if we could study here."

She sighed. "Come on, you've been holed up in your room all week."

"I just finished my paper, but I still have three tests in the next two days. All my stuff's here. Please," I begged.

She finally agreed and came by half an hour later. Hugging her as she entered, I realized how much I'd missed her.

"Mark, Ross, Zack, and Bill say hi." She told me releasing me. "I heard you worked out with the guys this morning. Was it good?"

"Of course, they're always fun."

"What do you think of Doug's new look?"

I rearranged the books on my futon, unsure if I could keep a calm facade. "I've never seen him without his stubble."

"His five o'clock shadow look was new this fall."

I had to change the subject. "So, how are you? Things good with Ross?"

She sat down on the futon with me and chatted about Ross and her classes, flag football, and volleyball. She updated me on almost everyone in the house. I was glad Doug didn't make the list. Whoever the next girl was, I didn't want to know about it.

She brought up Stephen, but gave up on the topic when I didn't engage. We got some study time in before Ross called to inform her the chapter meeting was over. She begged me to come to the house, but I shook my book in front of her face.

Thursday I met Mark for racquetball after my math test. It was fun playing with him and I could almost convince myself that things were normal again. After our games he tried to talk me into coming to the house and the volleyball game, but I had my excuse down pat. Thinking I'd need to come up with something different next week, I jogged back to my room for a quick shower.

My tutoring sessions ended at six, and Elise and I had dinner together. We were studying when Lila called just after nine from the gym. They were going out, and she wanted me to come along. Before I could get out my standard line, Zack ended up on the phone.

"Come out with us. You could use a break. Everyone's coming. I'll pick you up!"

He was right, I could use a break. But I wasn't going if Doug would be there. "Everyone's coming?"

"Yeah, I think. Hold on." It sounded like he pulled the phone away from his ear. I heard lots of background noise. "You coming out with us Doug?" I heard Zack say.

"Umm, yeah, no, I'm out tonight."

"Doug's out, but most everyone else is in. Are you coming?"

I looked over at Elise. Still wary of being stuck alone, I thought she might be willing to share a ride with me. I muted the phone. "Hey Elise, do you want to come out with us? Just for a while?"

She agreed, and I took the phone off mute. "Elise and I will meet you there."

"I could come get you, but okay." He gave the phone back to Lila who was overjoyed I'd agreed to come out.

I changed and freshened up. There was no way I was showing up in my comfy jeans, no matter who was or wasn't going to be there. I used Marissa's five-minute makeup routine followed by the five-minute hair fix. In the end, I left my hair down, still a little curly from the shower.

After I slipped on a turtleneck, dark jeans, and black boots, Elise handed me a cup. I swirled and sniffed it wondering just how strong it might be.

"Just drink it and thank me. You're going to have to lighten up at some point, or I'm going to go nuts."

I held our door open for her, locking it behind us. "Is that a ploy to get me to smile?"

"Yes, you're not going to pull off your little charade looking so depressed."

"I have an excuse this week. I have three tests."

She rolled her eyes at me. "Don't forget the paper."

By the time we got to the pub, I indeed felt more relaxed. Zack and Bill met us at the door. They each pulled me in for a hug, and we found Lila, Ross, Mark, and Stephen at the regular table.

Lila bounced over to me. "Wow, you clean up nice. I like the curls."

Elise took the seat next to Stephen, so I took the end spot. Positioned between Zack and Bill, I asked about the volleyball game.

Mark chimed in from the other side of Bill. "Amazing how smoothly it went and how much more focused Doug was without you there to distract him. Maybe you should study every Thursday night."

"Maybe I will then." I stuck my tongue out at him.

Zack wrapped an arm around me, squeezing my shoulder. "Hey, what are you saying? Manda's our mascot."

"Wow, a one-armed midget for your mascot? That's pretty sad," I said, leaning over the table to grab a carrot stick. After my great comeback, I almost missed the chair. Elise's drink was hitting me pretty hard.

"What did you give her?" He motioned to Elise.

"Hey, this is an improvement over earlier, believe me."

I shot Elise a stern look, and she laughed. As usual, my looks were ineffective.

"So what's the problem?" Zack asked.

"Nothing like two tests in a day to cheer one up."

"Well, you definitely need a beer," Zack said. "I'll get one for you."

"Oh, no, she doesn't need one," Elise said. She then whispered something to Zack.

"Diet Coke?" I asked.

I shifted my chair closer to Zack, preferring to talk to him over a conversation that involved Mark. I became aware of Zack's hand rubbing my back. How long had his arm been around me?

"I could help you study your bio if you want."

"What time is it?"

"Nearly midnight," he said, pulling out his phone.

"I should get back." The effects of my drink had worn off and the caffeine kicked in. I figured I needed another good hour of studying, so I went looking for Elise.

I found her on the dance floor, and she and Lila tried to pull me into their circle. "Are you ready to head back?"

She looked at her phone. After seeing the time, she stuck her lip out at me.

"I can take Manda back," Zack said, materializing behind me. "I was going to study with her anyway."

Elise jumped on his offer and rejoined Lila.

I didn't realize I'd agreed to study with Zack, but it seemed like a done deal now. Outside, it was chillier than I thought, and I shivered.

"Butt warmers?" he asked as we got in the car.

I nodded. His sport utility vehicle was top-of-the-line with leather and wood grain trim, and the seats got warm really fast.

He pulled out of the parking lot. "You have the old tests from the house, right?"

"What?" I had no clue what he was talking about.

"Copies of old tests. You didn't know we had a file at the house? I'm surprised Doug or Lila didn't tell you about it."

"I don't think so, maybe. They could have, but I don't remember."

"We should drop by and grab some copies. We can use the copier in Doug's room."

This was definitely not what I wanted to do. I couldn't see a way around it without him asking questions, so I agreed. How bad could it be? Doug wasn't disappearing any time soon, so I might as well get used to it.

We were five minutes from the house, and I was glad I didn't have more time to panic. Zack pulled up in front. We retrieved the files from the library and made our way up to Doug's room. All the way up the stairs, Zack bounced the rolled up tests on my head. I ignored him, but he didn't stop.

"Jeez!" I caught the pages mid-swipe as we entered the upstairs hall.

"Finally, a reaction. Bout time."

Just then, Doug's door opened and Blondie bounded out, her whole body wagging. She almost knocked me over, but Zack grabbed me around the waist before I lost my balance.

Doug came out of his room, and his gazed landed on me for a split second before he looked away. "She knew you guys were here before I did."

I leaned down to pet Blondie, and she pressed up against me, pinning me to Zack.

Doug pulled her away. "What's up?" He looked between us.

I straightened up, looking to Zack. "Can we use your copier to copy some tests?"

"Sure." Doug dragged Blondie into the room so Zack could enter.

I waited in the doorway, leaning my back against the frame. Between chemistry and biology there were probably thirty pages to copy. I was hoping it was a fast copier as the tightness in my chest seemed to be creeping up on me again.

"What are you doing?" Zack motioned to me. "Get in here."

I slipped into the room and leaned against the counter across from where Doug sat on his futon. As soon as I did, I realized it was the same spot he'd almost kissed me. There was nothing to be done about it, though. He released Blondie, and she crossed the small space to me. I rubbed her head, and after a few minutes, she collapsed beside my feet. I was tired of standing and jumped up onto the counter to sit down. It was too silent, and I swung my legs back and forth for distraction.

Zack crossed over to me. "You look uptight, Mini-Girl."

"I just have to get through these tests."

"So this little cloud will magically lift at what time tomorrow?"

"I would say two, but then I have my shrink appointment. Let's say three-thirty."

"Mark was giving you a hard time tonight."

I shrugged. "He always does."

Doug had been silent the whole time, typing away on his laptop. We were keeping our voices fairly low, but he was only sitting four feet away. "What's he giving her a hard time about now?"

I hesitated, letting Zack answer. "He said he was glad she wasn't at the game."

"That was nice," Doug said.

I finally looked at him and his deep blue eyes dug into mine for a split second before I diverted my gaze. Desperate for a different subject, I asked a general question. "So what's new here? I haven't been to the house all week."

It was a Hail Mary. I definitely wouldn't have pointed it out otherwise, but I didn't want Zack bringing up Mark anymore.

Zack crossed back to the printer. "The mixer's tomorrow night. You should come."

Doug spoke up right away. "She can't come." Again his blue eyes seemed to pierce through me for the briefest second.

Zack turned to Doug. "Why? It'd be fun, besides Anna is trying to recruit her anyway? She won't mind."

Doug stood. "She's not your girlfriend, so she can't come."

Why was Doug being such a jerk? It wasn't like I wanted to watch girls hang all over them anyway.

Zack turned to me, smiling. "She could be my girlfriend." He took my hands.

This was new. Was he trying to get a reaction from Doug? "Thanks, Zack, but Lila and I are seeing a movie."

He stuck his lip out. "It'd be more fun with you there." He poked my rib. I hadn't been tickled in a long time, and I jerked back instantaneously. He narrowed his eyes, smiling. "Ticklish are we?"

"No, I'm not." I gave him a stern look and slid as far back on the counter as I could, my knees to my chest. "Finish the copying." I pointed to the copier.

Zack obeyed and I relaxed my stance. I tried not to look at Doug sitting directly in front of me, but it was impossible. Growing impatient, I jumped down from the counter and stood beside Zack. "Are they done yet?"

"Last one. You tired?"

"I've probably got an hour left in me."

"Good, I'm starving. Do you have anything to eat in your room besides spinach?"

"I'll make you a sandwich, no spinach."

"Good, we're done." He swatted at Doug's head with the copies. "See you at the gym."

Doug didn't look up. There was no way Zack hadn't notice the change since last week. One of us would have to explain something and soon.

I followed Zack to his car. "Wow, Doug's like crazy-stressed about something. I haven't seen him like this in a while. He say anything to you?"

I was in front of him on the stairs, so I didn't have to look at him.

"No, I haven't really talked to him since Monday."

"Don't take it personally. Ever since..." Zack stopped. He didn't finish. Could this be about Zoey? He shook his head. "Never mind."

In my room, I made Zack a sandwich and he inhaled it. I rarely stayed up late these days, but his energy was contagious. Elise came in just before two. She was as chatty and perky as ever. When she ducked into the bathroom, Zack whispered, "Is she always like this?"

"Yes, but it's worse when she drinks."

"You up for quizzing?"

"As long as you are."

Although it was late, I loved the diversion. I wanted to be exhausted so I wouldn't think after he left. We went through the chemistry and biology tests, and I felt confident. It was good he'd copied the tests for me, even if it meant twenty minutes of torture with Doug.

"Are you working out with us tomorrow?" Zack asked as I escorted him downstairs.

I cringed. "What time is it?"

"Half past two."

"I'm going to pass."

"Will I see you at the house tomorrow night?"

I had to think a minute. "Umm, maybe, it depends on Lila."

"Okay." He feigned punching my shoulder. We exchanged goodnights, and I headed back up. Elise was waiting to pounce.

"Is there anything to spill? I saw you smiling."

"I was smiling?"

"You were."

"Fine." I went into the bathroom to get ready for bed.

One thing I'd learned about my grief was how easily it would sneak up on me. It'd been the same when Bubbe had passed in March. I'd expected to cry myself to sleep after seeing Doug, but I didn't. Then, when I woke alone in my room this morning, I couldn't keep the tears away. I drew in a deep breath, and tried to relax, willing the tears to stop. They didn't.

I heard a quiet knock on the bathroom door. I had to pull it together. I knew grief, and I could get through it. Those counseling sessions during my Bubbe's illness and after her death had prepped me for this very situation. Depression, I was in the depression phase I told myself. Repeating the five stages of grief to myself, I blinked hard, forcing the tears away. Denial, anger, bargaining, depression, and acceptance, I was almost through.

Kate opened the door, a cup of coffee in each hand. New tears welled up in my eyes. Damn emotions.

"Sweetie, what is it? What's wrong?"

I shook my head, dug my nails into my hand, and forced myself to look at her.

"Okay, well, if you want to talk, I'm here. Elise said you were out of coffee." She handed me one of the cups.

I wiped my tears with the back of my hand. "Thanks. Do you want to walk to class together? I'll be ready in half an hour."

The coffee helped me get moving. I started the shower, splashing cold water on my face. Makeup would be worthless, so I brushed my teeth and pulled my hair back in a ponytail. I grabbed my comfiest jeans and tank top and then looked through my sweatshirts. My fraternity hoodie was right on top. I threw it on the floor, choosing a gray Northwestern one instead. After gathering my things, I knocked on Kate's door, anxious to get out my room.

At the Student Union, we bought some muffins, and found a table. This was good. There were no memories of Doug associated with this place. I forced myself to relax. I had ten minutes, so there was no need to rush. But with no appetite, I only picked at the muffin.

Kate detailed her upcoming camping trip, further distracting me from my sadness. Tossing out our trash, we made our way to the chemistry building. We found Lila leaning against a wall outside the lecture hall.

She greeted me with a hug. "Late night? Any details I should know about?"

"Zack was really nice to help me study."

"And?"

"That's it. We dropped by the house to copy tests, and then studied in my room until late."

"You're killing me." She shoved me away. "But Elise was fun to hang out with. She's a crazy lady."

In between tests, I walked to the library but couldn't go in. It seemed shrouded with my depression. I found a secluded courtyard and caught up on phone calls and reviewed my calendar. I had several tutoring sessions. There was an away game, and I'd have to find an excuse for not joining my friends at the house. Starting to worry about how comfortable I'd become with lying, I realized I needed more to fill my days. My isolation was beginning to make me antsy.

Most of all, I was dreading my appointment with the counselor. I'd have to be honest with her about how I was handling my grief and how empty I felt inside. Worse, I'd have to tell her I was still deceiving my friends. Lying to them was not only wrong but probably psychologically unstable.

"Hi." A voice pulled me out of my misery. Stephen stood in front of me. "Can I join you?" So much for my secluded courtyard.

We made plans for a couple of runs over the weekend. Excited to have another non-fraternity activity, I stored his number in my phone. After my biology test, I had my counseling appointment. With a half hour wait, there was just enough to feel lonely again. Maybe, if I told Lila, I wouldn't feel as bad. As soon as the thought entered my mind, I talked myself out of it. As expected, the counselor was concerned I wasn't sharing my pain with my friends. Still, I wasn't willing to risk exposing Doug or myself.

Is this me?

Walking from the medical center to my dorm, I phoned Lila.

"Hey girlie, you free and clear of that psych stuff now?" she said when she answered.

"I am." I smiled despite myself.

"Whatcha up to now? Are you coming to the house?"

"I thought I'd go for a run since I missed my workout this morning."

"People here want to see you." Suddenly her voice was melodic. There was a pause and shuffling noise. "She's going to the gym!" she yelled into the background.

"Give me the phone." It was Zack. "Hey, can I come?"

"Didn't you already work out?"

"I'm always up for a workout, and I'm supposed to be your trainer, right?"

Even with feeling lonely, my habit of isolating beckoned me. Being alone was safe, but it contributed further to my loneliness. It was a vicious circle, and I was watching it swirl around me. In my current state, I'd probably never stop running.

He didn't wait for an answer. "If you still have some Gatorade, bring two. I'll meet you outside the gym in fifteen minutes."

There were a few seconds of background noise and Lila was back. "What's going on?"

"I guess I'm working out with Zack."

"I think he may be sweet on you," she half-whispered. "We still on for the movie?"

"You're crazy. He just wants to get out of working at the house. But, yes to the movie. I'll call you when I'm done at the gym."

Walking to my room to change, I considered Lila's assessment. Deciding she was wrong, I pushed the thought from my mind. I stuffed two Gatorade bottles into my workout bag, changed, and jogged down the stairs and to the gym.

Zack was waiting for me on the sidewalk. Maybe because of my obsession with Doug, I hadn't thought about how handsome Zack looked since my first day on campus. I berated myself, blaming Lila for initiating that thought. He closed the gap between us, picking me up and twirling me around.

He set me down. "That is okay now right?"

"Yep, noggin's good as new." I pretended to knock on my head.

"What are we doing?"

"Definitely a long run."

Neither of us said much as we stretched and got on the treadmill. I was focused on ridding my psyche of the unbearable feelings. Running helped, and although I put on my headphones, I still couldn't listen to music. I didn't know how far into my run I was when it felt like I was being watched. I turned, and Zack was staring. He chuckled and rolled his eyes.

"A bit serious today, are we?" He pointed to the readout on my treadmill. It read forty-four minutes and five miles.

I hit the stop button. "How long have you been watching?"

"Just a few minutes. You had me at four and a half miles" He threw me a moist towel. We cooled down and stretched out before heading to the weight room. It was packed with lots of seriously beefy guys. It made me nervous, and I shuffled closer to Zack.

"Don't worry," he leaned down to whisper in my ear. "They don't bite, at least not most of them. Just stick close."

Normally he would have set me up on a machine and then taken the one next to me, but today we had to wait in line. The atmosphere was so foreign I found myself being spontaneous with conversation for the first time in over a week.

Zack was bench pressing and his phone buzzed. "Can you get that?"

I dug in Zack's bag, and found the phone. Doug's name was displayed on the screen. I held it out to Zack. "It's Doug."

"Answer it," he directed without pausing his workout.

Ugh, I thought, reminding myself to breathe. "Hello."

"Umm, hi," Doug said. "Is Zack there?"

He didn't know it was me. Perfect! I held the phone out to Zack, and he shook his head again. I shot him an angry look.

"He's bench pressing right now."

"Amanda?"

Dammit. "Yes." I gritted my teeth fighting a sigh.

"Are you guys working out?"

"Yes."

"Well, tell Zack we have this little thing called a social tonight and he needs to be here." I had been totally right about Zack wanting to get out of work at the house.

"Okay, I'll tell him to call you."

"Thanks, Amanda."

So, now I was Amanda again? Did he have to say my name that way? I shook it off.

"What'd he want?" Zack asked, standing up.

I shook his phone. "Oh, so now you're available. The social? Ring a bell?"

"You're funny. Guess we should wrap it up."

As we were walking out of the gym, Zack's phone buzzed again and he answered.

"Sorry, I was finishing a workout with Amanda." He winked at me. "We're going to get something to eat. I'll be there in about an hour." Slipping the phone in his bag, he turned to me. "You want to get something to eat? Oh, and can I shower at your place?"

"Sure," I told him, surprised at my, now full, evening schedule.

"Perfect." He smiled, pointing the way toward his car.

I took my shower first and dressed while he took his. He pulled his shirt over his head as he came out of the bathroom, his hair still wet. His chest was perfectly chiseled, and I chastised myself again for this line of thought. I'd had enough humiliation at that house for a lifetime.

For dinner, we went to an Italian place in downtown Evanston. I had planned on making Lila meet me at the dorm, but I couldn't think of a way out of it, so I rode to the house with him afterwards. Stepping inside, my chest tightened seeing Doug.

"You're late."

Zack shrugged. "You knew I would be."

I pointed upstairs, eager to be away from Doug. "I'm going to find Lila."

I turned to go but felt a tug on my jacket. Zack pulled me towards him. "Hey, that was fun."

"Yeah, it was, thanks," I told him.

"She can't stay," Doug called from across the room. My heart rate jumped, and I envisioned punching him in the nose. Really? Again? He turned back as he walked away. "Nothing personal, Amanda."

"Jeez." Zack rolled his eyes, turning to follow Doug.

Finding Lila, we chose our movie and made our way downstairs. Passing through the front room, Zack called to me.

"Hey Manda, will you be back tonight?"

Lila answered. "The second this thing is over."

It was great to get out with Lila and the movie was perfectly mindless. Of course she had planned for us to arrive back at the house exactly at eleven. I tried to weasel out of going back with her, but she didn't go for it. Fighting a sea of girls exiting the front door, we found Ross and Mark cleaning up. Lila and I hung out upstairs and waited for them to finish. She waited until everyone was congregated to badger me.

"So, Manda's ditching us for the game tomorrow."

I rolled my eyes. Did she have to start with that?

"What?" Zack asked, bumping me with his arm.

"She's working. How boring is that?" Lila hit me on the leg.

Mark pulled a chunk of my hair. "That's lame."

I didn't care if I was lame.

Chapter 13

Thanks to workouts, tutoring, and babysitting, my weekend was Doug-free. Our Sunday night dinners were becoming tradition, and Lila, Ross, Mark, Zack, and Bill arrived just after five-thirty. Zack greeted me with his official hug-spin move.

"So Doug's bailing again, something about studying. I told him next time he had to call you, because I wasn't making excuses for him anymore."

It helped that we were both avoiding each other. I got Latino club, he got the fraternity house, and the gym was Switzerland. No one felt compelled to tease me at all, which felt like a first. As everyone filed out to get some studying done, Zack hung back.

"What are you up to the rest of the night?"

"Laundry." Laundry was the worst. You had to lug your loads down to the cold basement along with a handful of quarters and wait for a machine. It took hours, unless you were Lila. She'd complained to her dad, and he'd agreed to pay for a laundry service.

Mark wasn't out of earshot. "You could come to the house to do your laundry."

Zack tugged my arm. "Nah, come to my place. I have a washer and dryer in my apartment."

"I don't want to impose."

"Bring your books. I was just going to study anyway." He picked up my laundry hamper and set it next to the door. I gathered my books and computer, and he carried my laundry basket down to his car. At his apartment, I started the first load, and we settled into studying on his couch. I'd worried I wouldn't get much accomplished, but he was focused on his computer the whole night. Even with changing out the loads immediately, it was after midnight before I finally finished. Folding the last load and stacking it in my basket, I yawned.

Zack got up and stretched. "You could sleep here? You can have the bed and I'll take the couch."

Even in my studying overload state, I knew he was being ridiculous. "Right, so the super tall guy will sleep on the couch and the miniature girl will sleep on the huge bed? Deciding a sleepover was beyond my comfort zone, I declined the offer. I hoped I wasn't putting him out too much asking him to drive me back to my room. I mentioned it, and he was totally cool. When we arrived at my dorm, he helped me carry my laundry up to my room.

Convinced that Zack was romantically interested in me, Elise started asking about our evening the second he was gone. She was bummed when I told her nothing happened. I reminded her that she'd said I should stay away from him. She reminded me how boring I was. This I knew.

* * *

Try as I might to shake off the image with coffee and the morning news, I paced my dorm room floor, my heart racing. I'd woken suddenly from a dream in which I was falling off a cliff. The dream had loosened another memory or dream, I wasn't sure which. Freaked out, I called Elise, who confirmed it was an actual memory and not just some erotic dream about Doug. I couldn't get the moment out of my head: I'd shot awake, screaming and shivering uncontrollably. He'd wrapped me in his warm arms and held me tight against his chest.

Hoping a run would eradicate the memory from my brain, I threw on my workout clothes and ran to the gym. It was not to be, as Doug was the sole runner on the treadmills. I almost turned around, but he noticed me and I was trapped. I warmed up, trying to avoid looking at him. All I could think of was his smell, and his warm chest and huge arms encircling me. Did I mention the memory to him? No, none of what happened before mattered now, I reminded myself.

Taking extra time with my stretches, I thought about which treadmill to take. I preferred not to be next to his now gleaming chest, but it would look weird if Zack and Bill came in and I was at the other end. Fortunately, before the chasm in my chest fully re-opened Zack and Bill joined us.

The rest of my Monday was inconsequential, save dodging questions from Maria at the Latino club meeting. She was like a fly on honey.

"Hola, missed you last week. Where's Doug?"

I knew she didn't miss or care about me, just Doug. "He had other stuff."

She laughed. "Yeah, that's what they always say right before they dump you."

"We weren't..." It didn't matter what I was going to say, because she walked away before I could finish my statement.

My tenacious adherence to my Doug avoidance strategy meant I didn't have to see Doug again till Wednesday at the gym. Mark didn't care if I ever came back to any of the intramural games, and by six-thirty Thursday night, I thought I was in the clear for that day too. Five till seven, my phone buzzed. It was a text from Zack.

AREN'T YOU COMING TO THE GAME?

STUDYING.

OKAY, WELL, I'LL CALL YOU AFTER.

My phone rang at exactly nine. It was Zack.

"Hey, how was the game?" I asked.

"Good, we won. I'm going to shower and then come pick you up. I'll call when I'm right outside the door." He hung up before I could get in any excuse.

Guessing there was no use in resisting, I looked through my closet for something sexy. If there was any possibility Doug was going to be there, I was going to look hot. Elise was mixing drinks and handed me one. One drink and fifteen minutes later,

I found a cream lacey camisole top and soft leather vest at the end of the row. I pulled on some jeans and my fringed suede boots, impressed with my bold choice. I'd let my hair partially air dry, and the soft curls ended up being the perfect pairing to my outfit.

Zack buzzed when he was pulling up, and I took the stairs for speed. As I walked towards his sport utility vehicle, Doug emerged from the front seat. I forced myself to exhale, ducking past him as he held the door for me. I took the seat Doug had just vacated next to Zack.

Zack looked me up and down. "Hey, sweetie, you look good. Is that new?"

"Have you seen her closet?" Doug asked leaning forward. "She has enough outfits to never wear anything twice."

Why was Doug even in this conversation? My being angry at him felt easier than dealing with wanting him.

Zack gave me a confused look. "I didn't realize you were into clothes."

"Marissa and Lila stock my closet."

"Well, wherever they came from, I like it!" Zack squeezed my knee.

At the bar, I ended up sitting in the corner between Bill and Zack with Doug directly across from me. Zack shook a menu in front of me, asking if I wanted anything. My stomach felt queasy just thinking of Doug, much less sitting across from him.

"No, I'm good," I told Zack.

"I know that. But are you hungry?"

"Funny." I rubbed my hand along his stubbly cheek. It was an automatic movement, but I realized it could've been construed as flirting. I sat on my hands so I wouldn't touch him again. Why was I anxious about it? I wished Doug would disappear.

Zack, Bill, Doug, and I chatted at our end of the table for a while. Stephen showed up, and Lila waved him toward me. Doug had retreated into the world of his phone, and I was content to be entertained by Zack and Bill. Then again, my amusement could've been due to the shot Zack added to my soda. After a while, Zack started giving Doug a hard time about being on his phone.

"What's the matter? Trouble in paradise?"

Doug shook his head, and Zack took his phone from him. "You talked to her before we picked Amanda up."

Wanting nothing to do with this conversation, I got up to sit with Lila. Zack grabbed my arm. "Where are you going?"

"To talk to Lila."

"Save me a dance."

Thinking there might be something to Elise's assessment of Zack's feelings for me, I squeezed in between Mark and Lila. "I thought you'd never come talk to us. Any news from down at the other end? Looks like Zack is giving Doug a hard time about something."

Not knowing what my face might betray, I didn't look directly at her. "Some girl, from what I could tell."

"Probably Zoey, I hear they're talking again."

"Zoey, as in ex-Zoey?"

She nodded. "The very same. What about Stephen over there?"

"What about him?"

"You not into him? Only Zack now?"

"Zack and I are friends."

"Looked like some flirting to me."

"That's how we always are." It was true, but it wasn't. Tonight felt different. I pulled her up and pushed her towards the dance floor as a distraction.

Zack found me after a few songs and we danced together. It was crowded and there was barely any space between us. I found myself enjoying being close to him but Maria appeared out of nowhere. "Hola, Chica." She inserted herself between us.

"Hola." I smiled at her as Zack spun around behind me.

"Nice friend." She rolled her eyes and danced away.

I fought sticking my tongue out at her. Why was she always so smug? Could it be I hadn't gotten Doug just as she knew I wouldn't? Zack left to get water and I stayed on the dance floor with Lyla. When the band started its second set, I got a tap on the shoulder.

"Curfew." Zack took my hand and dragged me away from the group.

Following us, Stephen laughed at me. "You look like a kid being taken from an amusement park. I don't think I've ever seen you pout before."

Zack turned back to Stephen. "You haven't been around her enough. She has pouting down to a science."

I spun to face him, hands on hips. "I do not."

He leaned down so he was eye level with me. "It's actually one of the cutest things you do."

I followed him to our table thinking that now I may be into him. We gathered our jackets and Stephen picked up his glass of water.

"Are we running this weekend?"

I pulled out my phone and checked my calendar. "Sure, I'll text you."

Armed with his answer, Stephen headed back into the crowd. As Zack, Bill, Doug, and I filed out, one of the freshmen football players, Justin, approached us. We had calculus together and had chatted on the bus. "Hey Amanda, so this is your crowd? I thought you were a freshman?"

I stopped to answer him. "Yeah, I am. Do you know Zack, Bill, and Doug?" I forced myself to say Doug's name and motioned towards Justin. "Justin has calculus with me."

"I helped you that day on the bus, too."

Zack, Doug, and Bill formed a line beside me, and Justin backed up. Hesitating, he stepped forward and shook each of their hands. "Rowing, right?"

Zack took my hand. "Right."

Justin came to stand in front of me again. "I haven't seen you around lately."

"I haven't been taking the bus."

"Oh, well maybe I'll catch you here another time."

Without a free arm to gesture with I felt weird and shrugged. "Sure."

He turned and jogged to catch up with his friends at their car.

Doug turned to me. "Nice friend."

"What's wrong with him?" He didn't get to pick my friends, especially since he didn't want to be one.

Zack wrapped an arm around my waist guiding me towards the car. "Nothing if you want to get gang raped. His friends have a bad rep. You know that guy?"

"From class and the bus. You think he's a rapist because he's a football player? It's like saying you're stuck-up snobs because you're Greek and you row."

"We are stuck-up snobs. He may not be a rapist, but I can assure you lots of his friends are close to it."

"Okay, warning heeded." I held up my hand.

"Are you actually listening to us about something?" Doug asked.

I looked straight at him. "Not you, him." I pointed at Zack. It was a train of thought outburst, but I was damn proud of it. He looked at me wide-eyed for a second and then shook his head. I felt the familiar ping of his loss. Who was I kidding, ping? More like a stake through my heart. But I'd made my point and couldn't take the words back now.

Zack put his hand out for a fist bump. "Okay, we gotta get back."

There wasn't any conversation on the ride home, and I bounced my leg. Zack put his hand on it, stopping my motion. "Much adrenaline after that show?"

At my dorm, he put the car in park. "You're coming to the game on Saturday, right? You'll get to meet Zoey."

I bit my lip, trying to think of something fast. I didn't even know Zoey was back in the picture until tonight, and I certainly didn't want to see Doug with her. "Actually, I was thinking about going to see Tia."

"Your sister in Milwaukee?" Zack asked.

"It's been a couple of weeks, and I miss her."

"That'll make like three weekends in a row you've ditched us. How are you getting there?"

"I'll probably take a bus." I was pretty sure there would be a bus I could get there on. Feeling uncomfortable with how good I was getting at lying, the word pathological surfaced in my thoughts. The second thought I had along these lines was that I should be going to Mass and confession. I'd have to make a long list for that priest.

"Why don't we drive up together? I haven't been home all quarter."

I didn't know what to say. Zack's offer was unexpected, especially since it was for a make believe trip. All I knew was I didn't want to hang out with Doug and Zoey. Why hadn't I just kept my mouth shut?

Doug leaned forward from the back seat. "Aren't you forgetting rowing?"

"We could leave after. Would that work? I could pick you up by eleven at the latest."

What a hole I'd dug! "Wow, umm, maybe, I was planning to firm things up with Tia tomorrow."

"Think about it. I could drop you at your sister's and pick you up in the evening."

Uncomfortable with making plans with a guy I might be attracted to in front of one that I had been in love with, I fidgeted in my seat. "Okay, and thanks for the ride. Tonight was fun." I turned to see Doug opening my door.

I jumped out, and he closed it behind me. "Sorry about tonight. I didn't realize you were coming."

"No worries," I said, realizing that the drinks and Zack had served semi-nicely as distractions.

The next morning, my first task was to talk to Tia. She answered her phone immediately. I never called her at work, so I knew she'd assume something was going on. I explained that I wanted to visit and she peppered me with questions. Why this weekend? Why the short notice? Why wasn't I going to the game?

She and Ed were hosting an alumni club party and I was invited to join them. She indicated that she'd love help hosting. Then there was the inevitable question of how I was getting there. Deciding that I would get caught in a lie, I told the truth.

There was a few seconds of silence before she responded to my answer. "Zack, as in Doug's friend, Zack?" The tone was there. Tia was not my cheerleader sister. Although very sweet, she tended to be more critical. "So you're glomming onto Zack now that Doug's with Zoey again?"

Wondering how she already knew about Doug and Zoey, I defended myself. "No, I told Zack I was thinking of going to Milwaukee and he offered a ride. His parents don't live far from you." Damn, I didn't need this.

"But this all happened before you talked to me?"

"I was thinking out loud." That hadn't been a complete lie.

"And why do you want to come visit us?"

If I were Marissa, I would have played the drama card and acted hurt. "It's been a stressful quarter and I need a breather." That much was totally true.

"Sweetie, Thanksgiving is next week."

"You guys are closer than Champaign for a day trip."

"So you won't be staying overnight?"

"Not if I ride with Zack. He has rowing early Sunday."

Perhaps deciding she'd gotten all the information she was going to out of me, she acquiesced to my visitation plan. "Okay, well, that'll be fine. You can bring Zack to the party if you want. That way you'll know someone. I think he probably knows Zoey's friends, right?"

"Zoey's friends?"

"Yeah, she and a couple of people from her crowd live here, so we see them at alumni events." Aha, I thought, that was the reason she knew Zoey and Doug were back together.

As soon as I ended the call, my phone buzzed with a text from Zack.

THOUGHT I'D PICK YOU UP FOR THE GYM. IT'S FREAKING COLD, AND WE CAN FIGURE OUT TOMORROW.

SURE, THX, JUST TALKED TO TIA.

SEE YOU IN FIVE TO TEN.

FIFTEEN? DO YOU WANT COFFEE? ELISE MADE A POT.

BLACK.

KAY, SEE YOU IN FIFTEEN.

I put down the phone and found my workout clothes. Ten minutes later, I was downstairs with coffee in hand. As we drove I told him about Tia's party and he was excited to be invited. We parked in the gym lot and turning off the motor he turned to me. "Okay, so, my mom would love for you to come for dinner."

Zack's invitation caught me off guard. This had become a much bigger deal than I'd imagined. My day hanging out at Tia's watching football was turning into the social marathon of the season. Before I could say anything, Zack continued.

"You don't have to come. I think it'd be fun for you to meet my family. My mom's a little over the top, but—"

I shook my head at him. "That sounds great. I'd like that."

Thinking, Tia's main hesitation with my visit was that she would be entertaining for half her weekend, I figured this would be a good compromise.

Chatting about his family, we walked to the cardio area. Doug and Bill were already there, with machines picked out. We ran a quick three and then Zack and I paired up for strength training. Halfway through the workout, Bill came over and we switched partners. As long as I didn't have to be anywhere near Doug's bare chest, I was good.

He spotted me on the bench press. "So you seem better than a last week."

"Sorry, I didn't realize you were worried."

"Well you looked pretty distraught that day, but I guess you're allowed with the way your quarter's gone. Nobody else seemed to think anything was wrong."

My injury was nothing compared to the pain of a broken heart. I'd rather have my head smashed into a gymnasium floor several times than lose someone like Doug again. "I'm good," I heard myself say. It was a bit of a stretch, but I was on my way.

"Good to hear, and last night was fun. That was long overdue."

I agreed and we finished our workout chatting about sports. Grabbing some water afterwards, I checked my phone to find it was almost ten. I'd have to rush to get in a shower, change, and get to class. It seemed crazy, but being busy felt good. It left me no time to dwell on what I didn't have.

I made it to class in the nick of time. Afterwards, I considered not telling Lila about my trip with Zack. I knew I had to though, so I tried to work it in casually.

She grabbed my arm. "When did this happen? Did you guys hook up last night?"

"No. I wanted to see my sister, and his family is there."

"Because you'd call me immediately if you hooked up with someone, especially Zack, right?"

"Of course."

"Are you into him?"

Maybe, I thought, but that would be completely stupid of me. "No, we've just been hanging out."

"You were just hanging out with Doug, and now you're just hanging out with his best friend?"

Yes, hanging out with Zack, was stupid, psychotic, and reputation ruining, just like I thought. "Will it look bad?"

"No one's talking yet. After tomorrow, they may be. Does Mark know?" Feeling like every move I made had to pass through a committee, I rolled my eyes at her.

"Okay, well, tootles. I'll miss you." She gave me a hug. "We still on for Sunday night?"

"As always," I told her.

With biology, my counseling appointment, a tutoring session, and babysitting, the rest of the afternoon and evening flew by. It was a late night, and I was exhausted from my packed week. But I was happy that I would be able to wake up tomorrow and not worry about seeing Doug for two whole days.

* * *

I met Stephen in the dorm lobby the next morning promptly at eight, coffee in hand.

He pointed at my cup. "That is decaf right?"

"No, is that bad? I had a cup last week too."

"For someone with a head injury, yes."

I threw the cup in the trash at the entrance to the gym. We ran seven miles at a nine-minute pace, and I was happy that I was ready to run with Dad on Thanksgiving. Leaving Stephen to his weight training, I hurried back to shower and wash my hair. I was just about to finish drying it when my phone rang. Zack indicated they were putting the boats away, and he would be over in about an hour.

I finished my hair and consulted with Marissa on my outfits. Grabbing a bag, I packed the second one neatly inside. Zack texted me when he arrived, and I hurried down to meet him.

He jumped out and helped me juggle getting the coffees and my bag inside. In the car, I realized it seemed different. Maybe it was just that he was newly showered and his hair was still wet. The whole car radiated with his scent, unlike Thursday night when all I could smell was Doug. But maybe it was because this felt like a date.

As we got closer to Milwaukee, he asked about Tia and my family. I summarized their history, and before I knew it, we were pulling into the parking lot of their building. Upstairs, Tia greeted us at the door. She gave me a quick squeeze and then shuffled us off to meet Ed.

We found him in front of the big screen with his buddies. Seeing me, he grabbed me and twirled me around. After introductions, he showed us to the guest room to freshen up.

Zack plopped down on the bed as I brushed my teeth in the bathroom. "I like Ed. This is going to be fun! So why is it people want to pick you up and spin you around?"

"I would love to know the answer to that question." I poked him with the end of my toothbrush.

"I have to think on it." He took a long draw on his beer. I could feel myself becoming more attracted to him and wondered if there should be louder alarms going off in my head. We headed back towards the TV, but Tia caught me. She dragged me into the kitchen and immediately started giving me the third degree.

"I talked to Marissa. She said you guys aren't seeing each other. Is that true? Why did he want to come up with you? Isn't he a bit old?"

"He's a friend."

She stared directly into my eyes for a full minute. It was her interrogation strategy. I knew it well. All you had to do was stare back without looking away.

"Okay, fine." She threw her hands in the air. "You and your guy friends. I'll never get it. Here, help me refresh the chips, and I'll introduce you to everyone." She handed me three bags, and I followed her out of the kitchen.

Her circuit began with the guys watching the game. She asked Zack to join us so she could introduce him to people as well. He kept close to me, his hand on my back.

As we made our way into the dining area, a tall blonde girl crossed the room to us. "Zack, I can't believe it! You look great!" She inserted herself between us and wrapped him up in a hug. "What are you doing here? Wow, isn't it crazy that Zoey is down at Northwestern and you're up here?"

"Jessica, it's great to see you." He stepped back and grabbed my hand.

Talk about out of the pot and into the fire, I would just as soon have ducked away.

Zack lifted our joined hands. "Amanda, this is Jessica, Ashley, Jennifer, and Stephanie. They're friends of Zoey's from the sorority. Amanda is Tia's sister."

I greeted them, smiling and shaking each outstretched hand. These hands were connected to very long arms, and the arms to shoulders that towered over me. Each girl looked just as I would have expected from seeing the picture of Zoey in the yearbook, tall and beautiful.

"So what do you think about Zoey and Doug? Can you believe they're back together?" Ashley asked Zack.

He shook his head, looked at the floor, and then back up at her. I don't think I'd ever seen such a grave look on Zack's face. "Doug's never gotten over her. He's been miserable since she broke it off. I just hope it doesn't happen again, for his sake and mine."

Stunned at his raw honesty, I scanned the girls for their reaction. Each one stared bug-eyed and mouths agape at Zack. The truth was finally laid out in front of me. How hard would it have been for Doug to tell me earlier? A loud commotion from the TV room brought me out of my inner turmoil.

Zack motioned towards the TV. "I'm going to see what's going on."

They all looked between each other for an awkward moment. Jessica finally looked at me. "So you're a friend of Zack's?"

"Yes," I said, trying to shake off the intensity of the conversation. "A friend of mine is a brother, so we all hang out." I was impressed at how fast I put together a coherent explanation of how I knew Zack.

"So what happened to your arm?" Ashley asked.

"I hurt it playing volleyball."

Stephanie spoke next. "Wait, are you the girl Doug crashed into at the gym?" Like I needed to be reminded, this conversation was exactly what I'd come here to get away from. "And you know Anna, right?" She crossed over to stand beside me. "Anna said Doug was so upset about you getting hurt. It was so nice of him to help you out. She said you might rush in the winter."

Wow, that was a lot. "I'm thinking about it," I lied.

"You'd love being Greek. You meet so many girls who end up being your best friends."

I had the feeling this was morphing into a recruitment talk. Thankfully, Tia returned and saved me. "Can you help in the kitchen?" She turned to the four girls. "Sorry to drag her away."

"Not a problem. Good luck in rush. You'll love it," Stephanie said.

Thanking them, I excused myself to the kitchen.

Tia plopped a bowl of dip in my hand. "Wow, how'd you get yourself into that? Are you really rushing?"

"No, I was just being nice." I shuddered at the thought. That would be way too many females in one room for me. I made sandwiches for myself and Zack and made my way to the entertainment room.

I sat on the floor in front of him. He leaned in close and whispered. "So, you survived Jessica and her gang?" I nodded and he squeezed my shoulder. I lounged against his chair nestled between his shins the rest of the game. When the guests left, we helped Tia clean up and had her condo ship-shape in an hour's time. Thankfully, there was still football on, and Ed was so into the game he didn't have time to pick on me much. As it was, he only bugged me during commercials getting in a few head injury and one-armed girl jokes. He was definitely off his game.

Around five I excused myself to change and freshen up. Tia followed me into the guest room. Marissa had told her about my experience with Doug. Given her tendency towards criticism, I was wary of her response. Thankfully, Marissa had been thorough in her description of my relationship with Doug, and Tia was surprisingly supportive.

We left Tia's place right at five-thirty. Zack described his family on the twenty minute drive. He had three siblings. David, was a senior and just a few months younger than me, Dana was sixteen, and Joshua was thirteen. His mom required them to be home for Saturday dinners, so they would all be there.

We turned into an older neighborhood, with well-maintained homes and yards. The area reminded me of Bubbe's neighborhood where she'd lived in Chicago. Nervous, I fiddled with my sleeve.

He took my hand. "They are going to love you. But just so you're not caught off guard, my mom knows everything about you. She calls every day and won't get off the phone until I talk for like half an hour. So, I mostly tell her stuff about my friends."

I bit my lip. "I'm not nervous at all now."

Zack laughed, parking the car. We hopped out and made our way up the walk to the front door. Zack's mom opened the door before we were barely on the porch.

His mom crossed to me, wrapping her arms around me. "Oh, my goodness, look at her." She stepped back, placing her hands on each side of my face. "Such pretty skin, eyes, and hair...." She lifted a strand of my hair. "You said she was beautiful, Zack, but—"

"I told you she's not Jewish Mom."

His mom looked me up and down. By now my face was completely ablaze. "She definitely could be, look at her."

"I have my Bubbe to thank for my coloring."

Smiling, she pointed at Zack. "See, she has a Bubbe." She took my hand and pulled me into their house. Zack's father waited in the entry way.

"Zachary, Zack is here with Amanda. Entertain them while I check on dinner."

He shook my hand and led us into the front room. I leaned into Zack. "You said I was beautiful?"

"I think I agreed that you were pretty, but don't let it go to your head."

"How about some drinks?" his dad asked as we were seated.

"I'll take a beer, and she'll have a glass of red."

His dad got drinks from the bar, as his mom returned with appetizers. She moved into the hall and called out. "Dinner in fifteen minutes," then hurried back to the kitchen.

His dad slapped his knee. "Oh my, she's been so excited all day. She's been driving me nuts worrying about the dinner. You know how she gets."

Zack leaned towards his father. "She didn't have to do anything special."

His dad waved a hand in the air. "I know, but I couldn't convince her otherwise." He looked to me. "So, Amanda, you're a pretty brave little lady meeting Zachary's mother. How did you two meet?"

My face flushed again. This felt like a much bigger deal than Zack had portrayed it. Zack saved me. "Her dad is an alumnus of the fraternity."

"What are you going to do when you graduate?"

"Translating, probably. Maybe diplomatic protocol."

Zack's mother floated back into the room. "Oh, Zackary, what are you asking her that for? She has plenty of time to decide. And what are you doing giving her this wine? Her parents would kill us."

"Amanda's a freshman. She's a language major like Doug." Zack looked to his mother. "The wine will be fine, Mom, relax."

She wrung her hands together. "I guess, well dinner's about ready. I'm going to get your brothers and sister."

Zack heaved his body off the couch. "I'll go." Although the house was a good size, it seemed miniature with him moving through it.

His dad waved his glass towards me. "I would ask you about your arm, but I don't want you to have to repeat yourself at dinner. Sorry about my wife. She gets a bit excited, and you're the first girl Zack has brought home since high school."

"We're not—" I started.

He laughed. "I know. That's the one thing she actually bothered to tell me."

The sound of multiple bangs and bumps came from upstairs, and it seemed like the ceiling was going to fall in on us any second.

"Is it as noisy in your house? Abigail mentioned you have a sister here in Milwaukee, do you have any other siblings?"

"A younger sister, she's a senior in high school. Our house is a bit quieter."

"Ah, your dad must be a total wreck with three girls. I've only got one, and she worries me to death."

"He deals by being away a lot."

Just then Zack's sister appeared in the doorway, hands on her hips. "Are you going to stop them?"

He stood, waving her in the room. "They'll get hungry eventually. Dana, this is Zack's friend, Amanda."

Tall and blond, like Zack, she seemed to slink into the room. We exchanged greetings. I heard heavy footsteps on the stairs, and one of Zack's brothers darted into the room.

"Wow, what happened to your arm?"

"I hurt it playing volleyball."

"Volleyball? You don't look like the volleyball type."

I laughed and held up my cast. "That's probably why my arm looks like this."

Just then there was more commotion on the stairs, and Zack and his youngest brother half-wrestled each other into the room. Josh stopped short when he saw me. He wasn't as tall as Zack and David, but you could tell he was well on his way.

Just then his mom called everyone to the table. After the blessing, Zack's dad refilled the wine glasses. I made a mental note not to drink more until I'd eaten something. Zack's mom had made an amazing amount of food that all smelled wonderful.

As soon as the plates were filled, his mom asked about my Bubbe. Zack squeezed my hand under the table, and I took a deep breath. I told them how Bubbe, my dad's mother, was separated from her family and held in a concentration camp in France during The Holocaust. Her mother and younger sister were interned in Germany, and came to Chicago after the war. A year later, they learned Bubbe was living in an abbey in France. They were able to bring her to the U.S., but she had converted to Catholicism and only knew French, and the transition was hard.

His mother hung on my every word. "No wonder you're so interested in languages."

Dana leaned towards me. "Is your hair naturally curly?"

"Oh no, they're going to talk hair," David warned.

"You girls can talk after dinner," his mom said.

Dana shot a mean look at her brother. Then, the worst possible subject change came.

"Poor Doug, I'm so glad he's back with Zoey," Zack's mother commented.

"They're back together?" Dana asked.

"Seem to be," Zack said, looking to me. "Amanda hasn't met her yet."

"Wait, how doesn't Amanda know Zoey?" David asked.

"Amanda's only a freshman. I forget because it seems like she's been hanging out with us forever."

"You won't like Zoey," Dana said.

"She's met Anna and Zoey's other friends. You liked them, right Amanda?"

"Anna seems nice." At least that wasn't a lie.

"So are you rushing?" Dana asked.

"I'm not sure yet. I've met a lot of people and have gotten involved with a couple of clubs already."

"Smart girl, you don't need the extra stress," Zack's dad put in.

When everyone was finished, I offered to help with the dishes. I was glad when his mom accepted my help and Dana joined us. She asked more questions about my hair as we cleaned up. Finishing, I brought my bag in from the car and tried some of my products on her hair.

"I don't mean to be rude, I know you were really hurt, but I don't think I'd mind being nursed back to health by Doug Taylor. He is seriously the hottest guy ever."

I laughed despite myself. "Quite a few people think that."

"So you're pretty into Zack. He's not a bad guy, even if he is a pain sometimes."

She hadn't phrased the comment as a question, and her assessment surprised me. Was I into Zack? Did I think of him as more than a friend? I did find him attractive and enjoy being with him.

Zack tapped on the door. "Is everyone beautiful now?"

"Amanda is a genius," Dana said, smoothing her hair. "Thank you." She hugged me.

I squeezed her back. "You're welcome, but it's not me."

"She's not being modest, her sister dresses her. You should see her closet. Twenty pairs of shoes, a bazillion outfits, all picked out by Marissa."

Zack's mom poked her head in the doorway. "I think we'll play Monopoly if you guys are up for it?"

Zack looked to me, and I nodded.

"We'll be down in a few minutes," he answered. Then, he turned back to me. "Want a tour of the rest of the house?"

"Lead the way," I told him, excited to learn more about this guy who was becoming more attractive by the second. We walked down the hall to Zack's old room. Josh and David had shared a room until Zack moved to school, so now Josh had Zack's room. The room looked pretty much like I expected. The walls were covered with posters of athletes, models, and bands. Zack led me over to his corner of the room. There was a twin bed that looked like it would be way too small for him. On the wall, a set of shelves held trophies, books, and pictures. As I got closer I could see photos from the rowing team and fraternity. The trophies were three deep, sporting plates that indicated rowing, hockey, and cross country.

We paged through his yearbooks till his brother called us down for the monopoly game. When we joined his family downstairs, he pulled me aside. "Buy anything and everything. No survivors."

As partners, Zack and I sat across from each other. David flirted with me shamelessly, and Zack rolled his eyes. I studied him, with his long nose, broad chin and infectious smile, thinking he had a wonderful face.

Josh and Dana were focused on the win. Zack's dad sat behind me and coached me at every opportunity, which was always followed by complaining on Dana's part. I'd never seen people so serious about a game.

Zack's mom moved in and out of the room replacing drinks and snacks and correcting behavior whenever possible. Two hours in, they called the game, with David and Dana winning by a fair margin.

I thanked his parents, and we said our goodbyes. Halfway to the car, Zack grabbed my hand and pulled me to him.

"Tonight was good. I had fun. Thanks for coming."

"It was really good. I had a fun day. Thanks for driving." I dreaded heading back to the purgatory called Northwestern. Today had been a much-needed break. I hadn't realized just how unhappy I was. Definitely some changes were needed; I just wasn't sure what those were.

In the car, Zack patted my leg. "So I want details. Tell me things I don't know." He started peppering me with questions. "Do you play an instrument?"

"Piano, but not well."

He kept going, and I made him give an answer for each too. What was my favorite book? Who was my favorite author?

What was my favorite subject in school? What was my favorite place to visit?

"First person you kissed?" he asked after about twenty questions.

I hesitated, looking at him out of the corner of my eye.

"Mark," I said, covering my eyes. I couldn't believe I'd said it.

"Mark? Were you guys dating?"

"No, it was in seventh grade. We were playing spin the bottle."

"So you never dated him?"

"No, he's practically my brother." After we kissed that one time, we vowed to never do it again. It was too weird.

"So, who was the last person you kissed?"

This was embarrassing. It'd been way too long since I kissed someone, well, except Zack who'd kissed me on Halloween.

I smiled. "You!"

"I don't believe you, and that didn't count. You didn't kiss me back."

"I'm not lying."

He looked at me briefly. "Okay."

"So, what's with the inquisition?"

"Just gathering facts."

He asked for a soda, and I retrieved two from the cooler. Sipping the drink, I tried to think about something to talk to him about so he wouldn't continue the incessant questioning.

A big grin spread across his face. "So?"

I cut him off. "Nope, you can't ask any more questions."

"How about secrets?"

"What secrets?" I asked, rolling my eyes.

"I don't know. If I knew them, they wouldn't be secrets, would they? Something only Lila or your sisters know. Or maybe something no one knows."

"Tell me one of yours first," I demanded.

"Yeah, I don't have any. Your turn."

I totally believed he didn't have any secrets. Two months ago I would've been able to say I had none too, but my relationship with Doug had them piling up quickly.

His voice pulled me out of my mental spiral. "Who was your first, and how many people have you been with?"

I guessed he was talking about sex, which was a pretty personal topic, or at least it was to me. But, I'd had a really good day with him and found myself wanting to be closer to him. Plus, I sensed he was someone who could be trusted. I took a deep breath and said it. "I haven't been with anyone."

He looked at me, and then back at the road. "No one? Is this widely known?"

I was grateful for the darkness, sure my face was beet red. "Lila, Mark, Ross, and my sisters."

"So that's why they give you a hard time."

"Precisely."

"And it doesn't bother you?"

"What? No sex or them bugging me?"

He cleared his throat. "You do realize everyone else thinks it's sort of important."

"I do." There were a few moments of silence.

"I like knowing things about you." He rubbed my leg.

When I looked out the window, I realized we were almost back to campus. I dreaded going back to my room alone and facing my categorized life. His hand felt good on my knee, and I put my hand on his.

He gripped my hand and released it, making a turn into the dorm parking lot. "That drive flew by." He turned off the car.

Stretching my legs, I agreed.

He gripped the steering wheel, stretching out his arms. "I guess this is you."

We got out of the car and I retrieved my bag from the back seat. When I shut the door and turned around, he was inches from me. He took my bag and set it on the ground. When I looked up, he wrapped his hand around my neck, bent down, and kissed me. His warm lips and hand on my neck sent tingles down my spine. Unlike before, I kissed him back. Standing on my toes, I wrapped my arm around his back. His kisses became more insistent and his body pressed into mine, pinning me against the car.

Releasing my neck, he put his hand to my cheek. After a couple more short kisses, he stepped back. He traced his hand down my arm, and then took my hand in his. I looked up at him and he put a finger to my chin, leaning into me again. "I could kiss you all night." He looked towards my dorm.

I turned his cheek back so that he was looking at me. "I would like that." Had those words just passed my lips? Today had not turned out at all like I planned. For once this was a good thing.

In a second, his lips were on mine again. I stood on my toes, leaning into him.

He pulled away, setting his hand on my hips. "Did you think this would happen today? Did you want it to?"

I wasn't going to lie to him. I shook my head, raking my hair behind my ear. "No, I didn't realize you wanted this. I didn't know I wanted it until tonight."

"Wanted it when I kissed you or before?"

My face flushed, and I looked down. "No, earlier, at your house."

He kissed me again. "I wanted it too, and I'm glad it did." He spun my hand in his. "Are you seeing anyone?"

I'm not sure why but I hadn't expected that question. "No. I run with Stephen sometimes, but that's it."

"As long as you're not knocking bodies."

"Eww." I punched him, but he grabbed my hand, pulled me to him, and kissed me again.

"I want you to know that if we're dating, which is what I hope we're doing, I'm not dating around. It's only you." These words made me happy. A defined relationship was a good thing. He bent down and kissed me again. "Does that work for you?"

"Yes."

"Good." He smiled, swinging our hands between us. "I should walk you to your door. I have to be on the water at eight."

I didn't want the night to end. "I had a really good time today," I said, kissing him outside the door.

"Hey, you should come to the crew brunch with me tomorrow."

I definitely wanted to see him, but all of a sudden the relationship seemed overwhelming. Seeing him in private was one thing. But being with him, in public, possibly in the same room as Doug, scared me. Nonetheless, I accepted his invitation thinking I might as well pull the band aid off quick.

As I took the elevator to my room, I could still feel his warm lips on mine. He texted when he got home: HAD AN AWESOME TIME TODAY. CAN'T WAIT TO SEE YOU TOMORROW.

After replying to Zack, I sent texts to Marissa and Lila indicating I was back safe. Exhausted and happy, I fell asleep easily.

Chapter 14

The blare of morning news pulled me out of my sleep.

"Sorry, did I wake you?" Elise asked, turning the volume down quickly.

I pushed myself up on my good arm. "No, that's fine." Stretching, I tried to shake off the fuzziness from my sleep. I'd slept well and felt rested and happy. Happy, I was happy. It'd been too long since I could say that. Elise already had coffee in the pot, making it a perfect morning.

After my coffee, Elise crossed over to sit with me on my futon. "You seem happy. Does it have something to do with Zack?"

I cupped my hands over my ears, bracing for her reaction. "Yes."

I had to shush her so she didn't wake the whole dorm. As it was, Kate popped her head in through the doorway to make sure no one was hurt.

My phone buzzed, and I realized I'd forgotten my run with Stephen. Slipping on my gym clothes, I promised Elise I'd fill her in later. On the walk to the gym, I sent texts to Marissa and Lila. I had decided the night before I wasn't keeping secrets from my friends anymore. If they didn't like my choices, they would have to deal with it.

There was already a good morning text from Zack with details about the brunch. My texts to Marissa and Lila were vague "call me" messages. Meeting up with Stephen, I turned my phone off. I'd never get in my work out if they responded.

My run was great, and I zipped back to my dorm to have time to wash my hair. There was no point calling Marissa before ten, so the next task was to brave letting Lila in on my new dating status.

When I called, she picked up immediately. "Hey, I just got your text, what's up?"

"I thought you would want to know that Zack and I had a really fun day yesterday."

"And. . ." She waited maybe half a second. "OMG you didn't!" she screamed into the phone. "This is awesome! I am so happy for you!"

"What is going on?" I heard in the background.

"Don't tell Mark," I said quickly.

"He's not here, just Ross. Hold on."

"She hooked up with Zack," she said to Ross.

"No way, Mark's gonna freak."

"What, why?" she asked.

Great, this was a bigger deal than I thought. I relayed to her Mark's warning about Zack from the beginning of the quarter. Fortunately, she didn't share his opinion. Of course it could have been she was just excited for me to have any type of romantic relationship.

As we were finishing the conversation, Zack sent a text. I said goodbye to Lila and checked the message. They were just getting off the water. When I asked him what I should wear, he answered: CLOTHES ARE GOOD, BUT I WOULDN'T MIND IF YOU DIDN'T WEAR THEM.

HA HA, WHAT ARE YOU WEARING?

PANTS AND A SHIRT.

WHAT KIND OF PANTS?

WOW, THIS IS GETTING PERSONAL.

WHAT IS BILL'S DATE WEARING?

NOT COMING, NEITHER IS ZOEY. YOU MISSED HER AGAIN.

Almost wishing Zoey would be there, I finally got a description of Zack's attire out of him. I needed a dress and fortunately found one with side zipper. Just as I finished my makeup, Zack texted me that he was downstairs and that I should bring my computer and laundry for the afternoon. Hurrying to gather my things, my phone buzzed again. COME DOWN AND LET ME IN, YOU FREAK.

I slipped on my boots and went downstairs. As soon as he came through the door, he pulled me in and kissed me.

We took the elevator upstairs and he helped me throw my laundry and books into bags. "We still on for tonight?" Elise asked as we walked out the door. I'd forgotten about Sunday dinner, but we made plans to meet her for grocery shopping at four.

It was a short drive to the restaurant. Seeing Doug in the parking lot, I wished I hadn't come. Just three weeks ago, it was him that I wanted, but I pushed that thought from my brain. Getting out of the car, I stuffed my hands in my coat pockets and focused on steeping around the puddles.

Zack pulled at my arm. "You still good with us?"

I slipped my hand in his forcing a smile. "Yes, of course."

"Good." He pulled me to him.

Walking up the steps, I again focused on my shoes. "So, how was Milwaukee?" Bill asked as we reached them.

"Good." Zack and I said in unison.

"My family loved her." He squeezed my hand, and I looked to Doug for a reaction. I didn't see one. Why was I still wondering if he'd cared for me? Obviously he hadn't, our connection had been created by my psyche.

Doug's eyes were fixed on Zack. "Most people do." The words were light but his voice monotone.

Zack rocked back and forth on his heels. "It's too bad Zoey couldn't stay a couple more hours."

Mumbling some response, Doug turned to enter the restaurant. Zack motioned for me to go ahead of him. Wishing I could be anywhere else, I followed Doug and Bill inside.

The brunch was fun. The crew team was much bigger than I'd imagined. It turned out I'd only knew about half of the members. Zack introduced me to as many people as possible, including the coaches. He told anyone who would listen how I was going to be their new coxswain. Everyone rolled their eyes, along with me, when he detailed how he would whip me into shape once my cast came off. But by the end of the event, I almost believed him.

Zack and I sat next to Bill, with Doug directly across from us. Bill leaned into me as we were eating. "You and Zack, huh? Interesting way to shake things up."

I traced my fork around my plate. "Yeah, I guess."

As we were leaving, Doug approached us. "We need to talk about some house stuff. Can you come by later?"

He didn't look at me and I had to remind myself this is what we did. We avoided each other. Why did it still hurt? Because I still craved his company, no matter how it came. Couldn't we be friends now that we had both moved on?

Zack agreed to meet Doug at the house at five, which meant Zack wouldn't join us for dinner. I was disappointed, but it was probably better this way. It would give me a chance to share my news with Mark.

After the brunch, our studying session at Zack's apartment turned out to be more about kissing than work. This probably wasn't the best thing for my GPA. But driving to the grocery store, we made a pact to actually get some homework done later that night. With the end of the quarter looming, I definitely needed to.

We pulled into the grocery lot at exactly four to meet Elise. I wasn't sure if she expected Zack to tag along, but she didn't complain. After shopping, he dropped us off at our dorm. We were a little behind schedule thanks to Zack's need to provide humorous commentary on each shopping list item.

When Mark, Ross, and Lila arrived, Lila followed me into the kitchen to help. "Where's Zack?" Nervous about Mark's reaction to my news, I shushed her and hoped Mark hadn't heard. She shook her head at me. "Might as well face the music now."

She dragged me back to my room where Mark and Ross were waiting. Elise had bought some wine, so I poured glasses for all of us, thinking it would mellow Mark out. Lila baited me, asking how my trip to Milwaukee went.

"It was fun." I tried not to look at her, knowing I would blush and give it away.

"What did you guys do?"

This was tedious, but it was helping. Mark was like a brother to me, so I couldn't just tell him how attracted to Zack I was. Knowing how Mark felt about him, this wasn't going to be easy. I summarized the party at Tia's and described our evening with this family.

Lila continued her ruse. "So are you guys hanging out again?"

"I think we will."

Mark leaned forward and pointed at me. "Wait, what are you saying?"

"We'll probably go out again."

Ross hit Mark on the arm. "Dude, they hooked up."

Mark slapped him on the chest, and crossed the room to me. "We talked about Zack the first week you were here."

He wasn't happy, but there was nothing I could do. I didn't agree with Mark's assessment of Zack, and it was nobody's business but mine. I told him about my conversation with Zack the previous night. Mark admitted that Zack seemed to have reeled in his revolving-door girl habit this year. Still, Mark seemed to be stewing the rest of the evening.

Zack arrived just as we finished cleaning up. Mark intercepted him right off. "So, you and Manda?"

Zack looked to me and I rolled my eyes. Zack winked at me and then faced Mark. "Yep."

Mark put his hand out. "Okay, brother." They shook hands and that was it. I completely didn't get guys. Maybe it was some fraternity brotherhood thing.

Zack leaned down and kissed me. "Miss me?"

Mark put his hand up in front of his face. "Not in front of me though."

The next morning I worked out with Zack, Doug and Bill. Doug still wasn't acknowledging my presence, but I focused on my workout. I had an x-ray and orthopedist appointment that afternoon, and I hoped to get my cast off. It'd been over six weeks since the accident, and I was more than ready to have the use of both my arms.

Zack offered to drive me to the medical center. After checking in, we sat down in the waiting area. His phone rang, and he pulled it from his pocket. Looking at it and smiling, he handed it to me. "Here, you talk."

Caught off guard, I didn't check the screen for fear I'd miss the call. "Hello?"

"Oh, I must have the wrong number."

I recognized his mom's voice. "No, Mrs. Walters, it's Amanda."

She asked how I was doing and then about Zack. I told her about our day yesterday, and how sweet he was to come to my appointment with me. I finished the conversation by thanking her again for having me for dinner and handed Zack the phone.

He told her about our Sunday together, and stuffed his phone back into his pocket. "How much you want to bet she's ordering wedding invitations as we speak?"

I pushed his face away, laughing at him. It was only a few minutes before they called me back for the X-ray. Zack insisted on coming along, even when the tech said he should wait.

"She's a fainter," he said.

"I'm not going to faint getting an X-ray."

"You never know."

"Thanks for the vote of confidence."

The tech rolled her eyes and turned to walk down the hall. In the X-ray room, she and two other technicians positioned and re-positioned me and my arm to get all the films they needed. Next they sent us to the orthopedist's office to check-in and wait for the files to be sent over.

As we waited Zack's phone buzzed again. "Ugh." Zack showed me Doug's name on the screen. "I'm missing house dinner." He answered the phone. "Sorry, Doug. I'm at the medical center with Amanda. No, everything's good, just an X-ray and ortho appointment." They talked house business for a few minutes and Zack ended the call.

"Everything okay?" I asked when he put the phone down.

"He's annoyed. We're only supposed to miss so many dinners a quarter."

"And you've already missed too many?"

"He'll get over it, although I may have to clean toilets for a week. The Amanda excuse is wearing off I guess."

We waited a half hour to be called back to an exam room and a half hour more for the doctor. The X-rays showed that my arm was making progress, but I still needed at least two more weeks in the cast. Although I knew it might be early to get my cast off, I was disappointed with the news. Zack insisted we go to a steak place for dinner. I wasn't sure what proteins had to do with bone growth, but I loved being with him.

As I crossed the courtyard towards the classroom building the next morning, a hand lifted my backpack off my shoulder.

"Morning." Zack kissed me square on the lips and wrapped his free arm around my waist.

His smile was infectious and I temporarily suspended my worry about my GPA. "Did you just come from your workout?"

"Yes. Hey, I had a couple of things to ask you. First, are you coming to the co-rec football game tonight? It's the last one."

Realizing our relationship canceled the need to avoid Doug, I agreed to go.

"Good. Are you here for Saturday's game?"

"Yes."

"Good, Zoey's coming down for the game, so you can finally meet her. And you're going home for Thanksgiving, I assume?" I told him about my plans to ride with Tia and Ed to Champaign and back with my family Friday evening. He smiled and squeezed my hand. "Good, only forty-eight hours without you."

Out of the corner of my eye, I caught sight of Vivian. She'd stopped in the middle of the courtyard and was staring at us. I waved to her, and she walked over.

I introduced them. Zack displayed his winning smile and offered his hand to her. She stared bug-eyed at him, seemingly mesmerized. I had to catch myself before I laughed.

"Okay, well, I'll see you in class." She backed away, waving.

"Kay," I called after her.

"She's still looking back at us," Zack said.

I looked up at him, and he took my chin in his hand. Before I realized what he was going to do, he kissed me. It wasn't the simple quick kiss he'd used to greet me. It was a solid, please find a private spot, kiss. It caught me off guard, and my body reacted without me thinking. I stood on my toes and leaned into him.

He backed away before I did. "Well, I think we made quite an impression on your friend."

Cheeks burning, I hit him on the arm. "That was mean."

"But you liked it."

"Yes." I kissed him again quickly. "I have to get to class, though." I turned to go.

"Aren't you forgetting something?" He held up my backpack.

Late for class, I ran. Everyone was in their seats, but the professor thankfully wasn't there yet. Fortunately, Vivian had saved me a seat.

"OMG, that was Zack Walters. Are you guys dating?"

I nodded and put a finger over my lips to quiet her.

She looked confused. "I thought you were with Doug. Aren't they best friends?"

This was something I didn't want to be reminded of. "Doug was just a friend." I pointed towards the professor approaching the podium.

That night, I walked to the football game alone. At the fields, I scanned the rows for the fraternity colors. Finding them on the far side, I made my way around the outside. As I got closer, I realized the tall guy talking with Stephen was Doug.

"Hi," I said to them as I approached.

Doug nodded his head at me the same as he'd done for the last three weeks.

"Hi there," Stephen said. "I didn't expect to see you tonight."

"Well, there was some arm twisting, so here I am." I looked to where the players were warming up and found Zack. He saw me and waved as did Lila.

Stephen called for the game to begin, and he ran back and forth following the players. Standing here not talking to Doug was not what I wanted to do when I could be studying. Talking to him seemed like it may be less uncomfortable than not though. "So, how is your quarter?"

"Good. Yours?" He rolled back and forth on his heels.

I didn't take my eyes off the game. "Yeah, good."

The teams lined in front of where we stood, and Stephen stood beside me. "How's your running going?"

"I think I'm solid at my goal pace." He chatted with me about his new training regimen for a triathlon. Impressed that he could hold a conversation and mind the game, I mentioned it to him. "Can you really pay attention to the game and talk to me?"

"Sure, it's like riding a bike. You do it long enough, and it becomes automatic."

"I don't think my brain could ever work that way."

Doug stepped towards me. "What about when you translate? You convert between languages without thinking about it. It's the same thing."

Shocked he'd said more than two words to me, I stared at him for several seconds before I could respond. "I'm not sure I'm paying attention to two completely different things at once."

"I've watched you translate. You don't even seem to need to think about it. I'm not sure I've ever met anyone so fast."

Coming from him, I considered the assessment a huge compliment. "I guess, thanks."

Just then Stephen blew the whistle to announce the end of the first half and Zack jogged over to me. He rubbed my arms with his hands and pulled me into him. "You warm enough?"

When their play resumed, Doug again stood a few feet from me. I couldn't think of anything else to say to him, so I stayed silent. It surprised me when he spoke.

"Is your family coming up for the game this weekend?"

Feeling a little more confident, I answered. "Yes, and I'm looking forward to meeting Zoey."

"You're coming to the game with us?" His eyes bore into mine, and I had to look at my feet.

I took a breath and looked back up at him. "Zack invited me so..."

"Does your dad know about Zack?"

What did that have to do with anything? There was commotion on the field and he turned his attention to the game. Shocked, I couldn't take my eyes off him. He looked back at me then walked away without any explanation. Why did everything have to be so hard between us?

After the game ended, Zack asked if he and Bill could shower in my room. Thinking Elise wouldn't mind a couple of hot, freshly showered guys in our room, we drove to my dorm. As soon as we walked into the room, Zack flung his arms around Elise. She pushed him away, complaining that he stank.

"Did she tell you about our kiss in the courtyard?"

Embarrassed, I felt my face go hot.

"She did, you animal." Elise hit him on the arm.

He pointed at her. "That's one thing I am not. A bit of a show-off maybe." He turned to Bill. "Should I shower first or do you want to?"

"Go ahead. I'm dying to hear this story."

"You'll have to let me know how she tells it," Zack said, winking at me as he headed for the bathroom. I threw a towel at him.

They showered and were on our way to the bar in half an hour. Thankfully, there was a big crowd and it was easy to avoid Doug. I felt like we'd had a few good interactions tonight, but then he'd come out with the question about my dad. I didn't know how to interpret it, so I kept as far away from Doug as possible.

The next day my lab was quick, and I met Zack at the house. I'd worn a dress, excited to spend time alone with him before the Thanksgiving break. It was quiet with many of the brothers at classes, and we lounged on the couch chatting. He turned on the television to watch a show on injury rehabilitation, and I dozed off.

My phone woke me. It was a text from Marissa. Zack rubbed my back while we sent messages back and forth. When I finished, he grabbed my phone.

"Hey, I don't have a picture or a ring tone in here. We have to fix this." He snapped pictures of us.

"How about this one?" he asked pointing to where I was pushing his face away.

"I like it."

He played around with the buttons some more. "Okay, what song?" "How about 'Addicted' by Saving Abel?"

"Too racy."

He searched my playlists. "Or 'Superman'—no, 'Kryptonite' by 3 Doors Down. Get it?" Recalling from Mom's movies that kryptonite was Superman's weakness, it sounded perfect.

We were comparing playlists when Doug wandered out from his room. He approached us and stood there a few seconds, eyes on the television screen.

"Hey dude, study break?" Zack called to him. After what felt like an eternity, he acknowledged the greeting.

"Yeah."

"Cool." Zack nodded towards him. Doug didn't say anything else, and we went back to our discussion on music. Doug walked back down the hall to his room. Zack shook his head and cleared his throat, standing. "I'll be right back."

I watched Zack walk down the hall towards Doug's room. Sensing the growing tension, my chest constricted and suddenly I felt like I couldn't breathe. Grabbing my phone, I took the stairs two at a time. Thankfully it was warm for November, as I'd left my jacket. I walked towards the lake.

Whatever was going on between Doug and I would have to change or I was going to implode. I had no clue how to orchestrate a resolution. It was obvious Zack saw something was off with Doug too. His behavior left me thinking it had something to do with me. Would Zack guess the connection?

My world was crumbling. How had I gotten here? Why wasn't I brave enough to address this head on? To demand answers from Doug? Where was the girl who looked Carter directly in the eyes and called him a jerk? Where was the girl who walked away from Law in the middle of a cornfield?

My phone buzzed. I looked at the screen and read a message from Zack: WHERE DID YOU GO?

OUT FOR SOME AIR.

He asked if he could join me, and I texted where I was. Waiting for him, I realized I needed to be that girl again, to be courageous. Zack was a good guy and he'd been up front with me. If not for any other reason, he deserved my honesty.

He joined me on the beach. "You okay?"

I shrugged. "What's up with Doug?"

He looked up at the sky and back to me. "Yeah, about that, I guess Doug doesn't think we should be together. He thinks I will hurt you."

I couldn't believe my ears. Doug had crossed a line. He'd promised my dad he'd take care of me, but this was going too far. Why did he care? I didn't know how to respond, so I didn't.

"He seemed happy when you guys were hanging out. I need to ask you something again." He took my hand, forcing me to look at him. "Nothing happened between you guys Halloween, right?"

It was time for honesty. "Nothing happened. I liked him, but he didn't want a relationship with me." I hoped this was honest enough. I didn't think he wanted the grisly details.

"He never told you about Zoey."

I shook my head.

"I could tell, that night at the bar. You looked completely sideswiped."

I didn't know what to say. "Don't do that." He pulled me to him and kissed me. My body reacted without my head, and I forgot we were talking about Doug.

"Do what?"

I shivered and he wrapped his arms around me. "Bite your lip like that." He brushed his fingers across my lips. "It's the sexiest thing I've ever seen, and I'm not going to be able to resist kissing you when you do it."

I looked up at him. "So we're good?" If I knew one thing, it was that I liked Zack.

"Yes, we should get back though. I have to help close up the house for the break." We walked back to the house, and inside the stairwell he backed me against the wall. He kissed me, and I let myself get lost in it. My phone buzzed and I ignored it. He pulled away, taking my phone from my hand.

"Are you supposed to meet Lila?"

I stood on my toes. "Another kiss?"

"You should go meet Lila and get something to eat. I have work to do. Text me before you go."

Lila met me at the top of the stairs, hands on her hips. "There you are. You were kissing Zack, weren't you? I could hear your phone buzzing."

"Yes, so?" I nudged past her onto the second floor.

We ordered pizza, and she complained about her family as we ate. Her holiday drama was a good distraction from my swirling thoughts about Zack, Doug, and my crumbling world. Baby steps, I told myself refocusing on Lila. When she was talked out, I went to find Zack. Helping him check all the windows and doors, I got a text from Tia. I sent a quick text to Mark so he could meet us in front of the house. As I pocketed my phone, Zack backed me into a window sill for a goodbye kiss.

After a few minutes, I had to stop kissing him and compose myself. Zack helped me roll my bag out to the street. For once, Mark had beaten me and was waiting on the sidewalk. When Tia and Ed pulled up, Zack leaned in for a kiss. It was quick, and we only heard a minor complaint as Mark loaded his bag in the trunk.

Zack put suitcase in the trunk, kissing me again before he shut the lid. He opened the car door and leaned down to poke his head inside. He waved to Tia and Ed. "Hi guys, good to see you again. Happy Thanksgiving."

Looking a little shocked, they returned the sentiment. After another quick kiss, I ducked into the car. Ed didn't hesitate to comment as soon as the car was in gear. "Well, that happened fast. Weren't you just friends like five days ago?"

Tia turned to look at me. "You know he's a player, right?"

"Not anymore."

"You sure about that?"

I was surprised Mark chimed in. "He's definitely changed since last spring. He's only dated Kara this quarter. I haven't seen him with anyone else except you."

"At least you didn't hook up with Doug before he and Zoey got back together," Tia said, looking back at me. "That would've been embarrassing."

Hurt, I responded without thinking. "Why would you say that? If I liked Doug, then I would be hurt he was with Zoey. Isn't that more important than what people think?"

Mark cut in. "Wait, are you admitting you liked Doug and were hurt when he got together with Zoey?"

"I wasn't hurt that he got together with Zoey." It was a true statement, I was hurt before that. This conversation seemed like it might lead to me coming clean with Mark without having to really tell him outright. At least Tia's inquisition was good for something for once.

Tia turned around to face me. "You liked him."

Mark pointed a finger at me. "Ha! Caught ya!"

"So, I liked him. Nothing happened."

"But you're happy now? With Zack?"

"Yes."

"Good. See, it really wasn't that hard to admit, was it?"

"It doesn't need to be public knowledge."

"Why would it be? It's a non-issue."

I was grateful to be able to come clean and know Mark was cool with the info I dumped on him.

Tia turned around again. "Does Dad know about you and Zack?"

"I told him we were hanging out."

"Mmm-hmmm." She turned back to face front.

The rest of the drive was uneventful, with Zack texting me when he left the house and got home. Arriving late, I hugged my parents and Marissa, changed and brushed my teeth for bed. Sending a quick text to Lila and Zack, I climbed into my bed, glad that the Turkey Trot wasn't until nine o'clock the next day.

Chapter 15

I'd had a restless sleep but it felt good to wake in my bed, a real bed, and to hear the familiar sounds of my family beginning their day. It was only seven, but I needed diversion from recounting my dreams. In the kitchen I remembered Stephen's warning about running and coffee and poured myself a cup of half regular half decaf. I grabbed a muffin and shuffled over to see what Mom was up to. Already prepping food for Thanksgiving dinner, she was putting potatoes in a pot to boil.

Not even halfway through my coffee, Tia spoke up. "Did Amanda tell you she has a boyfriend?" She pulled Dad's paper down so he could see her.

"She told me she and Zack were hanging out."

I stuck out my tongue at her. "It's early. Why are you starting in on me already?"

"Because we only have thirty-six hours, and you are a crazy person these days."

"We talked about this in the car. Mark even thinks it's okay."

"I just wanted to make sure Dad knew."

"I'm an adult for Christ's sake."

Mom pointed the peeler at me. "Amanda, language."

Dad took another sip of his coffee and lifted his paper to continue reading. Ha, I thought. Tia, zero, Amanda, one.

When I finished my coffee and muffin, I went up to change. There was a text from Zack, so I shot him a quick reply. Putting my hair in a ponytail, I made my way back down to the kitchen to help Mom with the cooking. Marissa was up, and Tia had moved on to new prey.

With most of the dishes ready for final prep, Dad and I did a short jog around the block to warm up. After stretching, we drove the short distance to the race start. It was a fun tradition, and I was happy my injury hadn't kept me from it. Our wave started, and I kept pace with Dad.

As we ran, I updated him on how my courses were going. If felt good to be with him, talking about normal stuff. I'd missed his company, and our conversation grounded me. Nearing the end of the race, he brought up my dating situation. I assured him Zack was a good guy and I was happy.

"You have a good head on your shoulders," he told me. "Just remember to use it."

We finished the race in fifty-seven minutes after sprinting the last half mile into the college stadium. Dad was thrilled with our time, as it was a PR for him. He'd finally broken the sixty-minute mark.

Back at home, Marissa sat on my bed and caught me up on the latest in her life as I dried my hair. She had a lot going on with finalizing a college choice, making sure she kept up grades, and captaining the cheer squad. We chatted until Mom yelled for us to help with dinner.

Sitting around the table, we took turns saying what were thankful for. I had a pretty good list. I missed Bubbe, but I was alive and okay, my family and friends were healthy and happy, and my personal life and classwork were on an upswing. Barring the drama with Doug, I felt content.

As we were cleaning up in the kitchen, Tia pulled me aside. "You know I just worry about you, right? I don't mean to be critical. I just want you to be smart and safe." She hugged me and I squeezed her back, telling her I knew she cared and was trying to help. I didn't always like her delivery, but I knew her heart was in the right place.

We watched football until late. Snuggling with mom, I sent texts back and forth with Zack. His extended family was in from California, and it sounded like they had a full house. He told me his mom wished me and my family a happy Thanksgiving and invited me for Hanukkah. SHE'S DETERMINED TO MAKE YOU JEWISH, he joked in his next text.

That night I had awful dreams again and woke exhausted. But there was no time for more sleep, as we had the neighborhood football tournament. Dad had moved the schedule up so we could get to Evanston by five. Carrying my coffee cup across the street just after eight, I found Mark, Lila, and Ross huddled in a group, shivering.

Lila spoke first. "Your dad is a maniac." She lifted my cap up to see my eyes. "You look like hell."

"The man is right over there." I pointed to where he stood not two feet from us, a clipboard under his arm and whistle around his neck.

Lila linked her arm with mine and pulled me aside. "Are you okay?"

"Bad dreams," I told her, trying to dispel the images from my head. One was exactly the one I'd remembered having when I woke in Doug's arms. Each of the others had the same theme: I was falling, and when I hit, I died. Freaked out after a second night of these dreams, I'd already called my counselor. She'd said it was completely normal. Ironically, being in a safe environment gave your psyche the freedom it needed to process fears. Even with her assurances, I still felt uneasy.

Lila tugged me a couple more steps away from Mark and Ross. "Your family's worried about you. They've been asking questions. They think you look thin."

This was surprising. Why hadn't they said anything to me? Be brave and be honest, I reminded myself. I told her about the dreams and admitted it'd been tough with the accident and the stress of my scholarship.

"Mark brought up something about you and Doug."

"Mark was in this conversation?"

"Your dad stopped us a few minutes ago. Did something happen you didn't tell me about?"

I looked at the ground. "Yes, and no."

She grabbed my arm. "What is that supposed to mean? I thought we were best friends."

Coming clean about Halloween, I told her about avoiding the house and intramural games. She was angry, as she had every right to be. I explained my reasoning, and she agreed it was logical. She stressed that, even with good reason, I shouldn't keep things like that from her. Finally, she felt assured I had come clean and we walked back towards the scrimmages.

"So does this mean you're eating normally again?"

"Yes." I pushed her into Mark.

The games were fun. With Mark's family and Ross and Lila, our team won easily and Dad was happy with our victory. Walking back to the house, he noticed my cleats. "Hey girlie, what's with the pink? Are you like ten again? You didn't pay extra for the pink stripes did you?"

"Hey, you were the one who wanted me to be safe." I pointed to my shoes and then his. "Cleats, safe, running shoes not. Fourteen stitches, remember?" I shoved him.

"Actually I'd forgotten about that one. Although I'm sure we'll get the bill soon." He ruffled my hair. Not sure whether to speak with Dad about the concerns he voiced to Lyla, I decided against it. I hoped that in my time with them he'd seen that I was stable and eating healthy.

Back at the house, he was quick to rally everyone to get packed for the trip to Evanston. Pulling out of our driveway, just ten minutes off schedule, Dad suggested I invite Zack to join us for dinner. I messaged him, and he accepted right away.

After my parents checked into the hotel, Zack met us in their suite. He greeted Dad with a firm handshake. "Mr. Avery, It's good to see you."

"Mr. Walters, I'm glad you could join us." He motioned for us to sit.

"So Zack, you should know that I'm not entirely comfortable with the age difference between you and Amanda."

Zack looked to me, my face burning with embarrassment, and then back to my father. "I understand sir. I'm not sure how to alleviate your concerns. I've known Amanda a couple of months,"—Zack took my hand—"and I think she's amazing. I want her to be happy, and I plan to be around for as long as she'll have me." He winked at me and looked back to my dad.

My dad stood, offering hand to Zack. "Well, I wanted to be clear. Can I get you a drink?"

Zack stood and shook Dad's hand. "A beer would be great." When Dad was in the kitchen Zack leaned into me and whispered. "That was intense."

"Sorry," I whispered to him.

The dinner with my family was fun, and Zack seemed to fit in easily. Wanting one more night in a real bed, I opted to spend the night at the hotel and walked Zack down to his car at the end of the evening.

"That was fun." He slid his hand around my waist and leaned into me against the door panel. "Well, except for the first part," he qualified. "So tomorrow, you, me, Doug, and Zoey?"

"Yes." I tried to sound positive. With his body pressed against mine, I couldn't find much wrong with the world. We firmed up plans to meet at the house, and he kissed me goodnight. As I turned to go he grabbed my arm.

"With your dad's issues, I forgot about these." He pulled some photos from his jacket pocket. "I printed these out for you."

He handed them to me and I flipped through the prints. On the top of the pile were shots we'd taken with our phones on

Wednesday. Reaching the bottom of the pile I held up two of the images.

"You took these of me at the lake?"

"Yeah," he looked at the ground and back up at me, "you looked pretty standing there looking at the water. I couldn't help myself."

"Thank you." I told him and kissed him again.

The next morning, as Marissa and I approached the house, I could see Zack pacing. I'd sent him a text about an hour before letting him know we were on the way. We'd run into Kate, Jeremy, Stephen, Elise, and the football team on our walk across campus, and were late meeting him.

Zack spotted us and jogged to meet us. "Where've you been?"

"Didn't you know? Everyone knows Amanda." Marissa put her hand to her hip. "I'm going in." She rolled her eyes and marched off.

Ignoring her, he smiled, bent down, and kissed me. Walking inside, Zack caught me up to speed on the state of all interested parties. Doug's mom and step-dad were there. They didn't like Zoey, and his mom asked about me in front of her. This didn't sound like a good lead in to our introduction. Deep in thought, I chewed on my lip.

Zack bent down and kissed me square on the mouth, causing the brother next to us to punch him on the arm. "Get a room, dude."

"Zack." I hit him.

"I warned you about the lip thing." He took my hand and led me through the crowd to the back of the room. We found my parents talking with Doug's mom and step-dad.

Doug's mom crossed the space between us and wrapped her arms around me. "Amanda, I can't believe it. It's been such a long time. You look wonderful." She took my hand and stepped back. "Well, actually you look a little thin, but your color is better than the last time I saw you."

"Thank you, it's good to see you, too." I squeezed her hand and released it.

I felt a hand on my back and turned to see Doug. "You found her," he said turning to Zack.

"Where's Zoey?"

"Zack, you made it," a melodic voice sang out. I turned and a beautiful girl kissed him on the cheek and slid into Doug's arms. She could have been right off a New York runway. Tall, with golden hair, bright blue eyes, and perfect makeup, Zoey was nothing but stunning. Looking at them you'd have thought they just finished a photo shoot. Now I understood what Mark meant when he'd said I was only a six on Doug's scale.

"Amanda, hi." She smiled and held out her hand. "So nice to finally meet you. Zack won't stop going on about you."

I shook her hand and we chatted about academic majors, the house, and the football team. After a few minutes, she pulled Doug away to socialize. I couldn't help but watch them glide away. He was hers, and I was deluded to ever think for a second he might be mine. Kissing my neck, Zack broke my trance.

"You can't do that," I whispered.

"What?"

I couldn't help my smile as I tried to scold him. "My parents are right there."

"You were biting your lip again." He took my hand and I mentally vowed to embrace the good that was right in front of me. "So, what'd you think of Zoey?"

"She's beautiful," I said automatically.

"What else were you thinking?"

I thought for a moment. "Doug looks happy."

"Maybe so," he said and looked over at them. "One can dream."

A big cheer shook the room at half past ten. Zack pulled me towards the door and to the front of the procession. Reaching the stadium, we sat beside Doug and Zoey. She didn't speak to me until just before halftime when she asked me to go to the restroom with her.

She linked her arm through mine. "Everyone seems quite taken with you. Anna says you may rush. Any thoughts on which sorority you're interested in?"

Even though I had no intention of rushing, I knew there was only one right answer to this question. "I'm still on the fence about rushing. Your house will top my list if I decide to, though. I really like all the girls I've met from there."

"Think about it. Sororities are a great place to get leadership experience. It's important for your resume. So you're a language major? What are you going to do with that?" She shriveled up her nose. "You are double majoring, right?"

"Yes, chemistry."

"Wow, talk about grueling. Chemistry was hell."

Finally, we made it to the restroom. I wasn't sure how much longer I could hold up chitchatting with her. Unfortunately, there was a really long line. She put her hands on her hips and looked towards the front of the line. "This is going to take forever." We took our places in line, and she started again. "So, the whole arm thing, that was crazy. Doug feels so bad about it. But you totally seem fine now. I think Doug is right, though. You don't seem like Zack's type."

She seemed to spiraling into some sort of stream-of-conscious rant. I remembered she worked at a bank, and I was desperate to get the spotlight off of me. "So, you're in finance?"

"Yes. It's a good time to be in money management, the economy is so hot right now. I don't like Milwaukee much, but a lot of my friends are there. You met them, right?" I nodded an affirmation. "Of course, it's a pain now for me and Doug. I'm glad we're back together. It's just meant to be." She seemed to pause for dramatic effect. "He's going to do so well when he gets a job in Japan. I mean, he didn't make any money as an intern this summer, but at least he got experience overseas. I really have to get him to buy a different car, though. Can you believe he drives that thing?"

We were moving up in line, but not nearly fast enough. She seemed to love to hear her own voice. The way she talked about his car and the money he would make, I wondered if she really cared about, or even knew him. I felt sick. Even after everything, I wanted Doug to be happy. As soon as we were at the sinks, she started talking again. "Zack is totally hot, too. I'm sure he'll be a great boyfriend."

Desperate to get away from her and this conversation and feeling queasy, I walked out of the bathroom and into the soothing cold air. She followed me. "Anna really thought she and Zack were going to get back together. Have you seen her since you guys started dating? It's only been a week, right? She's probably not too upset, so maybe it won't affect your pledge chances. By the way, Doug's mom really seems to like you." She had barely breathed during this last string and grabbed my arm halfway up the flight of stairs. "Of course she would like anyone more than me, the girl who broke her son's heart. It's all working out fine now, so I don't know why she is still so bent out of shape."

She was drunk, and I hoped she wouldn't remember telling me any of this. I spotted Zack and headed straight towards him as fast as I could. Maybe it was time for me to drink something stronger than Diet Coke.

Zack was sitting on the other side of Doug. I kept my head down as I passed in front of him. Putting a hand on my shoulder, he stopped me. Surprised I looked up at him. "You don't look good. Are you okay?"

Before I could respond, Zoey said, "We had to wait forever, she probably locked her knees and is about to pass out or something."

I pulled away from him and into Zack's waiting arms. "You okay?" He looked into my face.

"Sure." I put on my best smile for him and Doug, who still stood facing me.

Zack handed me a soda and pulled me into his lap. He kissed my neck and whispered, "What did she say to you?"

"What didn't she say to me would be the better question."

At halftime, the stands cleared out and Lila and Ross as well as Mark, Bill, and their dates came to sit behind us. I moved behind Zack, so I could sit with Lila and get farther away from Zoey. After the game, we had dinner with my parents before they left for Champaign. On the drive back to my dorm after dinner, Zack asked me about my conversation with Zoey.

"It's stupid. I'm sure she was drunk, but the way she rambled on about her sorority, money, and cars, it was kind of too much."

"She is a very different person from you."

"Why did you want me to meet her so badly?"

"Because, I think you're awesome and I wanted to show you off." His reply surprised me as I'd thought it was more about me meeting Zoey than her meeting me. This made me happy. As he stopped the car, I kissed him. "Thank you."

He kissed me back with each kiss growing more insistent. The next thing I knew, I was backed against the passenger's door. When he stopped he pointed to the back seat. Getting out of the car, he popped open the back, flipped the seats down, and spread a blanket out.

"I'm sorry, but why are we hanging out in the back of your truck when you have an apartment?"

"Doug and Zoey are at my place. But that's only the second reason."

"And the first?"

He lifted me up onto the tailgate. "I'm not taking you to my apartment yet."

"I've been to your apartment before."

"If I took you there now, I wouldn't bring you back. We're not ready for that."

It was true, feeling the way I was feeling about him now, I wouldn't want to come back to my room much less choose to sleep alone on the couch in his apartment.

We listened to tunes and talked. Out of nowhere, he started tickling me. I screamed at him, curling up to protect myself. "New rule," he said, continuing to tickle me. "You get tickled when you bite your lip."

I tried to retaliate by wriggling my fingers under his arms. "Now you're in trouble, mister." He straddled on top of me and pinned my right arm to the floor.

"Hey, the disabled girl should get a handicap," I tried to say between laughs.

"I can't take any chances with you because you're Super Mini-Girl, remember?"

"Oh yeah, I'll have to figure out which power will get me out of this one."

"Good luck with that," he said lifting my shirt to expose my belly. Suddenly he stopped. "Oh my goodness, your stomach is so white it's almost transparent."

I tugged my shirt back down. "It's the moonlight," I said in defense.

The song ended and he fiddled with his phone until he found something else suitable.

"What does a girl have to do to get a kiss around here?"

He said nothing, but rolled over to face me, wrapped his arm over me, and gave me the most sensual kiss I'd ever experienced. I traced kisses down his neck to his chest.

I hesitated, and he lifted my chin so that I was looking at him. "You really trust me, letting me take advantage of you this way in the back of my truck."

"Well, there is a huge cast between us and I do have my knee strategically placed." I lifted my left knee up between his legs.

"Point taken." After another quick kiss, he got up, sliding out of the back of the truck. He lifted me to the ground and walked me to the door.

Sunday we spent the whole day at his apartment studying and doing laundry. We only left to go food shopping. In the evening we watched a movie. Thinking I never wanted to go back to my room or classes, I reluctantly let him drive me back to my dorm.

"Back to reality, princess," he said as he kissed me goodbye in front of my dorm.

With finals looming, the week flew by. On Thursday I found myself watching the volleyball game beside Doug. I tried to not think about the conversation we'd had the week before at the football game. Standing there in silence felt awkward and I decided to break the ice. "It was nice to meet Zoey."

Finally, he looked at me. "She was glad to meet you too. Hey, you weren't sick were you?"

"No, I must've locked my knees like Zoey said," I lied. So much for brave honesty.

"I was worried, you looked pale."

"I was fine."

"Good."

When he rotated out of the game the next time, he stood on the opposite side of the court from me. Later, I ended up across from him at the pub. He shifted in his seat, seeming unsettled, eyes mostly glued to his phone. I moved to sit beside Lila so that I wasn't monopolizing Zack's time.

Every time I looked their way Doug seemed to be looking at me. It made me uncomfortable, but I decided he must be staring off into space. After about a half hour, Lila leaned into me. "What did you and Doug talk about during the game tonight?"

I guessed Lila was in tune to our relationship, or lack thereof, since I'd finally come clean last week. "Nothing, I told him it was nice to meet Zoey and he asked me if I'd been sick."

"He can't seem to stop looking at you. I noticed it at the gym too." Great, now I had Lila being neurotic too.

Not fifteen minutes later, Doug pushed back from the table and left without as much as a goodbye to anyone. The next morning, we were halfway through our run when Doug arrived unshaven at the gym.

"Dude, what's with the stubble? Zoey won't like that," Zack said to him.

"Up late, studying." Doug looked at me and then started his run beside Bill.

"You seeing her this weekend?" Zack asked.

"Going up tonight."

"Goin' to Waukee," Zack sung in a deep voice. Doug hit him with his towel.

Chapter 16

The weekend was a blur of end of the quarter social events, studying, and my tutoring and babysitting gigs. The whole campus seemed on edge with the onset of the last week of classes, and I was no different. Not only did I have the pressure of getting my GPA up, but my cast was supposed to come off. I had horrible nightmares both Friday and Saturday nights and could only guess that these stresses were the cause. Zack suggested I sleep at his place. It was a tempting offer, for more than one reason, but there wasn't room in my psyche for anything new. I opted for a long exercise session and a late night with him, hoping to get a good night's sleep.

Shrill ringing woke me. I answered my phone without looking to see who it was.

"Amanda?" I tried to place the voice. I held my phone away from my ear to check the caller. "Doug?" I panicked. "Is everything okay?"

"Yes."

"Zack should be at his apartment. Did you try him? He said he was working out this morning."

"That's not why I called." There were a few seconds of silence. I wasn't sure if I was supposed to speak. He finally continued. "I wanted to know if you'd meet me for racquetball."

"I'm not sure what Mark said, but I'm not really good at racquetball."

"Will you just come hit the ball with me?"

Why? Was he trying to be friends? I wanted that too, just not at eight in the morning. "When?"

"Half an hour?"

I looked at the clock. It read eight nineteen. "I guess I can do that."

"I'll see you at the courts then," he said and hung up.

What just happened? I shook off the question, brushed my teeth, and called Zack.

He answered immediately. "What's up? I thought you were sleeping until ten." Just hearing his voice calmed me.

"Don't I wish. Doug called and wanted me to meet him for racquetball."

"Cool, I guess I'm working out with just Bill then."

"You think I should go?"

"Sure, why not? It'll be good for you guys." I wished I shared Zack's optimism. What was I supposed to talk to him about? "Drink some OJ and call me later."

Getting dressed, I found my racquetball bag and grabbed a bottle of juice from the fridge. As I walked to the gym, I tried not to think about spending an hour with Doug. Why had I agreed to meet him? Obviously, I had an inability to say no to Doug or Zack.

The racquetball courts were on the lower level and an attendant sat at the equipment counter. He pointed down the hall. "Court one."

I hesitated, confused. "Court one?"

"If you're looking for Doug, he's on court one." He again pointed down the hall towards the court. I still hesitated, so he continued, "Wee lass, yea big." He held up his hand at chest level.

My orange juice was finally kicking in. "He's not Irish." I shook my head, annoyed. Wee lass? Is that how Doug had described me?

The attendant said something else, but I ignored him and walked towards the court. Maybe I was being too harsh. But with only six hours of sleep, I wasn't in the mood.

Court one was on the end and didn't face another court as the others did. Doug stood at the end of the hall spinning a racquet in his hand. He was beautiful. No one would deny that. I set my bag against the wall.

"Did you get anything to eat?" He held up an energy drink. "I have another one of these if you want it."

"I had some orange juice."

Stretching, my mind raced. I tried to focus on what Zack said about this being a good step. It seemed more like torture.

"Should we play?"

My limbs were good and loose, but I'd been stalling. "Sure."

He held the door open and motioned me into the court. "How was your weekend? Zack said you were having nightmares again. Were they the same ones where you see your Bubbe?"

"What?" We'd been hitting the ball slowly back and forth, and I let the ball pass me.

"Were they the same ones as before, the dreams?" He tilted his head and stared at me for a moment. "We talked about them, before." He looked towards the far wall and served the ball again.

I tried to push the image of being held against his bare chest out of my brain. "I don't remember much from then." It was true, except for waking to his smiling face each morning.

"What about Homecoming?"

"Yes, I remember Homecoming." I retrieved the ball thinking I'd rather not.

"That was a good day."

His new topic distracted me from asking more questions about the dreams. The music threw me off, too. Instead of a high energy groove, it was some sappy love song. Maybe the attendant was pining for his girlfriend.

"Let's play a game." He served the ball. "What about the week before school started?"

I returned his serve and wondered where he was going with this. Homecoming? Orientation? What did they have to do with anything?

"That was a fun week."

"I don't think I have amnesia. I think they had me on some pretty heavy drugs. People forget things all the time."

"No, I wasn't—never mind." He shook his head.

He'd lost me. Between an abrupt song change and our odd conversation, I lost my concentration and missed the ball. How was I supposed to play racquetball to whiny love songs and stay on top of whatever point Doug was trying to make?

We managed to get a decent volley going, and I worked hard to appear upbeat. I'd imagined this to be a light conversation event, but his intense topic choices were weighing on me. I needed to keep him on mundane subjects, or I was going to explode. "How is your mom?"

"She's good. She thinks you're getting too skinny."

I couldn't seem to catch a break, so I tried again. "How was your weekend?"

"Not good. I broke up with Zoey, and it didn't go well."

I stopped and looked at him. "What? When?" I blurted out without thinking. If Zack knew about the break-up he hadn't told me. We'd been together most of the weekend, and I didn't think he would have kept this information from me.

"Friday, well Friday and Saturday."

I turned to face him. "I'm sorry." I wasn't sure which part to be empathetic about, the breakup or that it hadn't gone well.

"It's okay. It wasn't right." He served the ball again.

I had no clue what he was talking about, why he was saying these things to me, and what we were doing here. Yet another whiny love song started, and I was playing more horribly than

I usually did. I saw no point in this charade. I needed for him to say what he wanted to say so I could go. I focused on how I could get him to come clean. Out of the corner of my eye, I caught him shaking his head, and it put me over the edge.

"What?"

"You look frustrated."

Taking slow breaths, I was able to rein in my anger before I spoke. What I wanted to do was hurl the ball at his head. "Doesn't this music seem odd for racquetball?"

He paused, tilting his head. Coldplay's "Viva la Vida" started. It wasn't a sappy love song, but it reminded me of our dance Halloween night. He hit the ball again. "I actually like this one. Kind of fits me.

God, now he was being beyond cryptic. I was done. "Can we stop?" I caught the ball in mid-air.

He nodded and motioned towards the door. I walked ahead so I didn't have to look at him. Stuffing my racquet in my bag, I focused on breathing slowly. If he didn't have something definite to say, I was going to lose it.

I turned to face him. "We don't have to be friends. We just have to peacefully coexist."

He smiled. "So you've realized we can't be friends?"

He was the most infuriating person I'd ever met. How could you love and hate someone so much at the same time? I dug my nails into my hand and took a calming breath. Honesty, brave honesty, I thought. "No just that we don't need to be."

"We don't need to be, or you don't want to be?"

He was maddening. Right now, I didn't want to be. I kept my voice steady. "I'm okay either way. We just need to be civil for Zack's sake."

"Zack?" He inched closer to me and placed his hand on the wall beside my head. He bent down so our faces were barely a foot apart. "This isn't about Zack."

I opened my mouth to say something, but no words came out.

"Haven't you been listening to me for the past hour? I can't be friends with you because I can't stop thinking about you."

He couldn't stop thinking about me?

He moved his face to within inches of mine. "I broke up with Zoey. She's not who I want. I want you."

I studied his face, too shocked to speak. He wanted me? None of this made sense. He took my hand. His touch seemed to vibrate through my whole body. I should've yanked my hand away. I should've been throwing accusations at him left and right. He'd rejected me twice, and I'd spent weeks coming to terms with him not wanting me. Now I was happy with Zack. I looked at his hand holding mine and tried to wrap my brain around what he'd just told me.

"Please say something." His face was barely six inches from mine.

I pulled my hand from his. "You walked away twice." The words should've been flung at him, but they came out sounding more like a question.

"I know. I really messed things up. I should've figured it out sooner. I thought I was still in love with her. I couldn't be with you when I was still hung up on her. It wouldn't have been fair. I didn't mean to hurt you."

"But you did."

"I know, and I want to fix that. There's a lot I didn't tell you before, but I want to be with you."

"We argue all the time. I'm eighteen. I'm a freshman, and you're graduating in six months. Remember?"

"Yes," he admitted, replacing a strand of hair behind my ear. I batted his hand away and he placed it on the wall beside me. "I've tried not to want you, but it doesn't work."

He had tried not to want me? For how long? His watch beeped, and he turned it over. The hands were pointed at ten o'clock, and I was jarred back into the reality of my day. I had class and I needed a shower first.

"You're biting your lip."

His comment reminded me of Zack, and the heat from his body suddenly was too much. I put my hand on Doug's chest and pushed him away.

"I have to go." I bent to pick up my bag.

"You have to go?" He reached out to me.

I needed to put him off until I sorted through my feelings. "Yes."

He grabbed my arm before I could escape. "Please, there's more you should know."

"I can't hear any more right now. It's the last week of classes. I have two lab finals..." I held my arm up. "And this comes off today." He had no right to insert himself back into my life.

To my surprise, he released my arm. "Okay, just one more thing?"

I had no more patience left. "What?"

"Can I borrow your phone?" Why I complied, I don't know. Fortunately there were no calls from Zack to answer yet. Doug connected our phones and started punching buttons.

"What are you doing?"

"Just some tunes I put together. You know those in there that annoyed you so much." He motioned towards the court.

"You orchestrated those?"

"It was kind of amusing watching you get annoyed."

Now I was beyond angry. Had my reaction on the court betrayed me? Did he know I still cared? "Is it done? I need to go."

He held the phone out, and I wrapped my fingers around it to take it, but he didn't let go. "Can I call you?"

I looked at his face. His expression was pleading. Part of me wanted nothing more than to melt into him and be lost for days, erasing the pain of his absence. The other part of me wanted to punch him on his beautifully square chin.

I jerked my phone from his grip. "You have to give me some time." I turned and jogged down the hall and up the stairs. I was almost to the front doors when I spied Mark heading towards me. There was no escape. He'd already seen me.

"Amanda? What's the hurry? You look like you've seen a ghost." Great, I was as drained as I felt, and this was going to delay my escape.

"I was playing racquetball, and I'm running late."

"Racquetball? With who?"

Darn, I should have lied. But he would've known. "Umm, Doug. I'm really behind, and I want to get a shower before class." At least I had a workout for an excuse for looking pale.

"Doug? Why? OJ and muffin with me. Now." He pulled my good arm in the direction he was headed. I planted my feet, and he saw that I wasn't going to budge. "At least drink this on the way so you don't faint." He pressed an energy drink in my hand.

I took the drink and he released me. I sprinted for the gym exit, dropping the bottle in the trash just outside the exit. There was no way I was keeping anything down right now.

Somehow I made it to class with a couple minutes to spare. I slinked into a seat beside Lila, hoping to be camouflaged by my sunglasses. I had no desire to speak with anyone. If I could've stayed in bed all day, I would have. She and Kate were engrossed in conversation, and it was a while before Lila turned to me.

"So you must've heard the gossip from the gym." I slid my glasses off, thinking this was a safe topic. "Mark said you were playing racquetball with Doug, so maybe you saw them."

"Saw who?"

Her eyes widened. "Some couple. Supposedly, this guy put together this awesome playlist and asked this girl he was hot for to meet him. She totally ditched him, though. So sad. What a waste. Did you see them?"

"We were way down on the end." It was an honest answer at least. "How does everyone even know?" I was fighting hard to breathe normally. How did this stuff get out?

"Equipment guy spread it."

Drat, I knew I didn't like that guy. It was us. Everyone at the gym was talking about Doug and me. Zack would put it together. The professor came in, and we turned to listen to the lecture. Lila must have caught the shocked look on my face, because her eyes enlarged to the size of saucers. Hitting my arm, she started texting.

U?

I nodded.

AND DOUG?

I nodded again.

OMG, she wrote.

As soon as the professor left the podium, she pulled me out of the room and into the hall. "Spill," she ordered once we were away from the crowd.

"It doesn't sound like there's that much to tell."

"So everything was accurate? No wonder you were ghost white when Mark saw you. You told Doug to take a hike, right?"

"I'm not sure I even remember what I told him. I think I said he had to give me some time."

"Time for what? What are you thinking in that little brain of yours?"

"I don't know. I haven't had a second to think." I slid down the wall to the floor.

She sat down beside me. "I almost wouldn't blame you if you'd kissed him. It sounds so freaking romantic."

I told her the whole story.

"Damn, girl, he loves you."

"He didn't say that."

"He told his best friend's girlfriend that he wants her. He loves you. Do you still have feelings for him?"

I looked up at the ceiling, blinking my eyes to keep the tears from trickling down my face. Lila wiped away one that escaped.

"Zack is a good guy, he makes me happy."

"I know he does, sweetie." She wrapped her arm around my shoulders.

I tried to take in slow deep breaths to calm myself and stop the tears. As it was, people were already crossing to the other side of the hall to avoid us. "What am I supposed to do? Can I even trust him? What if I lose both of them? How am I supposed to decide?"

"You need time to figure out how you feel and what you want. But right now you have to get up and answer that damn phone, or I'm going to throw it against the wall."

I stood up and put on my sunglasses, declining the call from Zack. "How do I look?"

"At least you didn't put on makeup." She groomed my hair with her fingers.

As we walked out of the building, she bumped my arm. "Looks like round two," she commented, nodding ahead. Zack was standing directly in front of us, waiting. "I swear girl, what is it with you? All of a sudden everyone wants you," she whispered in my ear as we walked towards him. Normally, that would be a good thing, but not today. As usual, she was trying to lighten the mood and I appreciated her effort.

"Don't tell Mark," I requested before we reached Zack.

"I don't know nothin' bout birthing no babies," she said in her best Southern accent.

I stopped a couple of feet in front of him. He closed the gap between us, took my hand, and pulled me into a hug. His embrace was comforting. He loosened his grip a little and I looked up at him.

"I like your hair." He ran his fingers through my curls. "I wish I'd been there to see it when you woke up this morning, for more reasons than just this." He hesitated, studying me. "Can I have a kiss?" He wouldn't have asked before.

I nodded. Things were simple with him. I'd missed him this morning, and I had no clue what I was going to do with the information Doug had dumped on me. He bent down and gave me a long, hard kiss.

"We should talk, but lunch first. This way." He pulled me down the sidewalk. "I'm assuming you haven't eaten anything. There's a good sandwich place just off campus." He pointed in the direction we were headed. He talked about his workout and caught me up on everyone else's news from the weekend as we walked.

The café was crowded with people in business attire, and we snagged the last small booth. Our lunch came and he bit into his sandwich right away. I followed suit, anxious to know what he was thinking about the morning's events.

"So, interesting morning," he started as we walked away from the restaurant. I nodded. "Rumors are vicious. I'm assuming, since you let me kiss you and came to lunch with me, that at least the ending of this one is mostly true."

This was horrible. He was potentially being betrayed by his best friend and his girlfriend. "I didn't—" I started.

"I know you had no idea. I had no idea. Even if I'd been with you this morning, I would've told you to meet him. He's got balls. If he weren't trying to steal my girlfriend, I'd be proud." He stiffened, dropping my hand. "Do we have anything to talk about?"

I'd been staring at my feet, letting him lead me. Now, looking up, I realized we were in front of the biology building. "Did he tell you he broke up with Zoey on Friday?"

"No." He flexed his hands, curling and uncurling his fingers into a fist. "I know you had feelings for him." I wished I hadn't told him that. Then, a wide grin spread across his face. "But I'm not going down without a fight."

He led me over to a nearby tree, backing me into the trunk. I felt like I was in middle school again. The kiss was warm, insistent, long, and wonderful.

"So, am I still taking you to your appointment this afternoon?"

I nodded, feeling a little dizzy.

"Good, I'll pick you up around four, right there." He motioned to the street corner.

The alarm on his watch went off. "I'm going to be late." I watched him walk away. Could I be without him? Would it feel like it had when Doug left?

I made it through biology and chemistry lab, taking copious notes to stay focused. Finishing chemistry lab, Lila locked her arm in mine. "So, do you want the update from the house?"

"I'm not sure, do I?"

"Zack and Doug were fighting."

"Like fist fighting?" What had I done? They were best friends. I had to remind myself this wasn't my fault, this was Doug's.

"No, no, no," she said quickly. "Well, almost. Zack said something like, 'I should hit you' and they argued pretty loudly for a while before Zack stormed out."

"So everyone knows?" I leaned back against the wall.

"You couldn't hear specifics, so no."

She sat on a bench with me while I waited for Zack.

Chapter 17

Waking, I heard movement in the room. When I opened my eyes I was startled to see Elise's face, not two feet from mine.

"Hey, you," Elise whispered. "How do you feel? I have to leave but I wanted to make sure you were okay."

"What time is it? How long did I sleep?"

"Seven thirty, ten hours."

The cast removal had not been fun. Well, the cast had come off fine, but my arm hurt a lot hurt when I moved it. I took some heavy pain meds and they knocked me out.

She stepped back, putting her hand tc her hip. "So, I need to know why Doug was calling." Doug called me? Did I say he could? The whole event was so jumbled in my mind I couldn't remember. "What happened yesterday?" she demanded.

Knowing Elise was not going to be happy with this one, I blurted the story out and braced for her response.

"Why didn't you call me? Zack's an idiot. I would've told you not to meet that boy. Nothing good ever comes from you talking to Doug." She threw her hands up. "You are over him, right?

"I don't know."

"Zack was here when Doug called." She shook her head, gathered her things, and left for class. Anxious about my looming decision, I focused on my tasks for the day, including showering, washing and drying my hair, and getting to calculus, English, and international studies. With a new resolve, I reminded myself I could do this. If I could get through a traumatic head injury, I could get through this.

In the shower, it was hard to look at my arm. The skin was horribly white, the muscles shrunken, and the scar from the surgery was fiery pink. The doctor assured me the scar would barely be noticeable in a year. After drying one-armed just as I had for two months, I gingerly pulled on my shirt and put my arm in the sling. For once, I was happy my sleeves were too long and covered the scar that extended from my elbow down the length of my arm and onto my palm. Just the thought of my arm being sliced open made my stomach turn.

Zack called as I was getting dressed. "Hey, what hand did you pick up the phone with?" When I didn't answer he continued. "Just calling to see if you were awake. Last night was pretty brutal, eh?"

All I could remember was him finally convincing me to take the pain meds and falling asleep in his lap. Had we talked about Doug? "I'm sorry about last night. Elise said Doug called?"

"Did you tell him he could call?"

"I don't think so."

"I'm just driving home from the gym. We can talk about this later."

I put down my phone and slumped onto my futon. My arm throbbed. The way I felt about it mirrored how I felt about Zack and Doug. If only I could just hide under my covers until the quarter was over.

Being alone with my churning thoughts was making me crazy. Unsettled, I decided to walk to class. If I took the long route, I could slip into the classroom at the last minute so I wouldn't have to talk Vivian or anyone else.

On the way, I called Lila to scold her. "Why did you let me date Zack?"

"What?"

"Why didn't you tell me not to date Zack?"

"You're feeling guilty because you still have feelings for Doug." She knew me too well. "I didn't say it was a bad idea because Zack seemed good for you. It's not your fault. It's that jerk Doug because he can't seem to figure out who he wants."

In front of the classroom building, I spotted Doug sitting on a bench holding a cup of coffee and a brown paper bag.

"Lila, I have to go."

"What's wrong?"

"Doug's here." I hung up.

"Coffee and muffin?" he asked, approaching me.

Putting away my phone, I stood there. I wanted to scream. Why was he doing this to me? Maybe now that he actually wanted me, the pull would be gone. Who was I kidding? It wasn't gone and I knew it. I kept my distance.

"Did I say that you could call me?"

He ignored my question, holding the cup out to me. "The coffee is probably still warm."

Taking the cup, I took a sip. My stomach screamed at me, forcing me to remember I hadn't eaten since lunch yesterday.

He looked around. "Are you meeting Zack?"

"Later, you didn't answer my question."

"Not specifically, you didn't say one way or the other, so I took some liberties."

My phone's alarm sounded, signaling class time. "I need to go."

He followed me. As we reached the entrance, he touched my arm. "Can we talk later?"

"I have physical therapy, a bio lab final, tutoring, babysitting, and finals next week. I can't talk this week." Hadn't he heard me yesterday?

His eyes pleaded with me. "I need to explain."

By this time we were outside my classroom, and I caught sight of Vivian, who was motioning frantically to me.

"My class is starting." I should've turned and left. But I hesitated.

"Okay, I'll wait."

"Amanda," Vivian called.

"Go." Doug said, tilting his head towards my room. I wasn't sure if he'd meant he'd wait until the end of the week or the end of class, but I left him standing there.

Vivian grabbed my arm, pulling me across the room. This girl perhaps saw herself as much more of a friend than I regarded her as. I pulled my arm from her grasp and sat down, getting in a second bite of the muffin as the professor stepped to the podium.

She leaned over and whispered to me. "Wasn't that Doug? I thought you were dating Zack."

I tried to calm myself. I was frustrated Doug wouldn't give me space. He seemed adamant I hear whatever information he had for me. Maybe I should just listen and get it over with. I didn't want to be swayed by his story though. I wanted to figure out my feelings first. If only I had a day to stop and breathe.

After the lecture, I was thankful Justin stopped me to ask about my arm. It gave me an escape from Vivian. He was interested in comparing injuries and wanted to see my scarring. Wincing, I turned my arm over and moved my sleeve up a bit. My stomach turned at the pain of moving it, so I just showed them the lower part of my scar.

"Hey, where are you doing PT? You should come to the athletics department and get in the sauna." I needed more male attention like I needed a bullet in my head.

Doug wasn't waiting in the hall, but as I exited the building, I saw him standing across the courtyard. Again, he held a paper cup and a brown paper bag. The guy was not giving up. If he was being this adamant, it must be important. If I let him say what he needed to, maybe he would leave me alone.

"You're not giving up, are you?"

"Are you supposed to meet Zack?"

"Not until this afternoon."

"I have coffee and a sandwich. Please just listen to me."

"Fine, where?"

He pointed in the direction of the student union. Starving, I opted for my muffin and the hot coffee. He ate the sandwich as we walked. Taking the elevator to the top floor, we circled the level.

Finding no one, we chose a small table. He sat across from me, hands on his thighs. "There's no easy lead in, so I'm just going to say it. Zoey and I were engaged."

My breath caught in my lungs, and I felt my heart skip irregularly. I swallowed and tried to keep my reaction minimal.

He fidgeted in his chair. "We got engaged at Mrs. Chen's restaurant. Remember the one I took you to during orientation week?"

I nodded. Of course I remembered. How could I forget that night? That must have been why Zack reacted weirdly when I told him Doug had taken me there.

"It was in June, two weeks after graduation. She said yes immediately." He cleared his throat. "It wasn't like it was a surprise. We'd talked about it for months. But, the next morning she said she needed time to let everything sink in. That night she returned the ring."

Emotions swirled around me. My heart ached for Doug, but it also hurt realizing how much he cared for Zoey. I was frozen, not quite sure what to say. "I'm so sorry."

"I was only supposed to be in Asia for two weeks, but my dad got me an internship with a law firm and bank-rolled four more weeks. I had only been back two weeks when I met you."

He put his hands on the table. "I don't know why I took you there that night. Trying to erase memories maybe. I just enjoyed hanging out with you. Anyway, I shouldn't have. I drank too much, and then had to walk it off."

So that was the reason for the walk up to his rooftop. How stupid was I?

"Then, I realized maybe you'd misinterpret things."

This made me angry, but I waited.

He smiled and shook his head. "It should've been simple, really. But, you were everywhere."

Odd, I thought I had done such a good job at avoiding him. "I tried to avoid you."

"I saw you every day in the courtyard with your friends. And you were so smart and funny. And then you got hurt, the first time." He looked at the ceiling. "And then I crushed you on the volleyball court." He looked back at me. "I had to know you were okay. That's why I fought for you to stay. Then we became friends and that was good until..." He paused. "I liked being around you, I wanted to be with you. But I couldn't when I thought I still loved her. I don't know why I didn't just tell you. But you were the only one with no ties to her. It was really selfish."

He was silent for a few minutes. Amazingly, I was content to wait. Knowing how I felt after he'd broken things off with me—how I could barely breathe in his presence—gave me a little idea of how nice a Zoey-free space must have been for him. "Zoey and I got back together, and then you started seeing Zack. It bothered me more than it should have. I couldn't stop thinking about you."

All the tortuous glances, ones I wasn't sure if I'd imagined, were real. He shook his head and looked at me again. "I haven't been fair to you or Zack, and I'm sorry for that." He reached towards me. "But I couldn't not do something."

Hearing his side of the story was like seeing an alternate version of my life. "Thank you." He'd apologized and that was what I needed to hear. The other information explained his behavior, but in no way gave him an out. I looked at his hands, now flat on the table. Thinking if I touched him I may never go back, I sat on my hands. Truthfully, if I'd let my emotions take over, I'd have kissed him the day before. I owed Zack more than that, and I had no idea if a relationship between Doug and me would even work.

"Do you have any questions?"

A crystal ball, or maybe a magic eight ball, would've been nice. If only life were so simple. I needed to know this wasn't just about wanting to be with me more. If he had any feelings left for her, I couldn't be with him. "What if I weren't in the picture, would you have stayed with Zoey?"

"No, I'm not the same person I was six months ago. We don't want the same things anymore." I believed him. It was the feeling I'd had about him the whole time, like he was someone different with me. That he put on a charade for everyone else.

He pulled his hands from the table completely, and it took all I had to not reach out to him. "Will you give me some time?"

"Of course. Are you still with Zack?"

"Yes." It might have been an unfair advantage for Zack, but Doug was the one who'd come out of left field, so he had no right making demands.

His phone buzzed, and he stood and took it from his pocket. BLOCKED CALLER, I read before looking away.

"I told you she didn't take the breakup well." He put his phone back in his pocket. "Are you staying here?"

"I guess." It was all I could manage. I had half an hour until class, and I needed solitude. This empty floor was as good a place as any.

"Just call me if you want to talk."

I nodded, and he turned and walked away.

Sitting there for the next half hour, I tried to figure out how I would make this decision. I liked both of them, and the thought of losing either of them saddened me. Walking away from both was one option. I would meet other people. That thought only made me sadder. Making a pros and cons list got me nowhere, and I decided to try Dad's decision matrix approach. When my alarm sounded, I looked down at the paper and realized this type of analysis would never work. I tore up the paper and tossed it in the trash on my way out of the building.

Zack sent a text as I made my way to the lecture hall to confirm he'd be taking me to physical therapy after class. Finding my seat, I was glad to be in international studies where I could lose myself in the topic. Thanks to a great lecture and meticulous attention to my note taking, I barely noticed the fifty minutes pass.

The professor announced a quick break, and I walked out into the hall to stretch my legs. I sent Lila and Marissa texts. Marissa could almost always be counted on to have some drama going on, and today members of her cheerleading squad were quarreling again. It felt good to think of someone else's problems for a while.

After the last half hour of class, I walked over to the street where I was to meet Zack. I didn't have to wait long as he pulled up not two minutes later. Being with him reminded me why I was dating him, and I felt guilty about talking to Doug. My relationship with Zack was easy, and he made me happy. But was it enough? What if I loved Doug more?

"How was your day?" I asked as we drove to the medical center.

"Crappy, had to go to the house for lunch."

"Oh, sorry."

"Don't apologize, this isn't your fault. You talk to him?"

"Yeah, he was outside my classroom building."

"Stalking you, eh?" He shook his head. "Man, the guy's got it bad."

His tone was light, and I almost laughed. We pulled into the hospital lot, and he didn't continue the conversation. The physical therapy appointment went as well as it could have. I took a dose of Advil beforehand, and my arm didn't hurt as much as the day before. Afterwards, we ate at a sushi place. He was missing a house dinner, but he didn't mention it and neither did I. Our conversation didn't flow as easily that evening, but he didn't say anything until we were back in my room after dinner.

"So, he was waiting for you."

"I told him to give me some space, but he was waiting for me again after class."

"You didn't tell him to leave you alone?"

If I wanted to stay with Zack, I should have. But I hadn't. I didn't know how to respond.

"You're the only person I've met who could say no to him. I'm gonna go," he said finally.

I reached out to him, and he backed away. Saddened by his retreat, I tried to explain. "I thought if I listened to what he had to say, he would leave me alone. Zack, I like you, I like being with you, and—"

He cut me off. "I like you, too, but I need you to be all in. I deserve that."

He did deserve that, and much more, but I didn't have an answer. I wasn't sure I would choose Doug, but I couldn't tell Zack I was all in either. He pulled me into him and kissed me. It was hard and insistent, but he stopped abruptly and backed away.

He rubbed his finger down my nose. "We should take a break. You can call me when you make up your mind. I just need one thing."

"Anything." With my guilt stacking up, there was almost nothing I would deny him at this point.

"Anna may be ready to pounce. Will you go to the club with me Thursday night?"

I agreed to his request, and he turned and walked out the door. With nothing to distract me, I paced the floor. It wasn't good for my arm, which probably needed to be elevated. But it kept me from crying. I wasn't alone long, as Mark descended on my room.

Lila must have let everything slip, because he didn't waste time on small talk. "We've been friends since preschool," he started. After an hour of the not-so-friendly version of what are you doing with your life, the consensus was that I was crazy to dump Zack for Doug. It didn't matter that I hadn't even decided to be with Doug, or that just two weeks ago Mark has been chastising me for dating Zack.

It was midnight before I was able to shove Mark out of my room and got just fifteen minutes of quiet before Elise came in. By then, my physical pain had surpassed my mental anguish. Still, my throbbing arm and headache were a welcome distraction from my anxiety over the Doug-Zack issue. At least I could take the pain meds and drift off into oblivion.

I woke to my phone buzzing.

"Who is that?" I asked Elise, who held my phone in front of me.

"A text from Doug hoping your PT appointment went okay."

"So, you're reading my texts now?"

"I'm the self-appointed Doug monitor."

Getting up to brush my teeth, I rolled my eyes at her. Deciding to answer my messages later, I opted for an outdoor run rather than the usual gym workout. It was only thirty-two degrees outside, and the cool air helped me focus on my breathing rather than the swirling options in my head.

As I stretched out in my warm room afterwards, I read my messages. Mom, Dad, Marissa, Tia, and Doug's were all the same: checking in and asking how my physical therapy appointment went. I sent a group text to my family.

I messaged Doug separately. PT FINE. ZACK AND I ARE TAKING A BREAK BUT I'M DOING HIM A FAVOR THURSDAY NIGHT AND GOING TO THE CLUB WITH HIM.

His reply was immediate and simple. THANKS FOR LETTING ME KNOW. GLAD YOUR PT WENT WELL.

Not sure how I was going to ace my exams and make this decision, I forced myself to finish studying for the day before I entertained any thoughts about Doug or Zack. If I were fully honest, I'd rather just never make the decision. Realizing not making a choice would lead to an unacceptable outcome, I set a Sunday deadline for myself.

Lying on my futon and trying to fall asleep that night, I let my mind drift. My last kiss with Zack was still etched in my mind. He cared for me, and I cared for him. But Doug's voice creeped in. "I want *you*." And then I was wide awake.

I turned on my phone, thinking I'd listen to some music. Doug's playlist popped up, so I started it. I thought about how elusive he'd been. But now he finally filled in all the blanks. I knew everything. I got to the end of the playlist and "What About Now?" by Daughtry started. "You're biting your lip," I heard him say to me. This memory only circled me back to Zack.

Realizing I wasn't falling asleep anytime soon, I looked at my phone. No one would be up this late. Well, except Dad. It occurred to me he may be able to help. He'd talked me through some tough academic choices before, so I dialed his number.

"Hi, peanut, good to hear your voice. You're up late. Is everything okay?"

I took a deep breath, forcing mental courage down my wind pipes. I didn't like to need help, especially from him, and I was nervous about seeming vulnerable. "I need some advice on a decision I have to make."

"Is this about your courses? I thought you already registered last week."

"Yeah, I did. No, it's something else. I have sort of a big choice to make, and I'm having trouble with it. Can you give me some pointers on decision making?"

He asked if I'd try a pros and cons list and the decision matrix. Then, he suggested I think as if I'd made one choice and see how it felt. "Heck, I could make the decision for you, and you'd know immediately which one was right," he said.

I laughed. "Thanks Dad, but I need to figure this one out on my own."

"Okay, sweetie, you call back any time, okay?"

"Kay, Dad. I love you."

"I love you, too."

We ended the call, and I was glad I'd made it. His advice settled me and gave me a course of action. I picked up the journal Mom had given me for my birthday. I'd stuck the pictures Zack took last week in it. It was empty save the photos and some business cards. I spun the photo of me by the lake around on top of the book. How had I gotten here? Unfortunately, I knew exactly how. Now, I just had to decide on the right path out.

Exhausted and emotionally drained, I decided to hold off on Dad's decision making strategy for a day. I moved through the day like a zombie, napping after my classes. My phone woke me, and after the fifth text alert I picked it up.

Zack wrote. HEY THERE, EVERYONE SAYS YOU'RE MIA.

JUST NAPPING.

We still on for Nine? I'll Pick U up.

Yep.

Lying back on my futon, I decided to finally answer Lila's text and let her know I was going out with Zack. It wasn't five minutes before she knocked on my door, demanding more details. Seeing my near comatose state, she helped me with my outfit.

"Fix your hair half up and put on that royal blue shimmery top, black skinny pants, and some pumps. And no sling."

I declined her last demand, knowing I'd never make it through the night without my arm being supported.

"You know Doug will be there." She put the finishing touches on my curls. "It's the social finale of the season." I had no idea what to do with that information, so I took it as just that. "This could be interesting." Lila threw my shoes at me and pulled me out the door.

Hoping to feel more energized, we took the stairs.

Mark and Ross were waiting outside. "Took you long enough," Mark complained when we reached the car.

Just then Zack pulled up, and Lila gave me a hug before jumping in with Mark and Ross. Bill jumped out of the Zack's front seat, and I slid in beside him. My guilt was eating away at me, and the urge to bolt out of the car started to creep in.

"You look awesome." Zack squeezed my hand and put the car into gear before I could back out.

I told him I needed coffee, and he pulled one from inside the middle console. "Piping hot just for you."

Bill poked his head between us. "We have drinks for later, too."

When we got to the club, the line wound around the side of the building. We walked straight to the front of the line as usual. I wished I could remember the bouncers' names, as they were brothers at the house. But I only saw them when we came to this club. One of them almost took my coffee, but when I let him have a sip, he gave it back. Knowing the bouncers was definitely a perk.

"Doug got here about fifteen minutes ago, usual table." They waved us in.

Inside, Zack wrapped his arm firmly around my waist and guided me straight toward the table where Doug stood. Lila hadn't been wrong about this being the night to be out. Anyone who was anyone was there. Passing Justin and his buddies, Zack pulled me along.

As we approached the table, Doug's eyes seemed fixed on me. Zack put out his hand. "How's it going?"

Doug shook Zack's offered hand. "Good." I was surprised he sounded like it was any other night. But seeing the creases in his brow, I could tell it was forced.

Since I had no desire to be sober, I let Zack talk me into drinking shots with him. We hung out, talking and mingling until the music started. Dancing was exactly what I needed, so I found Lila. Even with the tension between Zack and Doug, everyone seemed to be having fun. Of course maybe no one else noticed they'd only said two words to one another.

Anna came over on our first dancing break. "Hi guys."

I was standing between Zack and Doug as I had been for the whole night. I felt like it was impossible to ignore. You shouldn't be here, my psyche screamed at me, but it was too late. Composing myself, I tried to focus on the conversation.

"She's flipping out," Anna was telling Doug.

"I know. I'm sorry, but there's nothing I can do."

Zack started thumb wars with me, and I lost focus. Maybe it was due to the caffeine two shot combo, but suddenly we were playing hand slap on the tabletop.

As soon as Anna walked away, Doug snatched my hand mid-air and placed it slowly on the table. Then, he spun and walked away, headed in the direction of the exit. I started after him without thinking.

Zack grabbed my wrist before I could get away. I turned back to him. He closed the gap between us, sliding his hand from my wrist to grasp my hand. "Is this the choice you want to make?"

Instinctively, I turned back towards the direction Doug had gone, but he was nowhere to be seen. I wanted to go after him. I needed to go after him. All this time I'd been just trying not to want him.

I spun back to Zack, who still held my hand. "I'm sorry, I have to go."

He released me, and I shot after Doug. When I got outside, he was gone. I scanned the parking lot hoping to find him.

"Doug went that way," one of the bouncers said and pointed towards the right lot.

"Dude, she's with Zack. Keep up man," another one said.

I ignored them and sprinted off in the direction the first guy had pointed. As I reached the end of the building, I found Doug's retreating form. I called his name and slowed my pace, my feet aching from running in my heels.

He turned immediately, and walked back towards me, stopping a couple of feet away.

"See, this is what I do. I get frustrated and I hurt you. You should go back and let Zack take you home." Seeing a flicker of anger in his eyes, I froze. "Go back inside."

I squared my shoulders, standing as tall as I could. "No, I'm not. I told you I was doing him a favor. That's what tonight was."

"You looked like you were having fun together. You should go back." He motioned towards the club.

I reached out to him, but he backed away and shoved his hands in his pockets. Before I could say anything, he stormed away. I trailed behind, nearly running to keep up. When he reached his car, he hit the roof with his fist. His intensity frightened me, and I hung back. He leaned over the car, placing both hands on the hood.

The pull towards him got the better of me. "Doug..." I stepped up to him, reaching out to touch his shoulder. He wouldn't look at me. I slid myself under his arm, so I sat on the hood facing him, and pulled him towards me. "It's always been you." Hardly believing the words had passed my lips, I continued, "Ever since the first day we met, that night you walked me to my dorm."

He looked down, and then back up to me. "I've been running around trying to keep you from getting hurt, and I'm the only one hurting you. I'm so sorry." He hung his head, and I lifted his face to make him look at me.

He pulled my hand from his face and placed it on the hood. "Would you have followed me out if you hadn't been drinking?"

I thought for a minute. Was I making this decision now as a reaction to seeing him walk away? That's when I realized it wasn't a decision I needed to make, it was me being true to my feelings. When it came to who I couldn't live without, it was Doug. Maybe, it wasn't the rational, safe choice, but I loved him and I couldn't walk away.

"Haven't you been listening to me? I had to come after you."

"It's late. If you don't want to go back in, I'll take you home. You should think about this again tomorrow once your head has cleared."

He was pushing me away again? No more. "I don't need to think about this anymore. I want to be with you." I tugged his jacket, pulling him closer to me.

His face was inches from mine. "Are you sure?"

I looked straight into his eyes. "Yes."

I leaned closer, touching his face. He placed his hands on either side of my head and closed the space between us. His lips touched mine, and my whole body melted into him. He was touching me, kissing me, finally.

He kissed my neck, sending shivers down my spine. Then he wrapped his arms around my waist, picking me up and twirling me around. "Oh my God!" He set me down and raked his hands through his hair. "I don't deserve you. You should've hit me at least twice by now." He backed away.

"You're forgiven." I pulled him to me, kissing him again.

At the end of the kiss, he pulled away, sliding his hands down my arms and taking both my hands. "So, we're good?"

"Yes, we're good." I kissed him again and he backed me onto the hood of the car. After a few minutes, whistles from a passing crowd forced us to resurface from our private world. "We should get out of here before that place empties." He cocked his head back towards the bar. "Are you coming with me, or do you need to go finish up in there?"

With the way I left, I doubted Zack wanted me to come back. "I'll go with you." I wrapped my arms around his waist and kissed him again. There was no way I was leaving him now.

Reluctantly I let go as he led me to the passenger door.

Neither of us spoke on the drive. My heart raced as I wrapped my brain around the reality that we finally were on the same page. "We should go out on a real date before you leave for the break," he said as he pulled into the dorm parking lot.

"Will you take me rowing?"

"Rowing? Can you even swim?"

"You promised." I used my best pouty voice.

"When did I promise?"

"That night at Mrs. Chen's." It was a stretch, as there wasn't an explicit promise.

"It'll have to be tomorrow early. We're locking up the boats Saturday."

"Really?" I slid to the front of my seat. Ever since he'd talked about being on the water at dawn, the oars hitting the surface rhythmically, I'd been waiting for a chance to experience it myself.

He reached for his door handle. "Okay, well it's late now, so—"I jumped out of the car and crossed over to meet him.

"Thank you."

"For what?"

"Rowing."

"I'm thinking I might not be able to say no to you."

"That's a good thing."

Not wanting the evening to end, I wrapped my arms around him. He backed me into the hood of the car and kissed me again. Our bodies entwined, and I lost all sense of time and place. When he stopped, I was lying on the hood of the car.

He pushed up away from me. "You're shivering."

"I'm fine." I gripped his jacket, pulling him back to me.

He took my hand and put it against his chest, and I realized how cold I was. "It's past curfew and it's going to be an early morning. You should get some sleep."

He was right, but I wanted to stay with him forever. Reluctantly, I agreed to go in.

Standing on my toes, I kissed him one last time. "I can walk myself in."

"I'll walk you."

I put my hand on his chest. "Doug, I want you to be my boyfriend, but you have to stop taking care of me."

He smiled, taking my hand. "I'm your boyfriend?"

Suddenly I was scared I'd jumped too far ahead. "Well, I guess we're dating now, right?" I squeezed my eyes shut, warding off any more games.

"Boyfriend works, and I'll try to be less protective."

I let out the breath I was holding. "Thanks." I kissed him again and took a skipping step towards my dorm.

His laughter made me turn around. "What?"

"How old are you?"

"Eighteen. Now, go home." I waved him off.

Although it was late and I was tired, I took the stairs to dispel my energy. After everything that had happened this quarter, things were good now. I'd been brave enough to be honest with my friends and follow my heart. This new decision probably wasn't going to be a popular one, but that was okay. Losing Doug was not an experience I wanted to live through again.

About the Author:

TRICIA COPELAND grew up in Georgia but now lives outside the mile-high city of Denver, Colorado with her husband, three kids, and multiple four legged and finned friends. An avid runner and paranormal fan, she also enjoys hiking, trivia, and Scrabble.

Connect with Tricia and other readers!

Facebook: facebook.com/TriciaCopelandAuthor

Instagram: instagram.com/tricia_copeland_brzostowicz

Twitter: @tcbrzostowicz

Pinterest: pinterest.com/triciacopelanda

Website: triciacopeland.com